"Who do you ride with?" he murmured, just loud enough for her to hear. "Speak."

She spat at him. The glob of spit didn't quite make it, splashing into the dirt. The raider lashed out with her unbound feet, catching nothing but dust. Twisting against the rope around her wrists.

There was a necklace at her throat, most of it hidden beneath her leather armour. The thing prickling the back of Garrick's neck started to move down his spine as he reached over, snagging the string, ignoring her bared teeth. Lifting it out.

Bones.

Polished white chips, threaded on the woven string.

Most raiders in the Tapestry weren't worth a damn. You could fight them off on a good day, stand your ground. But most didn't mean all. And there was one group in particular, a group who Garrick had only heard of, never actually seen . . .

Panic had a strange way of showing itself. For such a vicious emotion, it always came on gradually. The set of someone's shoulders. A tiny crack in another's voice.

It started to spread through the villagers behind Garrick the moment they saw the bones. The woman gave him a slow, twisted smile, and for the first time, she spoke. Above the trembling murmur of the crowd, her voice carried perfectly.

"You are so fucked."

And just like that, the villagers lost their minds.

THE BONE RAIDERS

The Rakada: Book One

JACKSON FORD

orbitbooks.net

Orbit
Hachette Book Group
1290 Avenue of the Americas
New York, NY 10104
orbitbooks.net

First Edition: August 2025
Simultaneously published in Great Britain by Orbit

Orbit is an imprint of Hachette Book Group.
The Orbit name and logo are registered trademarks of Little, Brown Book Group Limited.

The publisher is not responsible for websites (or their content)
that are not owned by the publisher.

The Hachette Speakers Bureau provides a wide range of authors for speaking events. To find out more, go to hachettespeakersbureau.com or email HachetteSpeakers@hbgusa.com.

Orbit books may be purchased in bulk for business, educational, or promotional use. For information, please contact your local bookseller or the Hachette Book Group Special Markets Department at special.markets@hbgusa.com.

Library of Congress Control Number: 2025935600

ISBNs: 9780316577694 (trade paperback), 9780316577717 (ebook)

Printed in the United States of America

LSC-C

Printing 2, 2025

For Jules.
I love you, dude. Let it rip.

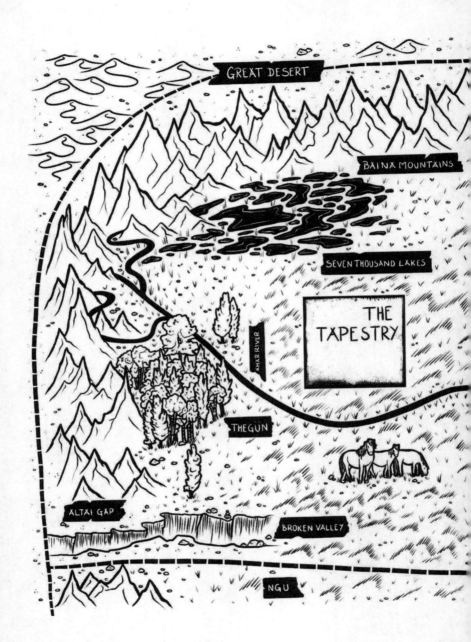

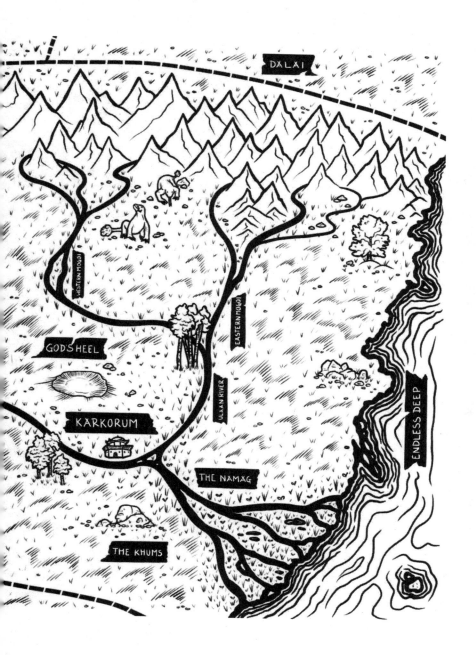

One

Garrick

"I was out taking a piss, and I nearly stood on her!"

Garrick slowly opened one eye. Which was a huge mistake, because that was when his hangover chose to announce itself by whanging hard against the inside of his skull. He closed his eye with a pained grunt, rolled back over.

When it came to pissing on people, he didn't want to know. He really didn't.

"Nearly kicked her in the head." The speaker was old Batu, just beyond the flap of Garrick's tent. The man was addressing a crowd, it sounded like: a hubbub of excited voices. "She was down in the long grass, all sneaky. If I hadn't been keeping an eye out, no one would have found her. No one!"

Garrick rather doubted that. Batu couldn't find his arse if the directions were tattooed on the back of his wrinkled hands. None of the villagers could.

A burst of agonising light lanced through his cracked eyelids. Someone, some deeply evil fuck, had pushed open the flap of his tent. He held up a hand, but it did no good whatsoever.

"Garrick, you need to come!" a hazy shape shouted. "Batu caught a raider!"

The shape vanished as quickly as it had appeared. Garrick propped himself up on his elbow, blinking, tongue sour in his mouth.

Raiders.

Been a while since any had come this way. The new Khan and his army were exterminating them, wiping them off the face of the Tapestry. All part of the Khan's grand plan for this land.

A raider scout that allowed themselves to be caught was a very poor raider indeed. Chances are, old Batu didn't know what he was talking about. Still, Garrick didn't trust the villagers not to cock this up. Somehow.

With a sigh, he found his way to his feet, doing his best to ignore the horrid pounding in his brain. To his left, his anvil sat, dark and silent. Tools nearby, arranged neatly on a wooden bench.

He would have given anything to stay inside; the tent was unbearably hot, dust hanging in the still air. But it would be hotter out there, where the twin suns could cook you in your boots.

Garrick supposed he'd be needing his axe, for show if nothing else. It lay propped against the fabric wall. His fingers closed on the weapon's worn haft. He slotted it into the sheath on his back as he stepped out, squinting into the searing midday light.

The blacksmith stood a head taller than anyone in the village. He was tanned and lined, but the skin at the neck of his sleeveless, boiled leather jerkin was still pale pink. Unlike the men of this land, with their neat goatees, his beard ran to his chest in a black river, flecked with grey rapids.

He'd come to the village a year before, a traveller passing through. He spoke the language, and had bartered for a place to sleep and a cracked bowl of millet broth. He'd ended up liking the place, and had stayed, offering his skills at metalwork. There were rumours of what had driven him from the west, whispers of scandal and betrayal. Garrick would only smile when asked, and say that it was a long time ago.

There were plenty of settlements just like this one in the massive, rolling grasslands of the Tapestry. It stood on a hillside, which ended in a cliff high above a rushing river. The colourful felt tents – *gers*, they called them in these parts – ran all the way up the gentle slope to the cliff edge.

As Garrick ducked out of his own *ger*, another villager brushed past him. This one was laughing – at what, Garrick didn't know, only that they sounded nervous and they were way, way, *way* too fucking loud.

Garrick clutched his splitting skull; he'd once been told that the fermented mare's milk they drank in these parts – *airag*, they called it – wasn't that strong. He briefly fantasised about finding the man who'd told him that, and beating him to death. The basic stuff wasn't, to be sure, but the people of this land had a way of distilling it that did horrible things to your brain.

He took several deep breaths. As he did so, and without really meaning to, he glanced to his left.

At the damned banner.

He'd been trying not to think about it; honestly, it was part of the reason he'd got so drunk last night. Soldiers had planted it two days before, at the bottom of the hill. Two white suns and a moon, crowned with orange flame on blue fabric, rippling in the warm wind. The Khan's Will, it was called.

Raiders weren't the only thing the Khan seemed set on exterminating. Villages like this one weren't part of his grand plan. Ditto for the many groups of nomads wandering the Tapestry, with their horses and wagons.

The old Khan had been content to let all of them exist, as long as they paid him tribute. The new one? *That* evil little prick wanted everyone under his thumb. Which was bad news if you happened to like living out in the grasslands of the Tapestry.

The Khan wanted an army. He wanted manned borders, garrisons at areas of strategic importance. The official reason was to be ready if Dalai invaded, from the north, or Ngu, from the south. Garrick rather suspected it was because the man liked the idea of thousands of troops at his beck and call.

And instead of scattered villages and roving bands of nomads, he wanted a single shining city, with a giant wall and leagues of farmland. Karkorum. His capital. He wanted everyone in the Tapestry in one place, where he could keep an eye on them.

That was the point of the banner. *Hello, villagers: those of you who can hold a sabre, deliver yourself to military training post haste. Those who can't, deliver yourself to Karkorum, and report for work. Those city walls aren't going to build themselves, and that grassland won't become nice, ordered rows of crops unless you put your backs into it.*

Didn't like the idea? Didn't fancy starving in a crowded, diseased slum, or suffering forced marches for no good reason? No problem. You could run, or you could . . . no, actually that was about it. Run, and hope you escaped the Khan's notice, or that one of the battalions roaming the Tapestry didn't come across you. *Good luck.*

The whole thing pissed him off. Life in the Tapestry was hard, but it suited him. Living in a nation-sized military camp did not.

Since the soldiers planted that banner, the whole village had been in an uproar. Everyone knew what moving to Karkorum meant – nobody came back from there. So they'd argued and debated and fought, and wasted valuable time.

Later today, the soldiers would be back, asking pointed

questions about why the villagers were still here. The kind of questions that usually ended up with someone's heart on a wooden stake.

Hangover or not, Garrick intended to be long gone before things got to the hearts-on-stakes bit. He had no intention of fighting in the army, or slaving away in the city, and he couldn't stop the Khan on his own. This land was finished, but he wasn't. He'd go north, over the mountains perhaps. To a place where they made booze that didn't hollow out your skull from the inside.

Still, he'd deal with this raider situation first – if it was indeed a raider situation. Least he could do.

He frowned as he took in the crowd: an angry, noisy mess of people surrounding their captive. The crowd was moving, dragging their prisoner up the narrow street between the *gers*, stepping past the village's single wagon – an ancient contraption with three remaining wheels, the bare axle propped up with wood blocks. In all the time he'd been here, Garrick had never seen it move. No one even seemed to know who it belonged to.

When this village decamped, headed to Karkorum to begin their fabulous new lives in service to the Khan, it would be the only thing left behind. A monument to what the Tapestry used to be.

He trailed the crowd as they dragged their prey to the edge of the cliff. The river sat fifty feet below, gleaming in the suns, reflecting a midday sky filled with puffy, billowing clouds. Beyond the river, shimmering grass stalks stretched to the mountains on the horizon.

He was going to miss this place. What a waste, to empty it of people, force them to live behind walls or in military camps.

There was a dusty, ancient wooden pole sunk into the ground near the cliff – Garrick had never got around to asking what it was for. Chances were, no one would know anyway. They were tying someone to it as he arrived, shoving her to sit on the dirt, binding her wrists above her head with a strip of rough cloth.

For once, old Batu had been dead right. This was no traveller. Travellers didn't wear paint. Hers was a jagged red slash, running from right temple to left jawbone.

"Found her skulking in the reeds, I did!" Batu bleated, to anyone who would listen. "If I hadn't had the boys with me, she would've run me through. Nearly took off Nugai's ear before we got her pinned."

Nugai grinned as several others slapped him on the back. Blood trickled down the side of his head, staining his beaded blue healer's headband.

The scout wouldn't stop struggling. She was young, twenty perhaps, with a round face and a hard twist to her mouth. Tall — over six foot, easily, with a body like a reed. Skin covered in nicks and scars, mementos of past battles.

Her hair wasn't cut short, like so many other raiders. Instead, she had a single long, black braid running down to her waist.

One of the villagers grabbed it, laughing as he wrapped it around the pole and tied it to itself in a clumsy knot, pulling the scout's head back against the hard wood. They'd taken her sash, and her faded grey *deel* hung open, the robe showing tough leather underneath.

Some of the villagers were passing the girl's sabres around. The fact that she had two weapons was strange in itself: fighting with twin blades was stupid. It looked flashy, but you couldn't defend yourself, or grapple. You'd get skewered if you didn't move like lightning. It was exactly the kind of fighting that they liked in the palace in Karkorum, funnily enough, where all you had to do was entertain the Khan while he had his breakfast.

"She's Black Hands!" someone shouted. "Has to be!"

"Not a chance," said another voice. "We sent them running ages ago."

Garrick grunted at that. There wasn't much *we* about it, if he remembered right. Just him.

"Arkan's Eagles then. None of them even know the right way to hold a blade, no surprise one of them got herself caught."

"Down by Arsi's tent." Batu was still going. "Found her myself when I went to take a piss!"

Garrick crouched, studying the scout. She caught his eye and actually snarled at him. It sounded forced, theatrical, like a mummer in some play.

He found he pitied her, just a tiny bit. If you had to pick a career with no future in the Tapestry, being a raider was at the top of the list. Even the ones still out there, which apparently included this young pup, were on borrowed time.

Awfully hard to make a living as a raider if there were no settlements left to raid, after all. *Or if the army is taking special pleasure in wiping you out.*

You could give up, of course. Pretend to be a villager, or try to join the army yourself. Just another citizen obeying your Khan's orders. But if they caught you . . .

There was something about this raider, though, that made the skin on the back of his neck prickle.

"Who do you ride with?" he murmured, just loud enough for her to hear. "Speak."

She spat at him. The glob of spit didn't quite make it, splashing into the dirt. The raider lashed out with her unbound feet, catching nothing but dust. Twisting against the rope around her wrists.

There was a necklace at her throat, most of it hidden beneath her leather armour. The thing prickling the back of Garrick's neck started to move down his spine as he reached over, snagging the string, ignoring her bared teeth. Lifting it out.

Bones.

Polished white chips, threaded on the woven string.

Most raiders in the Tapestry weren't worth a damn. You could fight them off on a good day, stand your ground. But most didn't mean all. And there was one group in particular, a group who Garrick had only heard of, never actually seen . . .

Panic had a strange way of showing itself. For such a vicious emotion, it always came on gradually. The set of someone's shoulders. A tiny crack in another's voice.

It started to spread through the villagers behind Garrick the moment they saw the bones. The woman gave him a slow, twisted smile, and for the first time, she spoke. Above the trembling murmur of the crowd, her voice carried perfectly.

"You are so fucked."

And just like that, the villagers lost their minds.

They all started shouting, bumping into each other, scrambling in their haste to get away. One of them still held the scout's sabres, nearly impaling another villager as he spun in place. A word kept coming up, rising above the tumult again and again.

Rakada.

Garrick didn't believe in the gods of this land. Didn't believe that Father Sky and Mother Earth had woven the Tapestry, thousands of years before. But he couldn't help himself thinking, just for a second, that they were vindictive bastards nonetheless. First the Khan's Will, and now this? What else could possibly befall this village?

He forced himself to look away from the woman's triumphant smile. "Enough," he bellowed.

Amazingly, they listened.

He turned slowly, taking in the frozen villagers. His hangover was gone. *This* was why they needed him: to be a steady hand when others wavered.

He couldn't protect them from the Khan's Will, no one could ... but he could stand firm against raiders. Even these raiders.

"Bayar," he said, his lips barely moving. The man with the sabres gazed up at him, trembling. "Get everyone to safety. Take them to the river, and follow it east. Where it widens, the grass is tall enough to hide in."

There was the sound of wood on leather as his axe slipped free. "The rest of you: with me."

"Do you know what the Rakada are?" one of the women snarled. "Do you know what they *do*?"

"You want your bones hanging from their horses, pale man?"

"It's a trick! It has to be! We need to fight."

"No no no. We ransom her, yes? Back to those monsters."

"The Bone Raiders won't care. Cut her throat, and have done with it! One less raider to fight later ... "

Garrick tested the weight of his axe. How much time did they have? Minutes? How long before the Rakada missed their scout? He listened hard, forcing his way past the panicked voices of the villagers. Listened for the sound of howling, carried on the wind.

The sound of rattling bones.

They didn't come. Instead, there was a very peculiar, rumbling growl.

Garrick turned, thinking it was too late, that the Rakada had already arrived. But the thing coming along the edge of the cliff towards them, from the north, wasn't a raider. It wasn't a soldier, come to carry out the Khan's orders.

It wasn't even human.

Garrick had heard stories of war elephants, in the kingdoms

beyond the mountains. He'd seen huge crocodiles in the rivers of the southern deltas. The thing walking along the cliff looked as if a sorcerer had melded the two, brought them together to create the single biggest creature Garrick had ever seen.

The lizard – that's what it was, a fucking *lizard* – was twice his height at the shoulder, with a massive, muscular body swaying from side to side. Scales the colour of summer grass. The tail swished the air, the end a thick, bony club the size of a boulder.

Four powerful legs stuck out, thick as tree trunks, the knees bent at ninety degrees. Feet with splayed, hooked claws as long as sabres. Garrick stared, mouth slack, amazed at how quietly it walked. Something that big shouldn't be able to move that silently. It wasn't fair.

And the head . . .

A full half of its length was taken up by a long, tapering snout; the teeth reminded Garrick of the knives he'd made when he was still an apprentice smith. Jagged and uneven. Behind the teeth was a forked tongue the length of a man's arm, purple as mountain flowers. Two horns stuck up from the top of its head, little nubbins of grey bone.

The crowd froze, trying to understand what they were seeing. Because *araatan* – that was the name for them, wasn't it? – didn't come into the Tapestry. They didn't come anywhere *near* the Tapestry. They lived in the distant Baina Mountains: solitary, retiring animals that ate goats and wild horses, along with any tragically unlucky tigers who got a little too ambitious with their hunting grounds.

Garrick had certainly never seen one – and definitely not one casually marching into the village, a hundred miles from the nearest mountain. It didn't make sense.

For a strange moment, he wondered if the captive scout might have summoned it – that *this* was the Bone Raiders' real trick, that they could somehow command *araatan*. But no, the bound woman was staring at the animal too, eyes huge and horrified.

The lizard's eyes found Garrick, each as big as his head, yellow and feral. Before he could even suck in a breath, it started to move faster, feet pounding the earth. Coming right for him.

Move, Garrick thought. And he did.

Not even close to fast enough.

An enormous, clawed foot took him at the waist. His left leg bent the wrong way, snapped like a twig as he crashed to the ground. Axe gone. He couldn't cry out, couldn't even breathe.

Hot breath on his face, stinking of old meat. Jaws, teeth, tongue, open wide above him. If he could just find his axe . . .

The jaws didn't snap shut. A bright point glowed inside them, and a wave of hot air buffeted Garrick, thick and syrupy. The screams of the villagers rose around him.

No—!

And then there was nothing but fire.

Two

Sayana

S ayana had grown up in the palace, in Karkorum.

From a young age, her parents made her attend court. Scholars filled her days, drilling her in manners and elocution, teaching her how to comport herself with grace and modesty. They taught her that there was a correct and eloquent response for every situation.

Unfortunately, her education didn't include what to say if you were tied to a pole while a giant lizard burned a man to a crisp in front of you, then ate him. So what came out of her mouth was: *"Holy fucking shit!"*

The beast bent its gigantic head down, snapped its jaws around the blistered, twitching hulk, and ripped it off the ground. Sayana yanked hard at her bound wrists, twisting back and forth. Which not only didn't work – at all – but ripped her skin to shreds and made her pull a muscle in her shoulder, because of course it did.

She was the only person actually trying to get away. Everyone else – everyone, every last soul in the village – just stared at the *araatan* in frozen shock as it swallowed its prey.

That lasted until the idiot holding Sayana's sabres dropped them into the dirt. The lizard immediately lunged forward, plucked him up in its jaws, and crunched down.

At that point, the entire crowd lost its collective mind. They scattered, screaming, scrambling. It was the smart thing to do, and very bad news for Sayana, because she was still tied to the pole.

"Hey." She gave her wrists, tightly bound above her head, another futile yank. She couldn't quite believe things had gone *this* wrong. "Don't just *leave me here!*"

The other Rakada weren't going to get there in time – they were probably still waiting for her to come back from her scout. The chances of them appearing to cut her loose were about the same as the lizard moving on without noticing a tasty and conveniently tied-up meal.

"Oh, Father Sky shit on your *heads*," Sayana yelled at the scattering villagers. She usually did her best not to take the names of the Weavers in vain, but honestly. She scooted round on her backside, trying to get behind the pole. It wouldn't help, but she had absolutely no idea what else to do.

Of all the raids to go completely wrong in the worst way possible, it just *had* to be this one, didn't it?

It had been weeks since they'd found a village or a band of nomads to raid: everyone was leaving, forced by the Khan to travel south to Karkorum. The Rakada were low on food, supplies, everything from needle and thread to spare stirrups, and they'd really needed this raid to go right.

Then that arsehole almost stepped on her, during her scout, and now this ... thing showed up. What was the fucking *araatan* even *doing* here? They lived in the mountains. They didn't hunt in the grasslands ...

One of her sabres was a few feet away, lying in the dirt, and you know what? She could contemplate the mysteries of *araatan* behaviour later. Preferably when she was very far away, and had drunk enough *airag* to make a horse black out.

Swallowing her panic, Sayana thrust her feet out to snag the weapon. If she could drag it close enough, even just get a toe on it . . .

She strained and strained, heel digging a furrow in the dirt, but it was no good. Too far. And it wasn't like there was another blade nearby; not so much as a skinning knife.

She was going to die here. The thought was cold, thin as a needle.

Sayana had never regretted becoming a raider. She'd hated the gilded cage she was born into, hated having every moment of her entire life chosen for her. Hated that she was expected to be quiet, obedient, submissive – to everyone. Her parents, her future husband, even the children she was expected to have.

No other raiders, as far as she knew, had grown up in the palace. But living in a village or as part of a nomad band wasn't much better. It was hard work, obligation, marrying who your parents told you to, working the jobs the elders demanded. The Tapestry was beautiful, but if you lived in a village like this, you didn't get to appreciate it. Your life was one of service, and for some people, it chafed and bit like a badly fitted saddle.

Being a raider meant freedom. Doing what you want, when you wanted. Riding under open skies, with nobody but your clan to answer to. It meant living a life where you could *enjoy* the Tapestry, *enjoy* the Weavers' work.

Whenever any Rakada doubted what they were doing, whenever anyone had second thoughts, Chimeg – their Chief – reminded them what this life offered. You could live in normal society, working from suns-up to suns-down doing what you were told, just to survive . . . or you could reach out with both hands and grab hold of what you wanted.

It was worth killing for. If you were smart about it – and the Rakada were – you never killed anyone you didn't have to. That was the price, and Sayana paid it gladly.

But there was a flipside: death could come for you too. You accepted the risk, accepted that any day could be your last (which meant you'd better make the most of the one you were currently living).

Sayana had always thought it was a fair trade. Until now, tied to this pole, which had made her start to question her life choices.

Her eyes landed on a stone in the dust, a little smaller than her fist. One of its edges was jagged, and it was just within range of her left foot.

No way. A stone wasn't a blade, and even positioning it . . .

Then again, it was that, or dinner.

There was only one way this went down. Only one way to get the stone where she needed it. Still, she cast her eyes skywards, suddenly regretting her earlier outburst. "Little help?" she asked, in case either of the Weaver gods were listening, and would perhaps take pity on her by conjuring up a handy sinkhole that would swallow the lizard.

To the surprise of precisely no one, this didn't happen. "Right," Sayana muttered. "Understood. Thanks ever so much."

She began kicking at the top of her left boot with her right, winkling her foot to help it along. The boot was good leather, worn and comfortable, and fitted snugly. Getting it off was agonisingly slow, and at every second, she was convinced that the lizard was going to turn around, look at her like she was an idiot, and then eat her.

Finally, her foot was free. She skittered the stone towards

her, snagged it between big toe and second toe, immediately dropped it. Picked it up again, foot muscles already starting to cramp, holding it as tightly as she dared.

She scooted her butt forward, away from the pole, sliding her back down the wooden surface – as far as she could, anyway, with her hands tied above her. Then she lifted her legs off the ground, bending at the waist, her abs screaming at her. She'd always been grateful for her hip flexibility, which allowed her to bend double with ease, but she'd never once thought it might save her life.

If she could get her feet up and over her head, get the stone to her questing fingers . . .

No good. There was still several inches between her feet and hands. She needed to get her butt and her lower back even further forward, squeeze out just a little bit more from her hips.

She thrust her head and torso out, away from her bound hands – and immediately jerked to a stop.

Her braid. It was still tied around the pole.

Sayana snarled in disbelieving fury, twisting her head back and forth, trying desperately to undo the loose knot. The others were always giving her shit about her braid. *You spend too much time trying to keep it clean, Sayana. Someone can grab it in a fight, Sayana. It'll get you killed.*

Well, fuck them. Just because she wanted to get as far away from the palace as possible didn't mean she couldn't keep at least one thing from her old life. All the same, she was *really* glad the rest of the Rakada weren't around to see that they were right about her hair getting her killed.

The knot came loose. Sayana gasped in triumph, pushing her lower back even further away from the pole, lifting her feet as high as they would go, toes screaming at her as they clutched the stone. Her core trembling, burning, fingertips stretched out.

With her luck, this was exactly when the lizard would notice her. She wouldn't just die, she'd die looking exceptionally stupid.

Her fingers brushed the stone's surface ...

And she had it. Gasping as she let her legs fall back, eyes on the lizard. Weavers' Breath, the beast was big; she was drowning in its shadow. It chewed on its prey, head bent, its back to her. That huge tail thrumming the air.

Slowly, she rotated the stone until the jagged edge faced in. The edge alone wasn't going to be enough. She'd have to use her hands to saw the fabric back and forth.

She got to work. Every time the stone slipped, even a little, her heart threatened to smash right out of her ribcage.

One of the villagers crept into view. The one whose ear she'd nearly sliced off, wearing the blue headband of a healer. He circled to the rear of the lizard, holding a rusted sabre. Why he chose that weapon when a perfectly good pair of sharp blades lay in the dirt by his feet, Sayana didn't know. Quite what he thought he was going to *do* with the blade was even more of a mystery; taking on an *araatan* with it would be like trying to kill a mountain with a tree branch.

"Over here," she hissed, pausing her work on the fabric for a second. "Cut me loose. I can help!"

She wasn't going to help. She was going to run as fast and as far as she could, but he didn't need to know that.

The man ignored her, focusing on the lizard. He raised his sabre, and in that moment, the beast twisted, lunged and ripped him off the ground.

"Oh, *come on!*" Sayana howled as blood spattered the dirt. She started sawing at her bonds again, frantic, back and forth, back and forth. She had no idea if it was working—

—and then her hands were free, springing loose so fast she wasn't ready for it.

She scrambled up, dust caking her one bare foot. Several *gers* were on fire now, black smoke curling into the blue sky. She darted forward, and grabbed her boot, followed by her closest sabre. She turned to get the other – and stopped.

Her weapons should have been next to each other in the dirt. Someone – maybe the healer, maybe the lizard itself – must have kicked the second blade out of reach. It now lay very close to the beast's clawed rear foot.

Fine, she'd lied about her braid being the only thing she'd kept from home. Her sabres were old friends, ones she used to sneak away from court to train with. And it wasn't just about losing something special. The thought of having her sabre end up in the hands of a clueless villager, one who could boast about taking it from a Rakada – a Rakada who ran away, no less – was impossible to stomach.

The beast had its back to her still, tail swishing, the thick knot of bone dragging a furrow through the dirt as it tore at the now very dead healer.

She wasn't going to waste the chance. She tiptoed towards the creature, trying to be as unobtrusive as possible, eyes on her lost sabre.

Almost there. She reached out a hand . . .

Which was when the beast swung its head around and stared down at her.

Three

Hogelun

By the time Hogelun noticed the lizard, it was right next to her.

She shrieked, kicked out at it, nearly toppling off her horse. The lizard, the size of an arrowhead, decided the rock it had planned to sunbake on wasn't worth the trouble. It vanished, a tiny green blur skittering off into the grass. Hogelun delivered an extra kick for good measure. Little arsehole.

"Sorry, boy," she muttered as she rubbed her horse's neck. Her horse, a brown-and-white mottled stallion named Hoof Monster, shifted in place, rattling the bones hanging from his saddle. Horses were generally disloyal bastards not worth naming, in Hogelun's opinion, but Hoof Monster had stuck around longer than most.

There were many things in the Tapestry to be scared of. Venomous spiders the size of a human hand. Storms with chunks of hail big enough to crack skulls, and yellow lightning that could blast you into the next life. Tigers that would tear your throat out before you could even say, "Hold on, is that a tiger?"

Hogelun was on that list too. She knew this because people who saw her coming, clad in bone, swinging her stone-headed club like it weighed as much as a throwing knife, frequently shat themselves.

But you could go back thousands of years, all the way to the First Riders, even beyond that to when Father Sky and Mother Earth wove the Tapestry, and you probably wouldn't find a single time when a little grass lizard had hurt someone.

Hogelun shuddered. It was just that . . . she couldn't stand the way they moved, that little slippy-slidey motion. Or the fact that they detached their tails to escape danger. She always had this image of the disembodied tail crawling its way up her leg, going for her throat . . .

Get a grip. They weren't *araatan*, after all, those horrible bastards who were the reason Hogelun would never in a million years go into the mountains.

She glanced over at Khunbish, but the smaller Rakada hadn't noticed her little lizard episode. Khun was crouched in the grass by her horse, contemplatively licking a stone.

As Hogelun watched, the licks became significantly less contemplative, like Khun was tasting something rare and delicious. Satisfied, she tucked the stone into her ratty old *deel*, which hung on her like beggar's rags.

"Hear anything?" Hogelun asked, jerking her chin at the village.

"Of course." Khun's voice was the whisper of a knife slipped from its sheath. She rolled her head, letting it flop down, her chin resting on the bulky leather pouch she kept strapped tight to the front of her body. "I hear your blood rushing through your veins and the muscles of your eyelids twitching like little insects beneath your skin."

Hogelun had long since got used to the things Khun said.

"No, I mean the others." She put a hand to her eyes, shielding her gaze against the twin suns. The Large Eye was particularly fierce that day, burning out of the bright autumn sky.

She listened hard, listened for the howls across the grass that would signal Chimeg's advance on the village. Nothing. No sign of their Chief. Just crickets, chirping gently in the waving grass.

The myriad bones that hung off Khun's scrawny frame clattered as she got to her feet. "Perhaps a wind sucked our dear Sayana into the clouds. Perhaps it carried her all the way to Father Sky, and even now she is one of his flames, eternal and clean. Such is the destiny for us all."

Hogelun pointed. "You dropped one."

Khun glanced around, then spotted the thigh bone in the dirt. "There you are," she said as she scooped it up, cradling it lovingly. "Mother has found you. There is no escape." She grinned at Hogelun. "I have too many memories. I am always misplacing them and having to find them again."

Hogelun wondered if it was worth pointing out that she'd done the finding, decided against it.

The two of them were a thousand yards south of the village, the cliff on their right. The other raiders – Chimeg, Erhi, and Sarnai – were to the west, hidden in one of the low scraggles of trees that sometimes broke the Tapestry's ocean of grass.

Hogelun would have much preferred to have Erhi here with her instead. But it turned out that if you seduced your lover for a quick roll in the grass and totally accidentally missed the start of a raid even *once*, you were marked for life.

So Erhi rode with Chimeg, and Hogelun was stuck with Khunbish until, as far as she could tell, the end of time. "Might actually come before this bloody raid gets going," she muttered.

"What's that?"

"Nothing."

Last thing she wanted was to engage Khun in a conversation about the end of time. They'd be here for *months*.

Hoof Monster stomped his monstrous hooves. Hogelun grimaced as she noticed the bloodstain on one of them – dammit, she thought she had cleaned that. Khunbish's own horse, a white pony named Midnight, with a bright blond mane, was skittish as Khun mounted him. Midnight lived in a perpetual state of terror from his rider, probably because Khun sometimes snuggled up with him at night and sang him sweet songs about the end of the world.

If you approached Hogelun and Khunbish, silhouetted against the horizon, you'd have been forgiven for thinking that they were mother and child. Then you'd get a closer look at them, and very quickly find somewhere else to be.

Maybe it was because of Hogelun, who had shoulders the size of muskmelons. She was twenty-five and had been this size since she was fifteen, which made her three brothers furious. Especially when they couldn't beat her at wrestling.

Then there was Khun, who could have been anywhere from forty to sixty (no one had got a straight answer out of her, and they had all given up trying) but who had a stare that went on for a thousand years. Her greasy, greying wisps of hair framed a narrow face, with a chin that looked like it could stab someone if swung at just the right angle.

Or maybe you'd decide to make yourself scarce because of the bones.

There were a lot of them.

Hogelun herself was rather proud of the hollow, jawless human skull strapped to her left shoulder, which she'd named Tiny. She was just as proud of the finger bones that fringed the edges of her *deel*. Those had come from a wagon train captain who had had the exceedingly poor judgement to call Erhi a raider whore.

Hogelun had also strapped several tibias to her forearms and biceps. Her necklace was made of gleaming, polished ribs, strung together with tough thread. Sometimes, she painted her entire head bright red, scalp to chin. But she was in a minimalist mood today, so she'd gone for a jagged red slash, one running from her left jawline to her right temple.

Khun's *deel*, predictably, was an osseous waterfall. She was a human hidden inside a mound of rattling white. It was a miracle she was able to move at all, or that Midnight hadn't collapsed from the weight. And Khun didn't paint her face and arms so much as just throw paint in the air and step underneath it before it hit the ground.

The bones were finicky, brittle, absolutely useless as actual armour. But when it came to raiding, they made all the difference.

See, Chimeg, the Rakada Chief, had this whole raider thing figured out. Sure, you could raid because you were genuinely fine with murdering and raping and stealing – what Hogelun thought of as evil raider shit. But what Chimeg had realised was that there was a way to enjoy the benefits of being a raider – the freedom, the sheer pleasure of existing in the Tapestry – while doing as little *evil raider shit* as you could get away with.

First, you raided as infrequently as possible. Raiding was dangerous! Each one carried the chance that someone, a villager with bigger balls than the rest perhaps, would put an arrow in your eye socket. Weavers knew, it had happened.

Second, when you did raid, you didn't rob people blind. You took what you needed *and nothing else*. That way, villagers focused more on rebuilding and moving on than half-baked and tiresome revenge missions.

Third — and definitely the most important — you made it so that when you *did* go raiding, you scared the absolute piss out of people. Even the ones with larger-than-average balls.

You cultivated a reputation that helped you avoid fighting altogether. A reputation that made most villages and nomad caravans simply give up, run for cover, leave their spoils behind for the taking.

And nothing, but nothing, built a reputation quite like human bones, rendered down from the corpses of those few who *did* actually stand up to the Rakada. That was Erhi's job, using various techniques and nasty-smelling compounds that Hogelun tried hard not to think about.

When you put all these things together, you made it a very poor idea for any villager to fight back. And if nobody did, if nobody got it into their heads to raise a weapon in the Rakada's direction . . . well, then no blood needed to be spilled, did it?

It wasn't perfect. The Rakada still took lives, if they had to. Hogelun justified it to herself like this: being a raider was a fuck of a lot better than the alternative. Better than the hard labour, village politics and child-rearing of everyday life in the Tapestry (*and arranged marriages*, she thought bitterly, *can't forget those*).

Raiders would exist whether or not the Rakada themselves did. Better to do it properly, with as little bloodshed as you could manage.

It wasn't noble. It wasn't virtuous. But it had given Hogelun every single thing she cared about in the world, and so she would raid until her own bones fell apart.

You do a couple of raids, you let the story spread about the bones, and then you get to spend the rest of the time doing whatever you wanted. In Hogelun and Erhi's case, that was usually fucking like wild rabbits, playing endless rounds of *shagai*, and getting drunk on *airag*.

Not that the Chief let them slack off when they did go on raids. *Fucking terrifying*, that was the aesthetic she had them aiming for, and Weavers help any Rakada who forgot that.

"Seriously." Hogelun turned to Khun, shifting in her saddle. Her thighs felt like they'd been immersed in a lukewarm swamp. "We've been out here for ages."

"Time is not important." Khun stroked the fat leather pouch on her chest. She had never told anyone what was in there and had always taken great pains to hide the contents.

The Rakada had a running bet going about what it was. Sayana thought it was a precious jewel of some kind, maybe one stolen from the palace. Erhi swore blind it was a baby bird that Khun kept as a pet, although Hogelun reckoned that, knowing Khun, it was probably just the remains of one. She had actually tried to look inside once; her wrist still hurt sometimes.

"I have waited an age for salvation," Khun went on. "Father Sky will not al—"

"Allow you to die yet, yes, I know," Hogelun said. "Heard you the first thousand times. Hey – you want some dried antelope? Still got a bit left."

Hogelun was the clan's cook and was rather proud of her skills with a little bit of salt and some woodsmoke.

Khun perked up. "Does it have tendon? I like tendon. It makes my teeth bounce."

Hogelun dug in her saddlebag, quietly appalled at how empty it was. It was great being a Bone Raider, but lately it had been getting harder and harder.

Raiding had always meant steering clear of Karkorum's army, but with this new Khan in charge, it had got bad. Really bad. Clans getting wiped out, hunted left and right, splintering as their Chiefs couldn't keep them together. A year ago, there'd been fifteen Rakada – a good size for a raider clan. But even the

Bone Raiders were mortal, and thanks to skirmishes with the army and a couple of other aggressive clans, they were down to six.

And that wasn't even the only problem. With every settlement being made to move to the capital, either as conscripts or forced labour, there simply weren't enough places to raid any more.

No matter where the Rakada went, they saw that fucking blue banner, with its white moon and suns. No matter how hard they looked, all they found was empty settlements. Even the game they sometimes hunted had made itself scarce. There used to be so many antelope and wild horses roaming the Tapestry; now, it would take days to find even a single small group.

Hogelun usually did her best not to think about it; she didn't have the brains to find a solution, which was why Chimeg was Chief, and she wasn't. But it had been getting harder to ignore, and for the first time, a little jolt of fear shot through her.

It had taken them weeks to find this little village on the clifftop. Weeks as their supplies got dangerously low. They needed nails, rope, wagon spokes, fabric to patch the holes in their *ger*. They needed preserved meat and fruit and vegetables. If they didn't get those things from today's raid, who in the hells knew when they'd have another chance?

She put it out of her mind, snagged a hunk of dried antelope from the bag. "Don't worry, Khun, got a lovely tendon right here for . . ."

Movement made her look up. A lone rider, cutting through the grass towards them from the north-west. Hogelun tensed – but then she relaxed.

Sarnai had a face that looked as if someone had punched her, repeatedly, and she'd let the bones heal badly out of spite. Nothing fitted, from her crooked nose to one eye that was slightly higher than the other. Like Hogelun, she used rib bones, but hers stuck up in an even fan from her shoulder blades.

There was only one Chief in the Rakada. But Chimeg, Erhi and Sarnai were the ones who actually decided what to do, who they were going to raid. Which was just fine by Hogelun.

Sarnai drew her horse up, flashing Hogelun and Khun a maddeningly calm smile. She might look like the result of an angry brawl, but Hogelun had never met anyone so calm and relaxed. "Either of you seen the Princess? Chief wants to know."

Khun brightened. Hogelun just knew that she was about to say something like *She slipped through a crack in reality*, so she got there first. "Why'd Sayana be with us? She's supposed to report to you and the Chief and Erhi."

"No sign yet." Sarnai leaned back in her saddle, scratching her uneven jawline. "Probably got lost."

Hogelun had her doubts, but it was hard not to look at Sarnai and not relax herself. Just a little.

"Oh – Hogs." Sarnai dug in her saddlebag. "Erhi said to give you this."

The fire apple she pulled out was perfect, crimson skin – speckled with delicious yellow pebbling – gleaming in the suns. Hogelun's stomach rumbled – this was so typical of Erhi. She knew how much Hogelun loved a good fire apple. Hogelun could already imagine what the first bite would be like, the sweet-sour-tart flavour filling her—

Sarnai took a giant bite, teeth crunching into the crisp flesh. Beaming, juice running down her chin, she tossed the rest to Hogelun.

Hogs caught it, glaring at her. "What the fuck?"

The other raider winked. "She said to give it to you. She didn't say how much of it I should give."

Hogelun took a bite of her own, then gave Sarnai the

Cut – putting her thumb to the underside of her chin, flicking it at her. "You are *such* a prick," she said, through a mouthful of fruit.

"Tendon," Khun said, thrusting out her hand and giving the apple a suspicious look.

Hogelun rolled her eyes, swallowed. "*Yes*, Khun, just give me . . . uh, what is that?"

That was a bloom of smoke spewing from the village. As Hogelun stared at it, a bright burst of yellow flame followed it.

"Oh good," said Khun brightly. "Fire."

"Weavers," Hogelun breathed, eyes growing wider by the second. "Princess, what did you *do*?"

Sarnai straightened in her saddle, her relaxed posture vanishing instantly. She said nothing, just stared at the blazing settlement, eyes narrowed.

It was difficult to see things at a distance in the grasslands, especially during the day, when heat haze could distort the horizon. And that was just from the grass itself; add fire into the mix, and picking out details was impossible – even if they weren't a thousand yards away. Hogelun shielded her own eyes, but she had no clue what had made the place they were supposed to raid suddenly go up in flames.

"Fire." Khun's delighted eyes gleamed between hanging locks of greasy hair and even greasier bone. Tiny knives appeared in each hand, as if by magic. "Fire fire fire *fire fire fire*."

In the distance, two trails of what looked like smoke shot into the sky. One orange, one bright crimson. Erhi's signal powder, which she made out of valley flowers and attached to her arrows in little bags. Bursts of colour against the blue sky. And a moment later: Chimeg's distant howls, rolling across the grass.

Hogelun unslung her club, hefted its comforting weight. It was four feet long, the gnarled wooden haft thick as a wrist, the stone head – still with a little bit of human hair and scalp smeared on the top – secured in place with leather straps.

Despite the distant flames and smoke, despite the hitch of worry in her chest, there was still the familiar thrill.

She loved this part.

"Well, all right then." Her voice was a deep growl. She cricked her neck, which felt weird, so she cricked it back the other way. "Let's fucking go."

Hogelun gave Hoof Monster some heels. The stallion exploded towards the burning village, the bones on his saddle rattling. Khunbish and Sarnai followed, and together, they thrust their heads back and unleashed a furious, wailing, air-shredding *howl*.

Four

Sayana

There was a moment — a long moment, a good few seconds — where Sayana thought the lizard would just keep eating. It had a mouth full of tasty villager, after all, and surely it wasn't going to abandon that just to go after her. Surely not. Not after she just escaped her bonds with nothing but a sharp stone and excellent hip flexibility.

Even when it crunched down on Nugai's body, swallowed, licked its jaws with that snake-like tongue, she thought she might get away with it.

She was still thinking these thoughts when the *araatan*'s tail whipped round and nearly took her head off.

Sayana yelped, flung herself to the side, the huge knob of bone on the end of the tail screaming past over her head. Her boot and her remaining sabre both flew out of her hands, vanishing into the dust, the lizard blocking out the world above her with its bulk as it moved, shockingly quick.

A curved claw slashed down, pinning the hem of Sayana's *deel* to the ground. She couldn't get the robe off, couldn't rip it loose.

At any moment, the rest of the Rakada were going to ride in and distract the beast. Aaaaaany second now.

Wide jaws filled the world above Sayana's head. She squealed – she hadn't even known she was *capable* of squealing – wriggling like a landed fish. Somehow, she yanked her arm free of the *deel* – just as the lizard bit down, the teeth punching into the dirt right where she had been a split second before.

Sayana scrambled to her feet, but one of her sabres happened to be in the way. It snagged her heel, putting her off balance, which landed her back on her arse in the dirt, and if there was a more infuriating way to fall down than tripping over your own weapon, she couldn't think of one.

She had an instant to register the bright point of light in the lizard's throat, and dived out of the way as a belch of flame scorched the air. The tent behind her, already smouldering, went up like a pyre.

The sabre, the one she'd tripped over, was right next to her. Without thinking, she snatched it up, then dropped it with a pained yelp. The blade and haft were intact, but blazing hot, the leather strapping burned away.

The whole village was burning, smoke and flame and the stench of boiling blood, the villagers screaming, and Sayana decided that she had had enough. They might have needed this raid to go right, badly needed it, but it wasn't her fault it had gone sideways. It didn't matter how much shit she would get from the others for losing her weapons – at least she would be alive for it.

The Rakada didn't run from their enemies, but Sayana figured that was more of a guideline when the enemy was a freaking *araatan*.

So that's what she did. She turned and ran. And the lizard, with an annoyed snort that Sayana felt in her stomach, came thundering after her.

The road leading down from the edge of the cliff was narrow. The *araatan* had to smash through the *gers,* closely packed on either side, and this slowed it just enough that Sayana started to get a little distance. It wasn't far to the bottom of the hill, but once she was there, she could vanish into the grass. Well, she didn't exactly know how that would work, but it was the best she could—

Her trousers were on fire.

She frantically started batting at her left leg, where the flames were, doing it without thinking. She was so desperate to put out the fire that she slammed right into the side of a wagon. It was sticking out from between two tents, a battered box of chipped wood and faded paint, and it knocked the wind out of her.

From behind – inches away, it felt like – the *araatan* roared, hot breath on her neck. She didn't bother to skirt around the wagon, didn't even wait to get her wind back. Gasping, retching, she simply scrambled up the side, finding handholds without looking, feet skittering against the wood. Her trouser leg was no longer burning, so at least she had that going for her.

She had to get over the wagon. Over, and away, into the grass. She got her balance on the angled wooden roof, took a single stride across it—

The *araatan* dipped its head, and hit the wagon at full, thundering speed. Flipping both it and Sayana into the air.

She didn't have time to scream. The wagon vaporised under her feet in a maelstrom of shattered wood as she flipped end over end, splintered wood everywhere. The *araatan* kept going, plunging straight through the space the wagon had been in, barely slowing. Sayana had just enough time to think that this was all really unfair before she landed hard on the lizard's back.

It was not a graceful landing. She hit it sideways, the narrow ridge of scales on its spine digging into her ribs, her legs flailing, grabbing hold and hanging on in sheer terror.

The lizard roared in confusion: not sure where its prey had gone, puzzled at the strange thing on its back, and clearly not connecting the two.

The smart thing for Sayana to do would have been to slide down, run while it couldn't see her. But at that moment, the lizard tried to buck her off, back legs kicking, and she instinctively dug in. Without even thinking, she grabbed hold of the nearest scales, which frilled up from its skin around the ruff of its neck. They were rough as rock, the edges shredding her palms.

The lizard thrashed in mad, desperate anger. If she fell now, there was an excellent chance it would stomp her to pieces – probably after she snapped an ankle from the height of the fall. So she held on. Swinging her body around, getting her legs across that ridge.

Ger fabric tangled around her as the beast crashed through two tents, a wooden pole nearly braining her. The *araatan* roared as it exploded through the last of the collapsed tents, back onto the narrow thoroughfare that divided the village.

A little boy sat cross-legged in the dust ahead of them, bawling his eyes out. Three years old, maybe. Face puffy and red, looking around for someone to make it all better, either unable or unwilling to move until they did.

And as Sayana took all this in, the *araatan* spotted the child. With a satisfied grunt, it headed right for him.

You couldn't be a raider unless you were very comfortable with killing people. And either very good at it already, or willing to get that way fast.

If you were smart about it, like Chimeg was with the Rakada, you did your best to kill as few people as possible. But there were always those who stood up to you, and if you wanted to keep living your life, riding free across the Tapestry, then you did what you had to.

Sayana had decided a long time ago that it was worth the price. That what she had – what they'd all chosen – was worth the smudge on their souls. The palace she'd grown up in had been toxic, vicious, a nightmare world of court intrigue and shifting alliances, a game she had no idea how to play. If she had to kill to get away from it, then kill she would. She wasn't ashamed of being a raider, or of what she'd done to stay one.

But some things, you didn't do. Ever. And one of those things was killing children. Or, in this case, allowing one to be killed in front of you.

So when the *araatan* spotted the child, Sayana did the only thing she could think to do. Ignoring her shredded palms and the screaming burn on her thigh, she held tight to the scales in her hands and pulled back. Dug in her heels too, like she would with a horse.

She might as well have tried singing the beast a little song. It utterly ignored her, continuing to charge at the bawling child, who stared up at the approaching monster in stupefied, unmoving terror.

There were two small nubbins of bone sticking up from the top of the beast's head. Sayana had no idea how she'd missed them, but as the lizard opened its jaws wide, she lunged forward as far as she could, grabbed the bony nubs, and pulled hard to the right.

She didn't expect it to work. All she knew was that she wasn't going to let this boy get torn to pieces without doing every single thing she could think of to stop it.

But as she yanked on the bone horns, the lizard—

Turned.

It wasn't the elegant, tight turn a horse might make. The thing was huge, after all, a galloping mountain. But it changed direction, tilting away from the child, roaring as it slammed headlong into the nearest tent. Sayana held on, eyes huge, not sure how in the nine hells this was working but too terrified to let go.

Something wrapped around her head – a piece of *ger* fabric, clothing, she didn't know, hot and heavy. And since she didn't dare take her hands off the horns, she had to furiously shake her head to get rid of the thing, hyperventilating in confused darkness.

As she finally got the fabric loose, the *araatan* remembered the person on its back. It bucked again, lifting Sayana off it and bringing her down tailbone first. Which fucking *hurt*.

In desperation, she pulled the other way, and once again, the lizard responded. It was as if it had no choice. As if it *had to* go where its head was pointed. All the same, Sayana had to pull with every ounce of strength she had.

She had broken her share of wild horses before – the stocky, ornery bastards that roamed the Tapestry – and this reminded her of doing it. You had to use the same unrelenting pressure, refusing to be dislodged no matter how badly the animal wanted you gone.

Without any prompting from Sayana, the *araatan* loosed a jet of flame, immolating yet another *ger*. And in that moment, she felt the strangest thing: amazement.

She was riding an *araatan*. Actually riding it.

Sure, she was only barely in control, could have been bucked off and trampled/eaten/cooked alive at any moment . . . but she was still steering it. Doing something that had never been done before, because no one had been stupid enough to try.

Right then, Sayana got a glimpse of the boy again. His parents had him, thank both the Weavers – she couldn't even fathom how they'd let him get away from them in the first place, but it didn't matter. They had him now. They were only a little older than she was, a man and a woman with ruddy, sun-damaged faces, and they were staring at her in total, stupefied awe.

Staring at someone on top of a snorting, rampaging, fire-breathing lizard. Staring at *her*, riding it.

There was a moment, just a few seconds, where Sayana forgot her terror. Where, for a fleeting instant, she actually smiled. Damn right they should stare at her in awe. She was awesome. *This* was awesome.

Or it was, until reality rapidly flooded back in. She had to get the beast out of the village. She had no idea what would happen then, but at the very least, she could make sure it didn't eat anyone else. In the next few minutes, anyway.

She pulled hard, the lizard fighting her, turning it south. Gripping the horns harder as she tore through the village, smashing *gers* aside, thigh muscles straining as she held on. Smoke ripping coughs out of her aching chest.

Five

Hogelun

Hogelun's howling record was twenty-six seconds of con-
tinuous noise.

There was a real art to it. Amateurs always tried to hold the
air in, let it out in a thin stream. But it was all in the diaphragm;
you had to control your core, tighten your stomach muscles.
Really put your back into it.

Hogelun hadn't come close to that twenty-six-second mark
in a while, but she had a good feeling about this next breath.
She inhaled deeply, head tilted back, already tasting smoke in
the air . . .

And then ahead of her, Sarnai suddenly peeled off to the left.
Away from the village.

Hogelun had just started her howl, and choked off with a
high-pitched, questioning little *Eep*? Sarnai was waving at them
to follow. *Frantically* waving.

For an instant, Hogelun had absolutely no idea what she was
doing. Then she looked past her, and saw.

The three of them were approaching the burning village from
the south, along the cliffs. Chimeg and Erhi rode from the west.

And rolling up behind them, in a huge thunder of dust, was a massive group of riders.

Riders clad in black. Riders with banners. Blue fabric, with white and orange shapes.

Hogelun stared slack-jawed at the Khan's soldiers: dark shapes against the puffy, billowing clouds on the horizon. It didn't make sense; why were the soldiers even *here*? Surely it couldn't be because of the Rakada. They hadn't even spotted the village until this morning ...

It wasn't the whole army, of course – just a battalion, no more than a hundred troops or so. But that was more than enough to wipe out Chimeg and Erhi. The realisation was a dull blade, slipped between Hogelun's ribs.

The Rakada and the Khan's army had always been at odds. But it had got worse over the past year – a lot worse – and it had whittled the Rakada's numbers down.

There used to be both men and women in the clan, getting along just fine, mostly ... but now, it was just the women left. Had been for a while. She remembered the Twins, Arsi and Arslan, who had died fighting soldiers at Antelope Rocks; Zinbar, who was almost as big as Hogelun herself, took an arrow in the gut. Still more had left, slipping away in the night, deciding that being a raider wasn't worth it any more. It made Hogelun sick – she couldn't fathom giving up this life willingly, not ever – but she wasn't stupid.

The problem was, they couldn't always face the army head on.

The Rakada had gone from fifteen, to twelve, to six. They didn't run from fights – it rather went against the whole *scariest-raiders-in-the-Tapestry* thing – but at some point, that idea met cold, hard reality. The reality of numbers: the bigger the battalion, the more chance the Rakada wouldn't make it out.

Usually, they could outrun a big group of soldiers. The more horses there were, the more they bunched up, slowed each other down. But today, the Weavers were clearly having a merry old time fucking with the Rakada. Not content with setting the village on fire, they'd decided to bless the army with speed, or better terrain, or fresher horses. The soldiers were going to catch Chimeg and Erhi – they were gaining on them already, running them down.

The Chief would no doubt have preferred Hogelun, Sarnai and Khun to get out of there. Save themselves. Well, in this case, the Chief could get fucked.

Khun took off after Sarnai, both of them heading for the Chief, for Erhi, for the army about to engulf them. Hogelun didn't hesitate; she gave Hoof Monster her heels, the horse obeying, going to a full-on gallop.

Sorry, Princess. You're on your own.

Arrows were already flying as they approached, black streaks against the blue sky, thudding into the ground around Erhi and Chimeg's horses. Hogelun didn't know who was going to reach the Chief first – the army, or the other Rakada.

Before she could resolve this, an arrow appeared in the flank of Chimeg's horse.

The animal's screech was audible even over the army's thundering hooves. It went down, its legs collapsing, nearly crashing down on top of Chimeg. The Chief only just managed to leap free, rolling hard. Her spear was still in its sheath on her back, and the roll was awkward, ungainly. She vanished into the grass.

Erhi was slightly ahead of her, crimson *deel* billowing as she rode, and didn't immediately realise that the Chief was down. When she did, she turned her horse back, nocking her bow, firing. But it was too late. The Rakada Chief was off her horse, an entire battalion riding her down.

As Hogelun urged Hoof Monster to ride even harder, Chimeg rose from the grass.

The Chief was compact and muscular, loose black hair flying around a block of a face. She wore no *deel*, as usual, just a thick, sleeveless leather tunic that ran down almost to her knees. She preferred sharpened jawbones as decoration, strapped to her forearms and shoulders. Her spear, shaft black from long use, held in one hand.

She stared down the oncoming soldiers. Even as the arrows whipped through the air around her – Hogelun actually saw one come within a few inches of punching through her shoulder – she didn't move a single muscle.

What is she doing? Hogelun had her heels dug so hard into Hoof Monster's sides that it was a wonder the horse didn't buck her off.

Still Chimeg stood. Unmoving. Facing the enemy.

When the Rakada were fifty yards away, when the soldiers were almost on top of her, she snapped her spear up like a striking snake, cocked back her arm, and hurled the weapon through the air.

It took one of the soldiers in the chest, hitting him so hard that he fell backwards off his horse. As he did, Hogelun caught a flash of red against his black uniform: his sash.

She didn't know much about how armies worked, but she knew that a red sash meant command. Chimeg hadn't just attacked. She'd stood and waited, and when she was damn good and ready and not a second before, she'd taken out the leader.

Panic rippled through the rest of the soldiers. They stopped launching arrows, just for a moment, breaking left and right in a confused, clumsy melee.

Sarnai had got ahead of Erhi. She reached down, trying to

scoop the Chief onto the back of her horse as the soldiers circled. Chimeg waved her away, eyes flashing. "What the fuck are you doing here?" she snapped, as Hogelun and the others arrived.

"Sorry, Chief," Sarnai said, sweeping hair out of her face as she flashed a relaxed grin. "Thought you could use a little help."

Hogelun barely noticed. It was Erhi she had eyes for, scanning the archer for any sign of damage as she brought her horse to ride alongside. There was none, of course – Erhi was immaculate, as usual, crimson *deel* spotless, her headband of bone chips perfectly positioned. She could have been sipping *airag* on a warm afternoon.

For half a second, Hogelun forgot about the army. Forgot about this absolute clusterfuck of a raid, and just took her in.

She couldn't help it. Erhi just did that to her.

The archer knew it too. She raised an eyebrow, quirking a smile as her horse's hooves hammered the dirt. She was deaf, but even on horseback, her hand signs were smooth and clear. *Riding in to save me, Hogs? I'm flattered.*

Hogelun didn't get a chance to reply. The soldiers were rallying. She whipped her head left and right, hunting for an opening. Every one she saw closed up immediately. She couldn't catch a glimpse of the soldiers' faces; it was all just a black blur.

Erhi was close by – Hogelun could sense her, just out of view on her left. The archer's drawstring creaked as she nocked another arrow. Hogelun didn't dare look round. She reseated her club in her hand, fingers drenched with sweat.

Behind the soldiers, the village burned, the sky black with smoke. There was something else too, a dark shape at the base of the fire. A shape that was moving. Hogelun didn't have time to work out what it was – she had more pressing things to deal with.

Chimeg let out a blood-freezing howl. Hogelun could see a

few of the soldiers' faces by now – young, scared. Pale under helmets that rose in a short, stubby cone. Threadbare black *deels* over thick leather. Bows and sabres held in trembling hands.

Hogelun had once asked Erhi how the Khan's generals kept their soldiers in check. Seemed to her that if they were forced to join up, they wouldn't want to be there. They'd desert or mutiny, and they'd be useless in a fight.

Erhi had made a face. *Some do,* she'd signed. *But you only have to punish a few before the rest fall in line. And anyway, they're being given weapons and told that a big part of their job is killing us. Raiders.*

Sure, half of these soldiers were fucking terrified – as you would be, if your commander had just been impaled in front of you. Even now, some of them were still shrinking back. But the other half? The other half looked excited about taking some raider bones for themselves. There was a good chance some had been raided themselves, back in the day; maybe one or two had even been in a Rakada raid . . .

Hogelun's mouth twisted. Wouldn't it be perfect, just fucking *apt*, if she got killed today by someone whose shitty little village she'd raided?

Khun flipped her knives in her hands, licking her lips. Again, Hogelun felt the urge to look in Erhi's direction, take in as much of her as she could. She didn't, because they weren't dying today, not a chance.

But right then, all she could think of was how the Rakada were being whittled down to nothing. One by one. Until there were hardly any left . . . and nowhere near enough to fight a force of this size.

Chimeg levelled a finger at the nearest soldiers. "Careful now. I'll be wanting my spear back."

Without another word, she drew her backup sabre, ripping it from her sash. She strode forward through the grass, giving a few experimental slashes. The soldiers stared at her in shock, because as their commanders would have drilled into them, approaching a mounted opponent on foot was madness.

Chimeg looked over her shoulder at the other Rakada. "Coming?"

Which was all they needed.

Khun attacked first, leaping off Midnight's back and zigzagging across the grass, gibbering mad nonsense as her knives flashed. Then Erhi was nocking and firing, Sarnai rushing after her Chief with her sabre drawn, and Hogelun was howling louder than ever as she rode hard at the soldiers. Her club parted the grass, the stone head launching upwards, Hogelun twisting her body to give it as much force as possible as it knocked two soldiers into the next life.

In a just world, the entire battalion would have broken and run after Chimeg absolutely smoked their commander. Unfortunately for the Rakada, the soldiers fought back.

Hogelun sort of lost track after that.

It always happened during a fight. This was the one thing she was built for, the one thing she never doubted about herself. If there was an enemy, and she had her club, she could let all her higher brain functions take a nice, long nap. The complicated, difficult bits of the world faded away, and all she needed to do was keep swinging.

Arrows shot past her face as blood spattered the head of her club, her arms, her face. At some point, she dismounted, boots digging into the ground as she swung again and again and again. Cuts blossomed on her forearms, a nasty one appearing on her shoulder, and she barely noticed. Just more scars to add to her tally.

She caught a glimpse of the Chief, off to her left. Chimeg had just snatched up her spear — but the moment she did, she had to drop it, getting her sabre up as two soldiers went for her, pinning her between them. One of their strikes sent her blade flying, and Hogelun's breath caught in her throat—

Chimeg didn't hesitate. The jawbones strapped to her long leather cuff had been honed with as much care as the blade on her spear. She spun in place, whipping her forearm around and burying them in the closest soldier's face.

"Yes Chief!" Hogelun roared, as Chimeg slashed at the second soldier. "That's what I'm fucking talking ab—"

Something smacked her in the back of the head.

She never saw what it was, but it made the whole world go wobbly for a minute. She came back, blinking, wondering why everything was sideways. Her club. Her club! Where was—

A shadow fell over her. A soldier, battle-crazed, teeth bared, driving a sabre towards her throat.

He didn't get there, because all at once, there was a blade sticking out of his chest. Sarnai ripped it free with a grunt, kicked the now very dead soldier sideways. "You're welcome," she said, winking at Hogelun.

Hogs shook her head, did it again. It cleared some of the fuzziness; the back of her skull was throbbing, pulsing with every beat of her heart, blood dripping onto her neck.

Hogelun spat, took Sarnai's offered hand, let herself get pulled to her feet. She wanted to ask what had hit her, how the fight was going, if the others were OK, if *Erhi* was OK. She opened her mouth and found that all she could say was "Fuck me."

Sarnai's grin grew wider. "Only if you ask very nicely—"

The arrow punched into her neck with a loud *thuck*.

Hogelun gaped as Sarnai fell, the smile still on her face. She crashed to the ground, her sabre skittering away.

It wasn't just that Sarnai was fearless, and lucky — up until the last few moments, anyway. She was one of Chimeg's most trusted people. The thought of her not being there, even as she lay dead in front of Hogelun, was almost impossible to take in.

She wasn't the first Rakada to die in front of Hogs. But this . . . it felt different.

The battle seemed to slow around her as she got to her feet. In that instant, she caught sight of Chimeg. The Chief had her spear back, but she was staring slack-jawed at Sarnai's body.

"Chimeg!" Hogelun yelled. The Chief didn't appear to hear her. A soldier came up behind her, and Hogelun's heart leaped into her throat — but at the last instant, Chimeg reacted, swinging her spear around and sweeping the woman's legs out from underneath her.

Erhi. She was off to Hogelun's left, her bow gone, her *deel* cut to shreds. She was going hand-to-hand with another soldier, her short sabre flashing as she defended. This time, Hogelun did move. But even as she forced her way to Erhi, even as she pushed and slashed and shoved and ducked, the horrid thoughts kept coming.

They weren't going to win this. There were simply too many soldiers. Chimeg had always said that she'd choose a few skilled raiders over a thousand badly trained soldiers any day; turned out, she was wrong. It would only take a hundred or so.

Erhi caught Hogelun's eye, a split-second glance. The archer didn't look like herself. She looked terrified, eyes huge, sweat pouring off her as she tried to dance away from her attacker. And Hogelun was too far, her club suddenly a dead weight in her hand, the back of her head screaming at her and Sarnai's blood still on her face. She wasn't going to make it, they were going to cut down Erhi in front of her—

In that moment, something changed.

It was as if the battle was suddenly running at half-speed. No, that was wrong — it was the soldiers. They were all staring in horror at Hogelun, sabres paused mid-swing.

For a second, Hogelun genuinely thought she'd scared the piss out of them with her approach. *Excellent.* She growled, hefted her club, took two steps towards Erhi — and stopped. Feeling dull, rumbling thuds rolling up through the dirt, suddenly aware that the soldiers weren't looking at her ...

They were looking at something over her shoulder.

When she turned and saw the *araatan*, thundering across the grass towards them, a hundred yards away and closing fast, a mountain with legs and teeth, Hogelun had the wildest thought. That the little lizard she'd chased off earlier had called its big brother for help.

The soldiers around her began to move, to scatter, but Hogelun just stared. Locked in place by sheer, bewildered terror. As the *araatan* blocked out the sky in front of her, she registered that there was something on its back.

Not something. Some*one*.

When she realised it was the Princess, the bottom fell out of her mind.

As the *araatan* reached the edge of the melee, it opened its mouth, revealing a glowing ball of flame in the back of its throat.

Six

Sayana

S ayana would have loved to take credit for crashing the
araatan into the Khan's army. It would have been so much
better, all things considered, if she could have said she'd spotted
what was happening, sized up the situation, and immediately
taken decisive action.

In reality, she didn't even *notice* the soldiers until the beast
was right on top of them.

She'd been so focused on getting out of the village – on riding
the *araatan* somewhere that wasn't filled with splintering wood
and whipping tent fabric and scorching flames, which didn't
have helpless little boys sitting there waiting to be eaten – that
she just didn't register what was happening in the grass at the
bottom of the hill.

She hung on with every muscle she had, coughing and spluttering, fingers locked in a death grip around the beast's stubby
horns. Wondering how in the nine hells she was going to get off
without being stomped, eaten, burned alive, or all three at once.

The *araatan* suddenly veered to the right, so sharply that
it nearly threw Sayana from its back. It accelerated too, going

from a trot to a thundering, rolling gallop – or whatever the galloping equivalent was for gigantic lizards with enormous legs. It was *obscene* how quickly it could move, how nimble it was for its size.

As Sayana got her balance, she became aware of a very large number of people in the grass in front of her. She had just enough time to register them as the Khan's army, to pick out the black uniforms and banners, and then the *araatan* opened its mouth and turned several of them to ash.

Sayana hung on for dear life as the lizard crashed headlong into the remaining soldiers, sweeping its head from side to side, snatching up one of them even as it knocked several aside. The soldiers who'd somehow managed to avoid the fire, the jaws and the swinging head panicked, dropping their weapons and falling over themselves to get away. Sayana would have been delighted, if she wasn't terrified out of her mind.

But there was something else beyond the terror. A sick satisfaction. Yes, she was barely in control, but Weavers, it felt *so fucking good* to smash the Khan's army for a change. She didn't have the first clue where they'd come from, but, at this point, it hardly mattered.

She glanced to her left, blinking back stinging sweat and sour smoke, and spotted the Rakada.

Hogelun, clambering to her feet. Chimeg next to her, blinking up at her in astonishment. Erhi too, eyes narrowed, like she didn't quite trust what she was seeing. Only Khun seemed unbothered by any of this insanity; she was waving, a wide grin on her face, like this was exactly how she expected Sayana to roll up. The only one she couldn't see was Sarnai . . .

The remnants of the Khan's army dissolved as Sayana crashed through their ranks, scattered them, sent them running in a hundred directions across the grass. In seconds, Sayana was through the fight. And as nice as it was to have scored a point for the raiders for a change, she was still stuck on the back of a very angry lizard.

She could steer it – but where was she planning on going? There weren't any convenient ledges she could leap to. There *was* a clutch of birch trees to the west, but even from here Sayana could see that the lizard would smash them to pieces. And even if she could somehow dismount, could somehow convince the *araatan* not to eat her, she couldn't stop it from going right back into the village.

Frantic, she looked around, but there was nothing. The birch tree grove in the distance, the village, the cliff running alongside it, the—

The cliff.

Before she could stop herself, before she could second-guess what she was doing, Sayana pulled hard on the left horn. Taking the lizard around in a huge, looping turn.

As she approached the cliff, a bird came in for a landing; it spotted the rampaging lizard, took off again in a wild flap to find somewhere that wasn't filled with violent, burning death.

Sayana had the strangest thought: she didn't want to do this. She didn't want to kill the *araatan*.

More than that: she didn't want to dismount. She didn't want to give up the feeling, give up steering this enormous mass of raw power. She kept picturing the shocked faces of the villagers, the soldiers – hells, the *Rakada*. Had anyone looked at her like that before? Ever?

But she had no choice. Because if she didn't kill it, the enormous mass of raw power would destroy her, and everyone around her.

At the last moment, the lizard appeared to understand what was happening. It roared in anguish, tried to force itself to stop, clods of earth flying as it dug in with its claws. But it was moving way too fast, with too much momentum.

Sayana got her legs under her, braced against the beast's back. She was probably going to snap that ankle after all ... but at least she'd be alive to heal from it.

Gravity took the *araatan*. As it rocketed off the cliff, and with her pounding heart trying to climb all the way up her throat and out of her mouth, Sayana slid off its back.

Her ankle didn't snap, although the impact shot up through her legs into her spine, in a way that she would absolutely be paying for the next day. She landed hard, rolled – but it wasn't just the *araatan* that had too much momentum. The beast – bellowing, furious – tumbled over the cliff ...

And she went with it.

For a split second, her world was a tumbling mass of rock and sky. Then she was brought up short, slamming hard against the side of the cliff, enough to knock the wind out of her lungs. She clung to the edge, fingertips taut and shaking, cheek scraped raw from the rock, face and arms smeared with dirt. Her burned thigh was agony.

The *araatan* was still roaring. A second later, the sound cut off with a heavy, wet thump.

It was the last thing Sayana heard before the blood rushing in her ears got too loud, underscored by a fierce, brutal ringing.

Hands reached over the cliff, grabbing her shoulders, under her arms. A few moments later, she was on her back in the dirt, blinking up at the blue sky. Still not a hundred per cent sure she wasn't dead.

Three black shapes slid into view above her head. She vaguely wondered if they were real.

"She lives," someone said. "As the prophecy foretold."

"Not now, Khun," said someone else.

More hands, and then Sayana was standing with the other Rakada – Erhi, Khun and Chimeg. Hogelun was a short distance away, bent over, retching her breakfast into the dirt.

Where did everyone's horses go? Why were they all on foot? And where was Sarnai? Why wasn't she—

Then she saw the look on Chimeg's face. Sayana closed her eyes, bitter dismay settling over her. She'd *liked* Sarnai.

Chimeg stood for a moment. She bowed her head and took a deep breath, a second. The shocked expression on her face melted away, and when she looked up, the old Chimeg was back. She studied the burning wreckage that used to be a village, then looked over at Sayana. "You do understand the meaning of the word *scout*, yes?"

Sayana blinked. "I—"

"Doesn't matter." Chimeg's face split in a smile. She strode towards Sayana, and wrapped her in a crushing hug. "Princess, I have no idea how in the fuck you did that, but you're bloody amazing. *That* was amazing."

Sayana didn't know what was more astonishing: that the Chief had complimented her, or that she'd got over Sarnai's death so quickly. Both felt too big to process.

Then again, she'd been through this before. They all had. Sarnai wouldn't be forgotten – they'd talk about her later, share memories, get fucked up on *airag* and celebrate her life. And then they'd move on, because . . .

Because it was all they could do.

Still, she couldn't help feeling like a fist had reached into her guts; reached in, twisted, refused to let go. In the aftermath of the fight – especially this fight, which Sayana still didn't quite believe had actually happened – Sarnai's death was too much to deal with.

Chimeg was still going. "I mean, you obviously weren't in

control – not beyond steering the damn thing." She let go of the hug, gave Sayana's shoulders a shake. "But still. Fucking incredible. We owe you one."

Sayana gestured at Hogelun with a shaking finger, speaking words that felt like they were piped in from another realm. "She . . . OK?"

She doesn't like lizards, Erhi signed. Her hand movements were shaky, clumsy. *What happened to your boot?*

"My . . ." Sayana looked down, blinking at her bare foot.

"Did you eat it?" Khun asked cheerfully, just as Hogelun stumbled up, face pale as a cloud.

"That—" The big Rakada cleared her throat, spat. The gob of saliva landed near Erhi's boot; the archer elegantly lifted her foot, flashing a look of mild annoyance at her lover, who didn't notice.

"That," the big Rakada said, "was an *araatan.*" Even in her shaky state, her hands signed for Erhi, the movements automatic.

"We're aware," Chimeg said.

"A giant lizard, running around the grass."

"Again: we all saw it."

Are you all right, my love? Erhi asked.

Hog's laugh was high and shaky. "Oh yeah. Terrific. Lovely day in the Tapestry, little raid, standard procedure, don't mind the *enormous fucking lizard* . . ."

How did you do that? Erhi signed to Sayana. *Get on top of it?*

They were all looking at her now. And she didn't have the first clue where to start. "It was sort of an accident," she said, feeling a little lame.

"You *accidentally* climbed on its back?" Chimeg asked. She shook her head, still grinning. "Nine hells, Sayana."

"How did . . ." Sayana's brain felt like the foam at the base of a waterfall: chaotic, constantly moving, white and hissing. "How did the *araatan* get here?"

"An ancient demon walks among us, feasting on our souls," Khunbish said, delicately scraping at the inside of her left nostril with her knife, the blade in far enough to make everyone feel super uncomfortable. Her other hand rested protectively on the leather pouch on her chest, as if she wanted to reassure herself it was still there.

Sayana's saliva felt just a little too thick when she swallowed, and there was still that hideous ringing in her ears. "I mean: why? What would make an *araatan* come down from the mountains?"

Chimeg and Erhi exchanged a look then. They'd spent years together in the Khan's army, before they became raiders, and had a way of communicating that the rest of the Rakada had never quite decoded.

The Chief rubbed her chin. "Here's what we're going to do. Hogs, you and I are going to head back, see if there's anything worth taking that isn't on fire. Erhi, keep an eye out for any more soldiers."

Sayana's eyes went wide. They'd needed a fresh haul of food, of supplies, and now . . .

How long before we find another village? Are there even any left?

Sarnai dead. Their raid target on fire. The army nearly wiping the rest of them out. Forget the *araatan*; short of actually dying, Sayana couldn't work out how the day could have gone worse.

The Chief turned to her. "Princess, you and Khun go down the cliff, see if you can't salvage anything from the *araatan*."

Sayana didn't even have the energy to bristle at the nickname. She just nodded.

Khun peered over the cliff, right at the edge, apparently not bothered by the fact that a strong breeze could knock her off. "The dreaming blood is swept away by the water of the ages."

Usually, they didn't pay too much attention to what Khun said. That way lay madness – or at least, that way lay confusion and exasperation and feeling like you needed to sleep with one hand on your sabre. This time, though, there was something in Khun's voice that told Sayana she needed to listen.

"Khun," Chimeg said patiently. "Use your words."

"It's not there. Our lovely little beastie."

"What?" Sayana stumbled to the edge, took a look for herself.

The cliff dropped fifty feet down to a field of scattered rocks, next to a shallow river; fast-moving, but not nearly wild enough to sweep away anything, let alone a huge lizard beast. There was a trail of black blood running from the rock field to the river, a smear that stopped at the water's edge. Little tendrils of the gooey blood bobbed in the current.

The *araatan* was gone.

Seven

Hogelun

G iant lizards could fuck right off.

That was Hogelun's considered opinion. They could fuck right off into the sun, then fuck off into the other sun, then just stay there until the end of time.

Her head hurt. Not like, I'm-going-to-start-bleeding-out-of-my-ears hurt, but still uncomfortable. Erhi had given them all a once-over, and no one had suffered any life-threatening injuries.

No one except Sarnai.

They'd buried her where she fell — what was left of her, anyway. She'd been dead when the *araatan* arrived, but her body had been caught in the lizard's flame. They'd removed their sashes and given her the blessings of Father Sky and Mother Earth, and . . .

Well.

Hogelun kept picturing that arrow, thudding into her neck. Another Rakada, murdered by the army. Another one sacrificed to the Khan's grand plan. Tears had pricked at Hogelun's eyes as Chimeg had said the rites in a calm, clear voice . . . but they never fell.

There was hardly anything left in the village to take. Its inhabitants were gone, scattered, and what was left was a burning, smashed wreck. Hogelun barely remembered digging through the rubble. After an hour, Chimeg called an exhausted halt, told the Rakada to head back to their wagon.

They never took it on raids if they could avoid it; it slowed them down, gave them something to defend when they should be attacking. Chimeg insisted that they hide it, stash it somewhere nearby before each raid, along with all their spare horses.

Which was dumb. Wouldn't it be better to be able to see it? Why leave it in a place where someone might stumble on it? But Chimeg had told them this was what they were doing, and Hogelun had just nodded. Chimeg was the Chief, after all, and there wasn't much point having a Chief if you were just going to ignore her commands. For this raid, they'd left the wagon in a clutch of rocky hills to the north-west, fifteen minutes' ride away.

As if mocking Hogelun's mood, the weather was perfect, the setting suns bathing the rolling hills of the Tapestry in burnished gold. The grass stalks waved in the wind, which smelled of juniper and soft earth. A thunderstorm gathered in the south, unheard lightning cracking green and yellow, but the rest of the sky was free of clouds. Birds wheeled high above the Rakada, turning in long, slow circles.

Normally, Hogelun lived for days like these. Riding with your clan, nothing ahead of you but everything you'd ever wanted. Not this time. This time, she couldn't stop her thoughts from boiling inside her head.

"Well, what was I supposed to do?" Sayana was saying to Chimeg, over her shoulder. The Chief sat on the back of Sayana's horse – an undignified position for a Chief, but it wasn't as if she had a choice. The Princess had managed to get a replacement boot off a soldier's foot, although it didn't fit her quite right. Khunbish, of course, was off somewhere unseen, doing ... whatever it was she did after a raid.

Sayana's horse — a mottled brown pony with a yellow mane — was new, so new that Hogelun couldn't remember its name. The Princess had a remarkable track record of letting them get lost or killed, often in ways that made no sense. There was one a few months back that was attacked by a bird of prey, while Sayana was fetching some water from a river. Birds never attacked horses, on account of not being able to carry them off to eat, and no one could quite work out why this one decided to have a go. The horse had bolted, vanishing into the grass, and leaving Sayana with a very long walk back to camp.

"Not get caught," Chimeg said. "You should *never* have been that close."

"How am I supposed to scout if I can't ... "

Hogelun didn't hear the rest. Right then, Hoof Monster swerved, avoiding a clutch of tough shrubs, and Hogelun's stirrup snapped. A little *plink*, and suddenly her right foot was hanging free. It wasn't even the leather; it was the actual metal. Rusty, sheared-off ends scraped her boot.

She stared in dismay. Were there any spare stirrups in the wagon? She didn't think so. And come to that, what was she going to cook them all tonight? Even with all the extra foraging and hunting they'd done lately, she had fuck all. And now they had to compete with the *araatan*, who shouldn't even *be* here.

An image of the little lizard from before flashed through Hogelun's mind. A tiny shape, vanishing into the grass ...

"Need a minute," she murmured, not knowing if Erhi could read her lips then, and not caring. She reined in Hoof Monster, dismounted, took a few stumbling steps. Stopped with her hands on her knees, breathing hard.

Erhi's horse, Windwalker, came to a halt nearby. It took the archer a few seconds to dismount — she had a special saddle, made of hard, oiled wood, that let her turn and fire while mounted. She appeared next to Hogelun, face knotted in concern.

Hogelun took several deep breaths. *I'm all right*, she signed.

It wasn't just the fucking lizard. She kept seeing Sarnai, the arrow sticking out of her neck. Kept thinking about how they could do nothing but bury her, how they hadn't even had time to drink to her memory.

Erhi straightened. *What are you cooking tonight?*

It was such a close echo of Hogelun's thoughts from before that she actually blinked in surprise. "What?"

She forgot to sign, but it didn't matter. *Tell me*, Erhi asked. *What's in the cookpot?*

For a moment, Hogelun's mind went completely blank. She had an absurd urge to tell Erhi that they were having roasted stirrup, and almost said it too. Why not? Nothing made sense any more. There were enormous lizards roaming the Tapestry when they should be in the bloody mountains, lizards that could burn you to a crisp and eat you whole. Probably the other way round too. Or both at the same time.

Fortunately, when Hogelun signed, her answer actually made sense. *Parsnip stew. With onions and herbs*. Yes, that would do it. She had enough for tonight, at least.

Could you put some garlic in there? Erhi asked.

You eat too much. Your breath always stinks.

Erhi raised a perfect eyebrow.

Not all the time, Hogelun signed quickly. *Just when you have garlic*. It was a stupid thing to say — Erhi spent so much time keeping herself clean, more than any of them. And she was proud of the paste she'd made so none of them lost their teeth – Hogelun had to remember that. *Your breath actually smells nice today*, she went on, *so . . . a bit of garlic shouldn't . . .*

Erhi patiently waited until Hog's hand signs faltered, still with eyebrow raised. Hogelun stopped, a hot, flustered feeling snaking its way across her shoulders.

When Erhi rolled her eyes, and gave her the Cut, tilting her head back and flicking her left thumb out from under her chin, Hogelun sagged a little. She didn't like insulting people, never had, even by accident, and definitely not her Erhi.

Despite her worry, she grinned back. She could watch that woman give her the Cut all day. Could watch her do anything.

Erhi and Chimeg had started the Rakada together. The Chief had already been thinking of quitting her army post – and the new Khan seizing power? That sealed the deal. She'd taken Erhi with her. Deserters were punished with death, so the two of them had become raiders. First with another clan, then striking out on their own.

Hogelun tried many times to work out why Erhi – cultured, thoughtful Erhi, with a mind the size of the Tapestry itself, who could wield a bow and concoct any powder and potion you wanted – had chosen her. Erhi, who had looked at Hogelun's clumsy, stammering infatuation, and decided: *Yes. This is who I want to be with.* Amazingly, incredibly, impossibly, she had chosen Hogelun.

Luck was in short supply for raiders these days, but every time she and Erhi snuggled in next to each other at night, her powerful arm wrapped around the other woman's slender frame, Hogelun silently thanked the Weavers that she had got that lucky.

Erhi leaned in, resting her forehead on Hogelun's. Even though she had to get up on tiptoe to do it. They stood there for a minute, swaying gently. Erhi's hair had come loose from her tight bun, the strands blowing in the wind and tickling Hogelun's nose, but right then she didn't give a fuck.

Erhi flicked the skull on Hogelun's shoulder. *Tiny says I can have as much garlic as I want.*

Tiny's an idiot.

Hogelun's eyes strayed to Hoof Monster's broken stirrup, and her heart sank a little. Still, she felt better than she did a few minutes ago. *What if we see another one though?* she signed. *Another* araatan? *What are we going to do?*

Ride hard in the other direction.

Obviously. Hogelun changed tack. *What I don't understand is, what are they doing here? In the Tapestry?*

Erhi studied the horizon. Hogelun waited patiently because she knew the archer would have a theory. She always did.

When Chimeg and I were in the army . . . Erhi's movements were hesitant, as if she was trying to line up her own thoughts. *There was all this . . . always these rumours about putting more soldiers in the Baina, along the border.*

Hogelun frowned. *Dalai's never invaded.* Dalai, the land to the north of the Tapestry and the Baina Mountains, was somewhere she'd never been.

And yet, suddenly we've got araatan *leaving the mountains.* Erhi pointed north – they were far from the peaks, but Hogelun could swear she saw them anyway, jagged shapes beyond the horizon. *The Khan isn't just making people leave the Tapestry and head to the city. He's conscripting a whole lot of them. Training them in camps, forcing them to garrison outposts on the border.*

OK, but—

Think, Hogs. Think about what that does to game. The archer spread her arms. *Kind of hard for a big lizard to hunt oxen and mountain goats if soldiers eat them all first.*

"And so they come out onto the Tapestry to find food," Hogelun murmured to herself. The air was hot, still, but she couldn't help shivering.

Still. If anybody could figure out how to survive, it was Chimeg and Erhi. The Rakada would be fine. All she had to do was focus on what was right in front of her.

Khunbish trotted by atop Midnight, the horse's eyes rolling wildly in their sockets. "I need elderflower," she called to Hogelun and Erhi. "Young stalks. Quickly, now, before the demons eat them."

She didn't stick around to check if the two of them obeyed, or if any elderflower-munching demons actually popped up. Just dug her heels into Midnight's sides, tearing off after Sayana and Chimeg.

Don't look at me, Hogelun told Erhi. *I'm not fighting any more bloody demons today.*

You never answered my question this morning, by the way, Erhi signed.

Hogelun cocked her head, and her heart began to beat a little faster, the way it always did when she'd forgotten something important. *What question?*

Would you rather live to a thousand with your current body, the same as it is now, or have an orgasm so amazing you die from sheer pleasure? She quirked her mouth, looking at Hogelun expectantly.

They'd started playing games like this. Silly would-you-rathers, which often led to long, rambling conversations that went on for hours. Hogelun hadn't answered this morning; she'd been distracted, getting ready for the raid, and hadn't given this question the attention it deserved. She should have. She didn't like not being able to answer.

But as she pondered it, she decided she was done

worrying – for now, anyway. Whatever was going to happen in the future, she knew what the next day would bring.

It would bring a hangover, because they'd be mourning Sarnai, but it would be a bittersweet sickness. Then, they'd take the wagon somewhere, let the horses wander and graze, and then they'd do whatever they damn well pleased.

Chimeg didn't just throw spears and stare down approaching waves of soldiers. Even the Chief had hobbies, and one of them, somewhat amazingly, was embroidery. She'd built up quite a collection of thread from their raids, and was working on a landscape, all greens and blues and glowing gold. She liked to sit on the top of the wagon, cross-legged, spear within reach as her fingers danced.

The Princess tended to hang around the wagon too, usually practising with those ridiculous twin sabres, or chatting to the Chief. Which didn't always work to their satisfaction – Chimeg liked being alone as much as Sayana despised it – but mostly, they managed.

Khun, for her part, liked to hunt – although having seen some of the bird and antelope carcasses she brought back to camp, Hogelun happened to think it was less of a hunt and more of a ritual disembowelment.

In Hogelun's case, what she usually wanted involved Erhi herself. Followed by a skin of *airag,* some tangy cheese and cured horsemeat, a little lazy *shagai* – which they played with the polished sheep's ankle bones she kept in a cloth pouch – and a long nap. Erhi, fortunately, usually wanted the same thing.

No work to do. No family or village elder to obey. Enough food and drink to last you day after glorious day. The whole Tapestry, ready and waiting. Hogelun studied the horizon, the billowing golden clouds rolling above waving grass, so lush that they looked like a velvet cloak, and found she couldn't wait.

Sarnai was gone, another Rakada snuffed out. But she hadn't died for nothing, because the rest of them were still here. Still fighting.

And whatever tomorrow would bring, it wouldn't involve *araatan*.

She considered Erhi then – just took her in. Took in the way the late-afternoon sunlight turned her skin to glowing, burnished bronze, how it made her hair seem like it was lit from within. A gentle breeze ruffled her *deel*, pushing the fabric against her body and outlining the curve of her breast.

And Hogelun told herself that it didn't matter if she made bad jokes, or forgot things, or didn't know how parts of the Tapestry worked. Erhi would be there – patient, calm, wildly smart, fucking delightfully gorgeous Erhi – and as long as she had that, Hogelun would be OK.

She bent down and kissed the archer, long and deep. "Well, you know which one I'm picking," she said, after they pulled apart. "Wait – do you *also* live to a thousand, in this scenario? Because if it's just me . . . "

Erhi smiled, held a hand to her cheek. *Come on. Let's get to the wagon, see what we've got left.*

Eight

Sayana

The Rakada's wagon was old as time, its four battered wooden wheels matched only by its even more battered sides, dented and scarred from thousands of miles back and forth across the Tapestry. If you had told Sayana the First Riders were the ones who built it, she wouldn't have believed you . . . but she would have had to think about it first.

Still, she was going to miss it now that it was nothing more than splintered boards and smashed wheels.

The suns were setting when they reached the place they'd left it, in the clutch of rocky hills west of the village. For a few seconds they just gazed at what remained: its side torn open, contents scattered, the dirt around it rucked up and trampled.

"Who did this?" Hogelun said, voice faltering. "Those soldiers?"

Wordlessly, Sayana pointed. Their spare horses were a little way away from the wagon. What was left of them, anyway.

Only one thing could have caused this much destruction. And she'd ridden it off a cliff a short while ago.

Unless there's more than one. The thought was chilling. Not just because it was obvious – there was no possible way there was only one *araatan* in the Tapestry – but because the idea of there being two of those things in the same area was too much to take in.

Sayana stood for a moment, grinding her teeth and trying not to throw a sabre at one of the tall boulders surrounding the wreck. Because the last thing she needed right then was a broken blade.

"The demons hunt us," Khun murmured. "We must cleanse our souls by cutting off and burning our little fingers."

She held one of her knives, but made no move to actually do this, to either herself or to the rest of them. Just stared at the wrecked wagon, her shoulders slumped.

It wasn't true of course – the *araatan* wasn't hunting *them*. It was an animal, and it was after food. It must have loved finding a group of tasty horses, all tied up for it. There wasn't a lot of space among the boulders, either; it probably smashed the wagon to pieces by accident, just by moving. The beast was hungry, and it was just the worst luck possible that it had come across their spare mounts.

A hot, blinding anger rolled through Sayana, because the *araatan* weren't supposed to be here. They were supposed to be in the mountains. But Hogelun had told her about Erhi's theory, shortly before they arrived: how the growing number of soldiers in the Baina had fucked with the food supply, forced the *araatan* into the grasslands.

Bad enough that the Khan was doing his best to exterminate raiders. Bad enough he was making it impossible to even *find* people to raid, marching them to Karkorum (whether they wanted to or not). He was forcing them to deal with giant, fire-breathing lizards. *And he probably didn't even know it was happening.*

A hunk of smashed pottery nudged up against Sayana's foot.

She gave it a hard kick, smashing it, sending the pieces bouncing off the rocks. It felt petty and pointless, but then, she was in a petty mood. *Fuck this day.*

"That was my favourite cookpot," Hogelun said.

Sayana's shoulders slumped. "Shit, sorry, Hogs. I didn't mean to—"

"It's fine." Hogs was rubbing her shorn head, back and forth, a rueful smile fixed firmly to her face. "Pretty sure it was busted already."

Sayana's burned thigh was in agony, and a horrible thought popped into her head: would Erhi be able to treat it? Would she have enough supplies? It was hard not to think about the rot setting in, the leg turning green and gassy . . .

She sat on the ground, eyes closed, trying to pretend this was all a bad dream.

They'd lost Sarnai. The raid had been a disaster. And now this. She didn't even feel any triumph from riding the *araatan* any more. *Should have figured it out earlier,* she thought bitterly. *Found it and rode it* before *it ate all our fucking horses.*

The Chief picked something off the ground. It took Sayana a second to see what it was, and when she did, she wanted to mount up and find the *araatan* and make sure it was dead.

Chimeg's embroidery.

The landscape she had been working on, with its bright colours and intricate details. Ripped almost in two.

The only time Sayana had ever seen their Chief relax, even a little bit, was when she had needle and thread in her hands. She didn't drink, never had, and Sayana had no idea when she last took someone to bed. Even when she played *shagai*, she looked like she was about to ride into battle. It was only her embroidery that could take her mind off the Rakada, even if just for a few moments.

Nobody said anything. They all just stood, watching her. The only sound was the night breeze, picking up, gusting around them.

"Search it," Chimeg told them, pointing to the wreckage. She dropped the embroidery in the dust. Stepped round it, like it didn't exist. "Khun, start a fire. We've plenty of wood, after all." A mirthless laugh. "If there's anything left to salvage, pile it up."

There wasn't much. A few bruised fire apples, missed in one corner of the smashed wagon. A couple of surviving arrows — Erhi's face twisted in hurt fury when she saw what the beast had done to her carefully carved shafts, which lay splintered and broken around the wagon. Thank the Weavers, she had enough healing supplies in her saddlebags to treat the burn on Sayana's leg, to fix up the rest of their scrapes and cuts.

They moved a short distance away, none of them wanting to be around the pieces of horse. The finished pile was pathetic, barely knee-high. They stood around, all of them staring at it as if it would magically double. Someone's stomach growled, and Sayana didn't even have the energy to raise her head and see whose it was.

She couldn't accept this. She wouldn't. She did not leave Karkorum and the palace and all of the shit her family put her through to let the dream die like this. She'd risked *everything* to become a raider, to live life on her own terms. This was not going to be how it ended.

"OK." She clapped her hands together. "We keep looking. There has to be another ... another village, or a wagon train, something we missed." She nudged Erhi. "Pretty sure we won't run into an *araatan* again. Not even we can be that unlucky."

No one said anything.

"So ... " Sayana licked her lips, which were summer-grass dry. "Tomorrow? We could try the—"

"We head south," Chimeg said. "The Namag."

Sayana stared at her, sure she had heard wrong. "But . . . but, Chief, there's nothing *in* the Namag. No one to raid. It's just marshes." She couldn't help but look down at the pile again. Everything they had left in the world.

If Chimeg heard her, she didn't show it. "We'll hunt on the way. See if we can build up our food stores. And there are berries and water pears in the marsh, enough for us to go on."

Water pears. Stunted, yellow fruit that grew in swampy areas, and tasted like it. "Chief—"

"We can't stay in this area." Chimeg looked at Sayana, as if only just noticing she was there. "Plenty of soldiers survived that little dust-up. They'll run to the nearest camp, which means that by tomorrow morning, this whole place will be crawling with troops. Not to mention, you know, the fucking giant lizards bumbling about. Best we lay low for now."

"Wasn't . . ." Hogelun rolled her tongue around her cheeks. "Aren't the marshes pretty close to Karkorum? Where the main force is? Shouldn't we try to . . . *not* be near there?"

Chimeg made a humourless *hmmph* sound at Hogs' question. "The army never go into the Namag." Her mouth twisted. "No people to conscript. No settlements or nomads."

"Too squashy-squashy underfoot." Khun ripped a cuticle off her fingernail, making all of them wince. She pondered the thin line of blood running along her fingertip. "Too many horses churn it up. Big patrols go nowhere." She shrugged. "And then they are eaten alive by the marsh ghosts who burrow into their eyes. I have witnessed this."

It might have changed, Erhi signed to Chimeg. *We haven't been to the Namag in a while*.

"Best option we've got." Chimeg picked up her spear from where it stood point-down in the dirt. She went to her saddlebags, retrieved a whetstone, started to sharpen the blade. "Before today, the army was wiping out raiders as they found them. We just moved to the top of their list. They'll be looking for us in particular, so we should be somewhere else."

"Chief." Sayana couldn't believe they were actually having this conversation. "We have . . . we've got nothing. Next to nothing." She pointed at the pile. "If we don't go on another raid—"

"We'll be fine," *Scrick-scrick* went the whetstone on the spear blade.

"But—"

"Oi." Hogelun didn't raise her voice often, but when she did, it could rattle rocks. "That's your Chief, Princess. What she says goes."

Sayana had got used to them calling her that. She didn't have a choice; once you got lumped with a nickname in a raider clan, that was it.

She rolled her eyes at it, mostly: *yes, yes, blah, blah, Princess Sayana left her cosy life at court in Karkorum to play at being a raider. Look at her ridiculous braid and her twin sabres.* She didn't care. She had more than proved herself on a dozen raids, and they all knew it.

But sometimes . . . just sometimes, when they used that nickname, it made her want to start hitting things.

Erhi's eyes glimmered in the firelight, her fingers dancing. *We do what she says. Show some respect.*

Sayana sat back, shoulders slumped. They did what she said, all right. And why not? They were the Rakada, after all. The Bone Raiders. Chimeg made them, and so nobody fucked with them. They all listened to her because she brought them open skies and lazy days and no obligation to anyone but themselves.

But what happened when there were no more settlements to

raid? When the *araatan* ate all the game? How could you be a raider when there was nothing and no one left to raid?

They had to attack. They couldn't just run, lie low, pretend it would all be fine when they emerged. But when she opened her mouth to tell Chimeg this, the words wouldn't come.

"What about . . ." Hogs cleared her throat. "What about Sarnai?"

They all shifted where they sat. Not meeting each other's eyes. Usually when someone was killed, they made a point of honouring them. Not just with funeral rights, but with drink and food and laughter and stories. Not to mention hangovers they could all be proud of.

But tonight, no one felt like celebrating. Not even a little.

"When we're in a better place, we'll remember her." The Chief rested her spear across her thighs. "I'll take first watch. The rest of you, get some sleep. At dawn, we're gone."

Nine

Sayana

By the time they reached the Namag marshes, early on their third day of riding, Sayana was pretty sure she was hallucinating. Either that, or the Large Eye really *was* a giant melon, floating in the sky and singing her a lullaby.

She slapped herself, then did it again, until it stopped looking like a piece of fruit.

They had been riding hard – as hard as their horses could take, anyway – but the boggy, sopping mud underfoot had slowed them way down. The standing water stank of decay, and the light from the melons – the suns, for fuck's sake, the *suns* – looked pallid and washed out.

They had to increase the amount of food they gave the horses, digging into their own supplies. There just wasn't enough vegetation for them to graze. Oh, there was some – sickly, watery grass, a few shrubs, clawing their way up until their leaves reached a few feet above the marsh. And thank the Weavers, the horses grazed as much as they could. Still, it was tough going.

That was without talking about the bugs. Sayana's arms were already covered with constellations of swollen bites.

She loved the Tapestry. She loved it more than life itself. Except for this part, which was the fucking worst.

There wasn't a soul around, not even a single bird in the sky. Was this going to be what things were like, from now on? Just constantly on the run? What was the point of raiding if they could never enjoy the spoils? If they had to run like hell right afterwards, keeping an eye out for the army, for *araatan*?

The others used to ask Sayana why she'd left the palace in Karkorum; why she'd abandoned a life of soft, pampered luxury for life as a raider. The fact was, even as a young girl, Sayana had hated it.

The luxury wasn't the problem – in truth, she sometimes still missed the food, and the soft beds and the palace gardens. But all those things came at a huge price. The palace and the court, even under the old Khan, had always been a pit of vipers. A place of bowing and scraping and poison smiles, of ambition and deception.

You couldn't trust anyone. Your dearest childhood playmate would cheerfully cut your throat, if it gave them a chance at a more prestigious marriage. Sayana had never known how deadly loneliness could be, until it hunted her through the palace corridors, every hour of every day.

And it would never stop. Not ever.

Her parents refused to help. They wanted her to be a dutiful wife, a mother, a quiet face in the crowd for the rest of her life. She'd offered to join the army, which made her adoptive mother's skin turn pale. She'd argued for an apprenticeship – perhaps to a court blacksmith, or to the eagle hunters. The person pretending to be her father turned all of it down flat. No, they had her entire life planned out, and she would be a good daughter and obey them.

Sayana had dreamed of running away. But to what? To a

village somewhere? To a group of nomads? Who could gain favour by dragging her back to the palace, when they found out who she was?

Even if she made a life for herself in a village or as a nomad, it wouldn't be much better than the palace. Less backstabbing and plotting, to be sure . . . but there were still arranged marriages. Backbreaking work. Rigid adherence to the words of the village elders. It would be exchanging one prison for another.

But then one night, she'd been practising her hated calligraphy, wondering if it would be so bad if she just picked up the ink pot and whirled it around her head for a bit. She'd heard her father talking about how they'd wiped out a group of raiders near the city.

She'd heard of raiders before, of course. She knew they existed. But as she'd listened, ink dripping onto her parchment, she'd wondered: *What if that could be me?*

And so three years ago, she'd left, and become one.

Fine: it had been just a touch more complicated than that. Planning her escape, slipping away one moonless night, had taken a while. Not to mention a truly staggering amount in bribes. But she fucking did it, didn't she?

She wasn't stupid. Raiding meant . . . well, it meant doing things she might not like. Stealing. Killing. She'd often wondered if she had it in her: to take a life, to put a blade through someone who stood in her way.

Turned out, it didn't matter whether she had it or not. The alternative – the loneliness, the desperation, the life of obligation – was far worse.

If she wanted to live, if she wanted to enjoy her one life in the Tapestry, she had to reach out and *take* it. And the fact was, people out here died all the time, from all sorts of things. From the rot, from animal attacks, from illness. Sayana didn't enjoy killing, never had, and she never pretended it was noble . . . but how was it any different to the other ways people in the Tapestry lost their lives?

She'd found a raider clan quick enough, a useless bunch called . . . Screaming Devils? Dark Beasts? There was that saying about how you never forget your first, but she had, because they were useless. And yes, she'd had to kill, although she tried to do it only if someone was coming at her with a blade.

She *did* remember the first person she'd killed, an old warrior with a limp, stumbling at her with a hunting knife in a night raid. She remembered the sound he made when he died.

Sayana never shied away from any of this. Never tried to pretend it didn't happen, because it did. And if that was the price – a few ghosts, a few bad memories – then she'd pay it gladly.

The Screaming Devil Beasts, or whoever they were, fell apart in a disagreement about who got to keep which horses from their raids. Still, she'd managed to learn a few things. And when Chimeg and Erhi swooped in to recruit the survivors, she was ready.

Alongside her, Hogelun was swaying on her horse, snapping awake with a startled snort. Khun, on Hogs' left, didn't even look her way. She just stared out into the distance, hunched and exhausted. Chimeg and Erhi were up ahead, both on one horse, shadows against the horizon.

Sayana found herself studying Hogelun. She did what Chimeg and Erhi said, and Sayana would give her this: she never pretended she knew better than they did. But Sayana wondered sometimes what Hogs really thought.

Hogelun was the first Rakada Chimeg and Erhi had recruited, and it had happened by accident. Like Sayana, she had left her family behind, because she and her parents (and her three brothers) had different ideas on the subject of arranged marriage – not to mention the fact that she liked girls instead of boys. Far better, she had figured, to roam the Tapestry and see what happened. And what happened was, Chimeg and Erhi tried to rob her.

She'd offered to cook them a meal instead. Somewhat surprisingly, they'd agreed, mostly because Hogelun went out of her way to make it sound delicious. They'd had many helpings of mutton grilled on the spit, washed down with some decent *airag* – well, two out of three, because Chimeg didn't drink. By the end of the night, Hogelun was hopelessly in love with Erhi, and Chimeg was telling her that they should all ride together.

Even raiders liked a good meal.

Was this what Hogelun imagined, when she signed up? That it would start to go this way? That they'd end up on the run, fighting for scraps, the Tapestry taken away from them piece by piece?

Sayana still couldn't believe Chimeg was letting it come to this. Both the Chief and Erhi were ex-soldiers, veterans of the Delta War with Ngu in the south. They had returned to Karkorum to find themselves outdated, stuck in an army that was being run by men with more interest in kissing ass than kicking it. It had taken years for them to crack, but crack they had, and they both deserted.

Erhi sometimes talked wistfully of her time in the army, but Chimeg never did. The Chief changed the subject whenever it came up. Sayana had asked Erhi about that once: *She did a few things she's not proud of,* the archer had signed. *But that's her story to tell, not mine.*

So far, it was a story they hadn't heard.

Khunbish was their most recent addition. They'd been camped in a ravine near the God's Heel, a year ago, and the bitch simply strolled up to the fire, entirely unarmed, the now-familiar leather pouch across her chest. Utterly ignoring the multiple sharp objects that were suddenly pointed in her direction, she straight-up told Chimeg that she was joining the Rakada.

Chimeg had disagreed with this assessment and moved to emphasise her point with a spear thrust to the throat. Ten seconds later, Sayana and every single other Rakada were in the dust, their weapons thrown into the darkness, with multiple sprains, bloodied faces, and, in Erhi's case, a broken pinky. Khunbish was sitting by the fire as if nothing had happened, digging into Sayana's roasted pheasant leg, the juices dripping down her chin.

After that, they decided it was better that she was on their side.

They never did find out where she came from; the only thing she kept saying, over and over, was that Father Sky wouldn't allow her to die.

There were others of course. The Rakada had been fifteen-strong, at their peak. Not just Sarnai – a horrid little jolt shot through Sayana's gut whenever she thought of her, but others too. Zinbar, who took that arrow in the gut. Ugan, who couldn't see for shit, and had fallen off his horse when a soldier cut the animal's legs out from under it. The Twins, Arsi and Arslan. The Rakada had got smaller and smaller, and Sayana didn't know how long the rest of them would last. Not any more.

And sure, some of the Rakada had slunk off. Abandoned the clan, when things began to get scary. Sayana didn't think that was much of an option; being a raider was punishable by death, even for her, with her family in the palace. Leaving raider life behind might buy you some time, but if even one person figured out what you'd been . . .

Sayana's head, already loose on her shoulders, had been gradually falling further and further forward. She was about to slip into a doze when she lost her balance, nearly toppled right off her goddamn horse. Just like Hogelun. She snapped up, her head jerking backwards so hard it made her neck hurt, blinking furiously. She had to stay awake. If she slipped off her mount into the mud, she'd never hear the end of it.

Of course, that resolve lasted about ten seconds. Sayana's mind wandered again, and for some reason, it landed on the eagle hunters. They were soldiers who took in the birds as fledglings, spent months and years bonding with them. Sent them spinning into the sky to hunt down game. Now *that* was a life Sayana would have accepted, if her parents had let her.

There weren't many of them left in the Tapestry – few anywhere, as far as she knew. Hunting with an eagle, while extremely impressive, wasn't exactly what you'd call efficient.

The ones in Karkorum were mostly for show, entertaining the Khan's court, and it was a status symbol to have one serving your family. Being an eagle hunter would have been fucking great.

The image dissolved, just another thought on the verge of sleep. Sayana was back on the *araatan*, crashing into those soldiers, terrified and hanging on for dear life. But more than that: excited, too. And in a weird way, kind of sad it hadn't lasted longer. She still didn't like that she'd had to drive the *araatan* off a cliff, that didn't feel good at all, not when—

She sat bolt upright in her saddle. Khun, off to her left, gave her a curious look.

Usually, Sayana's ideas came to her in dribs and drabs. Little fragments that she had to piece together. That was part of the reason, she was convinced, that Chimeg and the others turned down so many of them.

But this idea? This one arrived in a single, blazing bolt of lightning. Fully formed. Perfect.

"What is it?" Hogelun unsheathed her club. "Do you see something?"

Sayana's response was to drive her heels into the sides of her horse, sending her galloping in the direction of the two Rakada on the horizon. "Chief! Chimeg!"

She had to get this idea out before it faded, even a little bit. It was foolproof and brilliant and the answer to every one of their prayers.

The Chief said something to Erhi, who wheeled Windwalker about and rode back towards Sayana, hooves kicking up bursts of dirt. They met at the top of a small rise – Chimeg and Erhi coming from one side, Khun and Hogelun from the other, converging on her. All of them had their weapons out, Erhi standing in her stirrups, scanning the horizon. The horses chuffed and snorted – the kind of noises that made it clear they were really on their last legs, and if their riders didn't stop this stupidity, they would end up in gooey marsh water.

"What is it?" Chimeg shouted.

"The *araatan*!" Sayana yelled back.

"Shit – where?" Hogelun stood, forgetting about her snapped stirrup, and nearly toppled off her horse.

"You're saying it followed us?" Doubt filled Chimeg's voice now, as if Sayana had lost her mind.

"No, that isn't—"

"I'm not fighting a bloody lizard." Hogelun looked like she was going to pass out. "Won't do it."

In the background, Khun was chanting. A language Sayana didn't know, guttural and angry, eyes closed, knives raised to the sky.

Sayana put two fingers in her mouth and whistled loudly.

Then she had to stop doing that and calm her horse – the as-yet-unnamed animal was perhaps three seconds from kicking her off.

Chimeg studied the utterly empty landscape for a few more moments before rounding on Sayana. "Explain," she snapped. Then: "Khun, shut up."

Khun gave one final gargling warble, then subsided.

The idea was still burning fresh in Sayana's mind. She forced herself to take a deep breath, moved her hands carefully so Erhi understood too. "Look, I know how to fight back. Against the army. The Khan."

"Princess." Chimeg was dangerously calm. "It's been a very long couple of days. If you don't start making sense in the next five seconds, I'm going to stick one of those pretty sabres up your pert little backside."

Sayana ignored this. "The Khan wants to wipe us out, right? Well, what if we didn't have to run? What if we could take the fight to him and his army?"

Erhi peered at her, as if she'd misread her signs. *By having them . . . fight the* araatan? she signed, glancing at Hogelun in confusion.

How did they not get this? How were they not dazzled by its brilliance?

"By having them fight *us*," Sayana said. "Except this time, we aren't riding horses."

She slapped her mount's flank. "We're riding *araatan*."

Ten

Sayana

For a few seconds, the other Rakada just stared at her. Chimeg had an expression of polite confusion on her face, as if Sayana had just suggested they give up their life as raiders and come up with a set of fabulous dance routines to entertain the Khan and his court.

It was Erhi who cracked first. Her right cheek bulged, and she let out a helpless *pfft*, a burst of air, clutching her stomach in silent laughter.

That set them off. Hogelun and Khun nearly fell off their horses in hysterics. Even Chimeg couldn't help it, her mouth twisting as she tried to suppress a chuckle. Sayana stared in disbelief.

"I'm serious!" she shouted, which only made them laugh harder. "There's a way we could—"

"Enough," Hogelun could barely talk. "Please, stop. I can't."

Erhi dismounted and dropped into a crouch, tears pouring down her face. She looked up at Sayana, tried to get herself under control, completely failed to do so. Khun was howling at the sky.

Sayana goggled at them. "What is *wrong* with you all?"

Yes, it was a wild idea, she got that, but to have them laugh at her? After she had steered the damn lizard into the army, and saved them all? Weren't they even going to hear her out?

Chimeg was still smiling. She manoeuvred herself into the saddle, moving the horse to stand alongside Sayana's, clapping a hand on her shoulder. "Appreciated that, Princess. We needed to take some weight off. Maybe it was time we stopped for a bit anyway. See to the horses."

Sayana shook her head. "Chimeg, I'm serious. I know how we could—"

"Wait." Hogelun wiped her face. There was still a mad grin on it, like this was part of the game too. "You mean this. You want us to ride . . . those things."

"*Yes*. If you'd all just listen to me . . . "

Chimeg's hand fell away, and she looked at Sayana with something that might have been pity. Erhi slowly got to her feet, her hands moving shakily. *This is a joke, right?*

"Yeah." Hogelun's grin had taken on a very forced quality. "She's just having a laugh. Aren't you, Sayana?"

Sayana swung her leg over the side of her horse, dismounted. "Uh . . . again, no, not a joke."

"Let me see if I understand this." Chimeg gazed off at the horizon, as if she couldn't quite believe she had to have this conversation. "You manage to avoid getting eaten by that *araatan*, which I still don't understand, then you somehow end up on its back. You figure out how to get it to go in a certain direction – which I'm grateful for, by the way, don't get me wrong – but you still have to drive it off a cliff to make sure it doesn't kill you. And you think this means . . . we should all have a go?"

Erhi, no longer laughing, threw up her hands and started to root around in one of her saddlebags. Hogelun shifted on her horse, uncomfortable. Only Khun was looking at Sayana, eyes boring into hers. Sayana couldn't read her expression.

The thought, which had been so clear, started to fragment. She had to work hard to keep her voice steady. "Our horses. What's the one thing they can't do?"

When there was no answer, she had to stop herself from yelling in frustration. "They can't attack. They're fast, and they can get us out of trouble, but they can't actually fight."

"I dunno." Hogelun scratched her horse's mane. "Hoof Monster here took a chunk out of this one guy, about a year back. You've never seen so much blood." She waved at Erhi, attracting the archer's attention. *Hey – you got any* airag *left? Been riding all night, I could use a drink.*

It gives you stomach ache this early in the morning, Erhi signed back, distractedly. *You know that.*

Sayana was losing them. She spoke quickly, trying not to sound desperate. "If we were all riding *araatan*, there wouldn't be an army in the world that could stand up to us. The . . . the Khan could send every battalion he had, and we would just burn right through them."

How could they not see this? If they could ride the *araatan*, train them, use them when they raided . . .

Well. They could simply roll up to any village they wanted, get what they needed, without having to kill a single person. Who would stand up to them? Who would even try? They would never again run short of supplies, or food, or anything.

And the army! The Khan could make it as big as he wanted, fill it with conscripts, and it wouldn't matter. With even one *araatan*, the Rakada would stand a chance against anyone who came at them.

As for the Khan's plan, his vision for the Tapestry, where everyone was either a soldier, or an indentured worker in

Karkorum: fuck that. Good luck, dickhead. Try put your little Khan's Will banners down, see where that gets you.

Sayana's mind was very good at running away with itself, and it had a good sprint going now. Why stop there? Who said they even had to be raiders at all? They could keep the Khan and his army from fucking with people, and take tribute in return. Whatever they needed, whenever they needed it. They, and their *araatan* buddies, could have the ultimate life in the Tapestry.

She took a breath, managing to calm her thoughts for once. Best not to get ahead of herself. Their main goal should be to protect themselves from the army, make sure what happened today—*what happened to Sarnai*—never happened again.

"Don't you see?" Sayana said. "You can control them. That's how I steered the one I . . . the *araatan* in that village. You grab hold of the horns, yeah, those little nubs, and it goes where you—"

"Enough." Chimeg's voice made it clear that as far as she was concerned this idea of Sayana's had run its course. "Princess, I could drop you on anything in the Tapestry, and you'd be able to steer it by grabbing the back of its head. Because it's an *animal*."

"You don't under—"

"No, hear me. Steering a beast is a long, long way from controlling it. Not to mention you'd have to work out how to mount it without the damn thing biting your face off."

Hogelun shuddered at that, but the Chief didn't notice. "*And* do the same when you dismounted. *And* make sure that all the time in between, the *araatan* actually did what you told it to."

She tilted her neck to one side, wincing as she rubbed at a sore spot. "Do I seriously have to explain all this? This isn't a dog you can train to roll over. It isn't a wild horse that bucks for a bit and then gives up."

Chief, Erhi signed. *Can we stop for a while, like you said? Windwalker's running hot.*

"*I'm* running hot." Hogelun dismounted, put her arms around the archer, resting her chin on the woman's shoulder. "The last time my legs were this numb, I'd eaten one of Khun's mushrooms."

"Ah yes." Khun blissed out for a moment. "The Sacred Fungus of the Ancients. I grew it in my hair, you know. From but a single spore."

Sayana's thigh – which had been healing pretty well, thanks to Erhi's anti-rot goop – woke up with a vicious, stretching sting. "Khun," she said, desperate. "You get it, right? You see why we should do this?"

"So many pretty colours." Khun's voice was dreamy.

"No more." Chimeg dismounted, dusted off her hands. She crouched, started massaging Windwalker's legs, working out some muscle knots on his shins. "Hogs, get a fire going. Princess, you and Erhi get some water to boil. Khun and I will cool the horses, dig up something for them to eat."

Sayana put a hand on the Chief's shoulder. "You don't understand! There was—"

Chimeg moved so fast that she didn't have time to blink. The Chief dropped her shoulder, pivoted on her heel in the dust, and snatched Sayana's wrist. Held it very firmly, giving it just the tiniest twist.

Chimeg wasn't going to hurt her, Sayana was sure of that. Pretty sure. All the same, it seemed wise to stop talking.

"Princess," Chimeg said patiently. "The only reason you survived . . . whatever in the nine hells that was, was luck. You got luckier than anyone had any right to be. You could try that little stunt of yours again, and ninety-nine times out of a hundred, you'd be thrown off and eaten.

"You know what you should be doing? You should remove your sash, thank Father Sky and Mother Earth that you're still alive, and promise never to try anything that foolish ever again. You shouldn't take that as a chance to come up with more wild schemes that will probably get all of us killed. I'm trying . . . "

Abruptly, the Chief let go of Sayana. Composed herself.

"I'm trying to keep this clan alive," she said. "I'm doing everything I can to make sure we don't get overrun, and you're absolutely not helping. You don't know how to control the *araatan*. You don't know how to train them, and I would be extremely grateful if you'd stop pretending that you do."

"I didn't say *I* knew how to do it." Sayana massaged her wrist, wincing. "But there's someone who does."

"What do you mean, someone who does?" Hogelun said.

"Um . . . shit, yeah, I probably should have led with that."

The beauty of the idea had blotted everything else out, including how to actually convince the others to go along with it. But oh, it was beautiful, and if she could just get them to listen . . . "So you know how I grew up in Karkorum? Like, in the palace?"

"Oh, did you?" Hogelun's eyes were wide and innocent. "I had no idea."

"Get to the point," Chimeg snapped.

Despite the Chief's tone, a smile crept across Sayana's face. They were going to love this.

Eleven

Yesuntei

At the very top of the domed palace roof in Karkorum, there was a tiny platform. So small that it could only take one person. Yesuntei had no idea why it existed, but she sometimes liked to go up there. First thing in the morning, if she could. Breathe in the dawn air, take in the entire city in a single, slow sweep.

The palace and its brass dome were beautiful. But if pressed, Yesuntei would admit that the Khan's home wasn't her favourite part of Karkorum. No, the rest of the city, everything she could see at that moment, took that prize.

It was magnificent.

The palace sat on a tall hill, with two deep rivers converging at its southern base. On the northern slope was a sprawl of closely packed huts, walls made of mud and hard stone. Some were dwellings, for those who worked at court, but most of them were for the army: kitchens, mess halls, armories.

What always got Yesuntei, though, was the vast expanse of *gers* that stretched out beyond them, basking in the rising suns.

Thousands and thousands of families, who had chosen to

make their way to this great city. To devote their lives to replacing their old-fashioned tents with dwellings like the ones on the hillside. To build an impregnable wall around the perimeter, one that glorified the Khan.

They joined his army, too. Swelled its ranks, held dominion over the grasslands. They would defend the northern border, in the Baina Mountains.

She'd never intended to do this work: the work of building a great city, a great nation. She'd always assumed she'd be a life-long soldier, but after that . . . unpleasantness with her former battalion, she was lost.

Until Etugen, the Great Khan, recognised something in her that not even she knew existed. Her ability to plan, to see the entire picture, to deal with multiple complex problems at once. She was a good soldier, but this? She was born to do this. It was her great work: the work of helping to realise her Khan's vision.

It would take time − years, Yesuntei knew − but soon that vision would be a reality. A great city, a great nation. No more Tapestry, with its thousands of little nomadic bands milling about; just a single, unified land.

Hanggai. That was the name the Khan had chosen. And the city of Karkorum the glorious jewel at its centre.

When she climbed down the ladder to the dome's shadowy antechamber, the wind gusting her long black hair around her shoulders, Timur was waiting for her. The assistant was court-trained, fat as an adder in his robes. She hadn't told him where she'd be, of course, but he always knew.

Yesuntei stepped off the ladder, and stood. Under her immaculate black *deel*, her frame was as wiry and scrawny as a teenager, even though she'd seen thirty years. It was her damn stomach that made her this way. It felt uncomfortably tight, bloated and hollow at the same time. Always gnawing at her.

She headed for the spiral staircase, which led down to the balcony running along the dome's interior. Timur fell into step beside her.

"Let's have it," she said. Her voice reverberated under the brass roof, giving it an unpleasant edge. Below, the sound of the Khan's court was a distant, nervous whisper.

"Yes, *bahadur*. The outbreak of the black flow has spread to the western part of the city overnight. They require more healers."

Yesuntei grunted. "What else?"

"A protest near the river." They stepped into a narrow stone corridor, lined with colourful tiles, and Yesuntei's ears popped slightly – one of the quirks of how the palace was built. The air sat strangely, moved in unpredictable ways. "The usual nonsense. Food, sanitation, conditions at the worksites. The Guard was dispatched, of course, but it descended into quite a brawl before it was put down."

"Unimportant. Next."

Ahead of them, the corridor opened up into one of the lesser courts, a room of green jade and delicate sculptures, packed with scribes and courtesans.

"Those are the chief matters on your morning docket, *bahadur*." Timur's bland smile didn't reach his eyes. "Oh – forgive me, I almost forgot. A tiger has been attacking residents in the Crop District."

His eyes slid up and to the left, as if struggling to retrieve the information. "It has killed two already, savaged another. Last I heard, the Guard had cornered the beast in a granary. It should be dealt with shortly. If I may: what are your orders regarding the healers for the western—"

"A granary?"

"Yes, *bahadur*? So I am told."

"Take me there," Yesuntei said. She drove a fist into her side, resisting the urge to wince. "And fetch Tuya."

"*Bahadur*, it is just a tiger. Surely there are more pressing . . . "

Her assistant trailed off as Yesuntei's eyes bored into his.

It took a long time to get to the Crop District, on the city's eastern edge. The *gers* were densely packed, the spaces between them narrow and treacherous. It was easy for your ankle to vanish into a pool of unspecified muck, for the wooden board you were walking across to tip you over.

You couldn't use horses, either: once you got off the main road that split the city east and west, you had to dismount and walk. That would all change, of course, once they began replacing tents with permanent dwellings, but it would take time.

The whole place stank, sweat and shit lingering with the stench of cooked meat and burned herbs. Pale faces peered out at Yesuntei from the flaps of the *gers*, saw her black *deel*, with its red rose brooch of the Khan's Right Hand, and hastily ducked back inside.

Yesuntei wondered, as she often did, if they understood the weight on her shoulders. The task she had been given of lifting this city up. The difficulties she faced on a daily basis, and how they made it worse with every brawl and fire and pocket of disruption.

You couldn't feed a growing city by bringing in food from outside. At least, not entirely. They pulled as many fish from the river as they could, and it still wasn't enough. So the grass on the eastern side of Karkorum had been slashed back, the earth ploughed, crop fields created for the new citizens to work in. Millet, barley, wheat.

Simply getting enough water to the fields was an enormous task, but it had to be done. As Yesuntei arrived, citizens were already hard at work in the fields, backs bent. The enormous mud granaries ran along the southern edge of the fields. Only a third had been filled so far: big square blocks with wide entrances, silent and dark.

Most of the food went to the army – the vast, swelling ranks of soldiers charged with securing the grasslands. Yesuntei held no illusions about the conscripts' willingness to carry out the Khan's orders, but soldiers who were fed well and given sufficient *airag* rations tended to fall in line.

A group of Khan's Guard stood a short distance away from one of the granaries, weapons out – Yesuntei recognised their watch leader, Gantalgun, a man with a barrel chest and permanently red eyes.

"*Bahadur*." He snapped to attention, his men following. Trying and failing to hide the puzzlement on his face, his confusion as to why his commander, the Right Hand herself, was there. "We have the beast cornered."

He pointed at the granary. The suns were rising behind it, and it was dark as night inside the entranceway. There was a thick smear of drying blood at the entrance, vanishing into the black interior.

"And now one of our granaries is off limits to us." Yesuntei came to a stop, her hand resting on the hilt of her sabre, tucked in her black sash.

"I . . . *bahadur*, we were—"

"This animal should have been dealt with the moment it entered the District. You have archers, and heavy arrows. Why is it not dead?"

"It is . . . it is quick. We loosed several arrows, but it evaded us."

Yesuntei gestured to the fields behind her. "Does all this mean so little to you?"

"*Bahadur*, I can assure you—"

She stopped him with a raised hand, then turned to Timur, who was not-so-subtly trying to rub a spatter of shit off his sodden court shoes. "Where is my sister?"

Tuya arrived as she always did, in a cloud of angry dust. Didn't matter if she was on horseback, or striding across muddy, stinking ground like she was now; like most eagle hunters, she always looked as if she was emerging from a pitched battle.

Her *deel* hung open, sash barely knotted, sweat-stained tunic underneath. Her dark hair in a bun, loose strands sticking out. A scarred leather glove hid her right hand and forearm, although her eagle, Ayanga, was nowhere to be seen.

Tuya was shorter than Yesuntei, and far more muscular. But she walked slightly hunched over, neck bent forward, chin sticking out. "I was sleeping," she snapped at her sister, ignoring the men surrounding them. "First lie-in I've had in months."

"We need you." Yesuntei nodded towards the granary, noting how the workers in the fields had stopped, watching them closely. Good.

Her sister followed her gaze. "And you want me to go into your crop storage because . . . "

"Tiger. It's already killed two people."

Tuya closed her eyes in dismay. "I told you," she hissed. "I told you this would happen. You start working the Tapestry—"

"Hanggai," Yesuntei intoned.

"The *Tapestry*. You start hunting where you shouldn't, and it cuts into food sources. Tigers – and not just them, by the way, everything else out there – start looking for other things to eat. They start *roaming*, do you understand?"

Yesuntei was four years younger than Tuya, but sometimes – most times, actually – it felt as if it was the other way round. And if anyone else in this entire city who didn't sit on the throne had spoken to Yesuntei in that way, they would have been buried up to their necks in the dirt before the suns set.

She stepped in close to Tuya. "I am not prepared to sacrifice any more people dealing with this animal," she murmured.

"Except me, apparently."

Yesuntei gave her a patient smile. "You'll be fine. This is what you were meant to do. Besides, I'll be right there with you."

"No. No. You'll only—"

"I will not leave you unprotected. Not *ever*, do you understand? Not even with this. I will never ask you to take risks I wouldn't take myself."

Tuya lifted her head to the sky, as if asking the Father for a little help. When he declined to make an appearance, she swore under her breath, then lifted her chin in Gantalgun's direction. "You. Idiot. Did any of you hurt her?"

The watch leader cocked his head. "Excuse me?"

"The tiger. Is she injured? Or sick?"

Yesuntei decided it wasn't worth asking how Tuya knew the animal's sex. Gantalgun looked around at his men, questioning eyebrows raised, then shook his head.

"Fine." Tuya pinched the bridge of her nose. "I need meat."

"I don't—"

"*Meat*. Horse, antelope, doesn't matter. Get a big chunk of it."

Ten minutes later, Tuya was holding a dripping hunk of horse flesh in one hand, fingers digging into the soft surface. With a muttered prayer to whichever god happened to be listening, she jerked her chin at the darkness inside the granary. "Let's get this over with."

Yesuntei drew her sabre, and she and Tuya stepped inside.

The granary smelled dusty, and very slightly sour, like *airag* on the turn. Not to mention the delicate tang of spilled blood. For a few seconds, Yesuntei was utterly blind, enveloped in darkness.

Inwardly, she cursed – she should have planned for this. If the animal attacked now, she wouldn't be able to see it coming.

It didn't. Didn't make a single sound. They might have been entirely alone.

Slowly, they stepped further into the cavernous space. Until Tuya, standing a few feet ahead of Yesuntei, suddenly murmured, "Don't move."

The objects in the granary slowly resolved themselves. Yesuntei made out giant mounds of cut grains, bundled grass for horses. A wagon lay pushed into one corner, wheels removed . . . and on top of it, there was a hunched, dark shape.

As Yesuntei turned her head towards it, the shape moved. Just a little. Lifting a head the size of a man's torso, the wood creaking underneath it.

Yesuntei raised her sabre, doing it on instinct, fingers tightening on the hilt.

"I *said*, don't move." This time, Tuya's voice was a soft, urgent hiss. Her posture had changed, just a little. Her spine was straighter, her shoulders no longer hunched.

A sound came out of the darkness. It wasn't a growl, or a snarl. It was a low, guttural *hum*, a noise that seemed to vibrate the walls, roll through the hard-packed earth under their feet.

Yesuntei did not regret bringing Tuya here. It was an opportunity – one that she couldn't pass up. All the same, a little prickle of fear touched the back of her neck.

If the beast came for Tuya, she wouldn't hesitate: she would attack, put herself between the tiger and her sister, even if she died doing it. She wasn't going to let any harm come to Tuya, not ever, not to the only family she had left.

Let her work.

Slowly, Tuya went down to one knee, never taking her eyes from the hunched shape. She stayed kneeling even when the tiger got to its feet. For the first time, its eyes picked up the light from outside, tiny little flickers in the darkness.

"Hello there," Tuya whispered – and just like that, the tiger moved.

It was fast. So unbelievably fast, leaping off the wagon, the thrum in its throat filling the world. Even as Yesuntei's eyes widened, as she raised her sabre, she understood: she wasn't going to get there in time. And however good her sister was with animals, it wasn't going to be enough.

But before the tiger could reach her, Tuya let out a *scream*.

No, that was wrong. Not a scream. It was a shout that defied explanation: part growl, part yelp. It didn't sound human.

Tuya rocketed to her feet, swinging her arms above her head, making the noise again and again. The tiger skidded to a halt, roared, the sound shaking Yesuntei's gut. It was in the light now, big and tawny, a huge female with blood in her whiskers. It stalked to Tuya's right, teeth bared, huffing as it breathed.

Tuya's growl-yelp-barks were shorter now. Yesuntei caught a glimpse of her face, which was twisted and angry, eyes huge.

She wasn't speaking to the beast. That wasn't how this worked. Tuya had tried to explain it, years ago, tried to explain why she was so good with animals, in a way that others simply weren't. It wasn't magic – it was simply perception. Intuition.

"You have to show them," she had said. "You have to make them believe that you're stronger than they are. That you could hurt them, badly, even if they eventually killed you. Wild animals don't understand enemies or friends. They understand full bellies, and safe spaces. Make it easy for them to get those things, and they'll leave you alone."

Tuya's instinct, her natural abilities, had led her to become an eagle hunter, and after the Khan had recalled her to Karkorum to become an entertainer at court, she became the first choice for dealing with animals. It was astounding that the Guard hadn't thought to call on her to begin with.

Tuya lifted the hunk of flesh. The tiger's eyes narrowed, and it bent low, ready to leap – just as Yesuntei's sister tossed the meat, doing it with a contemptuous flick of the wrist. The tiger snatched it out of the air.

"Then you show them you can provide," Tuya had said, in that long-ago conversation. "That letting you feed them is easier than feeding on you."

Tuya wasn't taming the animal. You couldn't tame something that lived in the wild – that would take years. But if you established dominance, showed that you would be very difficult to kill cleanly – and gave your quarry an escape route – then you might walk away from an encounter.

If it was injured, or sick, or mad, then none of this would work. But a simple dominance play, in the right hands . . .

Tuya was making another sound now. Quick little huffs, drawn from the very back of her throat. She walked a slow circle around the animal, which swallowed the last of the meat, watching her, licking its lips with its enormous pink tongue.

Tuya caught Yesuntei's eye, gave a quick jerk of the chin. Yesuntei nodded, stepped slowly back into the light, never once looking away from the beast.

Gantalgun hovered on her left. "Back up," she snapped.

He and the other soldiers obeyed, giving the door a wide berth. Two of them were visibly trembling. Yesuntei committed their faces to memory – she would find out who they were later.

Tuya came out first, walking backwards, and the tiger followed. Padding into the light, blinking sleepily, as if just roused from a delicious nap.

"All right," Tuya murmured, when she was a few feet away from Yesuntei. "She's fed, she's calm, she's got an exit." She pointed to the east, in the direction of the grassland. "But I can't guarantee she won't come back, so—"

She didn't see Yesuntei lift her hand. A moment later, with a dull thud, an arrow appeared in the beast's neck.

Tuya screamed again – and this time it was a scream of horror.

The tiger howled as three more arrows struck its midsection. They were heavy arrows, useless over longer distances, but ideal for penetration. No missed shots this time; the beast was a clear, slow-moving target.

Blood spurted across the dirt, the tiger thrashing, trying to get to the nearest soldier. But its back legs were no longer listening to it, feet dragging.

Yesuntei had positioned her archers perfectly. She made Gantalgun fetch the best marksmen in the Guard, five of them lined up so that any arrows that didn't hit their mark would fall into the granary.

Tuya stumbled towards the dying beast, crashing to her knees next to it. It swatted at her, far too feeble. Trembling in a growing pool of blood, a strange wheezing noise coming from its throat. Eyes rolling in terror, as if it didn't understand what was happening, didn't understand why it couldn't get to its feet. Why it could no longer run.

A moment later, the eyes closed halfway, only the whites showing, and it fell still.

Nobody moved. Even the wind had stopped.

Tuya put a hand on the tiger's flank. Looked back towards Yesuntei, tears streaking her cheeks. She didn't need to ask the question – it was written on her face, clear as the dawn sky.

Yesuntei strode forward, ignoring the blood splashing her boots, and swept her sister up in a hug. Tuya fought, of course she did, but Yesuntei held her in place. "It's all right," she murmured. "You did so well."

She wouldn't understand, of course. She could never see further than what was right in front of her. But the moment Yesuntei heard where the tiger was, she spotted the opportunity. It's why she didn't order the workers in the field to be dismissed, why she made sure Gantalgun and his men were still in attendance.

By nightfall, the story would be all over the city. How the Khan's Guard pacified a ravenous beast. How they had ensured it would never return. The workers and soldiers who saw it would talk of nothing else.

The tale would grow, spreading through the *gers*, discussed over cookfires and skins of *airag*. By tomorrow morning, there would be stories of Yesuntei getting the beast to bow before the Khan himself.

She held her sister at arm's length, glanced back towards the assembled soldiers. "For the glory of Hanggai," she called.

"Hanggai!" they yelled back, even the ones that had been shaking with fear not thirty seconds before. Behind them, the workers in the crop fields took up the call, voices ringing out in the still air.

Tuya was silent. Yesuntei's grip on her shoulders tightened, just a little.

For a few moments, she thought Tuya might lash out at her. That's how deep the fury in her eyes was. And that would have been bad, because Yesuntei couldn't allow that – especially not there, in front of her troops.

She was surprised to find herself silently pleading for her sister to obey.

But Tuya had always been a good soldier. She complained, she griped, she snapped and snarled . . . but she obeyed. She obeyed her Khan, and she obeyed her sister.

"For the glory of Hanggai," Tuya said, speaking in a low monotone.

She twisted out of Yesuntei's grip, stalking away across the hard-packed dirt. Yesuntei didn't follow.

Timur appeared at his mistress's elbow. She hadn't even realised he was still there. "Congratulations, *bahadur*," he murmured.

Yesuntei didn't acknowledge this. There was still too much to do, and not nearly enough time to do it in.

"What's next?" she asked.

Twelve

Sayana

Turned out, the others didn't love Sayana's brilliant idea. Even after she laid out the amazing things she'd seen the eagle hunter do at court — like that one time the woman brought in a whole troupe of rowdy jackals, made them silent with a single command and had them do tricks for the Khan. Even after that, the other Rakada told her to fuck off. In exactly as many words.

Sayana would admit, her timing could have been better. Hitting everyone with it after a hard ride, on zero sleep, was probably not a good choice. But in the moment, the idea seemed huge — too big to contain, the kind of thing she had to get out, right there.

It was their second night in the Namag. Every third step was into stinking mud, and the mosquitoes threatened to drive Sayana insane. Her ears already ached from the number of times she had accidentally swatted them.

Her braid was fucked. It was tough to maintain anyway — every few days, she had to undo it, clean it as best she could. But unless she was prepared to specifically boil up a batch of mucky marsh water each and every time, that wasn't going to happen. The braid remained stiff, ratty. With little bits of dried mud in it, although Sayana couldn't for the life of her figure out how *that* had happened.

They'd managed to find one of the few pieces of dry ground in the marshes, a nothing little patch between two murky, ankle-deep pools, and had set up the clan's *ger*. It was Sayana's shift on watch; she sat cross-legged nearby, huddled in a blanket against the cold night air. In the *ger*, Erhi snored softly.

Sayana used to think she'd hate watch duty. Sitting by herself, with nothing to do but keep an eye out for anyone stupid enough to sneak up on them, sounded like torture. No one to talk to, nothing but her thoughts for company.

Turned out, there was a lot to see at night. Even when it was cold and quiet. When there were no clouds, Sayana could see the vast expanse of stars they called Father Sky's Beard: shades of white and pink and blue, painting the dark in a million pricks of light. She felt like a tiny speck of dust, beneath the notice of anyone important. A speck of dust that could go where it wanted and do whatever it felt like.

She liked how she could figure out what the weather would be in the mornings, purely based on which stars were hidden behind clouds. Wide-open sky, with everything visible? They'd wake up to chilly mist, water beading exposed skin. If there was a thunderstorm blotting out the northern horizon, lightning flickering in the dark sky, that usually meant an absolutely spectacular sunrise.

So yes, watch was nowhere near as bad as she'd thought. Except for tonight, when her mind was a nest of buzzing hornets.

She couldn't stop thinking about her little encounter with the *araatan*. It still didn't seem real — hells, the very fact that the beasts existed at all didn't seem real.

There *were* other large animals in the Tapestry. Oxen taller than a man, river fish with huge, sinuous bodies. Crocodiles in Ngu big enough to be mistaken for fallen tree trunks. There were even mammoths who walked the grass, once, although no one had seen one for a hundred years.

But all these other giants were gentle, placid. The *araatan* were . . . not. Not to mention that they were bigger than all of the others — maybe even bigger than the damn mammoths — oh, and let's not forget the fact they could breathe fucking fire. How did that even happen? Sayana could swear she had a lesson about it once, a dimly remembered tutor explaining it to her, but the details weren't there. Something about gases? Maybe?

She shivered. It was autumn now. The grass had started to turn golden brown, the tips creaking and rustling with dry whispers as the Rakada rode through them on their way to the marsh. Like most autumn nights, the sky was clear. The moon shone down, reflecting in the still water. There was only one, unlike the twin suns that rose each morning.

Sayana had never really understood why no one cared about the moon very much; everyone in the Tapestry worshipped Father Sky and Mother Earth, praised the suns, named them as the eyes of the Father . . . but nobody ever gave much of a fuck about the moon. It seemed unfair, really.

Unfair. That was a fun word.

A mosquito hummed around Sayana's ear. She resisted waving it away for about three seconds, and then thrashed her arms above her head, flailing, feeling ridiculous. Her skin itched so badly — both on her bitten arms, and on her burned thigh — that she genuinely contemplated jumping headlong into the cold, gloopy marsh water.

On the other hand, the only thing worse than itching was

explosive diarrhoea. So she sat, and breathed, and tried to study the sky. You couldn't see it from the palace—not really. Just little glimpses, through slitted windows . . .

A little while after she first joined the Rakada, Chimeg had pulled Sayana aside and quietly told her that she had to stop whining. Apparently, she had a habit of complaining about things, especially things she thought were stupid, or pointless. It was part of the reason the others nicknamed her Princess, and of course, she'd whined about that too.

Problem was, Chimeg was right. It was one thing to complain about something genuinely unfair; it was another to bitch and moan about, oh, latrine duty, or helping Hogelun prep their food, or having to track down specific herbs for Erhi. Just because you could spend most of the time living exactly how you wanted in the Tapestry didn't mean you could escape the boring shit completely.

If your Chief gave you a command, you listened. Especially if it was someone like Chimeg, who always gave herself the hardest jobs, who never complained, who put herself on the line for them every single day.

Sayana only had to think about what happened whenever they broke camp; Chimeg never cared whether her raiders believed in the Weavers like she did, but she wouldn't let anyone disrespect them. Mother Earth and Father Sky had woven the Tapestry, and so every time they moved on, the Rakada would pick up everything. Every piece of trash, every scrap of fabric, every gnawed bone from their evening meal. All of it. You didn't sully the Weavers' creation, not ever.

And Chimeg was always the first to start – she never issued an order, never told them it was time to make tracks. She just got up from the fire, and started collecting their debris.

That was just who the Chief was. So Sayana had taken a

deep breath, thanked Chimeg for her insight, and promised to be better.

Then she'd rewarded herself by eating two whole fire apples she'd been saving, because really, if you were going to become a better person you might as well have something nice to eat while you did it.

When Sayana was growing up, in the still, stifling air of the palace, her parents and their friends talked of raiders like their doom was inevitable. That their choices meant they would die horrible deaths. "They all know it, too," her mother had said, over the edge of her porcelain cup. "Deep down, every one of them knows their destiny is to die like dogs. They just want to take as many people with them as they can."

But raiders didn't live on borrowed time. They weren't just waiting to die like dogs − a phrase Sayana happened to think was insulting both to raiders and to the many hounds she'd been lucky enough to scritch behind the ears in her life.

But now . . .

For months, the Rakada had struggled. Struggled to find new places to raid, to stay one step ahead of the army. And the Chief's response was to just . . . ignore it. Keep going, just like always.

They'd discussed forming an alliance with the other clans − that was one option Chimeg *had* considered. But that was easier said than done. First, they'd have to find them, figure out where they were in the vast Tapestry − it wasn't as if the clans told people where they were going. Second, they'd have to convince them that the Rakada weren't planning to fuck them over the first chance they got.

Those two would have been bad enough. What killed the idea dead, though, was the simple fact that against the might of the army, it just wouldn't work.

Maybe they'd see off a couple of battalions. And maybe a few nomad groups and villages would go unmolested by the Khan for a time. But eventually, they'd come across a force too big to beat. The Khan simply had more men.

But an *araatan*, even one . . .

Sayana couldn't help but think back to how the soldiers had looked when she'd rode up – well, fine, when she'd somehow managed to steer the *araatan* into them. That look of stunned, horrified awe. Of *fear*.

Because an *araatan* could win a battle all on its own. Hells, you could take out the rider, get lucky with an arrow, but you'd *still* have the hungry, fire-breathing monster to deal with. Not like the *araatan* would shrug its shoulders and slink away, just because its mistress had fallen.

And Sayana could see all the way to the end of that particular line of thought. If they could defeat the army, the Khan would have no way of forcing people out of the Tapestry, and into the city. They'd choke off his air supply. The grasslands would be theirs. The army couldn't touch them. No more running, no more skirmishes, no more fallen raiders.

No more Sarnais.

As for raiding? There wouldn't be any need, once they had a lizard or two. No settlement would dare fight back. Fuck being a *Princess*; she and the Rakada would live like queens. They'd never have to worry about anything, ever again.

Sayana smirked. Even she could see that was probably a touch optimistic. And all this was contingent on the small, inconsequential matter of actually training an *araatan*.

But the Rakada wouldn't try. That was what got her. They wouldn't even *attempt* it. It wasn't just that Chimeg wouldn't budge – Sayana had expected that. No, what really got her was the others. They all blindly followed Chimeg, just fell in with what the Chief told them to do. Even Khun.

Of course, it was a long shot. Sayana had some notion that getting jackals to do tricks and using an eagle to hunt were a little bit different from convincing an enormous, toothy, fire-breathing reptile to let you mount up and control it. But at least she could say she'd tried. If it really was going to end, if the Rakada really were going down, along with everyone else in the Tapestry . . . then she could go with her head held high.

Autumn. In a few months, it would be winter, harsh and heavy and choked with snow. If the Rakada hadn't got their shit squared away, their food stores in good shape . . .

"Oi."

Sayana jumped, ripped out of her thoughts. It was Hogelun, face just visible in the light of the moon. The big raider had her blanket wrapped tight around her. "Get some sleep, Princess," she said, her words accompanied by a puff of white vapour.

Sayana hadn't even realised her watch was done. Her legs ached as she stood, complaining as she picked her way across the boggy ground to the *ger*.

But as Hogelun took her place, club resting on her thighs, Sayana came to a halt.

She could picture the eagle hunter's house in Karkorum. She could picture the woman in her mind. Images of unkempt hair, dusty leather, the expression on her face as she made her animals obey her every command.

If Chimeg didn't want to risk the Rakada raiding Karkorum, that was fine. She was Chief, and that was her call.

But she didn't get to decide what Sayana did, without the others.

The idea was so startling that her eyes actually widened. The city wasn't far. The Namag was slow going, to be sure, but once you were out it was no more than two days' ride across the Tapestry, if you were kind to the horse. A straight shot.

Even then, she hesitated, because what the fuck was she even thinking? Riding right into enemy territory, by herself, to kidnap someone?

But what she saw then was fifteen-year-old Sayana. With her fine silk *deels*, and her packed schedule of elocution and singing and formal dinners. With the battered, wooden practice sword she kept hidden away, taking it out only when she was sure no one was watching, spying on the soldiers training, peering through the slitted window in her room, mimicking them.

The girl who got out, who said: fuck that.

The girl who decided that the next person to tut quietly and tell her that one day her husband would bring her into line was going to get a blade stuck in their neck.

The girl who struck out on her own, found her people, made a life for herself. Who risked everything.

And Sayana saw that girl's face when she told her she was thinking about going on a solo mission to save her raider clan . . .

And saw her face when she decided not to, after all.

Before she could talk herself out of it, she'd made her way across to her horse. Halfway there, she glanced back towards Hogelun, who was seated with her back turned, still as a stone.

Sayana's saddlebags were stacked nearby. She quickly ran through what she had: some old turnips, a few wrinkled fire apples, a pouch of millet, a skin of water. It would have to do. She could replenish the water on the way, maybe even do some hunting. Once she was out of the Namag, there would be grass, enough for her horse to eat its fill . . .

Her horse woke with a clumsy huff, but Sayana managed to soothe him, murmuring gentle nothings in his ear, slinging her bags onto the saddle. This was going to be hard: she'd had a few hours of sleep before her watch, but that was all. Still, it wasn't anything she couldn't handle . . .

She put one foot in the stirrup—

—and slammed back down to the earth as Hogelun grabbed her shoulder.

"What the fuck are you doing?" Hogs spoke in a low voice, not a whisper. You learned that as a raider: if you wanted to speak without anyone nearby hearing you, you never whispered. Whispers always carried, no matter how quiet you made them.

Gently, Sayana removed the hand from her shoulder, gave it a quick squeeze. "I'll be back as soon as I can."

"That's not an answer." Hogs spoke through gritted teeth. "Chimeg told you not to—"

"I know. Just . . . just tell them I was up and riding before you could stop me."

Hogelun looked around, as if trying to find someone to back her up. Finding no one, she turned to Sayana, threw up her hands. "Think. Weavers' breath, Princess, *think*. You're heading right back into army territory – right back to their fucking headquarters. You're trying to . . . what, kidnap this person? And then somehow bring her back here, all without raising the alarm? And get to . . . if she could . . . " Words seemed to fail her. "This is . . . it's dumb. Really, really dumb."

Surely Hogelun wasn't going to try to keep her here? Because if that happened, everyone really would wake up, and then Chimeg would probably do something annoying, like confiscating all of Sayana's supplies.

"Yes," she murmured. "It's dumb. You know what would have been smarter? All of us doing it, backing each other up, having an actual, proper plan." Sayana stuck a finger at the *ger*, at the slumbering figures inside. "But since I got shouted down, I guess I need to do it myself."

"But you'll die." Hogelun sounded so sincere right then that

Sayana's will weakened, just a tiny bit. "They'll kill you, the second they see you. You do understand that, yeah?"

"I won't have my bones. I won't look like a raider. I'd just . . . I'd just be another person coming in from the Tapestry."

"And getting out? How were you planning on doing that?"

Sayana ignored the question. In one movement, she mounted her horse, swinging her leg over the saddle. Hogelun stared up at her, furious. Helpless.

"Sorry, Hogs," Sayana said. "I don't have a choice."

With a gentle tap of the heels, her still-unnamed horse began to move across the marsh. She stayed slow, doing her best to avoid sloshing the water, and thankfully, her mount obeyed.

There was a flickering little flame of worry inside her, but the faster she went, the further she got, the more it dwindled down to nothing.

Thirteen

Hogelun

Hogelun knew exactly what to do. She had to wake the others. Chimeg and Erhi had to know.

Maybe it wasn't too late – they could catch the Princess if they left now. Hells, they could catch the Princess anytime. It wasn't like they didn't know which direction she was going in.

She took two steps towards the *ger*, then came to a stop. Better idea: *she* should go after Sayana. Just ride up, tell the evil little bitch to turn around. If she wouldn't, then Hogelun would make her. She could snap the Princess in two with a look, and what was the point of being the biggest Rakada if you couldn't knock some heads together?

A few feet from her horse, she stopped again. Leaving now would mean that no one was on watch.

Sure, the Khan and his army never really bothered with the Namag . . . but what about other raiders? What if someone slaughtered the Rakada in their sleep, all because there was no one to raise the alarm? Plus, her damn stirrup was still broken, so riding would be difficult . . .

A mosquito chose that moment to whine in her ear. Hogelun swatted at it without thinking, and smacked herself in the head.

She had to wake the others. She *had* to. Erhi would know what to do . . .

Halfway back to the *ger*, she stopped for a third time. Sat down hard on the boggy ground. Hugged herself, shivering — she had tossed her blanket aside when she tried to stop Sayana, and couldn't see where it was in the darkness.

Behind her, Erhi gave one of those amazingly cute snores. Hogelun listened hard, hoping that Erhi would wake up on her own. But after a moment, all was silent. Except, of course, for the mosquito still buzzing around Hogelun's head.

Fuck the Princess. They *told* her this was a stupid idea, in multiple different ways. If she still wanted to do it, then that was her own problem. Hogelun had enjoyed having her around, but the Rakada existed before she arrived, and they would continue to exist after.

Wait, Sayana left? No, I didn't see her, she must have snuck off. What a pity. Well, we can't help it if she's an idiot, time to move on with our lives . . .

Hogelun let out a long, slow breath, pleased that she had finally put this to rest.

A soft footstep behind her. She scrambled to her feet, club held ready, spotting a figure over by the horses.

Hogelun drew breath to cry out, then paused. Because the figure was Khunbish . . . who was currently securing saddlebags to Midnight.

"Are you absolutely shitting me?" Hogelun spat. Quietly. Had everyone in this damn camp lost their fucking minds?

Quickly, she made her way over to Khun, sheathing her club on her back. Unlike with Sayana, she didn't touch the older

Rakada — Khun tended to express displeasure in particularly violent ways if you made contact unexpectedly. But she did hiss the woman's name, ask her what she was doing. Even though she knew already.

Khun studied her in the dim moonlight. "A journey in darkest night, into the darkest places. One should never make such a journey alone."

Hogelun had no idea how Khun even knew Sayana had left. She rubbed her forehead with a closed fist, eyes squeezed shut, trying not to think about what the Chief would say when she found out that she, Hogelun, had let not one but two of the clan just dash off in the middle of the night.

"Khun," she said, with what was frankly a much calmer voice than this situation deserved. "The Princess is an idiot. Her plan is one of the worst ideas I've ever heard. You helping her isn't going to make a single bit of difference."

Khun stroked her cheek. It was a surprisingly gentle gesture. "Mother Earth slumbers. Father Sky's eyes are closed. The Weavers do not watch for our Princess. She deserves my eternal protection, while I'm still here to grant it."

She cocked her head, sniffed the air rapidly five or six times, then hopped up on her horse. The pouch on her chest shifted, and she moved it back in place, stroking the leather. "I will set a fire for you in the ancient mountains," she told Hogelun, from her lofty perch.

Hogelun was going to scream. She really was. "Chimeg," she told Khun. "Your Chief . . . she . . . she *ordered* you, and me, to stay put here."

There was a rattle of bones as Khun slung her headdress on. "You fear," she said.

"I'm not scared. I was trying to—"

"Oh, but you do. You fear choosing. You fear it so much that you would let us ride into the dark. You hope that your lover will choose for you, or your Chieftain, or the gods."

Oh good, Hogelun thought bitterly. *She's lucid tonight.*

"You hope that if you cook your meals and raid who you are told to raid, everything will be fine." Khun rolled her head, in a slow circle. "You did not even choose to be a raider. You merely let it happen."

"Dog shit." Hogelun was dismayed at how small her voice was. She was so dismayed that she decided to do something about it, only she went too far and the growling voice she used sounded like she had a bad cold. "You do what Chimeg says, don't you? I didn't see you telling her to get fucked. You know, before. Why are you leaving *now*?"

But lucid Khun was gone, replaced by twisting-her-fingers-in-strange-shapes Khun. "He will not let me die," she sang happily, fluttering her fingers above her head, then gave Midnight gentle heels and took off after Sayana. This time, Hogelun actually gave chase, but it only lasted for a few steps before she gave up.

Her hands fell by her sides, clenched into fists. Khun's words rang in her ears.

In that moment, Hogelun would have given *anything* to be on a raid. A good, old-fashioned dust-up. She wouldn't have even minded if it was one of those raids where a bunch of villagers decided to fight back, making things difficult. Even raids like those were easy when you got down to it: you rode in, and if someone popped up in front of you, you swung your club until they changed shape and stopped moving.

The Weavers had made her the size she was so she would be really, really good at fighting. Why were they dropping this shitshow in *her* lap? Why didn't they give it to someone smarter?

She gazed helplessly as Khun vanished into the night, then turned and gazed even more helplessly at the *ger*.

She could wake Erhi and Chimeg now, and they'd be furious that she'd let Khun and the Princess go. Worse: they'd be disappointed. Hogelun could take that from the Chief, barely, but from Erhi?

She could do nothing . . . only, that might be even worse. *Why didn't you wake us? What's wrong with you?*

And if she did go . . .

If she left the camp undefended . . .

If Erhi woke up, and she wasn't here . . .

She closed her eyes. Hoping that when she opened them again, it would all have been a horrible dream.

No such luck. She had to decide what to do, and she had to decide right now.

Fourteen

Sayana

Dawn was breaking over the Tapestry when Sayana spotted the pond. It was as good a time to rest as any, and the water looked clean and fresh. Dragonflies hovered over the surface, zipping back and forth.

Sayana still didn't quite understand *why* Khun had decided to ride with her. She'd asked, naturally, when Khun had caught up to her, and the older raider had gone on a long monologue about the history of butterflies in the Tapestry, and after a while Sayana had stopped listening.

Was Khun actually going to be helpful? Sayana didn't have the first idea. She was only just starting to think about how she was going to do this — something she *really* should have considered before riding off into the night — but it was probably going to involve sneaking past groups of soldiers. Khun was many things, but she wasn't exactly what you'd call stealthy.

Still, Sayana had to admit: as much as she loved the idea of single-handedly saving her clan from destruction, she appreciated not having to do it alone.

She dismounted. "Let's stop for a bit. Give the horses some water, maybe get a couple hours' sleep."

Khun sprang off her mount's back. "You will water Midnight. I will hunt turtles."

"You'll . . . sorry?"

Khun jabbed one of her knives at the opposite side of the pond. "I saw one in the reeds. They are delicious with rock salt and birch roots."

Before Sayana could say anything, Khun had vanished into the grass. A warbling voice drifted back to her: "It likes to be scratched behind the ears!"

Sayana didn't know if she meant her horse, or the turtle she was hunting. It didn't seem worth it to ask for clarification.

She let their mounts drink, gave Midnight a scratch behind the ears (he gave her a withering look, but didn't object) and filled their skins. Then she just sat on a rock for a while, eating one of her fire apples and watching the suns come up. Watched as they spread warm, glowing light across the waving grass, burning away the early morning clouds. An eagle rode the thermals high above; as Sayana watched, it dropped into a dive, flapping its wings as it vanished from sight among the waving stalks.

For a second, Sayana's pulse quickened — but then she relaxed, irritated with herself. Catching the eagle hunter they were planning on kidnapping, before they even *got* to Karkorum, was about as likely as Chimeg giving Sayana a nice shoulder rub and foot massage after a hard day of raiding.

They were still a full day's ride away from the city. *Long way to go.* But they'd found water and the sunrise was pretty and no one was immediately trying to murder them. There weren't even any *araatan* sniffing about; Sayana's mouth twisted at the thought of what the other Rakada would say if she got killed by one, while trying to kidnap someone who could help her ride them.

She sat and watched the dawn, and waited for Khun to return with her turtle. She was still sitting there, forty minutes later, when Hogelun came thundering up.

Hogs was riding so hard that she almost drove Hoof Monster right into the pond. She brought her mount up just short of the waterline; the big bastard looked exhausted, half-mad eyes rolling in his sockets. His mistress didn't look much better; she was filthy, *deel* caked in dust, streaks of sweat on her shorn head.

She dismounted, stumbling a little on the landing, and pointed a shaking finger at Sayana. "Right. *You.*"

"Hogs?" Sayana clambered off her rock. "Where did you come fr—"

"I have been chasing you," Hogelun declared, taking big, wobbling strides towards her, "for the entire *bloody night*. Do you know how hard it is to track someone on horseback in the dark? No? Well, I do!"

Sayana blinked hard, as if this was all a dream. How did they not hear Hoof Monster behind them? And surely they couldn't have been that hard to follow – it wasn't as if Hogs didn't know where they were going . . .

"You chased us all night?" she said.

"*I didn't think it would take that long!*" Hogelun slowed for a moment. "I sort of got lost. There were a bunch of confusing rocks on this one hill, and I got a bit turned around and . . . look, it doesn't matter. You are getting on your horse and you are coming back with me and you are doing it right now. Where the fuck is Khun?"

She peered at Sayana, as if the woman was hiding in Sayana's *deel.*

"Hogs, listen." The younger raider held up her hands, palms out. "I'm going to Karkorum, and you're not going to stop me."

Hogelun barked a mirthless laugh. "Really? We're still doing this?"

"I know you don't understand—"

"No. I don't. Do *you* understand that if you keep being an arsehole, I will pick you up and drag you back myself?"

Sayana didn't really understand how Hogs thought that would work, but she took a hasty step back nonetheless – as anyone would, when faced with a gigantic, angry raider operating on no sleep.

Weavers, it would be great if Khun could pop up right now. It probably wouldn't help much, but at least it would give Hogelun two people to deal with, instead of just her.

"Please, please listen to me," she said. "If you do this, I'll . . . "

"You'll what?"

Inspiration struck. "I'll catch a lizard and put it under your blankets while you sleep."

"You wouldn't dare."

Sayana bared her teeth in a grin. "Watch me."

Hogelun chewed the inside of her lip, then shook her head. "Know what? I'll live. And I'm serious – you need to get on your horse and come back with me, right now."

"You're being completely unreasonable."

"*I'm* being unreasonable? You're the one who abandoned your clan for no good reason."

"How is saving all of us not a good reason? Use your brain, just for a minute, *please*?"

Under normal circumstances, Hogelun might have just rolled her eyes. Not today. Her eyes widened, nostrils flaring as she strode towards Sayana.

At that moment, there was a panicked shout, followed by Khun yelling, "Get back here! Tell me your secrets!"

Sayana turned to look—

—just as a dark shape exploded out of the grass behind her.

She spun, hands flying to her sabres, not quite quick enough. Whoever it was collided with her right hip, sending her sprawling. Her mind filled with a dozen scenarios, all of them bad. Soldiers, other raiders, Khan's Guard, Chimeg and Erhi.

Sayana scrambled to her feet, mud spattering her *deel*. Whoever had hit her was sprinting at Hogelun – and right then, Sayana realised that Hogs had no weapon.

And, as it turned out, didn't need one. Hogelun swung an enormous arm out, and knocked the person off their feet. Air left them in a startled gulp as they went airborne, back parallel to the ground. They crashed into the muck, Hogelun immediately on top of them, forearm jammed into their throat.

Khun was dragging someone else out of the grass, a small and very loud someone. Sayana had just enough time to register all this when Khun threw her quarry into the muck too, screaming nonsense at them from three inches away.

"Khun." Sayana dropped her hands from her sabres, darting forward and making sure the woman could see her. "Khun, Hogs, *stop*. They're kids."

Hogelun had seen it too. She frowned down at her captive, who was a boy of about twelve, with a hooked nose and a mop of dark, unruly hair. He was trying to bite Hogelun's wrist, and she had to lean hard into him before he stopped. "Don't touch him," the boy was shouting. "I'll kill you!"

The other one, underneath Khun, was even younger. Eight or nine. Unlike his brother – and they were brothers, Sayana could see the resemblance immediately – he was terrified. Breaths coming in little hitching gasps as Khun waggled a knife in front of his face.

"Stop it." Sayana pulled Khun off – normally, you didn't touch her, she didn't like that, but she wasn't going to let Khunbish threaten a child. She scanned the grass, wondering if the boys had other people with them, but no one appeared.

Hogelun grunted, dragging the older boy to his feet. "Right. Who in the nine hells are you?"

"Little thieves," Khun spat. "Stealing my turtles."

Sayana sagged. She'd thought these boys were trying to attack them – turns out, they were just running away. An entirely sensible response, when confronted with an angry Khunbish. It had been their bad luck to crash headlong into Sayana and Hogelun.

Sayana got between Khunbish and the younger boy, reaching out a hand for him – after making sure he wasn't about to rip a blade of his own from his sash. Both boys wore travel-stained *deels* over dirt-brown tunics, and the younger one had a fur hat of some kind, in the mud next to him. He blinked up at her, and after a moment, let her pull him to his feet.

"What are you doing out here?"

The younger one opened his mouth, but his brother got there first. "Don't say anything." He made an attempt to wriggle out of Hogelun's grip, and got precisely nowhere.

Sayana thought fast. She, Khun and Hogelun had taken off their bones, and they wore no face paint. If these boys were with anyone – a band of nomads maybe, or a group making their way to the capital – then it didn't automatically make them a threat.

"Let me go," the older brother snapped. "I'm a Bone Raider. You don't leave me alone, I'll cut out your skull and drink from it."

Sayana met Hogelun's eyes. Under the circumstances, Sayana was quite proud of the fact that neither of them laughed.

"Our whole clan's looking for us." The boy was still trying to twist away from Hogelun. "They know where we are, and they'll come, and they'll fuck you up!"

"Anyone out there?" Sayana asked Khun.

"The grass is silent as the heavens," Khun said. Which Sayana took as a *no*.

"Look, where are your parents?" It felt like a wild question to ask, but she asked it anyway.

She didn't expect an answer, and the older boy just scowled at her. But to her surprise, the younger one piped up. "They were supposed to come with us."

Hogelun must have let her attention slip, because suddenly, the boy she was holding wrenched out of her grip. She let him go, and Sayana tensed . . . but he just rushed to his brother, got between him and Sayana. Fists up – which looked ridiculous. In the light from the rising suns, they seemed even younger than Sayana had first thought. They were thin, too, their clothes hanging off them.

And all at once, Sayana understood.

"You were in Karkorum, weren't you?" she asked quietly.

"Just let us go," the older one said. But the fight had gone out of him, and he let his fists fall to his sides.

"We were all going to leave." The younger boy peeked out from behind his brother. "Mother and Father and Abaka, he's our other brother, but the soldiers found out and Abaka told us to run and—"

"Quiet," said the other, sending a worried look at Sayana and Khun.

But tears had started to glisten in the younger one's eyes. "They were going to make Father and Abaka be soldiers, even though they didn't want to." The words came out in a rush, as if they'd been held back for a long time. "They made Mother and Tarkhan and me work all day in the fields—"

"You're such a baby," the older one – Tarkhan, presumably – snapped. But there was fear in his eyes too, raw and fresh.

His brother went on. "And there wasn't enough food, and it was loud all the time and Mother got sick, so Father said we'd escape but then we tried and the soldiers they . . . and Mother told us to run and Tarkhan said . . . said . . ." He trailed off, dissolving into sobs.

His words hung in the still air. The eagle was back up again, circling, hunting for more prey in the grass.

Sayana struggled to take the boy's words in. How long had they been out here? Where in the nine hells were they *going*?

"We're not going to hurt you," Sayana told them. "And we're not going to take you back, nothing like that. Just . . . do you have somewhere to go?"

Tarkhan stared at her for a moment, defiant, but the fight had gone out of him. "The mountains," he muttered. "Father said there were people hiding out there."

Not to mention soldiers. Sayana wondered if she should tell the two of them this, only . . . only all at once, it felt too big. She had never been to the mountains, so who knew what was up there now?

"If you've been out here for a while, you've been hunting," she said. "Right?"

The younger boy sniffled, nodded. "Tarkhan has a bow."

Sayana wondered where the bow was, decided not to get sidetracked. "Plenty to hunt around here. Turtles, small game. Birds. Take all the time you need – we won't stop you. Will we?"

She directed the last bit at Khun, who grunted something ugly, but didn't object.

"I saw some wild horses to the south-east, earlier," Sayana said. "You might be able to break one, if you sneak up on it. At least you'll have a mount then."

Tarkhan looked like he didn't believe her. But after a few moments, he nodded. Slunk away, pulling his brother with him. Just before they vanished into the grass, the younger one flashed Sayana a small smile. Then they were gone.

The Rakada never saw the boys again.

For a long moment, the three raiders stood silently at the edge of the water. Nobody seemed to know what to say. Sayana kept running the younger boy's story through her head. The capital hadn't been an amazing place when she'd left, but was this really what awaited those who were made to move there? Was this what happened if they said no?

Sayana couldn't get her head around how pointless it all was. The army trying to wipe out the raider clans . . . at least she could understand that. She didn't like it, but she got it. This, though? Forcing people to live where you told them, working them to the bone, killing them if they fought back? What was it *for*?

But of course, she understood that too.

She turned to Hogelun. "If—"

"No." Hogelun shook her head. "Nope. Do *not* start with that shit."

"Hogs . . ."

"If you're going to tell me that you're doing this because you want to . . . I don't know, *save* everyone living in the Tapestry, then I'm going to laugh in your face, Princess. You're doing it because you want to keep raiding. Don't try to pretend for one second that you care about what's happening to people in Karkorum."

Khun said nothing, watching both of them closely.

"*Princess.*" Sayana folded her arms. "Remind me why you all call me that, Hogs. Wasn't it something to do with living in a palace? Growing up there?"

Hogelun huffed out an exhausted breath. "Get to the—"

"I know how people in the palace think, and I know what the Khan is like. I knew him before he *became* Khan. I know exactly how much of a flaming cunt he is, and what happened with those boys? That doesn't surprise me one bit. *Wake up,* Hogs. He's destroying the whole Tapestry, a Tapestry that *we* are a part of. And right now, I feel like I'm the only person in this entire land who is actually doing anything to stop him."

Her voice had risen, almost to a shout. She couldn't remember ever speaking like this before – it felt like the words were fighting each other to climb out of her mouth, like they *had* to get out into the world, like it was the only thing that mattered.

"So you can drag us back to Chimeg. Be a good little soldier for your Chief. But what happens then? We run? We keep raiding, and hope things change? What happens when I die, like Sarnai did? Or Khun?"

Khun cleared her throat. "Father Sky will not permit me to—"

"*We know*, Khun. Hogs, what if Erhi—"

"Don't," Hogelun whispered.

"Then listen. *Of course this is crazy.* Of course it's probably going to get us all killed. But it's better than sitting around doing nothing. We might never be able to ride *araatan*, and it might not make a difference anyway, but . . . but I'm still going to try." She lifted her chin. "Now you can come along and help, or you can run back to the Chief and wait until she figures it out. Something tells me, you'll be waiting for a while."

Her words rolled out across the water. A fish broke the surface briefly, scales flashing in the sunslight, vanishing in a burst of bubbles.

"Hey," Sayana said. "Where's your club?"

The weapon, with its big stone head, wasn't in its customary spot on Hogelun's back.

"Left it behind." Hogelun sounded miserable. "So Erhi wouldn't . . . so she'd know I'd be back for it."

Sayana didn't quite know what to say to that. She certainly wasn't going to point out to Hogs that her attempt at a message might be read as *I'm done being a raider, and I hate it so much I don't even want my club any more.* Absolutely not.

Still. It wasn't like Erhi was going to be any *more* angry if Hogelun came back in a few days, as opposed to one night.

"How about it, Hogs?" she said quietly. "Because we could really use the help."

Hogelun ran a hand across her scalp, flicking beads of sweat away.

"Fuck," she spat.

Fifteen

Sayana

When Sayana had that little conversation with her fifteen-year-old self, imagining how excited the girl would be that she was going on this insane mission, she forgot something rather important.

She should have remembered that coming back to the city she hated would bring up some shitty memories. Especially when she saw that palace on the hill, with its pointless brass dome.

It had been three years, and in that time, Karkorum had grown like fungus across a rock. A sprawling slum of battered *gers* spread out from the hillside below the palace. The grass around the city's edges was brown and dead, trodden underfoot by the constant procession of horses, people, wagons.

Sayana hadn't understood the full extent of the Khan's plan until now. Until she, Hogs and Khun were walking among the tents – well, not walking, not really. Pushing, shoving, squeezing, stepping. After riding on wide-open grassland, it felt like being strangled alive.

Turned out, getting into Karkorum was ridiculously simple. They just joined the stream of people making their way in from the Tapestry. No bones, which were stashed in a hollow under a rock a few miles away. Mostly, anyway; Khun insisted on keeping a few finger bones on her, both for luck and because she said she liked their shapes.

Sayana already missed her horse. They'd left him, Hoof Monster and Midnight tied up in a small copse of birch trees west of the city, next to a quick-flowing stream. They spent some time cooling the horses off, checking for leg knots, getting them fed and sleepy, and then walked the rest of the way.

There were soldiers everywhere – mounted, on foot, watching – and the people making their way into the city looked beaten down, fearful. The closely packed tents blocked the light of the setting suns, lacing the paths with shadows. Everywhere Sayana looked, there were exhausted faces. They huddled over meagre cookfires, mended worn clothes, and peered from tent flaps. Mothers wiped dirt off their children's faces, not bothering to do the same for their *deels*, which were crusted with the stuff.

Seeing mothers with their kids made Sayana think of the two brothers they'd met at the pond. How thin they were. The haunted, harried look in their eyes.

The sound was a low, steady murmur of coughing and muttering, the squelching of mud underfoot. The stench of smoke and sweat was unbelievable. A large section of the *ger* city had burned down, the tents nothing more than blackened hulks, still smoking.

"Can see why you didn't like this place," Hogelun muttered.

There was the constant gravelly hiss of whetstones on knives, small knots of people gathered in the shadows, starving eyes watching the three Rakada. They passed several people arguing with soldiers, and on at least one occasion, the argument turned violent. Sayana had to put a hand on Hogelun's shoulder to stop her from moving in as two men in black *deels* beat the living shit out of a man around her age.

"It's not our fight," she murmured.

"Fuck you, Princess," Hogelun flicked a half-hearted Cut in Sayana's direction.

Khun said nothing.

The feeling in Sayana's stomach had got worse, and she was surprised to find that she actually felt guilty. Which was ridiculous: *she* hadn't forced these people to live here, in the shadow of the palace. All the same: she'd been a part of the city, once. Maybe if she'd stayed, she could have . . .

Could have what? She left for a reason, thank you very much, and there was nothing and nobody that could have convinced her to stay.

One of the more enterprising arrivals had turned his *ger* into a tavern. It sat at the base of the hill, a dark hole, with hastily knocked-together benches and piss-weak *airag*. After a little haggling, Sayana traded some dried horsemeat for three cups of the stuff. Karkorum used *sukhes* – gold and silver coins – but they never quite filtered out into the Tapestry, and clearly, the people who lived in the tent city hadn't got around to adopting them.

They grabbed a table in the corner, ignoring the suspicious glances from the other patrons. One of them, a heavyset man with an oozing head wound, approached their table. Then he saw the way Hogelun was looking at him and made an abrupt left turn towards the door.

It was strange to see Hogs without that skull on her shoulder. She had left Tiny with the horses, and said that if anything happened to him, Sayana's skull would be the replacement. She took a sip of *airag*, then peered into it, as if looking for anything resembling alcohol. "Remind me of the plan?" she asked.

"I told you already," Sayana said quietly, doing her best to ignore her furiously itching thigh. "When we stopped to get water yesterday."

"Yeah, thanks, Princess," Hogelun replied, glancing at Khun, who had lifted the cup above her head and was gnawing on the underside. "Still a few things I don't understand."

"I'm not—"

"Like how you say you knew where this ... eagle person lived."

Sayana fought to control her irritation, and got her arse handed to her. "When I was here, she had her quarters on the east hill, just under the palace wall. People in Karkorum don't move very often, like I keep saying, so there's no reason she isn't still—"

"Oh yes." Hogelun rolled her cup between her hands. "Because the city clearly hasn't changed since you've been gone. You could probably just move back into your old room in the palace."

"Helpful, Hogs. Thanks." Sayana leaned forward. "How many eagle hunters do you think there are? When I was here, we had two, and one of them died right before I left. The other one—" Sayana couldn't remember her name, no matter how hard she tried "—let her eagle loose in this courtyard next to her house. We used to watch."

Hogelun chewed on this. Gave Sayana a tight, resigned nod.

"We wait here," Sayana said quietly. "Until it's late. We go up there, we get inside, we make it very clear to her that we need her help."

"And then we somehow convince her to lead us out."

That was the part of the plan Sayana liked the least. They couldn't just knock this person out and throw them over Hogelun's shoulder, not with this many soldiers around.

For this to work, the eagle hunter would have to lead them out herself; a knife in the small of her back should be sufficiently motivating. The woman was known – that much Sayana was sure of – so she could get them safely past any patrols.

"What's her name?" Hogelun asked. "This magical lizard trainer person?"

"I don't remember. And she didn't train lizards. She was just good with animals."

"Wonderful. Do you at least remember what she looks like?" Hogelun gazed sourly around the makeshift tavern. "Shame to do all this and then accidentally kidnap a royal prostitute or something."

"I like prostitutes," Khun said reflectively.

Sayana rubbed her nose. "Yes, Hogs, I remember what she looks like."

"What if she says no?"

Sayana set her barely touched *airag* on the table with a thump. "Are you a raider, or not?"

"Keep your voice down," Hogelun hissed, her eyes darting to the rest of the clientele.

"She helps us, we let her go free."

"And if she decides not to?"

"We persuade her."

Hogelun put her drink down too. "You are *not* going to bloody torture her. Forget it."

"Calm down." Sayana pushed the words through gritted teeth. "That was *not* what I meant."

"Then what *did* you mean?"

"Well ..." All at once, Sayana felt uncomfortable on the wooden seat. "I mean, we could make her think ... you know, we could ... "

"Weavers' bloody breath," Hogelun muttered.

"We *are* pretty good at scaring the piss out of people. That's kind of our thing. We wouldn't even have to do much, just leave her alone with Khun for five minutes."

Khun, who was currently sniffing the table, spoke without looking up. "I only need two."

"Brilliant." Hogs studied the table. "And if all that doesn't work? What then?"

Truth be told, Sayana had tried very hard not to think about that part. The Rakada only killed people who got in their way, and Sayana was pretty sure this particular case didn't count. They were never going to resort to torture, not ever, but if the eagle hunter still resisted . . .

Her plan had a bit of a gap there, she'd admit. Still, that could come later. Along with other important topics, like what she was going to say to Chimeg on their return.

They nursed their *airag*, eventually having to barter for a second round after it became clear that not even they could make a single cup last four hours. But finally, they made their way out of the tavern.

The night was cold, and the darkness hadn't improved the city. The Rakada had to carefully pick their way between the tents, taking extra care not to step into standing pools of water. The sky had clouded over, and there were no stars or moon to light their way.

Sayana had assumed that the people in the upper city – a term she had never used before but which slid into her mind like a nasty little snake – would have built some sort of wall between themselves and the sprawling mess of *gers*. She knew how they thought, after all, and most of them were snobbish pricks.

But there was no wall, not even a clear border. The tents and the actual buildings, with their rough mud walls and stone lintels, bled into one another. Gradually, the hard-packed dirt underfoot became flat stones, although there were still patches of mud here and there. There was hardly any light — nothing but the odd torch, hastily shoved in a wall sconce.

Sayana was pleased to find that she remembered most of the streets and alleyways, and there was a tiny pull in her heart when they passed a shop she used to go into with her mother, one where they ate curds sweetened with honey. She was less pleased at the number of soldiers around — standing in twos and threes between the buildings, leaning against walls.

None of them looked like they'd pose much threat — they weren't willing recruits after all. But it would only take one dedicated little fuck with a stick up his arse to shout for help . . .

After the third time, when they had to quickly duck back behind the corner of a building, Hogelun pulled Sayana close. "If you stand on my foot again, I'm going to bash your head in."

"All right," Sayana hissed. Khun was stroking the pouch on her chest, murmuring to it, as if telling it about the grand adventure she had brought it on. "We're getting close."

But were they? Sayana put a hand on the mud wall next to her. Despite the chill air, she was sweating. Also a touch drunk — clearly, that *airag* was a little stronger than she had thought. Usually, the stuff was piss-weak, but it was autumn, and something in the horse milk always made autumn *airag* lethal. She had to remember that.

And remember where the fuck this house is.

Sayana lifted her eyes to the clouds, silently asking Father Sky for a little luck. As usual, he declined to reply.

She dropped her head — then stopped. Looked up again.

The building they were next to was a single storey, low to the ground. If she reached up, she could just about get her fingers over the edge of the roof.

"Follow me," Sayana muttered. Then, before either Hogs or

Khun could protest, she scrambled up the side of the building. Trying to do it as quietly as humanly possible.

The roof was made of rushes, mixed with mud and laid over thin wooden beams. Gently sloped, so rain could wash right off (and run downhill into the *gers*, naturally). Smoke rose from short, stubby chimneys, and it made Sayana realise: there'd been no fires inside any of the *gers* at the bottom of the hill. Just small cookfires on the outside, far from the fabric walls.

She thought back to the burned section of the city – to the smoking ruins of the tents. The fire must have spread fast, with the *gers* this close together. An inside fire ban might make sense, after an inferno like that, but at night, those tents must have been dark, and freezing.

Reason number two thousand and twenty-seven why living in the city was the worst.

She'd seen these structures being built, seen men on top of them. The roofs should support their weight, if they moved carefully. They would get a better idea of where they were going, and they could avoid all the dedicated little fucks patrolling the streets.

Sayana peered over the edge. Hogelun spread her hands, staring up at her like she'd gone mad. Khun, however, was grinning, eyes flashing in the darkness. In seconds, she was on the roof too.

Hogelun muttered something ugly but reached out, letting Khun and Sayana help her up. It wasn't easy. Sayana wondered what might happen first: if her shoulders would tear out of their sockets, or the soldiers from around the corner would come to investigate Hogelun's hideous grunting.

But eventually, all three of them were on the roof. Hogelun stood, and as she did, one of her feet landed on a section of rushes.

Sayana snatched her back. "Careful," she murmured. "Use the edges — that's where the mud is strongest."

It wasn't just the risk of crashing through to the room below. The rushes creaked; the last thing they needed was some shopkeeper or court retainer squawking about how there was someone on their roof.

Ignoring Hogelun's murderous expression, she started picking her way along. If they'd dared to walk on the rushes, it would have been much easier. But having to stick to the edges of the sloped roofs made things awkward; when they overbalanced, there were very few places to catch themselves. Sayana kept her footsteps light, arms out for balance. Her hands were sweat-slick, a metallic taste in her mouth, like she'd bitten her tongue.

Most of the buildings — the ones not separated by a road — were close together. Close enough to hop from one to the next, anyway. Sayana didn't dare look back to see how Khun and Hogs were doing: if one of them fell, there was nothing she could do to stop it. She just concentrated on keeping them pointed in the right direction, aiming for the hill's eastern flank.

High above, the palace's brass dome shone in the dark night. Torches, placed at intervals around the base, lit up the metal. Soldiers walked between them, silhouetted against the glowing brass, armed with longbows. Hopefully, the three little figures on the roofs below were too small and distant to see.

Turned out, finding your way somewhere while balancing precariously on rooftops was a lot harder than doing it at ground level. The third time Sayana stopped, squinting into the low light, she could actually feel the frustration radiating off Hogelun behind her.

She was about to start moving again when there was a startled shout, below and to her left. Running feet, the sound of leather on metal as sabres slipped free of sheaths.

She had no idea what had got them spotted, but it didn't matter. They were going to have to fight their way out. Her hand strayed to the hilt of her right sabre; if they attacked now, leaped off the roof, and hit them hard and quick—

There was a scuffle, unseen, on the street below. Someone squawking about how he had permission to be here, he had spoken to the Khan himself. His voice cut off with a sick, wet thud.

Sayana let out a low, shaky breath. They waited for the scuffle to stop, for the street to fall silent again, and kept going.

It took ten more minutes of carefully picking their way across the rooftops before she found the courtyard she was looking for. This was definitely it. She remembered standing right there, in that corner, watching as the hunter loosed her eagle, sending it wheeling into the blue sky.

She'd been warned not to get too close, and after catching sight of the eagle's hooked talons, she didn't need to be told twice. Afterwards, she'd seen the eagle hunter go into . . . yeah, that house there. In the far corner. A smaller dwelling than the others, with a single lit torch on the outside wall.

No soldiers in the courtyard. No one around at all.

This might actually work. Assuming, of course, they could figure out how to get the eagle-hunter-whose-name-she-still-couldn't-remember past the soldiers they had seen on their way there . . .

As Sayana straightened up, a sudden gust of wind unbalanced her. She wheeled her arms, her balance slipping—

Hogelun grabbed her by the shoulders, steadied her. When she looked back, the big raider's eyes were huge.

Thanks, she mouthed. Hogs gestured at her to keep going.

She lowered herself down to the cobblestones, landing in a low crouch. Despite everything, she couldn't help but feel the same rush she got when they went raiding. Because wasn't this just another raid? Sure, there wasn't much howling and stabbing and rattling of bones, but they were still in enemy territory. Taking what they wanted by force.

"Quickly now," Khun muttered – so close to Sayana's ear that she jumped. "I can smell the Khan from here. He stinks of liver and onions." She sniffed the air for a moment. "And wild jasmine. That's not bad, actually."

The three of them crossed to the house at the far corner, boots light on the uneven stones. Like most buildings in the city, there was no door – just a thick fabric flap, pulled tight across the opening. As they got close, Sayana caught a whiff of what might have been bird droppings – a feral, bloody, sour smell. Made sense: it was a bird of prey after all.

This was the place, all right.

Sayana looked over at Hogs, raised a finger to her lips. Hogelun rolled her eyes, gestured at her to hurry up. With one last look around the deserted courtyard, she quietly pushed open the flap, and stepped inside.

Her eyes took a moment to adjust to the darkness. When they did, a relieved smile flickered on her face. Hanging in one corner was a thick leather glove, one she had seen eagle hunters use.

The interior was sparsely furnished. A trunk, the sleeve of a *deel* hanging from the opening. A rough rug on the stone floor. A small table, dotted with tools and scraps of leather. And in the opposite corner from where the glove hung: a single bed. A heap of blankets with someone sleeping underneath them.

The hunter was fast asleep, breathing heavy. Moving as quietly as they could, they took up positions by the bed: Sayana and Hogelun along one side, Khun behind them, knife ready.

There was only really one good way to quickly overpower

someone woken from a heavy slumber, and as Sayana had pointed out earlier, it was in line with the Rakada's skill set.

She looked over at Khun, who quickly licked the edge of her knife, and nodded.

In one movement, Sayana and Hogelun grabbed the blankets and the sleeping person inside them, and ripped them off the bed and onto the hard floor.

Before the eagle hunter could even cry out, Khun was in motion. She sprung forward, landing with knees either side of the woman's head. Slammed a hand on her mouth, cutting off the yelp of surprise and pressing the edge of her knife to the twitching throat.

From above her hand, the woman's panicked, horrified eyes stared out at them, huge as the moon itself. Breathing through her nose, rapid and fluttery. Despite the knife, despite the hand clamped on her mouth, she tried to scream again.

Khun leaned down, until her nose was an inch from the eagle hunter's. She shook her head, just once, and the woman's scream trailed off into nothing.

Sayana listened hard. There was no sound from the courtyard outside, no shouts, or running feet. Nothing but the woman's panicky breathing.

Step one complete. Now, all they had to do was get the hunter to lead them out of the city. Which shouldn't be hard, with a knife in her back.

Only . . .

Sayana couldn't help but notice the serious number of wrinkles on their captive's forehead, radiating out from those terrified eyes. The eagle hunter was older than her, she knew that much, but . . .

"Scream again," Khun whispered, "and I will eat your tongue. Understand?"

Slowly, she lifted her hand. Sayana got her first full look at the woman's face, and the bottom fell out of her stomach.

"It's not her," she said.

Hogelun's head swivelled. "I'm sorry, what?"

"I don't know who this is."

The woman pinned beneath Khun was in her early fifties, with thinning hair and a trembling chin. She looked like she was about three seconds from fainting dead away. Forget taming vicious lizards: Sayana wouldn't have trusted her to pet a dog.

"Sayana." Hogelun's voice was very low, and very calm. "Please tell me we didn't just break into the wrong house."

Sayana looked over at the glove, hanging on the far wall. There was no mistaking it: now that her eyes had adjusted, she could even see the talon marks from where the eagle perched. This *had* to be the hunter's house, so where was she? And who in the world was the trembling mess they had just ripped out of her bed?

"Tricksy, tricksy, tricksy." Khun looked as if she very much believed this was their quarry in disguise, and the only way to get to her was to start peeling back skin.

Sayana knelt down, looked the woman in the eye. "Where is she? Where's the hunter?" She had to snap her fingers in front of the woman's nose before she could get her attention. Even then, the woman just shook her head, shocked into silence.

"That's it." Hogelun was rooting around in her pouch. "We're done. We're getting the fuck out of—"

A flicker of movement from the door. Sayana spun around, had just enough time to register a black blur rushing at her before whoever it was smashed her into the wall.

Sixteen

Hogelun

They should never have trusted the Princess. All that business of *I know where she lives* and *people in Karkorum don't move very often*. Dog shit. Utter and total.

So when the new arrival sprinted towards Sayana and absolutely crushed her against the wall, Hogelun felt just the tiniest bit of satisfaction. Just a bit.

Then she moved. Because nobody did that to a Rakada.

Hogelun wrapped her enormous arms around the attacker's midsection, pinning them in place. Khun, of course, was quick off the mark too: springing to her feet, crowding the person and jamming the knife to their—

The attacker lifted their legs, using Hogelun's arms for leverage, and kicked Khun in the stomach. The older raider grunted, knocked back.

Hogelun was built for bear hugs. They could be warm and comforting, or they could crush the life out of you. She started to squeeze, cutting off the person's air supply. Her reward was a backwards headbutt into her chin, hard enough for her to taste blood.

Sayana reappeared, grimacing, sabre drawn. The attacker's feet found purchase on the floor, and she shoved Hogelun sideways. The two of them crashed into the leatherworking table, tools clattering everywhere. So far, the woman – and it was a woman, Hogelun could see that now – hadn't made a sound.

The person they'd pulled from the bed scrabbled on the ground for the doorway. Khun stopped her, planting a knee in the small of her back. She raised her eyebrows at Hogelun in a clear gesture of *Are you going to deal with this or what?*

Hogelun growled in annoyance, her jaw aching. "Stay ... still."

The woman did not stay still. Instead, she stamped down on Hogelun's instep.

The pain was like something from another world. Hogelun yelped, and the woman slipped free of her arms, lunged for Sayana. The two of them went down, grappling, the woman trying to wrestle the blade away.

A shaft of light from the doorway sliced across the woman's face, and Hogelun got her first good look. It was the eagle hunter. Hogelun had no idea how she knew this – she'd never seen the woman in her life – but sometimes, people just looked like what they were. The hunter had a hooked nose and flashing blue eyes, windburned cheeks, a messy ponytail. She looked like someone entirely comfortable with a huge bird of prey on one arm.

Hogelun limped over, trying to ignore the agonising pain in her foot. She reached down, gripped the hunter around the throat with a giant hand, picked her up – she had never actually picked someone up this way before, and was quite pleased at how easy it was – and slammed her against the wall so hard the entire house shook.

The woman bared her teeth, fought to squirm free. Hogelun reached for the knife in her sash, but her hand was just a little too sweaty, the woman moving too fast for—

Sayana arrived sabre-first, sticking the point into the eagle hunter's throat, deep enough to draw blood. Breathing hard, her own blood gushing from her nose.

Finally, the hunter stopped moving. A second later, Hogelun had her own knife pressed to the other side of the woman's windpipe.

It had been fewer than ten seconds since the hunter arrived, but it felt like hours. The hut was silent, save for everyone's laboured breathing, and the horrified moaning of the woman underneath Khun. No sound from the street outside. Somehow, their little dust-up hadn't attracted attention.

Hogelun couldn't *believe* how much pain her foot was in. Like the hunter had stabbed it, instead of just stepping on it. She pushed past the feeling, growling at Sayana, "Now what?"

The Princess shook her head, spraying droplets of blood. "Now we—"

Which was when Hogelun realised her hand was too close to the hunter's mouth

Teeth clamped down on her index finger. The pain blasted up her arm, twisting her face into a silent scream.

Between her foot, and her bitten hand, it was getting *really* hard not to take this personally.

Through eyes narrowed to slits, Hogelun realised that Khun had half turned in their direction, knee lifted just a little off the pinned woman's back.

The eagle hunter saw it too. "Odval," she spat. "Run!"

As terrified as the woman on the floor – Odval – was, she did what she was told. Khun made an attempt to pin her, but she was in just the wrong position. Odval bucked her off, hurled herself at the flap of fabric, stumbling out into the courtyard. And the second she did, she started screaming blue murder.

Outstanding. As Hogelun flicked blood away from a pair of appallingly deep teeth marks in her finger, she got her knife back in position on the hunter's neck. Khun and Sayana did the same, neither of them bothering to chase Odval.

With three blades at her throat, the woman finally decided to stop fighting. Her eyes, however, burned with a desperate need for violence. If they'd suddenly started glowing, Hogelun wouldn't have been the least bit surprised.

Outside, Odval was still yelling. The hunter flicked a glance down at Hogelun's bitten finger.

"Try it again, see what happens," Hogelun told her.

"Who *are* you?" the hunter said. When she wasn't shouting, her voice was surprisingly high-pitched. Delicate, even.

Khun waggled her blade in front of the hunter's eyeball. "We are your doom."

"No, no, we are *not* your doom." Sayana made the hunter look at her. "We need your help with something, so please just—"

The eagle hunter spat in Sayana's face, resumed her struggle. "Ayanga!" she cried. "Ayanga!"

Hogelun didn't know who Ayanga was, or how long they had until there were soldiers thundering through that flap, but it was probably measured in seconds. To Sayana, she said: "Plan?"

"Shit." Sayana wiped spittle off her face, blinking hard. "We . . . um . . ."

"Fuck me. At least one of us came prepared. Get her on the ground."

The hunter looked, for a moment, as if she was about to start up all over again. Then she flicked her eyes down at the two blades at her throat, back up to the one hovering an inch from her eye, and clearly thought better of it.

When they'd left the horses, Hogelun had packed the small pouch she kept on her sash. She almost hadn't taken the coil of thin horsehair rope from her saddlebags; mostly, she used it for tying up her mount, and occasionally Erhi, when the other woman was feeling frisky and demanding. In the end, she'd brought it with her to Karkorum, because she had a hunch that a kidnapping mission might require it.

In seconds, she had the woman's wrists tightly trussed behind her back. She began to work on the legs when there was the sound of running feet on the cobblestones outside. Many, many running feet, accompanied by angry shouts.

"Hogs?" Sayana said, glancing nervously at the entrance. "Little busy here."

Khunbish let out a screech and hurled herself out of the tent flap, knives flashing. Sayana followed, sabres up.

Hogelun spared a half-second's thought for the poor soldiers who were about to run headlong into a Khun tornado, then went back to her task.

"They'll cut you down," the hunter hissed, twisting her bound wrists. There was a lot of noise from outside now, and a *lot* of screaming. "You'll never make it out—"

Hogelun had ripped a strip out of one of the blankets, and took great pleasure in balling it up and shoving it in the woman's mouth. A second strip tied the gag in place, reducing the hunter's voice to muffled grunts. It was *really* kicking off outside the door now.

With a grunt of her own, Hogelun hefted the wriggling captive onto her shoulder. Her foot hurt so much that she almost couldn't do it — not to mention her finger, which was a whole new level of hell.

With her cargo, there was no hope of her being able to fight. Not well, anyway. She would just have to pray that Khun and the Princess had things under control.

Hogelun gritted her teeth and pushed her way through the door flap.

As she expected: clusterfuck.

Eight black-clad soldiers had trapped Sayana and Khun in a wide circle. Sayana was bleeding from a cut on her arm. Khun was unhurt, mouth twisted, lunging at a soldier who had tried to get in on her flank. The cobbles were already stained with blood from three bodies.

One of the soldiers went for Sayana. It made Hogelun's heart leap into her throat – the Princess still had her two sabres, like she was in some mock-battle in the throne room, all pirouettes and fancy outfits. There was no way she could—

Sayana spun, twisting away from the soldier's strike, sliding her back foot on the uneven ground. Perfectly balanced. She swung her left sabre, and the man went down with an agonised howl, blood gushing from a wound in his side.

But even as he did so, two more rushed Sayana, trying to cut her off from Khun. Someone, somewhere, was ringing a bell hard.

Hogelun had never felt so helpless. That feeling lasted precisely half a second before she realised that she did, in fact, have a weapon.

"This is for my foot," she snarled at the bound woman on her shoulder. "And my finger."

The hunter realised what was going to happen an instant before it actually did. She shrieked around her gag as Hogelun hefted her like a sack of grain, and hurled her bodily at the two soldiers.

One of them half turned, tried to dodge. Not even close to

fast enough. The eagle hunter took him out, his friend too, all of them collapsing in a heap.

Right then, a bird tried to take Hogelun's face off.

It soared out of the night, a silent nightmare of flapping wings and slashing talons. Hogelun only just managed to get her arm up and yelped as the talons raked across her wrist, gouging bright lines of pain.

She lashed out with her other hand, more on instinct than anything else. The strike hit the bird right in its side, below the wing. It whirled away, almost crashing into the nearest wall before gaining height and vanishing into the dark.

Hogelun had no idea how the eagle had even heard its mistress, how it had known what to do. It was sheer dumb luck that her hit had made contact, done enough to scare the bird off. She hadn't even known eagles attacked humans; they weren't the biggest birds around, or the most aggressive. Judging by the shocking amount of blood gushing from her arm, she clearly needed to rethink that.

In the back of her mind, Hogelun wondered why out of the three Rakada, *she* was the one getting all the hideous injuries. It didn't seem fair.

More soldiers were arriving now, what looked like every recruit in the Khan's army, running out of alleyways, calling for backup. Hogelun scooped her captive off the ground, swung the woman back over her shoulder. "What are we waiting for?" she shouted at Sayana. "Let's go!"

And they ran.

There was exactly one exit from the courtyard that wasn't clogged with soldiers. Hogelun didn't know why, and didn't care. She plunged down it, following Khun and Sayana, working very hard not to trip on the uneven cobblestones.

Her lungs were tearing their way out of her damn chest.

She put her head down and kept going, following the other two through the twisting passageways. She didn't especially appreciate being a beast of burden, but apparently that was her job tonight.

Heads stuck out of doorways, yelled when they saw the Rakada coming. That fucking bell was still going; whoever had the job of ringing it had clearly decided that this was their moment.

The three of them exploded out onto another courtyard, one further down the hill. They were at the border of the tent city – *gers* lined the southern edge of the open space.

Two soldiers blocked their path. One of them had a bow, already raised, arrow nocked. Hogelun had a split second to register this, register that the archer was aiming right at her, and then he fired.

For a heartbeat, she was certain that this was it. This was how she would die. She pictured Erhi, tried to see her face—

The arrow passed so close to her neck that she felt the air move. It thudded into the wall behind her, and she looked up just in time to see the Princess skewer the soldier in the chest. His bow clattered off the cobblestones as he fell, his quiver spilling arrows.

Khun had the other one backed up against the wall of a nearby *ger*; he made a grab for her, fingers snagging on her *deel*. Instead, he caught the strap of the leather pouch she wore on her chest. As he stepped back, the strap snapped, and the man—

Pulled the pouch right off her.

In that moment, it seemed to Hogelun that everything in the courtyard stopped moving. Even the captive on her shoulder ceased wriggling.

The soldier – a grizzled, older warrior with a flat nose and an unkempt beard – had Khun's pouch in his arms. Khun stared at him, a look of mild puzzlement on her face. As if the soldier had mentioned in passing that he was actually a horse disguised as a human, in town to see how the other half lived.

The man glanced down at the pouch. With a snarl, he tossed it away, lifting his sabre.

And Khun went *ballistic*.

Her expression was replaced by a look so nasty that Hogelun half expected the cobblestones to melt. She threw herself at the man, latching onto his upper body, legs wrapped around his midsection, howling as she plunged her knives into his chest again and again. Howling loud enough to shatter stone.

Blood splattered her face and arms, the wall of the *ger*, the cobblestones. The man died very fast, and fell very hard. Khun rode him down, hacking at his lifeless body.

Sayana yanked Khun off. It took her more than one try, and Hogelun thought there was a real chance the older Rakada would attack the Princess too. But with one last incoherent scream at her victim, Khun moved. She skittered backwards like a spider, ripping her pouch off the ground. Cradling it like a newborn. Fingers fumbling at the top flap, peaking inside.

Relief flooded her face. In that moment, Khun looked like a child. One who had been lost in the dark, alone, scared . . . and rounded a corner to find their mother, waiting for them with open arms. Her eyes glistened, and Hogelun could swear she was about to start sobbing.

Hogelun had seen a lot of shit in the time she had spent raiding. She had *done* a lot of shit. But that . . .

What the fuck was that?

More soldiers ran at them from behind. The one in the lead stopped when he saw the blood, staring in horror. He did it so suddenly the two behind crashed into him, the three of them tumbling to the cobbles. In any other circumstance, it would have made Hogelun laugh. Now, it just gave her a kick in the backside.

"Come on!" she yelled at Sayana and Khun, waving madly at them to keep going.

Seventeen

Yesuntei

When dawn broke over Karkorum, it found Yesuntei in the middle of a courtyard near the palace, trying to find a good reason not to murder the man standing in front of her.

There was already some blood on her boots — still tacky, despite the soldier who owned it having died hours ago. When she thought about it, what was a little more, really?

And if it would help bring Tuya back, Yesuntei wouldn't have hesitated. She would have cut this snivelling excuse for a captain down before the next word came out of his mouth.

But she needed to hear what he had to say, needed to understand exactly how this had happened. How (and why, in the name of Father Sky, *why?*) raiders had come into the Khan's sacred city, slunk through the shadow of his palace, and stolen the only family Yesuntei had.

" . . . Managed to avoid our patrols, *bahadur*." The man — she didn't actually know his name — stood at rigid attention, gazing into the distance past Yesuntei's shoulder. "My men were alert, as always, but . . . "

"Alert," Yesuntei said. Very calmly, and very quietly. Behind her, Timur hovered. He had the good sense not to speak.

The captain swallowed. "We found what appear to be footprints on the outside wall of a dwelling. They may have used the rooftops."

This time, Yesuntei said nothing. The captain, unfortunately, mistook this for a signal that he was doing well. "They may still be close by. There is a strong chance my lady Tuya may yet still be al—"

Which was when he saw the look in Yesuntei's eyes and wisely decided not to finish that sentence.

Yesuntei's stomach was worryingly calm. The gnawing, hollow feeling that had dogged her for years was nowhere, which was very, very bad. Whenever it vanished, it always came roaring back, worse than ever.

Her fingers were tight on her sabre hilt. She let go, curled her hand into a trembling fist. It was the only way she could stop herself from ripping her weapon from its sheath and swinging it until everything in front of her stopped moving.

"Leave," she told the man. He nodded so hard that his neck creaked, and a moment later, he was gone.

Yesuntei made herself breathe deeply. She slowly turned her head, taking in the mud-and-stone buildings, the cobbles, the looming palace. They looked as they always did – peaceful, serene. Civilised.

For the first time, it felt wrong. Yesuntei wanted the place to look like a battlefield: wrecked buildings, plumes of smoke, the anguished moans of the dying. The people in this city should have fought. They should have laid down their *lives*.

Instead, the only evidence that anything had even happened was a few dead soldiers, and some drying blood on her boots.

She had no idea who these people, these raiders, were. If they were even raiders: three women, wielding knives and sabres, dressed in unremarkable *deels*. No distinguishing marks or clothing of any kind.

Perhaps that was the endgame here: people from the tent city kidnapping the sister of the head of the Guard, demanding better treatment, better food . . . only surely no one in Karkorum would be that stupid.

"What about the woman?" she asked Timur, without turning around. "The one who was in Tuya's house?"

Timur gave his throat a gentle clearing. "We have spoken to her at length. She has not told us anything useful, even under . . . pressure."

Yesuntei's lip curled. She didn't know the woman who had been in her sister's home, this Odval. A weaver, one of hundreds who toiled in the depths of the palace, someone of no import. Yesuntei wondered if she was in on it, somehow, if she'd led the kidnappers to Tuya's door. But if that was true, then she had no cause to raise the alarm . . .

Unless she'd changed her mind. Unless she got scared.

Yesuntei turned and marched back towards Tuya's house. Maybe they missed something. She should have demanded Tuya move into the palace; it didn't seem important when Tuya returned to Karkorum, but oh, Yesuntei wished she'd been more insistent.

As she was about to duck through the flap, Timur stiffened. Yesuntei turned to look, and her heart sank.

A small group of men and women had entered the courtyard. They wore fine *deels*, a riot of colour, out of place against the drab cobbles and mud walls. At their head was a plump man, moving with the stiff-legged gait of someone with perpetually swollen ankles. He was in his fifties, with a beard as luscious and shiny as the orange silk of his *deel*. Sleepy, hooded eyes

looked out from his bland face, and he gave Yesuntei an indul-
gent smile as he approached. The people behind him were like
delicate, twittering birds.

Yesuntei stood tall, trying to keep her face neutral. She had
really hoped to have something useful, to have soldiers in the
field with a clear purpose, before Baagvai showed up.

He was an advisor to the Khan, one of those men who pro-
duced nothing and contributed even less, but somehow always
managed to find themselves in positions of high esteem. Mostly,
he left her alone – partly, she suspected, because he didn't
want to soil himself with the hard work of actually running
this place. Except here he was, walking towards her with that
maddening smile, like everything was as it should be.

"*Bahadur*," she said, the word tasting sour in her mouth.

"My dear Yesuntei." Baagvai had, annoyingly, a wonderful
voice: deep and musical. "I was devastated to hear of your loss. I
came as soon as I could." His followers made some appropriately
distressed noises. "If there is anything I can do, anything at all,
you need only ask."

Get out of my sight so I can find out what actually happened.
Yesuntei ached to say it, ached to pin this blob of a man against
a wall and gut him. Instead, she inclined her head. "I am
grateful."

"Tell me." Baagvai nodded to Tuya's house. "How did
this happen? How did raiders breach the walls of Karkorum
herself?" Leaning on the word *walls*, as if to emphasise that
Yesuntei hadn't managed to build them yet.

"We don't know if it was raiders," Yesuntei said stiffly.
"We're still gathering evidence."

Baagvai made a pained face. "Of course. The Khan has ex-
pressed a personal interest in the events of last night. He asked
me to find out as much as possible."

Yesuntei had to fight hard to keep her expression neutral. Baagvai, of course, didn't care at all that Tuya was missing. He saw this as an opportunity, something he could hold over Yesuntei. If she overstepped or threatened his position, then he'd whisper in the Khan's ear. It wouldn't take much. A few honeyed words.

She let her own sister be taken.

Perhaps she is under more stress than we believed.

I wonder . . . maybe she takes on too much. It might be time for less arduous duties . . .

"Please inform the Khan that this matter is well in hand," she said, making sure to keep her voice bland. Bored, even. "I will personally ensure that the perpetrators are brought to his justice."

She hated speaking like this, hated having to shape her words. But she had to be so very careful.

Baagvai bowed his head. "I am glad to hear it." He placed a hand on her shoulder, and she had to work extremely hard not to grab and twist, snapping all those fragile little bones. "Perhaps you will be good enough to keep my office informed. That way, I will be able to make my report to the Khan with full confidence."

Yesuntei briefly fantasised about what the Khan would do if she walked into court with Baagvai's head on a silver tray, laid it at his feet. "Of course, *bahadur.*"

She gave him a final nod, then stepped inside her sister's home. She thought for a moment that he might follow, and she knew, without a shadow of a doubt, that if he did, she really would kill him. But the only one who came through the door after her was Timur.

She scanned the wrecked furniture, the bed with its mess of blankets, the scraps of leather that dotted the floor. Her sister's eagle glove still hung on its hook in the corner. Yesuntei lifted it off, turned it in her hands.

Her grip tightened. She twisted, the old leather creaking. Harder and harder. They were going to take it all away. Everything she had worked for.

And on the heels of that thought came a wave of guilt, as sharp and bright as a knife blade. Who cared about Karkorum? Who cared about what she was trying to build? Her sister was gone, and that should matter more than anything.

She wouldn't be who she was without Tuya. Long before she'd been lifted out of her purgatory and given the great purpose of building up this land, long before she came to occupy her current position, Tuya had spoken for her.

Without wanting to, she pictured that day in the Khan's court – the old Khan, Ulagan, years ago. Tuya on bended knee before him, begging that her sister be allowed to . . .

Yesuntei squeezed her eyes shut. Tuya had risked everything for her, and now she was gone. And what was Yesuntei thinking of? Her position. Her *job*.

She hurled the glove away. It bounced off the remains of the leatherworking table, fell to the floor.

"We will get her back, *bahadur*," Timur said quietly. "Please do not worry. If they—"

Yesuntei rounded on him. "You forget your place."

The momentary flicker of surprise on his face sparked her guilt again, but only for a moment. She didn't want his empty promises. She didn't want assurances. She wanted answers. Evidence. Something to point her in the right direction.

"We start from scratch," she snapped, as the first hollow twinge shot through her gut. "I want to personally speak to everyone who saw these invaders last night. Every single one."

Timur's face was completely neutral. "Your will, *bahadur*."

He ducked out through the flaps. Yesuntei stood for a moment, then scooped the glove off the cold stone floor. As she turned to hang it back on the hook, a flash of white caught her eye. Something poking out from under the remains of the wooden table.

She crouched down, putting the glove to one side so she had both hands, and lifted the table away.

A bone.

And not an animal bone either; this one was human. Spend any time as a soldier at war, and you get to know the differences. Animal bones were rougher, lighter and less dense than the one Yesuntei held. And no animal bone would gleam the way this one did, even after polishing.

Why was there a human bone – a finger bone, Yesuntei thought, turning it over and over in her palm – under a table in her sister's house?

Abruptly, she stood, pushed through the door flap. The glove lay on the stone behind her, forgotten.

Eighteen

Sayana

Sayana spent most of the two-day ride back to the Namag rehearsing what she was going to say to Chimeg.

Confidence. That was the key. Presenting the eagle hunter's capture as an audacious act of superhuman bravery. Right into enemy territory! Right out from under their noses!

It was a good plan.

Until she got punched in the mouth.

Chimeg and Erhi were in the same spot they'd left them in. Deep in the marsh, the *ger* still standing, the two of them sitting around a dying fire. It was mid-afternoon, the clouds low, the air thick and cloying.

Sayana came to a stop and dismounted. Her thighs, chafed from so much riding, complained loudly.

Hogelun handled their prize – still bound and gagged, lashed face down over the back of the horse. They'd taken the gag out a few times, to give the woman food and water. It hadn't stayed out long, mostly because they got tired of hearing her tell them she was going to tear their arms and legs off.

She'd actually tried to make a break for it on one of their

stops, still tied up, hopping away across the grass. They caught her — because, come on — and tied her ankles to her wrists, which probably made her discomfort worse. She was still pissed, still staring at them with utter contempt, now laced with a leaden exhaustion.

Erhi didn't even look in Hogelun's direction. The big Rakada didn't appear to know what to do with her hands: clasping them behind her back, then at her waist, then hung at her sides. Her forearms and hand were still crusted with dried blood; a little rot had set in too. Nothing Erhi couldn't treat, but . . .

Sayana tried not to feel too guilty. She hadn't forced Hogs to come with her. But she got a little twinge of it anyway, good and sharp.

Khun was muttering to herself, still on top of an exhausted Midnight, patting her *deel* as if she'd lost something. On the northern horizon, a thunderstorm was building, black cloud shot through with shades of green.

Sayana cleared her throat. She'd been drinking water all day, but somehow she was still thirsty. "So," she said brightly. "We did it."

Chimeg said nothing. Poked at the ashes with a stick.

"This is the person I told you about. If we put her to work . . . " She trailed off. All that confidence she needed? It had chosen a great moment to make itself scarce.

Slowly, Chimeg stood. Sniffed, long and languorous. And finally, she turned, and walked over. Ambled, really.

"I know you told me not to," Sayana said, heat rising in her cheeks, "but I couldn't just do nothing. And we got away clean, so—"

There was a muffled yell. Sayana spun around, and the eagle hunter was charging right at her.

Somehow, the woman had worked loose from her bonds;

maybe she'd been doing it for hours, moving back and forth as they rode across the grass. The ropes still hung around one wrist, the skin beneath them raw and abraded. Her ankles trailed rope too, almost but not quite tripping her up.

Sayana grabbed for her. Exhausted, frustrated, far too slow. The woman hit her in the face on the run, fist glancing off her bottom lip. Her head snapped back, spit flying, stars exploding at the edge of her vision.

Chimeg didn't intervene. She simply stepped aside, and watched.

Sayana fell to one knee, fumbling at her sash, trying to draw a sabre. The eagle hunter managed to shake free of her ankle ropes, tearing out the gag and flinging it away as she took off across the marsh.

Hogelun jogged after her. Sayana wanted to shout at her to use her horse, not chase the woman on foot, but her face wasn't working at that particular moment.

With a warbling howl, Khun charged away, quickly overtaking Hogelun. Sayana didn't get to see how it turned out. Chimeg hoisted her off her knee, pulled her in very tight, and very close. Hand gripping the back of her neck, fingers digging in hard.

"Give me one reason," the Chief said, "why you should still be a Rakada."

"I—"

"Just one. Go on. A single reason why I shouldn't take your bones and your blades and stake you to the ground for the fucking *araatan* to find."

How about: I got us someone who can save our clan?

But of course, the words wouldn't come.

Khun came back, dragging the eagle hunter, knife to her throat and one arm twisted up behind her back. Midnight trotted at her heels, chewing on a piece of marsh grass.

They were followed by a puffing Hogelun, who finally approached Erhi, over by the campfire. The archer didn't even look at her. She just stood, slung her bow over her shoulder, and stalked away. Right past Hogelun's club, still standing straight up in front of the *ger* where she'd left it.

Erhi mounted Windwalker, and took off. For a few seconds, Hogelun looked as if she was about to give chase. Then she thought better of it, her shoulders slumping.

Sayana wanted to hug her, but she didn't think the Chief would be letting her go anytime soon.

Khun forced the prisoner to her knees in the dirt. Grabbed a handful of hair, pulled her head back. The woman snarled, but stopped fighting. For now, anyway.

"Chief, please," Sayana said. "If you'll just let me explain . . ."

"You did explain. We had a long chat about it, don't you remember?"

What Sayana remembered was getting shut down before she could actually say much, but it didn't seem wise to bring that up.

She pointed a shaking finger at the prisoner. "If there's *anyone* who can help us control those things, it's her. I've seen what she can do, Chief. She knows animals. How they think, how they move, how they—"

There was a thud as something hit the ground behind her. Khun yelped, just as a huge screech echoed across the marsh.

What now? Sayana spun to find Khun on her arse in the mud, and a giant eagle – the same eagle, she guessed, that attacked them in Karkorum – with its talons digging in the muck. Enormous wings spread, beak open, eyes flashing as it chirped.

"Oh, shit." Hogelun had gone pale.

How in the nine hells had it tracked them all this way? And

why had it waited? Why not hit them while they rode? Sayana didn't have the faintest idea.

The creak of a drawstring. Chimeg had a bow – the Chief didn't use them much, preferring to leave the archery to Erhi. But she could shoot, they all could, and at this range, she wouldn't miss. The eagle turned its beady eyes on her, its wings – dark brown, mottled with silver – beating the air. Khun circled, knives out.

"Wait!" the eagle hunter yelled. "Please – please don't hurt him. Let him . . . I'll calm him down, OK?"

As if hearing his mistress, the eagle chirped again, louder this time. Khun was muttering something about how she loved pretty birdies, waving her knives in the air before her.

"He's just trying to protect me." The woman slowly rose up off her knees. "I'll send him away."

Which, Sayana thought, would be an excellent opportunity for Tuya to command the bird to rip someone's throat out before the Chief could get off a shot. It was definitely what she would do.

Chimeg lowered the arrow tip. Just a little.

The woman wasted no time. "Ayanga," she said – then clicked her tongue, rapidly, several times. It reminded Sayana of the sound you'd make to get a slow horse moving. To Hogelun, she said, "Give me your *deel*."

"Uh . . . " Hogelun stared at her. "No. Fuck you."

"Hogs," the Chief said.

Hogelun gave the eagle hunter a wretched look, but did as she was told. She shucked her *deel*, then balled it up and tossed it to the eagle hunter. The woman grabbed it out of the air, wrapped it around her forearm.

The eagle still looked like it wanted to murder them all, then gorge on their intestines. But the hunter kept coaxing it, kept making that clicking sound. Eventually, with a last hiss at Sayana, it hopped onto the hunter's arm. She grimaced at the weight, bending her knees before straightening up.

The sight took Sayana's breath away. Tuya, bird on her arm, shoulders squared, never took her gaze off the eagle. Eyes narrow, calm but focused. Sayana hadn't realised how tall the woman was; it was as if taking the weight of the bird forced her to straighten up.

What must it be like to have that much control? To have a deadly creature close enough to rip you to pieces . . . and to have it trust you? To command it?

Tuya's eyes met Sayana's, just for a second. Cold and hostile, sure, but . . . there was something else there too. A fierce pride. As if she was daring Sayana to come and take this from her. Sayana's pulse quickened – sweat had broken out on her hairline, cooled by a sudden breeze.

The woman stroked the eagle's feathers, murmuring softly to it. Then, with a "*Hah!*" she lifted it into the air. It took off with a thick flapping of wings, gliding away across the marsh.

"Is that bird gonna come back?" Hogelun asked. She had retrieved her club, grimacing at the cuts on her wrist from when the eagle attacked them in the city.

"No. He . . . I've sent him hunting." Slowly, the eagle hunter raised her hands. Addressing Chimeg. "If you're trying to ransom me, it won't work."

Sayana seized the moment, stepping in close to her Chief – who had, after all, just seen the woman tame a vicious bird of prey. "She's good," Sayana said, leaning in close. "You just saw for yourself. I'm begging you, let's just talk to her, at least."

"You disobeyed a direct order," Chimeg snapped. "Put the whole clan in danger. Do you understand that, Princess? Does that register at all? I want her gone."

The woman's voice reached them again. "You can turn me loose. I don't even know who you are. My sister's probably looking for me, and she——"

Sayana ignored the hunter. "Chief, please."

But Chimeg was staring at the woman now, eyes narrowed. "What's your name?"

For a hopeful moment, Sayana thought the Chief might finally be seeing some sense. But there was something in her voice that she didn't like. Not one bit.

The woman licked her lips. Without her eagle, she looked hunched and timid again. "Tuya."

"And who is your sister, exactly?"

"Yesuntei. Her name is Yesuntei. She's——"

Tuya stopped, because there was the oddest sound coming from Chimeg. A kind of hissing, agonised groan. She lifted her face to the clouds, as if trying to make Father Sky himself hear her.

Yesuntei. Sayana's eyes widened.

Oh, I might have fucked up here.

"You took," said Chimeg, "the sister of the Khan's Right Hand One of the most powerful people in Karkorum?"

"I——"

Chimeg's voice rose in volume. "You stole Yesuntei's *fucking kin*?"

Khun had gone very still, hovering behind Tuya.

"You've killed us," Chimeg said. "Do you understand that, Princess? You've just ended all our lives."

Sayana knew who Yesuntei was, by reputation at least, from when she lived in the city. And there was no way she'd screwed up this badly. It wasn't possible. Not even the Weavers could be this cruel.

"Begging your pardon," Hogelun said. "Who the fuck is Yesuntei?"

"Oh, that's right," Chimeg replied, a mad grin plastered on her face. "You've never been to the city before, have you, Hogs? Not before last night anyway."

"Chief, come on." Hogelun waved a hand at Sayana. "I tried to stop her, I really did. I never meant to get dragged into—"

"No, no, please let me tell you. Because you wouldn't know who she is, would you?" Chimeg shook her head. "You really should have asked Sayana here. She could have told you *all* about her."

Hogelun looked over at Khun, who was circling Tuya, sniffing her hard. For the first time, the eagle hunter looked just a tiny bit smug.

Chimeg spoke again: "She was part of an elite unit inside the army. Got turfed out when it was discovered that she was torturing prisoners." She grimaced. "Nasty little habit of digging graves for people who weren't dead yet.

"But oh, that isn't the end of dear old Yesuntei," Chimeg went on. "Bitches like her don't die easy. See, the new Khan decides he needs someone like her around, so he pulls her out of the dungeons and gives her a job building up his new city. She believes she owes him a blood debt, and so she swears to protect him. *And* to carry out his vision for the Tapestry."

She jerked a chin at the horizon, in the direction of Karkorum. "Even before Erhi and I left the city, you knew not to fuck with her. People who did had to get used to breathing dirt." Her eyes flicked to Sayana. "And you just stole her sister. The only family she has."

Sayana still didn't believe it. How could she have missed that the eagle hunter and Yesuntei were siblings? Had she known once and forgotten? Or had it just never occurred to her to ask?

But by the time she'd left the city, she was sick to the back teeth of it, sick of every single person at court. The endless backstabbing and lies, the politics. She'd stopped caring who was related to whom. Maybe she'd known once – known that Tuya was the sister of this Yesuntei person – but it was a dusty scroll deep in the recesses of her mind.

"It's fine," Sayana said – or heard herself say, because the words seemed to be coming from somewhere about three feet over her head. "She doesn't know it's us. The Rakada, I mean. We weren't wearing our bones and—"

"I was," Khun says.

Oh, that was right. Of course. Khun had insisted on holding onto a few tiny bones, and had made ugly faces when Sayana told her no.

Weavers, she was going to have a stroke. She really was.

"I kept some for good luck." Khun patted her *deel* again. "The tiniest little finger ran away somewhere. Not good luck at all, I suppose."

Sayana closed her eyes. Picturing the fight in Tuya's house, the escape afterwards. The bone could be anywhere. That might be a good thing – they'd covered a lot of ground in the past two days – but she couldn't depend on that.

Was there a tiny bit of her that was glad she wasn't the only one who'd fucked up here? Of course she was.

"Perfect," Chimeg said. "So now there's evidence."

And with that, she nocked another arrow, aiming at Tuya – and this time Sayana knew, with absolute certainty, that she was about to loose.

"Wait!" She leaped forward, got between the two of them. Facing Chimeg, hands out. "Just wait one damn minute."

"Move," Chimeg snarled.

Sayana glanced back over her shoulder. To her surprise, there was no fear on Tuya's face. When the eagle attacked, *that* was when she'd shown fear – when Chimeg was aiming right at the bird. Now, when she was about three seconds from getting an arrow through the throat herself: nothing. She stared right at Chimeg, lip curled in a snarl.

Chimeg's face was thunder, echoing the storm on the horizon behind her. "Princess, if you don't get out the way, I swear to the Father and the Mother I will shoot you first, then her."

"But *why*? Chief—"

At that moment, Chimeg got a good look at Tuya, and loosed her arrow.

It whipped past Sayana, and Tuya jumped as the shaft buried itself in the dirt several feet behind her. It must have missed by a hair, if that, a single last-second twitch of the drawstring.

Chimeg was already nocking another arrow, Tuya tense behind Sayana, not sure whether to run away, or run right at the Chief.

"Why don't we just let her go?" Hogelun said, the words coming out in a blurred rush. "If we don't hurt her, her sister might—"

"Ah yes," Chimeg growled, arrow tip tracking Tuya. "The fearsome and powerful Rakada, too scared to hold onto a prisoner. Too *weak*. You think that story won't spread?"

Sayana couldn't believe she was hearing this. Chimeg was worried about their reputation? They could come back from that, but it would be awfully hard to return Tuya when she had an arrow through her throat. That was about as final as it got.

Khun was studying the sky, as if none of this was happening.

Right then, Tuya decided enough was enough. She sprinted at the Chief, only just dodging the second arrow as Chimeg loosed it. She had no weapon, no chance in hell; Chimeg might be a poor shot, but her hand was already going to the knife in her sash, the bow cast aside as Tuya ran at her.

Sayana snatched at the hunter, putting an arm around her midsection, forcing her to stop, her body between Tuya and the Chief. "Wait," she hissed in the woman's ear, barely able to hear herself. That's how hard her heart was pounding. "Just give her a second."

"What the fuck is *happening* right now?" Hogelun sounded wretched.

Sayana turned in place, arms outstretched, leaning back against Tuya. She'd stopped fighting, for now.

"Listen." She looked her Chief in the eyes. "I fucked up. I admit it. But the army's after us anyway, right? They already want to wipe us out. What difference does it make if Yesuntei—"

"Because now she'll want us *specifically*," Chimeg spat. Sayana had never seen her this angry. "We had options before. Now, the only thing we can do is run. Hope we have enough of a head start."

"There's another choice, and you *know it*." For the second time in two days, it was like the words were trying to bust out of her all at once, each one fired like an arrow. It was startling, and a little scary . . . but Weavers, it felt good.

Erhi had crept closer. Hogelun turned towards her, started to say something, then trailed off when Erhi flashed her a warning look.

Tuya's hand brushed her side. She was going for Sayana's dagger, stuck in the front of her sash, and doing a poor job of it. "Stop," Sayana muttered. "I'm trying to save your life here."

"Great job so far." Tuya's breath was soft on Sayana's ear, her voice barely above a whisper.

"Just . . . just don't move."

When Sayana spoke this time, she signed too. Erhi's lip-reading was fine, but she didn't want the archer to miss this. She didn't want *any of* them to miss this.

"We let her go, we kill her, we run . . . it all ends the same way. Dead, dying, hounded out of the Tapestry. So this Yesuntei person comes after us, so what? How does that change anything? Whether it happens tomorrow, or a month from now, we still end. All of us."

Chimeg said nothing.

"If we really are going to die," Sayana went on, "if that's really our fate, no matter what we do, then I don't want to do it because we ran out of places to hide. I don't want to spend my last months scared. I want to fight. This place . . . " She swung her arm out, taking in the Tapestry. "Have any of you actually looked at it? *Really* looked at it?"

A smile cracked on her face. One she was only dimly aware of. "It's amazing. It's always been amazing. Every day, I wake up, and I have to . . . to *pinch myself* that I get to be out here. So go ahead: laugh at me, call me an idiot, a Princess, shoot arrows at me – your aim is shit, Chief, just by the way – but don't tell me I'm wrong.

"I want to fight for what we have. I want to ride straight at the Khan, on the back of a fucking *araatan*. And if it doesn't work?" She spread her hands. "Then at least I can say I tried."

For a few seconds, nobody spoke. And then, from behind her, Tuya said, "I'm sorry: you want to do what on the back of a *what*?"

"Oh yeah," Hogelun said. "Probably should have mentioned that."

Sayana didn't look around to see Tuya's expression. She was staring right at her Chief, not daring to look away.

Slowly, very slowly, Chimeg lowered her dagger.

And started to laugh.

There was no humour in it. None whatsoever. It was an exhausted, weary chuckle, one that only became a laugh because it had nowhere else to go.

"You know what?" she said. "Sure."

Sayana blinked, not daring to believe what she just heard. "Really?"

"Why not? What choice do we have now?" Her mad grin was back, sliding onto her face as she locked eyes with Sayana. "But you're the one that's going to do it. You, and her."

She gestured to Tuya, who by now was staring in undisguised horror. "You're going to find an *araatan*. You're going to convince it not to eat you. And when it does – because it will – both of my problems will be solved in one go. You ..." A steady finger pointed at Tuya. "And her."

The eagle hunter stepped back like Chimeg had cursed her. The Chief got in close, looming over Sayana, silhouetted against the sky.

"I'll never forgive you for this," she murmured. "No matter what happens. I'll never forgive you for forcing my hand."

She gave Sayana one last, disgusted look. "Get to work. *Princess.*"

Nineteen

Yesuntei

Military camps usually smelled like shit. And sweat. And overcooked food, and the heavy fug of illicit *airag*. A noxious, heady miasma, that the wind always picked up and gleefully dispersed for miles.

Not this one, though. This particular camp didn't smell of anything.

It lay in a field of jagged boulders, a few miles west of the city. Technically, the unit was supposed to be in the barracks, on the hillside below the palace – which is where all soldiers not on a posting lived. But when the captain of the unit simply known as the 8th declared they were making camp in the rock field, no one from the city or the palace complained.

If anything, Yesuntei suspected that whichever bureaucrat signed off on it did so with a private sigh of relief.

Naturally, they knew she was coming long before she got there. Jochi strode out to meet her, marching from behind a boulder that was only slightly larger than he was.

He wore full armour, despite the heat of the day: leather and tarnished iron, over a grey *deel*. A conical helmet too, perched on his mountain of a head: dull gold, with a simple inlay of green leaves. His long, flowing beard, flecked with grey these days, reached almost to his waist.

The corners of his mouth curved upwards, just a tiny bit, as Yesuntei dismounted. "*Bahadur,*" he rumbled.

"Don't you *bahadur* me." Yesuntei wrapped him in a hug – or tried to anyway, she never could get her arms around him. He chuckled, then squeezed her back. It was gentle, by his standards, but still forced the air from her lungs.

Jochi barked a laugh. "You've got softer, in that palace of yours." He playfully swatted her shoulder, and she had to work very hard to keep her balance. "Like squeezing a feather pillow."

She flicked him the Cut. She hadn't made the gesture in years, and it felt strange. Forced. Then again, nothing felt right today. She'd spent a sleepless night, her gut tearing at her, burning and aching.

Timur wasn't with her today. This was no place for him.

"I heard about your sister," Jochi said, as they moved deeper into the boulder field. There was the faint clanging of metal on metal now, echoing off the rocks. "A poor display."

He meant the soldiers in the city, not her, but Yesuntei felt a jab of that familiar guilt all the same. Guilt at not forcing Tuya to move into the palace; at not getting the damned wall built.

She might not have been on guard the night Tuya was taken, but this was still her fault. And she'd already seen the stares, picked up on the whispers in the corridors of the palace.

The unit's camp was in a large clearing in the centre of the rock field. *Gers* on one side, a neat and uniform grey that matched Jochi's *deel*. Cookfires in front, ashes already swept away. Horses stood in a single neat bunch in one corner of the clearing, stock-still, all of them in full armour.

There were perhaps a hundred soldiers. Men and women, stripped to bare chests and breast straps, in the middle of training. Yesuntei couldn't see a single practice sabre: the 8th fought with edged blades. Blood stained the dirt from a dozen cuts, trickling down hard muscle. On one side, a long line of troops shot arrow after arrow into straw targets shaped like human torsos. The nearest soldiers snapped to attention as she and Jochi entered. After a momentary pause, they went back to their training.

The soldiers made way for her, and she exchanged nods with the ones she knew. It had been a long time since she'd ridden out with the 8th; she considered that part of her life as finished and done. But now, she couldn't help but wonder what would have happened if she'd been allowed to stay. If the old Khan and his court hadn't demanded her removal.

"It's always good to see you," Jochi said. "But I cannot help you. Not without the—"

"We found this in my sister's quarters." Yesuntei pulled the finger bone out of her *deel*. Jochi took it, brow furrowed, turning it this way and that. "You've been out there a lot more than I have lately. Does it mean anything to you?"

He held it up to the suns, squinting, sucking his bottom lip. "How do you know it didn't belong to Tuya?" He tossed it back to her with a smirk, a challenge in his eyes. "Maybe she took it as a trophy. Maybe that ridiculous bird of hers brought it back from a battle somewhere."

On any other day, Yesuntei would have found Jochi's little performance charming. He liked to do this, liked to amble around his subject. But today? Today, she simply didn't have time for it.

She stepped in close, spoke low and fast. "You know where this came from." She held the bone up between them like a weapon. "Tell me. You owe me that much at least."

One of the nearby soldiers paused in his training, looking over at them. Jochi barked a command, and the man hurriedly got back to what he was doing.

"If they *were* raiders," he said, "and I have my doubts ... then the bone gives it away. Clan name is Rakada – people call them the Bone Raiders. Never seen them myself, but you mention that name in the Tapestry and people start praying to the Weavers for salvation."

"And they ... carry bones?"

"Wear them, actually. So the rumours say, anyway."

Yesuntei closed her eyes. *This* was the answer she was looking for.

At last, she had a name. Something to focus her anger on. She could actually feel it, coalescing into a bright point, a burning sensation behind her sternum.

It was a power play, that much she was certain of. These Bone Raiders, these ... Rakada ... they planned to ransom her sister back to her. Or perhaps just hold her as a hostage, ensuring that they were left alone to keep terrorising Hanggai.

A bitter, satisfied smile flickered on Yesuntei's face. They were about to find out just how bad a mistake that was.

She and Jochi had been in Ngu together. The southerners had crawled out of their swampy delta, thinking they could take the Tapestry for themselves. They should have known it was a bad move, and Yesuntei and the 8th had shown them why.

It hadn't taken long. Turned out, you only had to bury two or three squads of soldiers alive before the rest decided that, actually, their little half-arsed invasion wasn't really worth the trouble.

The old Khan, who was fat and lazy and had never ridden into battle in his entire useless life, had disapproved of these tactics. He had tiresome ideas about honourable combat and facing your enemy on the battlefield head-on, and didn't appear to care that hundreds of men would die in the process. When he demanded that someone take responsibility, Yesuntei had been the one dragged to a cell.

She was the 8th's commander, after all.

In hindsight, she saw it as a strange blessing, because when the Khan keeled over stone dead from a heart attack, the new one had found a use for her. He'd pulled her from her cell, gave her responsibility, shared his *vision*. A vision of Hanggai, a new nation. One that would never be invaded again. Not by Ngu – not that they would dare, not after Yesuntei broke them – and not by Dalai, the nation beyond the mountains, with a military that rivalled Hanggai's own. The only way to stop it happening was a unified nation, strength upon strength.

The new Khan had told her a simple truth: that she was meant for greater things than leading soldiers. Then he'd taken her out of her dark, stinking cell, lifted her up, and given her a chance to prove it.

Jochi had been given command over the unit after Yesuntei left. A fine choice. But he was far more rigid than her, far less imaginative, especially when it came to annoying things like chain of command. Which is why he was now smiling – a small, sad one, a smile of deep regret.

"Before you say anything," Yesuntei started, but he cut her off.

"You have the Khan's Guard," he said. "Good soldiers, all. Their commander will do what you say."

"Forget the Guard," Yesuntei snarled. "You and I both know that they'd never survive out there. I don't want them. I want *you*."

Jochi shook his head, and her heart sank. There was only one option she had left now, and she would have preferred not to use it.

"Without the Khan's orders," he was saying, "I cannot give you my soldiers. You know that."

"You mean these?"

She'd rolled up the parchment carefully, tied it with a strip of orange fabric. Jochi's expression stayed the same, but there was just the tiniest change in his eyes as she handed it over. The smallest flicker of surprise.

Jochi's lack of imagination was a problem. He couldn't be bribed, and while he might be persuaded around to her way of thinking, it was a very flimsy *might*. As for blackmailing him? Perhaps by threatening his sons, or his wife? That could go wrong in so many hideous ways. Which left only one option.

Jochi unrolled the parchment. Unlike many soldiers, he could read, but he barely bothered checking over the words. Instead, his gaze was drawn to the seal in the top right corner. The Khan's Will – a smaller version of the one displayed on his banners. Blue and orange inks, expensive, and hard to get. Yesuntei had been sure to secure an ample supply months ago – just in case.

She hadn't gone to the forger herself, of course. She hadn't dared, not with that oily shit Baagvai skulking about. But she had plenty of ways to access the palace dungeons . . . and the poor prisoner had been so eager to keep his remaining toes. She had to admit, he did fine work, and he did it quickly.

Yesuntei folded her arms, waiting patiently for Jochi to look at her. He knew the order was false, of course. He would be insane to think otherwise; she could have pulled it out when she first arrived, simply shown him the orders and have done with it. Jochi was many things, but he wasn't a fool, and they knew each other too well.

But he didn't dare accuse her of lying. In the back of his mind, he'd be thinking: *What if she isn't?*

Under ordinary circumstances, Jochi would trust his gut. He'd ignore that little voice. But this time, trusting his gut would mean questioning the parchment in his hand, with its blue and orange seal done in ink found only in the palace.

That was where she had him. There were terrible, terrible punishments for falsifying the Khan's Will — Yesuntei had administered a few of them herself. If Etugen ever found out that she'd had this parchment mocked up . . . well, even she didn't want to think about it.

But she could read Jochi's thoughts, as if they too were on parchment. *She knows the penalty for this. Would she risk it? Would she really be that mad?*

He could call her out, of course. Accuse her of lying. Only thing was, if the order *was* genuine, and he sent her away empty-handed, the result would be just as catastrophic for him. Possibly for his sons, too, both soldiers stationed in the mountains. The Khan tended to react badly when his orders were questioned. When his seal wasn't met with instant and total obedience.

Was Tuya worth the risk? Yesuntei had asked herself that several times, before she came here. All of this for one person. All of this deception.

But in the windswept quiet of her quarters, she'd decided: yes. For Tuya, for her sister, it was worth it. Always, and for ever.

Jochi finally looked up at her, and just for an instant, Yesuntei was sure she'd made the wrong choice. That he *was* about to call her out. If that happened, she would have to work very quickly.

But after a few moments, he nodded. No mistaking the look in his eyes this time: resignation. He knew he'd been beaten.

She felt no satisfaction. This was the only way. And using it meant that riding out with Jochi and the 8th, far from

Karkorum, could get difficult. He wouldn't forget this. Wouldn't forget how she trapped him.

"These Bone Raiders," he said. "They will be hard to root out."

"Then let's get digging."

As he barked orders to his troops, Yesuntei found that the finger bone was in her hand again. Her lip curled in contempt, and she tossed it into the rocks.

Twenty

Hogelun

At this particular moment, there were a lot of things Hogelun had to worry about.

With everything that was happening, they hadn't had a chance to hunt, and were down to their very last scraps of food. There was some antelope meat, plus a few shrivelled vegetables and some millet. *A feast*, she thought bitterly.

Her Chief was still deeply pissed at her. She knew this because every time she tried to talk to Chimeg, the woman told her to fuck off. That was a pretty good hint.

There was this woman Yesuntei, who Hogelun hadn't known existed until two days ago. Not only did she apparently want them all dead, but was quite capable of making it happen in various unpleasant ways.

There was the prisoner, the eagle hunter, who had protested so loudly that training an *araatan* wasn't possible that they'd had no choice but to gag her again.

Oh yeah. The *araatan*. Almost forgot. They were literally, at that very moment, trying to track down a giant, ravenous lizard, when the sensible thing would be to get as far away from it as possible.

But all of those things paled in comparison with this: Erhi wouldn't talk to her.

Hogelun had been prepared for an argument. She'd expected a fight. What she hadn't anticipated was for the archer to completely and totally freeze her out.

She rode alongside Erhi as the Rakada headed north, moving her hands so much she lost control of Hoof Monster more than once. The archer didn't reply. Barely even looked at her.

After a few hours of this, Hogelun stopped being annoyed and started being angry. The anger became fury, and the fury dived into a kind of desperate pleading. And *still*, Erhi said nothing. Her hands never strayed from her reins. She didn't speed up, didn't drop back, didn't do more than occasionally glance in Hogelun's direction. Just kept riding. When they stopped to give the horses a break, to cool them down and let them graze, Erhi made a point to turn her back.

Eventually, Hogelun herself put some distance between them. She didn't know what else to do.

Before they shut her up, the eagle hunter had spent quite some time telling the Rakada that they were idiots, that they were all going to die, that there was absolutely no way to pull this off. But amidst this, she'd actually given them something useful.

In theory, she'd said, it wouldn't be too hard to find an *araatan*, even in a place the size of the Tapestry. In the mountains, the beasts favoured deep caves, big enough for their huge frames; they'd probably seek out similar spots in their new environment.

If there was one thing there was a shortage of in the Tapestry, it was caves, both big and small. But there were a few, and the advantage of being a raider who went back and forth across the whole Tapestry was that you usually knew where to find them.

They could have gone back to the village they'd raided a few days before. There was, after all, the *araatan* Sayana had ridden off a cliff. It had survived the fall – somehow, Hogelun hadn't quite worked that out yet – and would presumably still be in the area. But they didn't need Tuya to tell them that an injured *araatan* wouldn't exactly be amenable to training.

Instead, they rode until they met the Western Mogoi – the river that ran past the village and its cliffs – and followed it east. Miles rolled by under their horses' hooves. Above them, Hogelun thought she could just see Tuya's eagle, riding thermals.

Tuya herself sat on the back of Sayana's horse. Still gagged and bound, hands in front this time, holding on tightly to the saddle. Every so often, she looked over at Hogelun, shaking her head, as if desperately trying to tell her that this was a bad idea.

Hogelun would have told her that she was right. And also that there was fuck all either of them could do about it.

She was prepared to ride through the thunderstorm they saw brewing in the north, but it burned off. Left behind a glorious day, too, the suns beaming down out of a cloudless sky. From horizon to horizon, the wind sent ripples through the grass, waves of vibrant, rolling gold and green.

They hadn't seen a single soldier or army camp since they left the marshes. Not one. The ride was smooth, easy, the air hot but not desperately so. It was the kind of day that Hogelun usually longed for, and so rarely got, and she dearly wished they weren't ruining it by trying to befriend a ravenous *araatan*.

For what felt like the thousandth time, Hogelun spurred Hoof Monster to a trot, until she was level with Erhi. The river had widened, little froths of white appearing in the current, the water hissing gently.

"Are you hungry?" After all, Erhi was angry, but even angry people had to eat. "I dug up some wild carrots the last time we stopped."

She leaned in close, hands moving to match her words. "The others didn't see me. At least, I'm pretty sure they didn't. You get first pick. Want some?"

Erhi studied her for a moment, then turned away. Hogelun's heart sank.

"They're really good," she said, even though Erhi wasn't watching. As proof, she lifted one out of her saddlebag: a fat vegetable, bright orange, practically glowing in the midday sunlight. Hogelun's stomach rumbled just looking at it.

Nothing. No response.

Fuck it. If Erhi was going to continue to act like Hogelun was a piece of shit on her boot, then Hogelun was done trying to persuade her. If she had to be miserable, she shouldn't have to be hungry too.

As she lifted the carrot to her mouth, Erhi's hands flashed. Hogelun nearly dropped the vegetable in surprise. "What?"

For a horrible moment, she thought she'd missed it. That Erhi was going to turn away, not bothering to repeat herself. But instead, the archer fixed her with a look of contempt, and signed, *I nearly burned your fucking club.*

Club? What in the nine hells was Erhi talking ab—

"Oh!" She'd left her damn club behind, so Erhi would know she was coming back. "Shit! Yes. Well. I . . . thanks for . . . not doing that."

She touched the club's heavy stone head resting between her shoulder blades, as if reassuring herself that it was still there.

I thought you'd left, Erhi told her.

I did. Fuck, that was absolutely the wrong thing to say, she could see it on Erhi's face. *I was coming back. That was the point, because I wouldn't just leave my club, you know?*

It had seemed like such a good idea at the time. So very clever. An eloquent, simple way of telling Erhi that she'd return soon. Now, she just felt stupid. Everything she did was *stupid.*

Erhi's hand movements were jagged, angry. *I thought I'd done something—*

Abruptly, she stopped. Let her hands fall to Windwalker's mane, looking away from Hogelun as she sped up. Hogelun watched her go, feeling more or less exactly like a piece of shit scraped off a boot.

A moment later, they reached their destination.

Hogelun wiped spray off her face as she brought Hoof Monster to a halt on the cliff edge, alongside the other Rakada. Here, the river plunged over a sheer drop, perhaps thirty feet down. It met a broken mountain of boulders, splitting into a dozen smaller waterfalls, a hundred. At the base of the rocks, there was a wide, inviting-looking pool, sparkling in the sun, shimmering with broken reflections of the clouds.

Sheer rock walls bordered two sides of the pool, but on the western side there was a muddy, fertile shore, exploding with moss and shrubs. Alongside it, the river resumed its course, meandering through the birch trees, as if it hadn't just been shaken to bits by the plunge.

Hogelun had been here before, a few times. If this place had a name, she didn't know it. In the past, it had just been a convenient spot to water the horses, to camp for a few nights before moving on. Good memories mostly. But now, as she took it in, there was a sick, dry taste in her mouth.

As a rule, the Rakada didn't use caves like the one behind the waterfall. Chimeg didn't like it – didn't want to give anyone an opportunity to trap them. And they never stayed in one place long enough, anyway.

There'd been some debate between Erhi and Chimeg about whether or not to come here — if there were other people, or worse, the army, things could get complicated. Then again, as Erhi had pointed out, if an *araatan* had set up shop here, then there was a good chance everyone else would have got the fuck out.

Khun had her arms raised to the sky, head tilted back, speaking in a language Hogelun didn't know. And honestly, she was only halfway sure about the speaking part: Khun was either saying a prayer, or trying to dislodge something sharp from her throat. To Hogelun's surprise, the leather pouch normally strapped tight to the old raider's chest was off, carefully tied to her saddle.

"Right." Chimeg dismounted, feet landing in a puff of dust. "Your show, Princess."

Sayana gaped at her. "What — now?"

"Yes, now. Let's get this over with, come on."

Tuya was still making desperate noises behind the gag, shaking her head so hard that Hogelun thought it might snap right off her shoulders.

Hogelun found her voice, and this time, it wasn't Erhi she spoke to. "Chief, I don't think this is a good idea."

"No shit," Chimeg muttered, tying her black hair back in a ponytail.

"For Sayana, I mean. We can't just . . . she'll . . . "

She'll die. That's what Hogelun wanted to say. But the words wouldn't come, because surely Chimeg wasn't going to force the Princess to go in there? She was an idiot, but she was still Rakada. She was still one of them.

Only: Chimeg didn't give Sayana an out. Didn't offer a

convenient little smile, or shrug. Just jerked her chin at the falls.

There was a moment when Hogelun thought the Princess was going to protest. But then her face hardened, mouth set in a thin line. She hopped off her horse, peered over the edge. "If you can camp at the edge of the—"

"Sure, Princess," the Chief said. "We'll just camp right outside the entrance of an *araatan* cave, even though we don't know for sure it's in there, and it might come back from hunting at any moment." She squatted, tapping gently on the rocky edge with a closed fist. "No, right up here's just fine."

"What if I need help?"

"Princess, if you end up fighting an *araatan* inside a cave, then having more of us there is just going to give it a larger meal."

Hogelun's instinct was usually to throw her club in with the rest – shying away from a scrap didn't feel right. But this particular scrap would involve going into the cave, and that just wasn't going to happen.

"I'm not going to risk the rest of us over this," Chimeg told Sayana. "You want to do it so badly, go right ahead."

"Fine," Sayana said, far too loudly. Her fingers found the hilts of her sabres. "I'll see you in a bit."

"Mfffnfnfggmmff," Tuya said.

Wait. Erhi came round the side of her horse, held something out to Sayana. A small leather pouch with a slim drawstring. *This might help,* she signed, after she passed it over.

Sayana held up the pouch, squinting. "And this is . . . ?"

It will calm the araatan *down, if it gets angry.*

Which was about the maddest thing Hogelun had ever seen Erhi say. "I'm sorry," she says, forgetting for a moment that the archer was still pissed at her. "Since when do you know how to calm a . . . a fucking lizard monster?"

The archer hit her with a level gaze. *It may work. It may not. I did my best.*

Sayana sniffed the pouch, recoiled. "Smells like antelope dung."

Yes, that's what I make it from.

"When did you even—"

While you were in the city. Erhi did a masterful job of ignoring Chimeg's glare. *I was not idle.*

"What, did you find an *araatan* to practise on?" Hogelun asked.

Of course not. Outside of the dung, it's a blend of wolfclaw root and black clay. We use it on wounded humans, but I've seen it work on horses too. She turned to Sayana. *You will need to smear it on a blade, deliver it that way.*

"Great," Sayana muttered. "Super easy then."

"You'll find the four of us waiting here when you get back," Chimeg said. "And trust me when I say, none of us are coming down to—"

There was a delighted "Whoop!" as Khunbish flung herself off the cliff.

The rest of the Rakada stuck their heads over the edge just as she landed with an enormous splash. For a good five seconds, there was nothing but bubbles. Then Khun broke the surface in a spray of droplets, bedraggled hair trailing. She spat a stream of water, began backstroking around the pool.

Chimeg spoke in a weary monotone. "*Most* of us aren't coming down to help."

"How in the hells did she even survive that?" Sayana muttered.

"Father Sky won't allow her to die," Hogelun said automatically. "Hey – why don't we send *her* into the cave?"

"Why don't you shut the fuck up and get a fire going?" Chimeg snapped.

Sayana tucked Erhi's little pouch in her *deel*. Taking the eagle hunter with her, very much ignoring her muffled protests, she mounted her horse and headed north, hugging the edge of the cliff.

Twenty-One

Sayana

It didn't take long to get down to the pool. The cliff meandered north for a mile or so, then sunk into the rolling hills around the river. Once Sayana doubled back, it was a matter of a few minutes before the space between the birch trees filled with cool mist, and the hiss of the falls.

Others had been here. Recently, too. There were the remains of a cookfire, with ash that still looked fresh. A child's toy, a snatch of colourful fabric in the shape of some animal, dropped at the base of a tree. An *airag* skin sat nearby, empty and deflated.

And of course, there was a Khan's Will, too. The blue banner was knocked over, trampled into the muck. No telling when it was planted. Sayana couldn't tell if it had been knocked over by mistake, or on purpose. She hoped it was the latter, and that whoever had done so had jumped up and down on it a few times for good measure. Certainly looked that way.

Tuya's muffled protests became louder the closer they got to the pool. As they broke through the trees, her horse's hooves digging into the soft mud at the water's edge, Sayana decided she'd had enough. She yanked the gag out, so hard that the eagle hunter nearly toppled off the saddle.

"Ow." Tuya massaged her jaw with her still-bound hands. From the far end of the pool, Khun gave them a cheerful wave.

Sayana hopped off the horse, pulling Tuya down with her. Above them, Chimeg was just visible through the spray.

"Sayana, yes?" The mud had spattered halfway up Tuya's calves. "I know we haven't exactly talked much since—"

"And we're not going to talk now. Get moving."

"Listen to me. Please, please listen. You can't train an *araatan*. You can't ride it. It's a wild animal."

"So are horses. We break those all the time."

"So are hor—*Are you serious?* A horse doesn't breathe fire if you annoy it. A horse doesn't bite you in half if it's hungry."

As it happened, Sayana had been on the receiving end of *plenty* of bites from pissed-off horses, although right now it felt a little weak to say so.

Tuya kept talking. "If we go in there, and there's an *araatan*, we die. I don't know how else to explain this."

"I've seen what you can do." Sayana leaned in close. "I've seen you get jackals to jump through hoops. You've made snakes dance for the Khan, and you control a fucking eagle." She looked at the sky, although right now, there was no helpful drifting bird to prove her point. "You just have to do the same thing here."

Tuya's head flicked side to side, rapidly, as if searching for an escape. She lingered on the waterfall, and Sayana had to snap her fingers to bring her back. "Don't even think about it. If you come out before I do, Erhi'll put an arrow in your throat."

"And if you die, and I don't? What am I supposed to do then?"

"Not going to happen."

"You don't understand. The jackals, all of that — it took months to train them. It took ages to even get them not to tear my throat out when I stepped into their cage."

"I don't need you to train the lizard today. Just help me convince it that we aren't a threat. We go in, we say hello, we——"

Tuya wasn't even listening. "I had teachers, people who'd done all of it before. I don't know a single person who's ever controlled an *araatan*."

"I have." She'd already told Tuya about what happened in the village they'd tried to raid.

"That wasn't *control*. That was just a . . . an animal instinct. It didn't have a choice."

"Are you not even a little bit curious?" Sayana asked, trying to ignore the worry in the back of her mind. "All your work with animals, and you've never wondered?"

"Look." Tuya's voice was hushed. "I trained with my eagle in the mountains — I was there for a whole year. We didn't see *araatan* often, but you know what we did when one popped up? We got the fuck out of there."

She pointed a shaking finger into the cave, lifting both bound hands to do it. "They can smell and see better than we can. Their hearing isn't great, but that's about the only thing they can't do. If there's one in that cave — and it's a big if, because it might be out hunting, and then it'll be between us and the exit if it comes back — it'll smell us the second we step inside."

There was a moment — a real moment, huge and clear — when Sayana almost turned back. Because Tuya was right. This *was* insane. It didn't matter if she'd once, briefly, controlled an *araatan*; this was different. If they stepped inside that cave, there was a good chance — almost a certainty, actually — that they wouldn't survive.

She could make as many impassioned speeches as she liked, believe in saving the Rakada with all her heart, but none of that would stop her being eaten by a giant lizard.

She'd tried very hard to deny it, ever since she first rode away from Karkorum. But now, staring into the desperate pleading eyes of the person who could supposedly get this done, she almost backed out.

Almost.

There are some things that are buried so deep in us that nothing – not even the world ending – will dislodge them. Some people believed that family was more important than anything, or that it was their duty to obey their Khan no matter what.

Sayana's was simple: if you didn't like the life you had, you built a new one. And you had to be willing to die to protect it. Because if you weren't, then it wasn't worth having.

The Khan and his army were taking it all away. Piece by piece. With every person they forced back to the city, every camp they set up, every attempt they made to exterminate the raiders, they chipped away at the life Sayana had built. And if she was prepared to kill to keep what she had, then she should *damn* well be prepared to die for it.

But do you have the right to risk Tuya's life, too?

The question sat in her mind, solid and uncomfortable. She didn't know how to answer.

There was a smart way to do this, and a dumb way. If the *araatan* wasn't there, and arrived at the pool while they were in the cave, there was nothing they could do. But if it was inside already . . .

"I swear to you," she told Tuya. "If you help me do this, if you even just *try*, I'll give you safe passage. I'll get you back to Karkorum, unharmed. Back to . . . "

Something flashed in Tuya's eyes, and Sayana trailed off.

Back to Odval, was what she meant to say. Tuya's partner, the one who'd been in her bed when they'd entered her house.

But Sayana got a strong sense that bringing her up right now wasn't a good idea — not if she wanted Tuya's help.

Was Odval Tuya's wife? Lover? She had no idea, and just by the way, what did it matter? What the fuck did *that* have to do with anything? It wouldn't help them figure out how to train the *araatan* . . .

Another nasty little jab of guilt: there was an excellent chance Chimeg really would kill Tuya, sooner or later. Better that than leaving a witness, one who might give her sweet sister information about the Rakada. *Problem for later.*

The eagle hunter brought her back. "You realise you're not going to defeat the Khan with one *araatan*? The man has an entire army. This is pointless."

"I didn't literally mean I wanted to defeat the Khan . . . "

"Those are the exact words that came out of your mouth."

"I just want . . . " But it was too much. How to explain to Tuya that this was about staying in the Tapestry? About survival? Here, facing a climb up to the unknown space behind the waterfall, all of it felt a million miles away.

Tuya hung her head. Groaned, long and low.

"If you really want us to go in there," she said, "then here's what's going to happen. You're not going to ride the beast today. Maybe not ever. This is going to take time. Right now, all we can do is make ourselves known, let it know we're not a threat, hope it doesn't jump to any conclusions. And understand this, raider: in there, my word goes. I say we leave, we leave. No questions. Understand?"

Sayana nodded.

There was a tumble of slick rocks leading up to the space behind the waterfall. Sayana cut Tuya's bonds — there was no way she was going to make it with her hands tied. "If you do anything stupid . . ."

"Yes, yes, got it," Tuya snapped.

"I'm serious. One move I don't like—"

"Can we just do this? Please?"

Khun was sunbathing on a rock at the far side of the pool, looking happier than Sayana had seen her in ages. She had a sudden urge to join her, to just curl up on a rock like a . . . well, like a lizard. She bit her lip, kept climbing.

Behind the waterfall was a long shelf of rock, protected from the spray by an overhang. It was still deafening in there, but not as bad as Sayana thought it would be. The cave entrance was a little way along the shelf: a hole between two rocks that reminded her of a cat's pupil, narrow and slitted. Although *narrow* was relative – it was still huge, and wide enough to allow an *araatan* to squeeze through.

Predictably, it was pitch-dark inside. Sayana knelt on the wet rock, pulling out the torch she'd shoved into her sash. It was barely worthy of the name: a hefty stick, its tip wrapped in grass and rope, soaked in antelope fat.

With her flint and sabre, she struck sparks. The fat caught, guttering to life. The light it gave off was flickering and inconsistent, but at least it was enough to see by.

The opening might have been narrow, but the passage inside was wider than Sayana had expected. The ceiling hung low, and the place stunk of mould and mildew. But the ground was level, easy to walk on, and the spray only came in a few feet. Sayana studied the floor, looking for any sign that an *araatan* had been there, but the light cast too many shadows.

"Wait," Tuya said.

"What is it? You see something?"

"You said you saw me with my jackals."

"That's right."

"You're a raider. I only did that at court, in Karkorum. How—"

"I used to live there." Sayana trailed a hand down the damp rock wall, peering into the torch's flickering light.

"I don't understand. You . . . did you work in the palace? Who were your parents? Did they—"

"Doesn't matter. Haven't been back there in years. Well, I mean, until . . ." Sayana waved at her. "You know."

What would it have been like, Sayana wondered, to have known Tuya then? Probably unsatisfying – the eagle hunter would have seen her as nothing more than the daughter of a wealthy family, someone to treat with deference and distant, mild contempt. Nothing more.

Tuya was silent for a moment. Then, she said: "That was how you knew where to find me, wasn't it? You knew the right part of the city to look."

Sayana didn't answer.

The cave sloped gently downwards. There were a few marks on the walls that might have come from scales scraping along them, but it was impossible to be sure. There were bones, too: broken and desiccated, littered across the floor. Sayana knew a little bit about bones – obviously – and these ones came from small animals. Too small for an *araatan* to eat, surely?

A prickle on the back of her neck. *Other creatures might use this cave too . . .*

The passage curved gently to the right. Sayana briefly wondered how it had formed – what process led to this deep fissure in the cliffside. Impossible to tell.

Tuya came to a sudden stop. She thrust her hand out to warn Sayana, then snatched it back in, as if remembering that she was a captive.

"What is it?" Sayana whispered.

"Shh." Tuya stood stock-still, head cocked.

Sayana could have sworn it was her imagination . . . but was there a gentle slithering sound, somewhere far out of sight?

"Still want to go through with this?" Tuya murmured.

In response, Sayana gave her a gentle push.

She drew her sabre, sweaty fingers clutching the hilt. Quickly, she pulled out the pouch Erhi had given her and popped it open. The substance inside felt like tree sap; it stuck to her fingers, gloopy and thick. She smeared it on her sabre, wiped the rest on her trousers.

When she tried to pull her hand off, it wouldn't come. There were a few seconds where she just yanked at it, heart climbing all the way up her throat, sure that this was the moment the *araatan* would choose to fill the dark with flame.

Her hand came loose with a sucking pop. Tuya shook her head in disgust, but said nothing.

A few seconds later, Sayana's mouth fell open.

She expected a deep cave. Maybe for the passage walls to widen a little. What she didn't expect was for them to open all the way up into a gigantic cavern. A jagged, hollow space under the cliff. Forty feet wide? Sixty? Sayana couldn't be sure. The far wall was visible, but in the flickering light of her torch, it was impossible to tell how big it really was; shadow bathed the stalactites hanging from the ceiling, the stalagmites rising from the rocky floor.

The *araatan* lay in full view, next to one of the biggest.

Every cell in Sayana's body wanted to turn tail and run. She didn't move, didn't dare, didn't even breathe. Beside her, Tuya had turned into a statue.

"It's asleep," she murmured.

And it was. Sayana wasn't exactly familiar with how *araatan* behaved, but the beast's eyes were closed, its back rising and falling as it breathed. It was just as big as the one Sayana had ridden, back in that village.

There was dried blood, smeared across the floor. Burned weapons, the remains of what looked to be a cookfire. Whoever was here when the *araatan* arrived, they weren't here now.

There was something wrong with the beast's side. In the low torchlight, Sayana had to work hard to make it out. Bent and broken scales, twisted back, with actual chunks missing from the flesh beneath. Big, gaping wounds, the blood shining in the low light.

That's impossible.

But even as she tried to push the thought away, she *saw*.

Saw the nubby grey horns, the frill of scales at the neck, the exact shape of the mouth that almost bit her in two. And the wounds . . .

If you were protected by tough, layered scales, and you fell fifty feet off a cliff onto a field full of jagged rocks, you'd have wounds that looked like that.

This wasn't *just as big as the one she'd ridden in that village.*

It *was* the one she'd ridden in that village.

They knew it had survived. But somehow, this *araatan* had crawled its way downstream. Miles and miles from where it had fallen. It had made it all the way here, wounded, in pain, seeking out a place to hide.

For a moment, Sayana's terror was gone. She was just in awe.

Tuya slowly turned her head to look at Sayana. *Injured*, she mouthed. She backed away into the passage, swiping a hand across her throat.

Sayana didn't argue. She didn't know much about animals, but hurt ones tended not to take kindly to people getting in their space. Slowly, taking great care not to trip, she followed Tuya.

Her foot caught on something, a raised bit of rock maybe, and she looked down for a moment to steady herself. When she glanced back, the *araatan* was looking right at them.

Twenty-Two

Hogelun

T here was always plenty of salt in Karkorum.
They sent it from the mines in the mountains, regular barrels of it. More than enough to go round. But in the Tapestry, all you had were occasional salt licks – the brackish water at the edges of lakes, where animals congregated.

Nasty business, getting the raw material out of that. You needed to boil it for ages, strain it, and Hogelun didn't always have the time. They sometimes scored some salt on raids, usually when they hit a wagon train, but not always.

Still, she had a tiny bit squirrelled away, and grimaced as she dusted it all into the pot. At least the flavour of her stew would probably turn out all right, even if there were very few chunks of antelope meat in it.

She squatted over the fire and peered into her second-favourite cookpot. Tongue sticking out from the side of her mouth, wishing she had some herbs. Just some sage, or dried marjoram. She needed to do a better job of keeping an eye out while they were riding, looking for the little green clumps . . .

A hand appeared over Hogelun's shoulder. It held another

pouch, this one made of soft leather. The hand was attached to Erhi, and as Hogelun took the pouch, the archer quickly walked back to the cliff edge. Sat down next to Chimeg.

Hogelun held the pouch in her cupped hands for a moment. Wondering if this was a peace offering, or if Erhi just didn't want bland stew. When she opened it, there was a small mound of grey-green herbs inside.

She shook a tiny bit out onto her palm, sniffed, used a moistened fingertip to bring a shred of leaf to her mouth. Not marjoram or sage, nothing she'd ever tasted . . . but not bad. Nice little mineral edge to it. And cooking might bring that out more, deepen the stew's flavour. Worth a try, for sure.

She threw most of it into the pot, gave it a stir to dissolve. The liquid was already coating her carved spoon, a good sign. Hogelun frowned at the pot, wondering if she should thin it. It might be too thick in the end; you never could tell with antelope . . .

For fuck's sake. The stew was fine. She just wanted to keep tinkering so she didn't have to sit down next to Erhi, and feel that frosty goodness coming off her in waves. And she definitely didn't want to think about *araatan*, or really, any lizards at all.

Then again, she'd apologised. Multiple times. And Erhi didn't own the cliff edge. If Hogelun wanted to sit down for a minute, take in the Tapestry on this fine afternoon, then that was what she was going to do. All the same, she had to give herself a very stern talking-to before she made her way over.

The archer didn't look her way. Chimeg sat on Erhi's right, sharpening her spear. Below, Khun was still swimming laps.

Hogelun sighed. "Thanks," she said to Erhi, moving her right hand down from the front of her chin. "For the herbs."

The response was a curt nod.

Hogelun cleared her throat, tapping her thumbs together above her folded hands. "Hey, Chief, how long since the Princess—"

"Twenty minutes." Chimeg held up her spear, flicking the edge of the bladed head.

Silence fell once again. Hogelun hated every bit of it. She turned to Erhi, about to embark on yet another apology, when there was a huge, flapping burst of noise. Tuya's eagle had landed on the cliff edge a few feet away from her, head cocked, as if wondering where its mistress was.

They stared at it, and it stared right back.

Slowly, Erhi picked up her bow, which had been lying next to her on the cliff. Hogelun held out a hand. Signed *wait*.

The eagle scraped at the dirt with a talon, as if hunting for worms. Then it took off, swooping down the falls and over the pool. Khun hooted in delight.

"Pity." Chimeg returned to her spear. "Could have been some extra meat in the stew tonight."

"They actually taste terrible," Hogelun said before she could stop herself, leaning over and talking across Erhi. "Like someone left the meat out in the suns. My dad caught one when I was a kid, and no matter how many herbs he put in there—"

Abruptly, Erhi stood. Stalked away into the grass.

Hogelun hated disappointing Erhi, couldn't stand the thought. Normally, she'd be grovelling, desperate to get back in the archer's good graces, terrified she'd gone too far. Right now, though? She'd gone through that stage, hours ago, and the anger roared up inside her like a snake exploding from its burrow.

She was on her feet so quickly that she nearly toppled off the edge of the cliff. Ignoring her Chief's startled "Careful!", she grabbed a small stone, hurled it into the grass on Erhi's right.

Erhi hated it when someone did that to attract her attention.

She spun round, a murderous look on her face, but for once it had precisely zero effect.

"What is your *problem*?" Hogelun shouted, signing with sharp, jerky movements. "You don't talk to me, then you do. Then you stop talking to me, then you just hand me some random herbs for cooking. Then when I'm just telling the Chief a story—" Chimeg was doing a good job of studying the sky "you storm off like I gave you the Cut. I don't care if you hate me, Erhi, just . . . just hate me properly."

Erhi raised an eyebrow. *What does that even mean?*

"You know exactly what it means! Chief, back me up here."

"Oh, why don't we pretend I already have, and go from there?" Chimeg said.

"I have *apologised*," Hogelun told Erhi. "Over and over and over. I'm just repeating myself at this point."

Erhi's signs were deliberate, and hard. *You hurt me.* Hands shaking as she twisted them for the word *hurt.*

As angry as she was, as much as she knew it was coming, the words still dropped Hogelun's heart into her stomach.

"I tried to bring the Princess back," she said. "I really did. But then . . . well, I thought I was doing the right thing. I thought I was helping us."

Erhi's shoulders slumped. She looked away for a moment, staring off across the grass. Plucking at the sleeve of her *deel*. Eventually, she signed, *The Rakada is just a name. And it's only the five of us now, after Sarnai died. If you do something for the clan and you hurt me in the process, or anyone else, then you hurt the clan. It's that simple.*

The anger and frustration clouded Hogelun's brain. Erhi made it sound so easy – like something Hogelun should have always known.

She didn't know what to say. Doing this, especially with

Erhi ... it was like trying to find her way down a stony hill, on a cloudy night when the whole world was pitch-dark. Every step could bring disaster.

A moment later, Erhi sat next to her. On her left, this time, putting Hogelun between her and Chimeg.

"I really am sorry," Hogelun signed. Hating herself for apologising, again, but not sure what else to do.

Silence for a few moments. Hogelun was looking down at the pond, watching Khun sunbathing stark naked on a rock, when Erhi tapped her on the elbow. *What was it like?*

"What was ... what like?"

Karkorum. There was a wistful look on Erhi's face. *Did you go past the weavers' district? Does Egu still have his shop there?*

"I ... I'm not sure. I wasn't really looking."

He did the most amazing silk work. I had two deels *from him.* Erhi wrinkled her nose. *They lasted about ten seconds out here, though. Dust tore them to pieces.*

Hogelun had a sudden image of Erhi striding across the Tapestry in a shiny, flowing *deel*, middle of a raid, cutting down enemies and looking fabulous while she did it.

I'm guessing the soldiers were all recruits? the archer asked.

Hogelun thought back to the raw, young warriors they fought through during their escape. "I think so."

"That figures," Chimeg said. "You start filling an army with conscripts, you get a bad army. Even if you bribe them with better food than the rest."

Undisciplined. Erhi shook her head. *We did patrol plenty of times, when we were still serving.* She flashed an evil smile at Hogelun. *You'd tried to kidnap someone when we were there, you wouldn't have made it ten steps.*

"Hey, Hogs," Chimeg said. "Remind me to tell you about the time Erhi here fell asleep on guard duty, one minute before our superior showed up. My legs still hurt from the run he made us do."

Erhi flicked her the Cut.

And for a long moment, Hogelun was somewhere else. A place where she and Erhi lived in Karkorum – only it demanded nothing from them. A place where they could wake up under a roof every day, where Erhi could have as many fabulous silk *deels* as she wanted. Where she could visit her favourite shops and come home to Hogelun's cooking.

But underneath it all, a worry: she couldn't do this to Erhi again. Couldn't disappoint her like she had. She needed to be better, because life without Erhi in it . . .

It wasn't worth living.

"I like that, by the way," Chimeg told Erhi, snapping Hogelun out of her thoughts. "That bit about hurting the clan if you hurt the people in it. Smart. I might use it when I—"

That was as far as she got, and then the *araatan* exploded through the waterfall.

Twenty-Three

Sayana

It was amazing what you noticed when you were about to die horribly.

The eyes of the thing that was going to kill you, for instance.

The dark pupils were rounder than Sayana remembered, the iris a deep, glowing yellow. They were *old* – and not in terms of this particular beast, either. They were the eyes of a species whose ancestors had walked the Tapestry long before the First Riders came, whose fire had shone on Father Sky's face when he and Mother Earth were still young.

The *araatan* got to its feet slowly, haltingly – one of its back legs was hurt, the claws dragging in the dirt. Towering over Sayana and Tuya. There was a half-second where Sayana thought it was too wounded to fight, that it wasn't going to attack. That it just wanted to be left alone.

Then it let out a jagged roar, and fired a huge tongue of flame right at her.

Tuya shoved her hard, knocking her out of the way. Sayana landed tailbone-first, the fire baking onto her face as it scorched the rock wall of the cavern. She scrambled backwards, her tongue feeling like it was going to choke her. She couldn't get a breath, couldn't stand.

The *araatan* charged.

It was appalling – no, actually, it was fucking horrifying – just how fast the thing could move from a standing start. Sayana got a split-second glimpse of the lizard filling the world in front of them, and then she bolted.

She and Tuya entered the passage at the same moment, running side by side, searing breath filling their lungs. And behind them, the *araatan* gave chase: a thundering, bellowing storm front. Its back leg might have been injured, altering its gait, but Sayana had zero doubt that if she slowed, even for a half-second, it would trample her into paste.

And if it sent out another dose of its fire breath, right now, there was nothing they could do. Nowhere for them to go.

As they reached the entrance, as blessed, wonderful light blinded her, the air behind Sayana turned warm. *Hot.* There was a hissing, crackling roar, and the tunnel walls compressed the sound, made it a thousand times worse. The *araatan* unleashed its fire, and Tuya and Sayana hurled themselves through the waterfall.

Sayana didn't bother worrying about whether there were any rocks where they'd be landing. Given the choice between being cooked alive and throwing herself into a pile of jagged boulders, she'd take the boulders. Every time.

But if there were any, Sayana and Tuya didn't hit them. The world became a whirling mess of spray and steam and sky; an instant later, dark water rushed into Sayana's lungs. She was coughing, spluttering, breaking the surface, frantically swimming, trying to get to shore, get to the horses, get away—

The *araatan* crashed through the waterfall. Sayana felt it rather than heard it, a deep *whoomph*, followed by a gigantic splash as it impacted the pool, the wave sweeping her and Tuya towards the shore.

Dirt under her hands, her knees. Sayana didn't hesitate, scrabbling up onto the bank. Khun was there, yelling at her to hurry, pulling her to her feet. Tuya. Where was Tuya?

Then Sayana saw her. On the other side of the pond, scrabbling across a broken bed of rocks. The eagle hunter stumbled, regained her balance, feet skidding on the wet surface.

The lizard was a fast swimmer. It churned up the water, body moving like a snake's as it pushed its way towards the shallows, swinging its massive head as it came out of the pond. It looked dazed, as if it didn't quite know where it was. Sagging down a little on its injured side, claws digging into the mud.

There was no possible way Sayana was going to get to Tuya. She could see that already, a dull realisation that cut through the sharp, bright terror.

It was over. Her plan had failed, in the most spectacular way possible.

Khun was screaming at her. Sayana wasn't even sure she was using actual words. For some reason she couldn't fathom, Khun was naked.

The older Rakada pulled her towards her horse, which even now was going absolutely nuts, yanking at the tether that tied it to its birch tree.

They couldn't fight the lizard. They couldn't tame it. The only thing they could do was get the hell out of there. At the very least, Sayana could make sure that the lizard chased her rather than Tuya; she owed the eagle hunter that much.

But before Sayana could attract the beast's attention, it fixed its gaze on Tuya. Growled, long and low, as it moved through the water towards her, sending up spray with each step. An arrow thudded off its scales, a second – Erhi, shooting from above the falls. But it wasn't going to do a single bit of good.

Tuya had nowhere to go. To her left, the rocks ran up against the wall of the cliff, mossy and slick. To her right, there was at least twenty feet of broken stone, ending in a clutch of trees. The kind of path that took time and care to navigate. Time Tuya didn't have.

Sayana had brought her here. Taken her from her city. And now she was going to watch her die.

Tuya, down on all fours, looked back over her shoulder. Stared at the injured, angry, rampaging *araatan*. At any second, the beast was going to mount the rocks.

Sayana yelled at her to run, fighting off Khun.

Only, Tuya . . .

What the fuck is she doing?

She'd got up, standing awkwardly on the wet surface, facing the *araatan*. Lifted her arms overhead, fingers spread. And slowly, carefully, she made her way across the rocks.

Towards the beast.

Sayana was clenching the hilt of her sabre hard enough to make her fingers ache. She couldn't move, couldn't even think what to do as this insane woman advanced on the single most dangerous creature in the Tapestry.

But then, Tuya's body began to move in a way Sayana had never seen. Her entire bearing just changed: a thousand micro-movements, happening all at once. Chin thrust out, shoulders spread wide, eyes narrowed. She got taller, her posture more erect. Like she wasn't only pretending but believed, absolutely believed, that she was ten times her size. Standing eye level with the *araatan* on the broken rocks.

The lizard ignored all of this, and lunged anyway.

Tuya didn't flinch. Just kept moving forward, face twisted

in an animal snarl. She was making the oddest sound: a kind of short, sharp bark, audible despite the rushing water.

The lizard's charge only lasted a few feet. That big tail was still swinging as it stumbled to a halt in a spray of mud and water, started backing up, growling again, eyes never leaving the hunter.

Sayana's mouth fell open. The *araatan* was ten times Tuya's size . . . and it was backing away from *her*.

It was injured, angry. But somehow, Tuya was making it think twice. And it wasn't just intimidation; this was something more, something deeper.

She slowed her advance. Ten feet from the *araatan*. Eight. Body still huge, moving with exaggerated strides. And as Sayana watched, she slowly held out her hand.

The lizard's growl became subsonic, that huge tongue flicking the air. Sayana couldn't believe what she was seeing: stopping the big beast in its tracks was one thing, but touching it?

Everything went away, everything except Tuya and the *araatan*. Her barks had changed, becoming softer huffs, like she was trying to empty the air from her lungs. And then, very slowly, and very gently, she placed a hand on the tip of the *araatan*'s snout.

Rested it there.

The *araatan* was still growling, that tail still swishing, sending up plumes of water, and Sayana was sure that at any moment it was going to snap. Lunge forward, tear Tuya's arm off. It would take less than a second.

The whole world held its breath, as if Father Sky and Mother Earth had joined hands and stopped time itself.

The air was full of spray. Sayana didn't know if it was from the flame hitting the waterfall, or from the *araatan*'s path through the shallows. The suns turned every droplet into a glinting jewel, a glittering cloud of light. And through the cloud, Tuya looked at her and . . .

Smiled.

It wasn't a smug smile. It wasn't even triumphant. It was a smile of pure, simple amazement. A child's smile, when her mother showed her a magic trick. The smile of a woman whose lover was finally home from battle, without a single mark on them. The angry twist to Tuya's face, the one Sayana had thought was more or less permanent, just . . . vanished.

It was one of the most beautiful things Sayana had ever seen. In that moment, she would have done anything for Tuya. Anything to keep that smile on her face.

It fucking *melted* her.

The *araatan* snorted. Its swishing tail slowed, the bone club at the end sending up a plume as it impacted the water. There was a screech from overhead – Ayanga, Tuya's eagle, swooping in low, carving through the jewel-box spray.

Tuya let out one final, sharp bark. The lizard's whole body was shaking now, that injured back leg slipping in the mud.

Sayana didn't move. Neither did Khun, although she still had a death grip on Sayana's shoulder. Tuya dropped her hand, and the lizard backed into the pond, swinging its enormous body around and awkwardly swimming across. Carefully clambering up the rocks under the falls, unbothered by the water pounding on its back.

It slunk through the spray. For a second, that big bone club at the end of its tail stuck straight out into the open air, as if the waterfall had sprouted a new rock formation. Then it was gone.

As if the *araatan* had never been there at all.

Twenty-Four

Sayana

"So." Hogelun clapped her hands, squeezing them together a little too tight. "That was fun."

Half an hour after the *araatan* left, there was still some spray in the air. It hung around in defiance of natural law, glittering in the late-afternoon suns.

They were all at the edge of the pool. Khun still hadn't put her clothes on – Sayana couldn't even see them piled anywhere. Their horses were in the birch grove nearby, the five of them standing in a tight, nervous circle.

Tuya sat cross-legged on the shore, her back to them. She'd told Sayana she needed to think. None of them had suggested tying her up again. The memory of her smile remained in Sayana's mind, bright and stunning.

I still don't believe it. It was the third time Erhi had signed this. She squinted at the pond, as if expecting the *araatan* to break the surface and come for them.

"The world of the spirits shifts and changes," Khun said. "But what we saw was as real as the fungus under my little fingernail." She stuck the grimy digit in question in Erhi's face; the archer pushed her away, grimacing.

Chimeg, so far, had remained silent.

"So, Chief?" Sayana asked her, unable to stop a grin breaking across her face. "Still think this is a bad idea?"

"Very much so."

"Exactly, it was . . . wait, what?"

"To be clear." Chimeg rolled her left shoulder, wincing. "I'm still not entirely sure how that happened, but we're not exactly riding the beasts into battle yet, are we?"

"I *did* ride it into battle!"

"If I remember correctly, you rode it *out* of the battle."

Sayana couldn't believe what she was hearing. Did she imagine the whole thing? Was she really the only person to see Tuya put a hand on the beast's snout?

"I mean . . ." Hogelun frowned. "Chief, that *was* pretty incredible."

"Exactly." Sayana snapped her fingers at Hogs. "Thank you. Has anybody ever done that with an *araatan* before? Ever? Khun, could you *please* put some clothes on?"

"What?" Khunbish barked, as if she were hard of hearing. Then she looked down at her naked body, and sauntered off without another word.

For the second time in days, Sayana only had a single boot; the other was somewhere in the depths of the pool. It meant she was a little lopsided, and when she swung round to face Erhi, she nearly fell into the mud. "You shot it with an arrow, and it didn't even notice. That's how angry it was. And Tuya . . . she stopped it. With no weapons, nothing, not even her eagle."

Erhi's signs were hesitant. *It's impressive, I will grant that.*

Sayana was about to keep going when the Chief held up a

hand. "Tell us what happened." She nodded to the waterfall. "In there."

The events in Sayana's mind were a little jumbled, shaken to pieces by the rush of adrenaline, but she managed to lay it all out. When she told them about how this *araatan* was the same one from before, Hogelun nearly choked.

When the tale ended, Chimeg looked over at the eagle hunter, still sitting silently by the edge of the pool. "How did you do that?" she asked.

Tuya didn't reply.

The Chief's voice turned sharp. "Hunter. Answer me."

"It wasn't angry," Tuya said, without turning around. "It was scared."

The Rakada all looked at each other. "OK," said Chimeg. "So that didn't really answer my question . . . "

Slowly, Tuya got to her feet, brushing off her trousers. Like Sayana, she was caked in mud, her *deel* soaking wet. "It was injured, and weak. It was terrified."

They waited for her to continue. She didn't. The eagle hunter was lost in thought, looking at them without seeing them. Khun came marching up, mercifully fully clothed, munching on a leaf.

"How did you know?" Sayana asked. "About it being scared?"

Tuya blinked. "Oh. The . . . the tail." She mimed waving it back and forth. "It's a fear response. I've seen it on smaller reptiles." She appeared to notice Sayana then, as if for the first time. Their eyes met, just for a brief moment. "And you saw its flame," Tuya went on, glancing over at Chimeg. "Didn't you? Compared to what they normally do, it wasn't all that strong. That injury really knocked the wind out of it."

Still almost turned us to ash, Sayana thought.

Tuya pointed at the waterfall, the cave beyond. "It's hiding. Trying to save energy."

"Begging your pardon," said Hogelun. "But that didn't stop it from nearly eating you."

It was angry, Erhi said. *And you calmed it. How?*

Tuya cocked her head. "Sorry . . . I don't sign?"

Erhi rolled her eyes, and Sayana translated. The eagle hunter stared at the ground, thinking hard. "I . . . can't really describe it. There's—"

"Dead dog shit," Chimeg snapped. "You spoke to it, somehow. Told it to back off."

"I didn't *speak to it*. It's not language – that's not how it works. I just figured out what it wanted." There was a strange longing in Tuya's voice. "It wanted to be safe. It didn't want to fight."

"You do remember the part where it tried to burn you alive?" Hogelun said.

"We surprised it, in its den. And it's injured, so, of course, it lashes out, but . . . but you have to look past that. See what it really wants. You show it you aren't worth the trouble."

"Which *still* doesn't answer my question." Chimeg had a look on her face, one that usually meant she was about to express her displeasure with the point of her spear. "How do you know what to do? How does it work?"

Tuya's familiar anger came rushing back. Her shoulders were stiff with it. She tried to speak, stopped, tried again. Sayana got the sense that this wasn't easy for her; that she didn't know how to describe what she did, any more than Sayana knew how to describe how people breathed without thinking about it. It just . . . was.

Eventually, Tuya looked over at Erhi. "You. Lady. You're good with that bow, yeah? How did you get that way?" Tuya signed a motion of shooting a bow. Not a particularly good sign, either.

Erhi slowly tilted her head, studying Tuya with a faint look of distaste.

"That's really rude," Hogelun said.

"Yeah, you shouldn't do that," Sayana echoed.

Chimeg raised an eyebrow. "Maybe leave the signing to people who know how."

Tuya had the good grace to look embarrassed. "Fine, yes, sorry."

Khun spoke around her leaf. "I will cut your face off for this disrespect, and wear it as a hat."

"Just ignore her," Sayana said, as Tuya took a hasty step backward. "She doesn't really mean it."

Practice, Erhi told Tuya. *Hours and hours of it. Time spent with many, many bows over the years. At rest and in motion on horseback.* She signed rapidly, the movements blurring together, and Sayana had to work hard to keep up and translate. *But what you have is not just practice. It's more than that.*

"It's magic, is what it is," murmured Hogelun.

"This is the point." Sayana drove a fist into her open palm. "That's exactly what I was telling you all. I knew someone who was good with animals, and here she is, and you just saw what she does. Why are we standing around debating this?"

"It *is* a lot of practice," Tuya said. "It's ... you have to learn to read body language. The way they stand, how their heads are positioned, ears ... although *araatan* don't really have ones that stick out. You have to pay attention to how *you* move, how you stand, what your shoulders are doing, your chin and hands. It's like horses — they communicate through their bodies."

She shrugged, nodded to Erhi. "You can shoot arrows. I can

read wild animals. I can pick up their state of mind, work out what they really want. Calm them if I have to."

She spread her hands. The mud on her palms had dried to a thin crust. "But . . . look, what you all want, to ride them . . . that kind of thing would take years. If it's even possible at all."

But there was an invisible question mark at the end of that sentence. Sayana didn't even think Tuya was aware of it.

"Chief," she said, quieter this time. "Give me a chance here. We can do this."

Chimeg chewed on her lip for a few seconds, then waved a hand at the eagle hunter. "Go sit somewhere else for a bit. We need to talk."

"And don't even think about running off," Hogelun told her. "Or . . ."

She looked over at Erhi, who mimicked Tuya's awkward attempt at signing *archery*.

"Of course," Tuya said, voice bitter. She complied, heading back to the edge of the pond, sitting with her arms around her knees. Far enough away that she couldn't hear them.

Sayana turned to Chimeg. "Before you say anything—"

The Chief immediately cut her off. "Yesuntei knows it was us who took her sister."

The change of subject knocked Sayana a little bit, and she faltered. "Chief, it was . . . it was one bone. Maybe they didn't even find it."

Chimeg gave Khun a dirty look; Khun grinned back at her, benign and unconcerned. "We have to assume the worst," the Chief said. "That Yesuntei knows it was us, that she's coming—" she ticked these off on her fingers "—and that we have no idea how long it might take her."

"Yeah." Hogelun sounded contemplative. "But we haven't

seen anyone in a while. Fair bet nobody knows where we are right now."

Sayana flashed her a smile. "Tapestry's big. Even on a fast horse, she'll have to search for a long time to find us. And—" she pointed at the waterfall "—she doesn't know what we're doing yet. We've got a bit of time to play with."

"Not much," Chimeg said darkly.

Erhi's hands moved. *She will wonder why we have not sent ransom demands. She will wonder why we have her sister.*

"Let the bitch wonder," Sayana told her.

"Come on, Princess," the Chief said. "When Yesuntei gets here – no, not a bloody word, it's a *when*, not an *if* – our only option would be to use her sister as a hostage. And even then, we'd still have to run. We'd spend the rest of our lives running. Plus, your little project will try to escape every chance she gets. Or turn that lizard against us."

She waved at Tuya. "That *was* amazing, what she did, but it didn't actually change anything. Maybe we could use her to . . . I don't know, guarantee our safety. Get to somewhere it isn't worth Yesuntei following."

"*No.*" Sayana blurted it out before she could stop herself. She wouldn't let this slip away. Not after everything they just went through.

The Chief's words were in her head, from before: *I'll never forgive you for this. No matter what happens. I'll never forgive you for forcing my hand.*

As awful as that sounded, it also meant she had nothing left to lose.

"I don't know what else I can do for you, Chief." Her words tasted like unripe apples, sharp and bitter. "We just saw something impossible, and if that's not enough to convince you, then I'm out of ideas." She stuck her chin out. "But when we're run out of the Tapestry, just remember what happened today. Remember that I *tried*."

Before the last word was even out of her mouth, Chimeg was moving.

The Chief crossed the space between them in a single heartbeat, and then there was a dagger point digging into the underside of Sayana's chin.

She stopped talking.

Chimeg's face hovered above her, eyes narrowed to slits. "I thought you'd die today." Her voice was a low, dangerous monotone. "I really did. I didn't like it, but you insisted, so I thought I'd give you the chance. You're still here. But you know what that *didn't* get you?" The tip of the dagger dug in, just a touch. "You don't get to talk to me that way. Ever."

"Oh, hells." There was no strength in Hogs' voice. Erhi and Khun were dead still. Sayana couldn't tell if Tuya was watching or not.

She was going to do it. The Chief was going to kill her.

And on the heels of that thought came one she didn't like very much at all: Chimeg didn't want her in the Rakada. Maybe she did, once, but those days were gone. She could talk as much as she liked about how she was glad Sayana didn't die, but that didn't mean Sayana couldn't shake what she'd said before. About how her and Tuya dying would solve all Chimeg's problems. The words of a Chief too stuck in her ways to change.

Sayana refused to look away. The Chief wanted to do this? After everything? Fine. She wouldn't make it easy.

Erhi gently put a hand on Chimeg's arm, and pulled the dagger down.

It's as if it snapped Chimeg out of a spell. She blinked, and let Erhi pull her away, nearer the trees. The two of them turned their backs to the others, hiding their signs.

"Sayana." Hogelun sounded very calm. "Would it be possible, do you think, for you to have a day where you *didn't* make our Chief want to murder you? Can you just try?"

"Working on it." The shakes had started, because if Erhi hadn't got involved . . .

Tuya was watching, looking over her shoulder at them. Sayana had never felt further from her Chief than she did at that moment.

Chimeg came back, Erhi following. Sayana braced for her to have a second go, but she stopped a few feet away. Arms tightly folded. Despite the hot suns above, their side of the pool was in the shade now, Sayana's bare skin pimpling.

"Erhi," Chimeg said, speaking through gritted teeth, "has reminded me that it took spine to go into that cave."

The archer's expression was a careful blank.

"And," the Chief went on, "that you risked no one but yourself. And her, I suppose." She gestured to a puzzled Tuya. "So: you've earned yourself a little more rope."

Sayana was grinding her own teeth together now. Chimeg was acting like this was a gift. Like she was bestowing it from on high. Her bare foot was sticky with mud, starting to itch. All the same, she'd take what she could get. "Appreciate it," she said. "I won't let you d——"

"Ten days."

"Chief." Sayana spread her hands, disbelieving. "That isn't *nearly* enough time. We're not going to be riding the *araatan* ten days from now."

"For the love of . . . " Chimeg pinched the bridge of her nose. "I don't need you to be *riding* it. But I do need to see that it's possible. Ten days, and then I want to see some progress."

Sayana jerked a chin at Tuya. "How was *that* not progress?"

"Don't pretend you don't understand. That was her saving

her own skin. It's a very, very long way from commanding the *araatan*. So yes: ten days to show me it's possible. If I'm not satisfied after that time, then we kill your hunter, and we run. Same thing if the lizard kills you. Either of you."

She levelled a finger at Sayana. "I'm not fucking about here, Princess. You don't like those terms . . . actually, I don't care if you don't like those terms. You'll take 'em."

Hogelun cast a worried look at the falls. "What if Tuya trains the thing to attack us instead?"

Sayana couldn't stop a second, even more worrying thought from muscling its way in. *She might just stall for time, until her sister finds us.*

She flicked a glob of mud off her forearm. Both were possible. This was a big risk — not that any part of this ridiculous idea wasn't.

Except: she kept seeing that smile, through the spray. That glorious smile. Kept hearing the question mark in Tuya's words, the way she spoke about the *araatan*.

"We will watch her." Khun clapped a hand on Sayana's shoulder, squeezing so hard that it felt as if her arm was going to pop out of its socket. "The Princess and me. We will study her every move, close-close. If she wants to turn the beastie against us, we'll know."

Sayana could have kissed Khun. If kissing her was a thing one could do without getting punched in the face.

"Brilliant," said Hogelun. "Because there's no way I'm going in there, ever."

The Chief called Tuya back. Ayanga had swooped down, perched on his mistress's arm, studying them with beady, suspicious eyes.

This time, Chimeg didn't speak. She gave Sayana a pointed look, jerked her chin at the eagle hunter.

Guess it's my show.

"Here's how this is going to go," Sayana said. "You're going to train the *araatan* for us. Get it to accept us, get it to do what we need."

She did her best to make it sound like there was no choice. It was a lot harder than she thought it would be; if this didn't work, there was a good chance Tuya would end up in a shallow grave.

The hunter raised an eyebrow. "Did you not listen to a word I said? It could take months. Years."

You've got ten days. Sayana didn't dare say it out loud. If Tuya knew about the arbitrary deadline, she really *would* try something stupid.

"Doesn't matter," she snapped. "We're not negotiating. You disobey, you try to escape, you grab a weapon, and it's over. Got it?"

Chimeg shot a sideways look at her. The Chief hadn't missed the fact that the deadline hadn't entered the conversation. Sayana kept talking, eyes never leaving Tuya. "You might think your sister will save you. I can promise you that if she tries, she'll get to see what your guts look like."

Tuya looked at all of them. As if truly seeing them for the first time. "You really want to do this?"

"We do," Sayana said.

A long moment, then the eagle hunter pointed at Erhi. "That goopy sleep shit of yours. Can you put it on an arrow?" Erhi nodded. "We need to treat its wounds. It won't be much use to us if it dies of the rot. You'll need to shoot it, get it all sleepy so we can heal it. Or try, anyway. Can you do that?'

Erhi's nod this time was a little less firm.

"We're also going to need meat. Antelope, gazelle, wild horse. Lots of it."

Sayana grimaced. *That* was going to take some doing; finding herds of game in the Tapestry had been getting harder and harder. Still, they had no choice.

Chimeg rolled her shoulders. "You heard the woman," she told the other Rakada, while clearly speaking directly to Sayana. "We want to make this work, we do what she said. Get hunting."

It was impossible to miss the meaning there. *This isn't going to work. You're going to fail.*

Sayana didn't mean to clench her fists, but she did anyway. Because when this worked, when she and Tuya trained that *araatan*, she was *never* going to let the Chief forget it.

Hogelun glanced down. "Don't tell me you lost your boot *again*?"

Twenty-Five

Yesuntei

Yesuntei sat on a bucket and watched the raiders die.

The bucket was made of sturdy wood, secured with thick metal bands. It wasn't quite large enough to sit on comfortably; she had to keep shifting position.

There were fifty or so raiders – a large group, a disorganised rabble calling themselves the Thunderhead. Not the Thunderhead*s*: Thunderhead singular. As if they were some sort of movement, a unified force threatening Hanggai.

Yesuntei scoffed. *Unified.* In past years, raider groups had attempted to band together, stand up against the might of the Khan. It rarely worked. A disloyal, undisciplined mass of vicious bastards usually found it difficult to maintain a workable command-and-control structure.

When she and the 8th found them, just south of Gangara Lake, they were involved in some sort of argument. Civil war. Dust-up. Yesuntei wasn't quite sure what the correct term was, or even what the disagreement was about. Not that it made a difference. Faced with a hundred mounted warriors, bearing down on them across the waving yellow grass, the raiders scattered.

Tried to, anyway.

At first, the captives claimed they knew absolutely nothing. Then Jochi and his men had a little talk with them, and the ones who survived admitted that they may once upon a time have heard of the Bone Raiders, but they had certainly never seen them. No idea what they were talking about.

Yesuntei didn't take part in any of this.

She was too busy with her bucket.

In theory, Jochi's method of interrogation made sense. They spoke to each prisoner individually, and if what they said didn't match up with the others, they started taking lives.

It worked well with prisoners of war — they were part of armies, they had commanders, they talked to each other. With raiders? A bunch of disparate scum roaming the grass in loose clans? It was pointless. There was no raider code. Nothing that prevented them from selling out other clans. Hells, the less competition, the better. But usually, the clans didn't speak, didn't keep tabs on each other's movements. A raider with a knife to his throat would say anything to save his skin.

Gradually, Jochi and his men whittled away at both the Thunderhead and the stories its members were telling. All garbage. Jochi kept asking questions, but at that point, it became clear, at least to Yesuntei, that this wasn't going to get them anywhere.

Perhaps they had chosen the wrong raiders to target. They might have better luck if they simply cut their losses and moved on, hunted down another clan. One more willing to tell them where the Bone Raiders might have gone.

The noises coming from the bucket were getting louder. Yesuntei kicked it hard with her heel, and the noises stopped.

A few feet away, near a line of kneeling prisoners, which was now in the very small single figures, Jochi straightened up. Blood drenched his black *deel*, and he looked exhausted. Yesuntei allowed herself a wry smile; she thought he'd have more stamina.

"Useless." He spat on the ground, passed his sabre to one of his men. "I've met oxen who knew more than these idiots."

Yesuntei said nothing. Her sabre rested across her knees, pristine and free of blood. She wore her armour – scarred plate the colour of an *actual* thunderhead, over toughened leather and a plain yellow *deel*.

Her helmet lay propped in the dirt nearby. She always took it off as soon as she could; it was hot and uncomfortable, and while she accepted that it was better to wear it than get an arrow through the skull, she preferred to get rid of it as soon as possible.

Jochi wiped his face. He hadn't mentioned the orders again: that parchment she'd conjured up with the Khan's seal. But Yesuntei had to wonder how long that would last. She was running out of time, and if they couldn't get results soon, he might start asking awkward questions.

"We should head east," he said. "If these Bone Raiders wanted to cover as much ground as possible, they would go where it was easiest."

Still, Yesuntei said nothing.

"You know my thoughts on this." Jochi glanced at the bucket. "It's the reason you lost your command in the first place. I would have thought that was enough."

Yesuntei had always found it strange that some interrogation methods were accepted in the Khan's army, and some were not. No one had ever told her about a line she shouldn't cross. No one said a word until she crossed it in the first place.

"We tried your way." Yesuntei nodded to the line of very dead raiders. "Didn't really get us anywhere."

"And you think you'll have better luck?"

Yesuntei stood up. That had always been the problem with Jochi. Sometimes, his will failed him.

She kicked the bucket away. It bounced off across the dirt and flattened grass, coming to a rest near one of the bodies.

The head underneath stared up at Yesuntei. She'd give this one credit: he looked less terrified than they usually did. More defiant. In her experience, people buried up to their necks in densely packed dirt tended to endlessly plead and beg.

This one had gone quiet now, jaw set tight, sweat pouring down his face. Unlike his raider friends, most of whom looked as if they'd been dragged behind a horse for a few miles, his short beard was neatly kept, his head fully shaved.

Yesuntei waited until he'd got a good look at the pile of corpses that used to be the Thunderhead. Then she nudged the side of his temple with her foot. "Up here."

He spat at her. He couldn't tilt his head back very far, so the spittle didn't do much more than dot her boot.

She favoured him with a benign smile. "I don't suppose you have any idea where the Bone Raiders went?"

The warriors of the 8th were watching. Hopefully, Jochi would keep them in line – not that it mattered, because this was happening no matter what.

"Of course." The Chief of the Thunderhead – she didn't remember his name – glared up at her. "When I last saw them, they were up your mother's crack."

"Hmm." Yesuntei said. "Seems unlikely. Are you quite sure?"

"We will rise again, a thousand strong, and sweep over—"

"Yes, yes, and you'll overthrow the Khan and make me your whore and burn Karkorum to the ground. Can we just get past that, please?" She crouched down. "The time of raiders is over. Even you have to understand that. But it seems our dear Rakada didn't get the message, and they took someone very close to me – I assume so they can bargain for their lives."

Her stomach was acting up again, the vicious, gnawing emptiness creeping back.

"I'm not asking for much here," she said. "I really am willing to let you live, if you give me just the tiniest little hint about where they might be."

When the response was another pathetic little fleck of spit, Yesuntei sighed. She stood and walked over to the giant pile of earth a few feet away. After all, when you buried someone, that dirt had to go somewhere.

"Let me tell you a story." She scooped a couple of handfuls up. A poisonous millipede snaked over the back of her hand, and she flicked it away. "When I was young, I was so angry, all the time. I had no reason to be, you understand – my sister Tuya and I grew up in Karkorum, and we wanted for nothing. Our home was comfortable, our parents worked in the palace and we had everything we needed."

The pile of earth was slightly behind the Thunderhead Chief, and he couldn't twist his head around far enough to look. Yesuntei made her way back over to him and began to pack the soil carefully around the back of his neck. He had a fold of skin there that really was quite unattractive.

"I was ... difficult," Yesuntei went on. "Young and stupid and furious at everything. I fought, insulted my mother and father, and Tuya ... I hated her most of all. She was the golden child, the one who was going to be apprenticed to the eagle hunters. It had been planned for years.

"No one knew what to do with me. There was talk about having me join the army, but the recruiting officer laughed in my father's face. They weren't going to waste time on someone like me."

More earth, packed in tight around his neck and chin. He fought it, of course, snapping his head from side to side. But Yesuntei had done this many times, and she built a mound around his head, so there was too much dirt to push out of the way.

"Tuya, however, wouldn't take no for an answer. She demanded the army find a place for me and ignored me when I told her I didn't want it. I fought her, too. More than once. But she wouldn't stop until she ended up in front of the Khan himself — the old one, I mean, Ulagan — begging that I be allowed to join."

She cradled the man's head, made him look her in the eyes. Pleased to see fear in them, finally.

"She risked her placement with the eagle hunters, her entire life . . . for me. So that I could have something too. She never gave up on me, not once."

Despite everything, despite the gnawing in her stomach and the danger Tuya was in, this memory still glowed. Blazing with light inside her. She looked over at Jochi, the barest smile sneaking onto her face. He didn't smile back, which was fine. He wouldn't interfere.

"Tuya gave me everything," she told the half-buried man. Patting more earth around his mouth, careful to avoid his snapping teeth. "The army taught me discipline and structure, and taught me to serve something greater than myself. My whole life, I'd been hunting for meaning, and my sister gave it to me. No one has ever given me a greater gift."

It didn't matter that her exit from the army had been less than ideal. That was nothing, a little blip, because she never lost her love of service. That stayed with her. Even in the dungeons below the palace, in the darkness of her cell, she knew she'd be able to serve again one day.

The new Khan had honoured that. More: he'd understood her

true gifts, how effective she would be at building Karkorum. Building his nation. For a moment, she could see it. A great and glorious walled city. A land ready to defend itself against anyone who threatened it. Citizens united in praising their Khan's vision.

All because of Tuya.

Yesuntei shook her head, chiding herself for drifting off. "Do you understand what that's like? To have nothing, no reason to live, and then be given purpose? Of course you don't. You've never had a purpose, beyond taking whatever you want, whenever you want it."

Her voice didn't change: calm and even. Gentle. "You and every raider in Hanggai are swine at a trough, gorging yourselves. And now, you've taken my sister. The most important person in my entire life."

Only the nose and eyes were showing now. He was taking desperate breaths, quick and sharp. Yesuntei continued to pack the earth in tighter, aware of the muttering from the troops behind her, and not caring. "I'm going to take some of the dirt away from your mouth, and you're going to give me something useful about the Bone Raiders. You have exactly one chance, and then I'll finish what I started."

She reached in and pulled a handful of earth away. When he finally found his voice, dirt-crusted and gritty, he said, "Please—"

Immediately, Yesuntei began packing the earth in again.

"Wait. Wait! The marshes!"

"What about them?"

"They . . . they hide there, sometimes. In the Namag. When they need the heat to die down."

Perhaps the man saw the disappointment in her face, because he kept talking. Words coming very fast. "You said . . . you said your sister was an eagle hunter, yes? Right? We saw an eagle. A couple of days ago. In the Namag."

"You saw an eagle," Yesuntei said, voice flat.

He licked his lips. "I remember, because you don't usually get them in those parts. We hadn't had anything to eat for a while, so Baltun tried to shoot it."

Yesuntei didn't know who Baltun was, but she suspected he was now one of the corpses behind her.

"It was on the north-eastern edge of the marshes," the man went on. "Didn't think anything of it ... not until just now when you said ... "

Yesuntei tapped her bottom lip. The north-eastern edge of the Namag wasn't a lot to go on, even if it narrowed the search area down dramatically. It was the thinnest of thin threads, but ...

But it was a thread nonetheless. And if she was going to find the Rakada, she had to pull on every single one.

"Good boy," she said, patting the man's head.

A shadow fell over the two of them. Jochi. "How do you even know he's telling the truth?"

Yesuntei rolled her eyes, retrieved the bucket. The buried raider stared up at her, understanding dawning. "No. Please—"

"If we find something, we'll come back and dig you out," she told him. "On my honour. Shouldn't be more than a few days."

"*No*—"

Yesuntei pushed the bucket down, driving it into the dirt. Covering the man's head. He'd be fine, for a few days, assuming a jackal or a tiger didn't come sniffing around. And if his tip turned out to be a good one? She'd send someone to dig him out. She was a woman of her word, after all.

If his information got them nowhere, then ... well. It was no great loss.

And at least they'd save themselves a return trip.

Twenty-Six

Sayana

Tuya's voice was hushed. "Whatever you do, do *not* make any sudden moves."

Sayana spoke without looking at her, mostly because she couldn't tear her eyes away. "It's barely awake."

The *araatan* was sprawled on its side at the far end of the cave, like a cat basking in the sun. Belly rising and falling.

"OK, then," Tuya said brightly. "Make sudden movements. I'm sure it'll be fine."

Something Sayana had discovered about Tuya: she loved sarcasm. *Loved* it.

From above, on the shadowy shelf of rock that ran along the left side of the cave, Khun cackled. They'd set torches around the chamber, which turned it from a pitch-black space into a mostly pitch-black one, but it was the best they could do.

It had been surprisingly easy − almost suspiciously easy, in fact − to subdue the *araatan*. After they'd crept in, found it curled up, Erhi shot it from the passage. At first, it had gone nuts, thrashing around wildly. But in under a minute, the thrashing had calmed, the beast sinking into an uneasy slumber. Erhi had been pretty smug about that.

Tuya had volunteered to tend to its side, treating the flesh with another of Erhi's concoctions – a paste of wild pears and six different kinds of root that she used to stop the rot, whenever any Rakada got injured. Effective, if a bit itchy; Sayana's thigh was still driving her insane, days after it got burned. By this particular *araatan*, actually. Couldn't forget that.

A little of Chimeg's needle and thread to patch the beast's wound – fine, a *lot* of thread – and it was done. Raw and puffy, already weeping, but closed. Sayana watched with guilty fascination from a distance, sure that at any moment, the lizard was going to wake up and lose its fucking mind, in which case they'd be down one *araatan* tamer and have to make a very quick exit.

There'd been nothing that Tuya could do for its wounded leg, although she'd said it wasn't broken. "It was probably healing *before* it chased us through the waterfall," she'd said.

That was a day ago. Now, after a fitful night of sleep, Tuya and Sayana stood a safe distance from the beast. A *very* safe distance. It would have been amazing if there was a giant chain to hand, ideally one that had links as thick as Sayana's biceps, but all they had was rope. Which would be about as useful as an edict from the Khan decreeing that henceforth, no *araatan* was permitted to bite anyone.

The other Rakada were by the pool outside, tending to the horses. Hogelun had given a hollow laugh when Sayana suggested they come watch the process. "Princess, I would rather wash the Chief's sweaty underthings for a month than go into that cave," she'd said.

"It wakes," Khun crooned from her perch. She was right. The *araatan* was slowly getting to its feet, swinging its giant head from side to side. Sayana tensed, fingers finding the hilts of her sabres.

The scales weren't just a uniform shade of drab green, as she'd thought. They captured the torchlight, shimmering in shades of purple and ochre. And as the beast swung its head in their direction, fixed curious, sleepy eyes on Sayana, she couldn't help but notice other details. The way the muscles in its neck stood out, the way it held its head.

It. They didn't even know if it was male or female. Was there a way to tell? There must be, although at this precise moment, Sayana couldn't summon up enough saliva to ask Tuya. She certainly didn't plan on bending over to check out its undercarriage.

As it stared at them, the *araatan* gave off another of those low growls. It turned, twisting, trying to get at the wound on its side.

"Well," Sayana told Tuya, not taking her eyes from the beast. "At least it doesn't *immediately* want to kill us."

"It might if you don't lower your voice." Tuya sounded half resigned, half scared out of her mind. "OK. First rule of approaching any wild animal: don't."

"Helpful. Thanks." Apparently, the sarcasm was rubbing off on Sayana.

"Second rule: if you're forced to approach one by a bunch of crazy raiders, give it a meal it doesn't have to fight for." She gestured to the passage behind them, where there was a butchered antelope carcass. "Let's bring it in, slowly. And I mean *very* slowly."

The antelope wasn't heavy. Kind of scrawny, actually. When they were a few feet from the passage, holding the carcass between them, the *araatan* suddenly snapped its head up. Nostrils flaring. Sayana had no idea why it hadn't smelled the dead animal until they brought it in — another thing she'd have to ask Tuya, when her heart wasn't beating quite so fast.

Every part of her was screaming to drop the carcass and get as far away as possible. But they kept moving forward, twenty feet away, fifteen, even as that stomach-shaking growl built and built. Khun's eyes glittered in the shadows, watching.

Just as Sayana was sure that the *araatan* was going to lunge at them, Tuya nodded at her to lower the carcass, mouthing the word *slowly*.

They did. Then without taking their eyes from the beast, they stepped away. Sayana had managed to retrieve her boot from the pool, had made an attempt to dry it; it was still disgustingly damp, squelching with every step.

With one last growl, the *araatan* took a hesitant, woozy step forward. Another. Sayana expected it to sniff the carcass, perhaps even push at it with its snout—

The beast exploded, covering the last few feet in a rapid, lumbering gait, back leg dragging. It snatched the antelope, crunched down. Gave the meat a single shake, then turned away, filling the cave with wet chewing.

"Let it feed," said Tuya. "When it's settled, we'll leave. Come back later with another meal."

"You're taking this very slowly for someone who already put her hand on its nose."

Tuya either didn't notice Sayana's tone, or pretended not to. "I still don't exactly know how I did that. I just . . . did what felt right. But I don't want to risk it again, not in here."

"So, what, we just feed it a few antelope until it likes us?"

"It's not a dog. It's not interested in *liking* us. It doesn't want to be friends. It wants food, and warmth, and to breed. Our job, if we actually live long enough, is to convince it that harming us won't help it get these things. It's to convince it that we are *safe*. Nothing more."

The lizard swallowed the last of the antelope, tilting its neck upwards and letting the meal slide down with a thick *glorp*. It reminded Sayana of how it swallowed the healer in that village on the clifftop, and she shuddered.

"How long will that take?" she asked.

"Yes, because I've clearly done this before, and know everything there is to know about taming *araatan*."

Sayana missed the days when they'd kept her gagged. Those were simpler times.

Tuya sighed. When she spoke again, she sounded more thoughtful. "It's not going to die from rot, but it's still in pain. If we can provide it with food, then it might – *might* – let us get close to it again. If . . . oh, shit."

The lizard was turning. And this time, it wasn't just studying them from a distance. It was walking back over.

"The beastie approaches," Khun sang.

"We're aware." Sayana took a quick step back, only for Tuya to reach out and grab her upper arm.

The eagle hunter hissed out of the side of her mouth. "Don't. Move."

Which was the least-likely-to-be-followed advice Sayana had ever been given.

The *araatan*'s head swayed from side to side as it limped over, eyes glimmering in the torchlight. Khun was moving, soft footsteps as she stalked along the rock ledge.

If they took off now, they might be able to make it into the passage. But even as Sayana had the thought, the lizard came within fire-breathing distance. All it had to do was let loose a single puff of breath, and that was it.

Ten feet became five. Three.

The lizard's breath on Sayana's skin: hot and damp, making her think of blood and swamp water. The scales on its face were much smaller than the ones that covered its body, and they were a different shape: regular, knobbly, little diamonds, instead of flat, uneven rectangles. Its mouth was closed, but it was all too easy to picture the teeth behind it, rimmed with saliva.

There was a moment when Sayana thought it was going to focus on Tuya, but no, it was coming straight for her, and she had to work very hard to keep her bladder in check.

The *araatan* sniffed Sayana: big, wet snorts, running its nose up and down her body, inches away. It let out a single, soft growl, and that nearly made her turn tail and run right then. She could tell herself that she was ready to die for their lives as raiders as much as she liked, but she would prefer it didn't happen in here.

Despite herself, she looked up. Right into its eye.

For the second time, she marvelled at the way it glimmered in the torch flame. With more light, the yellow iris was a deeper shade. It reminded Sayana of grass in late summer, the tips bronzed to a dry gold.

There was an instant where the eyes looked almost human. There was no intelligence behind them, not exactly: just an awareness. As if it was seeing Sayana for the first time.

The lizard gave off another thunderous snort, then turned away. It happened in the space of a second, the beast's massive tail dragging in the dirt behind it, passing just short of Sayana's feet.

She hadn't inhaled for a while, and it felt really good when she did. She looked over at Tuya; there was the ghost of a smile on the hunter's face. Not quite the level of what Sayana had seen at the pool yesterday, but it still sent a dazzling little jolt through her.

Despite her sarcasm, despite the simmering resentment in her eyes whenever she spoke to Sayana, she was . . .

The words wouldn't come. But it did make Sayana wonder what Tuya was like when she was off by herself, in the mountains. Just her, and her eagle. Not a single other person around. How did she stand? Did the lines on her forehead smooth out?

Some people used a smile as a tool. A weapon. Chimeg was a little like that, actually. But with others, their smile . . . it gave you a glimpse into who they were at their best.

It wasn't even that Tuya buried that smile, or tried to hide it. She couldn't, not with how she was around animals. But you could tell it didn't come out often.

Tuya held her gaze for an instant longer, then looked away. Sayana had the wildest urge to reach out, touch her cheek.

What the fuck am I doing?

A tiny huff of a laugh escaped her, barely audible. She shifted, letting her hand slide off the hilt of her sabre.

In the space of an eye blink, the lizard turned back, and lunged. There was no warning growl. No roar. Just sudden, looming *teeth*.

This time, Sayana reacted first. She grabbed Tuya and pulled both of them backwards, crashing to the ground as the lizard's jaws snapped shut in the space they'd been in an instant before.

The next few seconds were a yelling, panicked scramble as they bolted for the entrance, hot breath urging them on, and *now* the beast was growling, the sound filling the air like a million angry bees. At any second, Sayana was expecting that breath to suddenly *burn*, for the world behind them to fill with fire.

But the lizard didn't follow them into the passage. When Sayana dared to look back over her shoulder, it was turning away again. Stalking over to the far side of the cave, where there were still a few scraps of antelope meat scattered across the floor.

She watched until she was absolutely sure it wasn't going to come at them again. Blood rushing through her veins so hard that she felt like she was going to black out.

Hands on her shoulders. Then Tuya slammed her against the wall of the passage, face twisted in an angry snarl. "What is *wrong* with you?"

Khun was there. Sayana had no idea how she'd even managed to exit the cave; she appeared from thin air, knife held to Tuya's throat.

Tuya didn't even notice, eyes blazing with fury. "No sudden movements. I told you. What is it going to take for you to listen?"

"I didn't *make* any sudden . . ."

But she had. She'd dropped her hand off her sabre. But how could that possibly have triggered the lizard? It hadn't even been *looking* at her . . .

"Get this straight." Tuya's teeth were gritted so hard it was amazing she didn't pull a muscle. "You have to be predictable. You *cannot* surprise it, not ever, and definitely not if you want it to trust you."

She smacked Khun's hand away without looking, and abruptly headed up the passage in the direction of the waterfall.

Sayana's voice was a choked gasp. "Where are you going?"

"To get another antelope."

The tunnel fell silent, with nothing but the sound of Tuya's receding footsteps. Sayana's face was rich with sweat. "You all right, Khun?"

Khun beamed, absently sawing at a lock of her hair with the knife. "Oh yes!" She cut off the end, rolled it in her fingers for a moment, then stored it carefully inside her *deel*. "I'm having a *wonderful* time."

Without another word, she skipped off, following Tuya.

"Right," Sayana muttered, suddenly feeling very alone.

She closed her eyes, sagging back against the damp rock wall.

This is never going to work.

Twenty-Seven

Hogelun

It was probably a bad idea to go for a swim when there was an *araatan* nearby, but Hogelun couldn't help it.

It had taken her all day just to track down a measly little herd of antelope for that stupid lizard. She'd been sweaty and itchy, and in the late-afternoon sunlight, the pool looked like it had been placed there specifically to tempt her.

Chimeg had told her to keep one antelope back to feed the Rakada. Hogelun had kept sneaking glances at the pool while she gutted their kill, and eventually, she'd decided: *fuck it*.

It was heavenly cool under the water. Hogelun spun for a few seconds, feet in silky mud, blowing bubbles out of her nose. Then she came up in a burst of spray, rivulets running down her bald head.

Not that she planned to stay in here for long. She cast a nervous glance at the waterfall; it wasn't that she expected the *araatan* to come bursting through at this precise moment, but best to keep an eye out all the same.

The Rakada had set up camp a ways back from the pool, at the edge of the trees. Chimeg had gone to dig a latrine pit, which was something that had always impressed Hogelun. Anybody who volunteered to dig a big hole so that others could shit in it was clearly a person of quality.

Erhi sat cross-legged on a rock near the edge of the pool, carving arrows. She always took as many as she could from whoever they raided, but pickings had been mighty slim lately. A hummingbird flitted near her head, fat from summer wildflower nectar, hovering for a moment before zooming away.

"You should have a dip." Hogelun plopped down on the rock next to Erhi, splattering it with water. "It feels amazing, when you get used to it."

Erhi gave her a thin smile, went back to carving.

Hogelun barely noticed. For the first time in weeks – months, even – she actually felt good. And why not? Decisions had been made, a course set, Erhi was . . . well, less pissed with her. Yes, there was the *araatan*, out of sight behind the falls, but if it did decide to come thundering out again, Hogelun had a decent head start.

Erhi stopped carving for a moment, laid the arrow across her thighs as she took a drink of water from a skin. Hogelun tilted her own head up, basking in the suns' rays. Behind closed eyelids, the world was lit up in reds and yellows. Delicious, shifting shades of orange.

"What would you rather be?" she asked, hands moving automatically. "A fox or a tiger?"

She squinted at Erhi in the bright sunslight, but the archer was staring into space, her arrow forgotten. Hogelun brushed her knee, then repeated the question. "Because I figure, a tiger sounds good at first, because nobody messes with you, and you look gorgeous. But foxes just seem like they have more *fun*, you know?"

Erhi puffed out her cheeks. *I don't know. I'll think about it.* She toyed with the arrow in her lap but didn't move to finish it.

Hogelun's heart sunk a bit. Surely Erhi couldn't still be angry with her? After their little blow-up on the clifftop?

She began to sign the question. Erhi stopped her with a hand on her thigh, a small smile on her face. *We're fine. Not everything's about you, you know.*

"Then what is it?"

Erhi waved at the waterfall. *It just feels wrong.*

Hogelun snorted. "Which bit?"

Using my medicine like this.

"What do you mean?"

When I trained as a healer ... Erhi's movements were hesitant. Awkward. *They told us it was a sacred art. Our knowledge meant we had an obligation to keep the people around us alive.* She rolled her eyes. *A lot of it was nonsense – we had this one instructor who wanted us to believe Father Sky himself had chosen us to become healers, instead of just the recruiters.*

She ran a finger along the half-formed arrow. *It's not sacred, what I do. It's just chemistry. Properties of roots and herbs and types of earth. But I learned to help humans, not* ...

Again, she waved at the waterfall. Khun and Tuya were just emerging, making their way down the rocks.

No sign of the Princess. She probably hadn't been eaten, otherwise Khun might be moving with a touch more urgency. Maybe. You never knew with Khun.

Hogelun frowned. "I don't get it. You offered that sleep goop to the Princess yourself. *And* your magic anti-rot stuff."

I had no idea if it would work. If I'd suggested using my healing on an araatan *when I was training, my instructors would have thrown me out.*

"But isn't it good? That it works?"

Her answer was a see-sawing hand. *This is a me thing. Like, imagine if you cooked that antelope* — Erhi nodded at the carcass, hanging from a tree a short distance away — *with some herbs and some rock salt, got it really crispy and juicy* . . .

She let her hands rest, a dreamy look in her eyes.

"Bit hungry then?" Hogelun asked.

Well, I am now. Erhi shook her head. *But imagine if you did all that, and the rest of us got together and decided to feed it to a wolf, and the wolf liked it.*

"What are you on about? Obviously a wolf would love that."

What I'm trying to say is . . .

"I'd have packs of them following me around, hoping for more." Hogelun grinned. "Actually, that sounds lovely, having a bunch of wolves doing what I tell them. You think that would work?"

There was a flash of irritation on Erhi's face. *Hogelun. You need to be quiet and listen to what I'm saying.*

Hogelun knotted her fingers in her lap. *Just a joke,* she thought — but didn't say. She felt small, suddenly, without fully understanding why.

Erhi scooted around until she was facing Hogelun, still sitting cross-legged. *Point is, you'd be annoyed. You didn't set out to cook for a wolf, even if the wolf ended up enjoying it.*

"I do see what you're saying, but . . . this is good, right? It'll help the Princess make it out alive. And if another *araatan* comes at us, just put it to sleep. Win-win."

Erhi smiled. *You seem pretty calm about being so close. To the* araatan, *I mean.*

Hogelun wondered about that. There *was* the familiar twitch of fear as she did so, the deep-down jolt of anxiety at being this close to the *araatan*. But . . .

Before she could follow this thought, Tuya walked up. The eagle hunter looked exhausted, dark circles under her eyes.

"Going well, then?" Hogelun said.

"We need another antelope." Tuya squinted in the bright light.

Chimeg was back in the camp, doing something with her saddle. Hogelun gestured at the other two carcasses, stacked nearby. "Help yourself."

"We're going to need more. You understand that, yes?"

Hogelun leaned back, arms straight, peering up at this person who was supposed to be their prisoner but apparently thought she could dish out commands. Behind Tuya, the Princess was coming down the rocks, and even from this distance, she didn't look happy.

"You want to try hunt more than three antelope in a day, be my guest." Hogelun scratched her scalp. "We'll get some more tomorrow, so——"

She could tell Erhi had spotted something. The archer had tensed, leaning forward slightly on the rock.

There were figures emerging from the trees at the far side of the pool, all on horseback. Hogelun counted eight. No, ten.

Erhi sprung to her feet, and Hogelun followed, hissing a curse. Her club was behind her, too far away, leaning against a tree next to Erhi's bow. They'd let their guard down. Surely Tuya's sister hadn't found them already? There's no way they would have——

"Hold." Chimeg appeared between Erhi and Hogelun, hand raised.

The dark figures resolved themselves. Six men and four women, dressed in a motley collection of yellow *deels* and worn leather. They were led by a stick-insect of a man, even taller than the Princess, with a few wisps of greying hair clinging to a bald head. Someone – possibly a small child, or a blind person – had drawn what was supposed to be a human hand on his forehead with black pigment.

"Ugh," said Sayana, materialising on Hogelun's left. She had both of her sabres out, but let them fall by her sides. "*These* arseholes."

The Rakada weren't the only clan in the Tapestry to try and cultivate a legend around them. The problem with the Black Hands was, they weren't actually very good at it. They were clumsy, undisciplined and only about one out of every three raids actually got them what they wanted.

Their leader, with the bad comb-over, was Oktai. He'd managed to keep them together over the years, mostly by dishing out harsh punishments to anyone who stood up to him. Also by ensuring that no one in his clan was smarter than he was; given that he was as mentally agile as a bag of rocks, that was actually quite an achievement.

"Well." He beamed at the Rakada. The effect was ruined by his few remaining teeth. "This looks cosy."

"Did you want something, Oktai?" Chimeg asked. The Chief hadn't even bothered to unsheathe her spear.

Oktai scratched the underside of his chin. "Just the usual. Some water for our horses, maybe some river roots if there's any left. Oh, and whatever food and supplies you happen to have with you."

"Hmm." Chimeg pretended to consider this, lifting her eyes to the clouds as if asking Father Sky for his opinion. "No."

Oktai gestured to the rest of the Black Hands. "Sorry, I should have realised you'd never learned how to count. There's more of us than there are of you."

The Rakada Chief shrugged. "So I see."

One of the other Black Hands – a woman with a nasty-looking

cut on her jawbone that had a mild dose of the rot – hopped off her horse and darted forward, hissing in Oktai's ear. The two of them had a whispered conversation, with many glances in the Rakada's direction. Chimeg waited patiently.

Oktai waved the woman away, trying and failing to disguise his annoyance. "I wasn't clear," he said to Chimeg, speaking as if she were the five-year-old who'd drawn the hand on his face. "More of us means we can just kill you and take what we want."

Hogelun cocked her head. "Does it, though?"

There was a moment where she thought he really was going to try it. Which would have been deeply annoying: Hogelun had been having a decent afternoon, all things considered, and she didn't want to ruin it by killing people. Still, at least they'd have plenty of food for the *araatan* then . . .

She winced. Probably a bad idea to give the beast humans to eat if you were trying to get it not to eat *you*.

Oktai's shoulders slumped, just a tiny bit. He chuckled, as if this was what he had planned all along. "Ah, that's all right. Just seeing if you still had the stones, you know?"

He sucked his teeth, studying them, hands on his hips. "Bone Raiders, eh?" he said, to no one in particular. "I do a bit of bone raiding myself, from time to time." He grabbed his crotch at this, and in case they missed his meaning, gave a couple of thrusts as well.

"Wow." Hogelun turned to the Princess. "That's clever. You ever hear that one, Sayana?"

"No." The Princess widened her eyes. "Not sure I get it, either. Whatever could he mean, Hogs?"

"Bone!" Khun suddenly shouted. She stalked over to Oktai – she was at least a foot and a half shorter than he was, but it didn't stop him from taking a startled step back. She pulled a human rib from somewhere, and waved it in his face, inches from his nose. *"BONE?!?"*

Hogelun actually pitied Oktai. No one should have to deal with Khun without proper training.

Chimeg folded her arms. "Look, Oktai, we're busy here. You can water your horses, but then it would be delightful if you and your . . . your little *gang* would fuck off."

Khun was still menacing Oktai with the rib. He beat a hasty retreat, climbing back onto his horse.

"Surprised you're sticking around yourselves," he shouted to Chimeg. "Heard you kicked a hornets' nest."

His gaze landed on Tuya. It occurred to Hogelun, a little too late, that the hunter could have run if she wanted. Snuck off somehow, while the Rakada were distracted.

But she hadn't.

Chimeg sounded bored. "And where did you hear that?"

Oktai gave her another one of those disgusting grins. "I hear all sorts of things. Lots of information around, if you know where to dig it out."

Hogelun had to work hard to keep her face neutral. This was the closest they'd come to confirming that Yesuntei was, in fact, hunting for them. And if Oktai really had worked out what was going on, there was every chance he'd just sell them out.

The Chief had gone very still. The kind of stillness that usually meant things were about to get very ugly, very fast.

Oktai actually laughed. "Relax, Chimeg. I like being a raider, and I like being alive. Pretty sure that if I *did* whisper in that bitch's ear, at least one of those things would stop. She's not the merciful type, even to those who help her."

He puffed out his cheeks. "I don't really care very much, to be honest. We're heading for the desert. Us, and some other clans.

Arkan's people, the Skyflame, Red Jackals, couple of others. Tapestry's turning to shit these days."

"Not much in the desert either," Chimeg said, only barely moving her lips.

Hogelun puffed her cheeks. There *were* nomads in the Great Desert to the west – more than a few groups eked out a living there. But it wasn't much of a life. If you didn't fall into a sinkhole or end up choked to death in a sandstorm, it was only because you'd already got lost and died of thirst.

"Least we won't have the fucking army hunting us everywhere." For the first time, bitterness crept into Oktai's smile. He spat, the gob of saliva splashing into the pool.

Hogelun stared in mild horror; she'd been looking forward to another swim.

"Hard enough out here as it is," Oktai went on. "And the more of us there are, the better chance we'll have."

Is this really what they'd decided? To abandon the Tapestry? Had it got so bad that they'd willingly choose the desert?

The woman with the jaw wound piped up. "You could come," she told the Rakada. "We're meeting the others in ten days, in the Broken Valley. Then all of us—"

"*Solmon.*" Oktai probably imagined his growl was commanding, but it came out as more of a squawk. Solmon bowed her head, but Hogelun picked up a significant eye roll.

"Forgive her," Oktai said, turning back to the Chief. "She didn't really think that one through. Sorry about this, Chimeg, but the rest of us have no desire to fuck with Yesuntei. That's *your* problem, and I'd prefer you didn't bring it to the rest of us."

Translation: stay the fuck away from the Broken Valley.

Hogelun gave an eye roll of her own. Nasty place, that: she had no desire to head back there, for any reason.

Oktai jerked his chin at the waterfall. "We've hidden out

in there a few times. Not a bad spot, all told, although it won't be enough to save you when that bitch from Karkorum comes riding up. Unless you've got a pet *araatan* or two stashed in there, or something."

The Rakada said nothing.

Abruptly, Oktai spun his horse. "Always good to see you, Chimeg. And all the best of luck with your Yesuntei problem." He flicked a finger at the sky. "Hope you sent a few prayers in his direction lately. You're going to need all the help you can get."

Twenty-Eight

Sayana

The *araatan* had stopped eating.

Stopped doing much of anything, actually.

It lay against its chosen stalagmite, curled into a tense ball. Sayana would have thought it was impossible for something with legs that tall and chunky to actually curl up; then again, the word *impossible* wasn't a feature of her life much these days.

Other than an occasional growl, the damn thing might have been dead. It was the morning after the beast almost took her head off, and any hope they had of making progress had shrunk to almost nothing.

It was hot in the cave — hot, and muggy. Sayana and Tuya sat on the shelf of rock, their legs over the edge. They'd both shucked their *deels*, which were bunched around their waists. Sayana had always thought her arms were nicely toned, but Tuya put her to shame. She watched a trickle of sweat run down Tuya's right bicep, pool in the crook of her elbow.

"What?" Tuya said, noticing Sayana staring.

"Nothing."

Khun squatted nearby, clacking two small rocks together. Not tapping out a beat, just making little, irregular, maddening taps, interspersed with the occasional apocalyptic mutter.

"Is it sick?" Sayana asked Tuya. She'd been trying not to put that out into the open, but there it was anyway. "The rot?"

Tuya chewed her lip. "The wound looks fine, at least from here. Then again, like I keep telling you, I'm not an expert."

If the lizard *was* dying, if Erhi's medicine hadn't been enough to save it, then maybe they'd be better off getting out while they still could. Finding another *araatan* . . .

But after all they'd been through, the thought of doing this again – finding another cave, hoping a lizard was home, risking horrifying, violent death as they started from the beginning – was just too much for Sayana to deal with right now. Not to mention Yesuntei getting closer and closer.

"Do you think maybe it just . . . I don't know, doesn't like antelope?" Sayana said. "Got tired of it?"

"Don't be stupid." Tuya didn't have the energy to actually sound annoyed. "They're not picky."

"Maybe we should try something different anyway. Erhi says she saw a herd of wild horses to the south of here."

Tuya waved at the passage. "Be my guest."

Tap. Taptaptap. Taptap . . . tap.

"Khun." Sayana spoke through gritted teeth. "Please stop th—"

Khunbish shrieked, leaping into the air and hurling a stone at Sayana. It struck her on the shoulder, hard enough to sting.

"*Woah*—" Tuya ducked, scrunching her head down.

Sayana stared at Khun, rubbing her shoulder. "What in the nine hells was *that* for?"

"Sorry." Khun held up her hands. "I forgot you were here. You startled me."

"You *forgot* I was *here*?"

Tuya lifted her gaze to the ceiling. "We're doomed," she muttered.

Sayana snorted. Tuya stared at her for a beat, then gave out a low murmur of a laugh. Their eyes met briefly; Sayana looked away first, as the *araatan* sent out another low, rumbling growl.

The stone Khun threw had a sharp point, and it had nicked the skin of Sayana's shoulder, a dot of blood welling up. Her thigh had healed up to the point she barely noticed the itch now, so she guessed she was due for another injury.

She should go outside, stick her shoulder in the waterfall, rinse out the wound. Maybe grab some of that anti-rot stuff from Erhi, because even a small cut could turn bad if you let it. That's just what they needed: both an *araatan* and a Rakada down with the—

Her eyes went wide.

Waterfall.

"When did it last have something to drink?" she said.

Tuya rubbed her eyes. "Sorry?"

"The *araatan*. When did it last have any water?"

"I don't know. I wasn't . . . where are you going?"

But Sayana was already scrabbling down the slope, heading for the passage.

Chimeg was the only Rakada in the camp when she made her way down. The Chief was repairing a damaged saddle, eyes narrowed in concentration. "Do we have anything that could hold water?" Sayana asked, breathless from her scramble down the rocks.

"Yes," the Chief said, without looking up. "They're called skins."

"No, bigger. Something that could carry a lot of it."

"Why?"

"*Chief!*"

"All right, calm down. We've got some spare fabric for the *ger*, that might do it." She waved at their supplies, stacked in neat piles over by a nearby tree. "Certainly keeps out the rain, but what are you—"

Sayana didn't hear the rest. She tore through their goods until she found the thick, rough fabric. There were three patches, rolled up tight. Big circles, four feet across, enough to repair any holes in their tent. She grabbed one that didn't have smaller bits cut out of it and sprinted for the falls, ignoring Chimeg's questions.

Tuya was outside the entrance to the cave when Sayana got there. Sayana braced for the onslaught of questions – only, Tuya didn't ask any. Her eyes were shining, and without a word, she grabbed the trailing end of the patch and helped Sayana hold it under the rushing water.

Which turned out to be a spectacularly bad idea, because the waterfall nearly wrenched it out of their hands.

Somehow, they managed to hold on, crimping the edges until they had a makeshift vessel. It was heavy, dripping water, Sayana's hands screaming at her from trying to hold onto the wet fabric. But together, they somehow managed to manoeuvre it into the passage.

Khun met them halfway down. "You can come back, I promise I won't throw anything else at y—"

"Get big rocks," Sayana hissed, through gritted teeth.

The older Rakada pondered this. "You want me to throw bigger rocks at you?"

"*No*, Khun, just get a bunch of rocks and put them in front of the lizard."

A thought occurred, a nasty one: they were about to make a lot of fast, unfamiliar movements in front of a creature that had shown, more than once, that it didn't appreciate things moving in fast and unfamiliar ways.

Then again, the *araatan* was different today. Like it had no energy. There was a chance they were wrong . . . but Sayana didn't think so.

It took long minutes, and lots of standing around with arms straining while Khun built a circle of rocks in the middle of the cave. The *araatan* watched, silent, and Sayana tried not to think about what would happen if it decided to attack at this particular moment.

It didn't. And eventually, after much swearing and cursing of Father Sky's name, Sayana and Tuya lowered the miraculously-still-half-full vessel into the circle. The rocks propped up the edges, keeping the water in place.

Sayana's arms felt like they'd been filled with wet sand. She and Tuya backed up, moving over to the cave entrance.

A full minute went by, and still, the *araatan* didn't move.

Sayana's heart sunk. What the fuck did the beast *want*, then?

She stared at the thing, willing it to react. For once, she wasn't scared at all. She had discovered, to her surprise, that it was very hard to be both terrified of something and annoyed by it; it really was one or the other. Useful info, to be sure, but that didn't give them any idea of what . . .

But then, the lizard unfolded itself. Sniffed the air, looked in the direction of the vessel. Grunted once, lumbered over to it, and lowered its massive head. It didn't drink like a dog, lapping with its tongue; instead, its giant mouth opened and closed, slurping in water in thick gulps.

In seconds, the vessel was empty. The *araatan* sniffed it, then turned and retreated. Halfway back to its stalagmite, it stopped, swinging its head from side to side. One yellow eye found Sayana, blinking slowly.

"More." She had no desire to wrestle with the falls again, but they had to keep going. "We need more."

"I will help," said Khun.

Three times, they brought the lizard water. Three times, it drank its fill, and only on the fourth did it turn away from the vessel, sniffing it once before retreating. The three of them were dripping sweat. Sayana wasn't even sure her arms were attached to her body any more.

The *araatan* settled back by the stalagmite, scratching its side with its hind leg once, then lay still.

Tuya gave Sayana an exhausted nudge. "Good . . . thinking. I should have . . . figured that out."

As she pulled back, their hands brushed. Very slightly, for a single instant.

Sayana glanced up, without really meaning to. Tuya wasn't looking at her; she was staring intently at the *araatan*. The corners of her mouth turned very slightly upward.

Water droplets in the air, glittering like jewels. Tuya smiling, joy on her face . . .

Khun tapped a finger on the side of Sayana's head, knocking her out of her thoughts. "I don't understand how its brain works. The waterfall is just there. It could have gone whenever it wanted."

All Sayana could do is shrug. She had no idea why the *araatan* hadn't gone to find water on its own. Maybe the rot really was setting in. Then again, if it was, there was nothing they could do about it.

But on the heels of that thought came a more startling one: she didn't want the *araatan* to die.

And not just because she wanted to ride it one day.

This thing, this beast, survived a fall off a cliff, and what must have been a hellish journey downriver to this cave. It was hungry, and scared, and it had lost the only home it had ever known when it was forced to leave the mountains. It was just doing what it could to survive. It deserved to live.

Like the Rakada did.

"All right." Tuya's voice was a croak. She linked her fingers, stretched her arms overhead, face contorting. "Let's just . . . just give it a minute. Then we can . . ."

Except: the *araatan* didn't need a minute.

It got to its feet, snuffling at the ground, its back to them. Then, in a long, languorous movement, tail bumping against the stalagmite, it turned and began plodding back in their direction.

"Still thirsty, I think," Khun murmured. Except: the *araatan* ignored the bowl. Marched right past it.

The three of them stood very still. The lizard had a piece of shredded antelope flesh between its jaws, a morsel it must have scooped off the floor. The distant noise of the waterfall seemed louder then, filling up the cavern, hissing in Sayana's ears.

When it was a few feet away, the beast opened its mouth, and let the shred of meat drop to the floor. Then, without a second glance, it turned away. Headed back the way it came.

Sayana jumped when Tuya grabbed hold of her upper arm, squeezing hard. The eagle hunter looked as if someone smacked her in the head. "It shared its meal."

Sayana opened her mouth to speak, but no sound came out.

"It shouldn't be doing that." Tuya spoke more to herself than Sayana. "It's . . . it's a reptile. They aren't pack animals. It shouldn't even understand what we *are*."

Khun flashed an evil grin. "It likes you," she said, nudging Tuya hard in the ribs. The *araatan* had curled up again, its back to them.

Sayana's throat woke up, finally. "We gave it water, didn't we?"

"You're not listening." Slowly, Tuya crouched, never taking her eyes off the *araatan*. "It takes months — *years* — to build that kind of trust. You have to do the same thing over and over and over. This lizard . . . it's making connections. I've never seen that before. Even when I trained Ayanga . . . that bird's one of the smartest creatures I've ever seen, but he wouldn't even let me get close for a whole season."

"So we can do it?" Sayana asked. "We can ride it?"

Tuya barked a laugh. "Don't get your hopes up there. There's a big difference between this thing sharing its meal, and actually listening to instructions. That's going to take time."

Abruptly, she stood, heading for the rock shelf on the other side of the cavern.

"Where are you going?" Sayana called after her.

"I need to think."

Before Sayana could reply, there was a whistle from inside the passage. Chimeg's face was just visible in the torchlight.

"Go," Khun said. "I will keep an eye on the animal witch. I will peer into her soul."

The animal witch in question looked a million miles away, perched on the edge of the rock shelf, studying the still form of the *araatan*.

"Chief," Sayana said, when she caught up with her on the rocks next to the waterfall. "You won't believe what just happened—"

"We're heading out for a while." Chimeg gestured to the edge of the pond, where Hogelun and Erhi were busy with the horses.

"Heading out . . . where?"

"Now that we know Yesuntei's after us for sure, we need to get ahead of her. And unless you think we can all decamp to somewhere else with your lizard friend . . . "

She gave Sayana a meaningful look, letting the question hang in the air.

"No," Sayana said. "But Chief, we—"

"I'm not planning to sit here and wait for Yesuntei to come riding up on her schedule. Time to make her think we're somewhere else." She sniffed, nodded, as if that settled it. "We'll be back in a few days. You and Khun stay here, keep working. And stay hidden – last thing we want is someone catching you idiots out in the open."

"What are you going to do?"

Chimeg's lip curled in an evil smile. "We're raiders, Sayana. We're going on a raid."

Twenty-Nine

Hogelun

Bad idea, Erhi signed.

Hogelun shifted in her saddle. "We haven't seen anyone else in *three days.* My arse is—"

If you mention the blisters on your arse one more time, I'm going to knock you on it.

Chimeg said nothing, just gazed sourly at the northern horizon.

The three Rakada were on a low hill, and the landscape ahead was the kind of thing Hogelun loved. Or would, if her backside wasn't so raw. Below them, the wind rolled in languorous waves through the long grass, all the way to the mountains in the north – closer now, much closer, but still nothing more than dark shapes.

Father Sky was showing off. To the east, there was nothing but brilliant blue skies. To the west: a titanic thunderstorm, an absolute monster, mercifully far in the distance. A rolling hellbroth of black cloud and cracking yellow lightning. A river – one of the Western Mogoi's hundred tributaries – snaked its way through the grass between the Rakada and the mountains, running from the clear skies to the storm clouds. Wide, lazy, sinuous, reflecting the suns so brightly that it was hard to look at.

And on the southern bank, just visible: a wagon train.

The four wagons were connected, a pair of horses between each one, with a cohort of strong animals at the front. That meant it was army, because they were the only ones stubborn enough to do it that way. It was always much smarter to keep your wagons separate, so you could fan out if you had to.

Bad design or not, there was a reason the Rakada didn't raid wagon trains. Multiple reasons, actually. For one thing, they moved fast. Say what you wanted about small villages, but at least they tended to stay still.

Plus, the trains were usually packed with soldiers. They ferried supplies and equipment from Karkorum out to distant encampments, or brought resources back to the city from the mines. Even before the new Khan started tearing the Tapestry to pieces, the army didn't take kindly to being attacked.

"He's going to hit the storm." Chimeg pointed, tracking the path the wagon train was taking. "Even if he cuts south now, it'll still roll right over him. Fucking amateur."

"It is *not* a bad idea," Hogelun told Erhi. The train was turning south now, as if the pilot had finally twigged that he was about to ride into a storm that could turn the wagons to splinters. "The whole point of this raid is so that that Yesuntei bitch thinks we're operating up here, instead of at the falls. What difference does it make if it's a village or a wagon train or a couple of nomads on a single sick horse if—"

Numbers.

"I . . . what?"

Erhi didn't quite roll her eyes, but the sullen look on her face said it all. She'd been like this ever since they'd left the falls, lost in her own head, like she'd rather be doing anything but this. Hogelun had kind of been hoping that hunting for a raid target would give Erhi some of her fire back.

But the further they'd got from the others, the more silent and brooding the archer had become. Hogelun had caught her staring sullenly at Chimeg, whenever their leader's back was turned – something she couldn't remember ever seeing Erhi do.

The three of us attacking a train won't do any good. Erhi's hand movements were jerky, impatient. *We don't have the numbers to make a dent. Which means the pilot and the soldiers send us packing, laugh it off as an inconvenience. Maybe this particular story doesn't spread, or takes too long to.*

She shrugged. *With five of us, we could pincer attack it, maybe take down a couple of soldiers, disconnect one of the wagons. With just three, it's impossible.*

Chimeg wasn't looking at Erhi. She was studying the horizon, chewing gently on her bottom lip.

"But . . . " Hogelun said, desperate. "This . . . it's the whole reason we're out here!"

You're not listening. You never listen. Erhi pointed at the distant wagons. *The Chief and I were army once. We know how these things work. They don't put raw recruits on wagon trains – those are career soldiers only. They know how to fight.*

"Yeah, I get that." Again, that *small* feeling. And irritation, too, as much at herself as Erhi; she should have known this, she *did* know it. She'd just . . . just forgotten. Hadn't been thinking.

Erhi clicked her tongue, turned Windwalker. *We'll track east, see if there's a settlement along the river. No way we're hitting these wagons.*

Hogelun – stewing, sore, hungry, arse cheeks burning – was too exhausted to reply. She nudged Hoof Monster with a foot, turning him too.

"Yeah, he'll still hit the storm, no matter what he does," Chimeg murmured. She still hadn't moved.

The other two stopped. Hogelun cocked her head. "Uh . . . we know?"

She looked over at the storm, without intending to. It was a monster. Sheets of pounding rain were visible, even at this distance. No hail, not with the clouds that shape – you got used to reading storms out on the grass – but the lightning strikes alone would be enough to blow you out of your boots.

Slowly, Chimeg turned to them. A very small and *very* sly smile spreading across her face.

When she told them what she wanted to do, Hogelun just gaped at her. "That's—"

"Insane. I understand that."

"We'd—"

"Yep."

"But what if—"

"It's worth the risk." The Chief reached into her saddlebag. "Get your bones on."

Hogelun's own hands were moving before she could stop herself. Chimeg was right: the idea was utterly mad. But it was a billion times better than passing the wagon train by and hunting for another settlement, so fuck it, if they could . . .

She paused. Erhi was staring into the distance, mouth tight, slowly shaking her head.

"Erhi?" Chimeg was holding a jawbone, hovering it above her sleeve. "Got something to say?"

It took Erhi a few moments to start signing. *You know, you've been saying yes to a lot of bad ideas lately, Chief. Never thought you'd be pushing out some of your own.*

Hogelun goggled at her. Erhi and Chimeg had always seemed

like they could read each other's minds – no, more than that, like they were one mind split between two bodies.

"Excuse me?" Chimeg said mildly.

You go along with the Princess when she forces our hand, instead of exiling her like you should have. Then, you leave her behind with that eagle hunter when all of us should be working together to fight Yesuntei. Erhi jerked her chin at the wagon train. *And now this.*

"This is the best option under the circumstances." Chimeg sounded like she couldn't believe she was even having this conversation. And Hogelun had spent enough time around Erhi and Chimeg to recognise when one of them was signing with particular care and intent.

Erhi ignored her Chief. *I told you I'd always follow you. But I also told you I wouldn't do it blind. I get that you're the Chief, and normally? I'd follow your orders. But when two out of the three of us know that order's going to get us killed—*

"Uh, I think it's a good idea, actually." Hogelun heard herself say the words, but it was as if they were coming from somebody else.

Erhi ignored her. Straight up didn't even look at her. *Then it's time to consider if what you're saying makes sense.*

For no reason at all, Khun's voice popped into Hogelun's head – like the little psychopath was right there with her. *You fear choosing. You fear it so much that you will let us ride into the dark. You hope that your lover will choose for you, or your Chieftain, or the Gods.*

Chimeg started to sign again – something about how Erhi needed to simmer down – but Hogelun got there first. She waved her arms wildly – which didn't make a lick of sense, because Erhi was five feet away, not fifty, but whatever. "Hey. Hi. I can talk for myself, thank you."

There was a very strange sensation prickling up and down her spine. Like someone jabbing a tiny, thin needle, a thousand times a second. Strange . . . but somehow, welcome. She almost shivered, but whichever part of her had the reins wouldn't let her do it. "I'm with the Chief. We can take the wagon train, if we're smart about it."

The most startling thing happened to Erhi's face. It went through three or four emotions in half a second: surprise, anger, confusion . . . and a hurt, stunned look that nearly made Hogelun take back what she'd said. It made her feel like there was a heavy piece of metal in her stomach, twisted and rusty, corrosive. For a horrible half-second, she was certain Erhi was going to tell her to leave, that she never wanted to see Hogelun again.

But then Erhi's face softened. She closed her eyes, lifted her hands in an apology.

You're right. I don't speak for you. That wasn't fair of me to say. But listen . . . She turned to the Chief. *This isn't smart. If we get killed, then Khun and Sayana will never know.*

Chimeg digested this. After a moment, she reached out, put a hand on Erhi's shoulder.

"Do you remember when you and I first left Karkorum?" she said, pulling her hands back and signing the words. Hogelun couldn't remember ever seeing Chimeg look so tired. Like every word was having to be dredged up from a deep well inside her.

Chief . . .

"I had no idea what to do. Just this . . . this half-arsed plan. If I didn't have you there, it would have gone to pieces, all of it. And it wasn't just that you trusted me: you let me trust *myself.*"

Chimeg rubbed the heel of a hand into her right eye. "We're having a . . . a tough go at the moment. I don't like any of it. But we're on this course, and I trust you − no, I trust *us* − to get this done."

She thumbed over her shoulder, at the storm and the wagon train. It had turned back towards the river now, as if the driver had given up trying to avoid the storm and was just going to power through. "Are you with me?"

Erhi's sign was immediate. *Of course.*

Hogelun felt like she had just missed a sabre strike, as if she'd ducked and felt it whistle past overhead. Her mind filled with a hundred possibilities, each more horrifying than the last, and each coming back to the same place: that momentary startled anger on Erhi's face, when Hogelun spoke for herself. An anger that said: *We're done.*

She shook it off. Fuck that. Erhi understood, apologised. End of discussion. Surely?

The three of them studied the distant wagon. The huge storm front, crackling with lightning.

Hogs, Erhi said. *You got any* airag *left?*

"A bit. Why?"

Well, if we're really going to do something this stupid, I feel like it would help to be hammered.

Hogelun tossed Erhi a skin. Then she rolled her shoulders, staring out across the grass.

This was going to be fun.

Thirty

Hogelun

Hogelun had to raise her voice to shout over the thundering rain. "This is the worst idea *ever*!"

"It'll be fine," Chimeg yelled back. At least, Hogelun thought that was what she'd said. She couldn't be sure because of all the bloody lightning strikes. The bolts detonated on the hills around them, booming across the grass.

The safest place to be when you encountered one of the thunderstorms that periodically slammed into the Tapestry was somewhere else. Preferably under cover, with a cup of *airag* and a warm blanket. But if a storm *did* catch you out in the open, then you made damn sure it was somewhere with high points that could attract the blistering lightning strikes.

Hoof Monster stamped his feet. He wasn't usually bothered by storms – none of their horses were – but even he seemed to sense that standing in the middle of one wasn't the smartest idea in the world.

Erhi shook her head, sending rivulets of water flying. She looked miserable, and Hogelun couldn't blame her. She'd been right about the storm not dropping hailstones, at least, but the rain was pounding so hard that it may as well have been.

The river sat on a wide flood plain, and the pilot – who clearly had *some* brains in his head, even if he was slow to use them – had wisely decided to turn away from it. Or maybe someone had told him that even if it was too late to avoid the storm, he should probably try to not be in an area prone to flooding when a million tons of water fell from the sky.

The Rakada had picked a clutch of rocky hills for their ambush, south of the flood plain, directly in the path of the wagons. They had to ride like all the demons of the nine hells were after them, too, to get there before the wagons did. Even then, Hogelun had worried that they might be too late.

But so far, no one had arrived – and it had been long enough to make Hogelun wonder if they'd made a giant mistake. She glanced at her Chief, not liking the grim expression on Chimeg's face.

The water was pooling, lapping at their horses' ankles, drowning the thin shrubs that clung to life at the base of the hills. Hogelun wiped droplets out of her eyes – and froze. Peered into the murk. She couldn't hear a damn thing, but there was a dark shape coming towards them.

Chimeg and Erhi saw it too. In the next instant, Hogelun caught the shape of the oncoming horses, the blocky form of the wagon beyond.

"Ready!" Chimeg shouted. The Chief bristled with jawbones strapped to her forearms and shoulders. Erhi's *deel* hung heavy: fingers and toes, arranged in intricate patterns.

Hogelun herself had a human ribcage wrapped around her chest – she'd had it for ages, and this seemed like a perfect opportunity to try it out. And of course, she had Tiny, her pet skull, squatting on her shoulder. Couldn't ride into battle without him now, could she?

None of them wore any paint, which would wash away in the rain – but with this many bones, it hardly made a difference.

Hogelun unsheathed her club, seated the haft in her hand.

Here we go.

Chimeg raised her spear, and she and Hogelun unleashed a furious howl. As one, the Rakada launched themselves directly at the wagons.

Raiding a train this size wasn't something the Rakada could usually do. There were just too many soldiers, too many ways to die horribly. Even with all five raiders, it would be a tall order. You had to find a way to scare the absolute piss out of them. To come from where they would least expect.

And three bone-clad raiders, riding directly at you out of a pounding thunderstorm, lit by lightning, weapons drawn, howling their heads off, their horses' hooves kicking up giant sprays of water and mud?

That would do it every time.

The wagon's horses saw them first. They were already spooked by the rain, by the pooling water under their hooves, and the sight of the Rakada put them over the edge. They pulled to one side, trying to get out of the way, eyes rolling. The pilot – a tiny man with a thin beard, perched on the wagon's running board – yanked at the reins in confusion.

A split second later, he spotted the Rakada.

Hogelun actually saw the bottom fall out of his mind. His eyes went huge, and he scrabbled backwards on the seat, dropping the reins in a panic and clawing his way up onto the roof of the wagon.

There was a soldier on the running board beside him, grey *deel* soaked, water streaming from his conical helmet. His reaction was a little less panicky, but only a little. As Hoof Monster reached the wagons, he drew his sabre, one hand on the edge of the roof for balance—

Erhi's arrow took him in the chest, and he toppled out of sight.

In seconds, the Rakada were past the wagons. As one, they swung their horses around, Hogelun squeezing her eyes shut as a lightning blast lit up the surrounding hills. The wagons themselves were swerving, the movement of the spooked horses at the front rolling back down the train.

An arrow split the air over Hogelun's head, vanishing into the dark. She didn't see who shot it, and didn't bother looking. As Erhi and Chimeg went right, she hooked left.

She really didn't like what had to happen next. Still, you couldn't scare the shit out of someone just by riding past them.

Hoof Monster wasn't keen on getting close to the wagons. Hogelun felt a tiny bit guilty about that, but she just didn't have the agility to leap from the saddle onto the wagons – like Erhi was doing at that very moment, the graceful bitch.

Dark shapes scurried over the wooden roofs, shouting orders lost in the hammering rain, trying to work out what in the fuck was happening. Hogelun got as close as she could, half standing in her saddle, grabbing hold of the rain-slick edge of a wagon roof. Grunting, she swung her outside leg over, getting a foothold on the running board.

Her toes slipped.

For a horrible, wild moment, her feet were kicking free in open air, the only connection to the wagon her screaming fingertips on the edge of the roof.

With a yelp, she flattened herself against the shuddering wood, hyperventilating, her toes only just resting on the running board. Hoof Monster, deciding that he'd had enough of this shit, accelerated away.

Find you later, boy.

Hogelun grunted as she began clambering along the side of

the wagon towards the rear. A head appeared over the edge of the roof, capped by a conical helmet. A sabre flashed down at Hogelun, but she was faster, grabbing a fist of *deel* and yanking. The man yelped as he flew over her head, flipping out of sight. The storm was so loud Hogelun didn't even hear him hit the ground.

She inched around the back corner of the wagon, finally getting an actual foothold on the running board, enough to climb onto the roof. The surface was gently sloped, the water streaming off it.

There were two archers there, both crouched, hunting for targets. Neither of them were looking at the rear of the wagon. Hogelun unsheathed her club, and in one movement, swept them both right off the side.

The swing nearly made her lose her balance. She got her weapon under control, bending her knees. The wagon was bouncing and shuddering as it thundered through the hills; if she didn't do this right, she'd be following those two archers.

Ahead of her, on the next wagon over, Erhi and Chimeg were dancing. Chimeg's spear whipped up in a huge arc, spraying blood and water, frozen in a lightning strike. As she arrested a swing, a sabre crashed into one of the sharp bones sticking up from her bicep, snapping it clean.

Erhi moved like the lightning itself. She snatched the whirling shard out of the air, spun, drove it deep into a soldier's eye socket.

Even for the Rakada, that was a wild move. Hogelun couldn't help but grin as hot, delightful adrenaline prickled through her body. Would any other raider clan attempt this? Would any of them have the guts?

Something thudded into the wood next to her foot. She snapped her head up, panic surging. If there was an archer taking aim at her—

But it wasn't an archer. It was a soldier, young and panicked, poking his head up from the seat of the wagon she was on. Hogelun ducked as he hurled another object at her; it splattered against the wood, showering her with . . .

Hogelun looked down at her boots, spattered with white gobs of flesh. Apples. The idiot was throwing apples at her.

If she fell off the wagon after being hit by a piece of fruit, she was pretty sure she'd be able to hear the Rakada's hoots of derision from the afterlife.

She had nothing to throw back, so she did the only thing she could. She pointed, levelling her finger at the pilot, as if marking him. "*No*," she shouted.

He froze, arm cocked back, stopping in the act as effectively as if she'd stuck a knife through his head.

Just as Hogelun stepped towards him, someone far more competent pushed him out of the way.

He wore a red *deel*, the pounding rain turning it as dark as his thick, luxurious beard. His helmet was gold instead of steel, and his sabre – his very *large* sabre – was polished to a mirror shine.

Hogelun wasn't very good at army ranks, but this one didn't strike her as basic infantry.

The soldier didn't yell nonsense at her. He certainly didn't throw fruit. He just set his feet, knees bent, two hands on his sabre hilt.

Hogelun gave him the widest, most evil smile she could. Hefted her club, and *howled*.

To his credit, he didn't flinch. Just narrowed his eyes, and stalked towards her on the slick, unsteady wagon roof. No doubt he'd trained for this, trained to face an enemy in single combat, to clash blades with a worthy opponent.

Which meant he was utterly unprepared when Hogelun lifted her club, and brought it down hard onto the wagon's roof.

The wood splintered, the stone head of the club punching into it. Hogelun was prepared for the shock wave that rippled through the roof – the soldier wasn't. The hit didn't quite have the strength to knock him over, but he paused, fighting for balance on the rain-slick wood.

For anyone else, the club might get stuck, but Hogelun wrenched it free in less than a second. As the soldier steadied himself, Hogelun lunged towards him and slammed the stone head into his midsection. His ribs cracked, and he fell backwards, toppling out of sight.

From the next wagon over, Chimeg paused in the act of ripping her spear out of some poor bastard's belly to point at Hogelun, an approving look on her face. Hogelun grinned back.

She'd made quite a hole in the roof with that hit. As she glanced down, someone inside the wagon shot an arrow at her face.

She only just managed to avoid getting skewered through the eye socket, twisting away with a *"Whoa"* as the arrow whirled into the storm. The movement unbalanced her, and she came within a split second of tumbling off the wagon. Instead, she went to one knee, blinking in astonishment.

Who took a bow inside of a wagon? It's not like the damn thing had windows the archer could aim out of . . .

Chimeg's voice: *"Hogs!"*

She and Erhi were still one wagon over, a cut above the archer's eye oozing blood. She was gesturing frantically at the ground below the train. Chimeg was holding off two more soldiers, jabbing her spear at them. As a second arrow shot out of the hole, Hogelun leaned over the edge of the wagon roof.

There was far too much water down there.

It had been at the horses' knees less than a minute ago, but now it was touching their chests. They were going nuts, still galloping, but slowing as they had to push through the torrent. The wagon wheels were entirely underwater.

Hogelun's eyes went wide as she realised where they were.

The flood plain.

The big, flat area running next to the river.

The one place you really, *really* didn't want to be during a storm.

Somehow, the panicking, idiot pilot had steered them right onto it.

Hogelun had never given too much thought to the mechanics of flood plains. When the advice for not getting caught in one boiled down to *be somewhere else*, it didn't seem worth it to dig into the details. She had no idea how fast the water would rise, or at what point the wagon and horses would be swept away.

Pity. She'd really been looking forward to getting hold of that idiot with the bow inside the wagon, hauling them out, and doing horrible things to them. But the Rakada needed to find an exit, and quickly.

She wiped water out of her eyes, squinting at the landscape, trying to pick out details between flashes of deafening lightning. It would be so wonderful if there was a nice, gentle slope out of the flood plain, one they could steer the train up before they drowned.

Instead, there was a cliff − well, fine, not a *cliff*, but a place where the land dropped down in a sheer wall. As if a past flood had torn off a chunk of the hillside, leaving a vertical face behind, maybe ten feet high.

There was no way they'd get to the front of the train in time. They *had* to separate the wagons.

Erhi had clearly realised the same thing. She quickly clambered down from her wagon, managed to get herself onto the back of the horse pulling the one Hogelun was on. She waited a beat for the Chief to follow, then leaned off the side of the horse, and sawing at the strap connecting it to the wagon in front.

Hogelun shoved her club into her sheath; someone was going to have to steer them out of this mess, and apparently, that someone was her. She made her way over to the front of the wagon, swung down, plopped onto the pilot's seat.

Only: the soldier who attacked her with fruit was still there, somehow, staring at her from a pale, shocked face. The reins clutched in his hands.

"Give me those." Hogelun snatched them away. Erhi cut the straps, and the wagon lurched sideways.

Something hit Hogelun in the midsection. It was the soldier – he was on his feet, eyes wide with panic, and as Hogelun stared in confusion, she realised he'd punched her. A pathetic excuse for a punch, but still.

"What are you *doing*?" she snapped. He punched her again, getting her in the chin this time.

Oh, fuck this. With one hand fending off the soldier, another pulling at the reins, Hogelun steered the panicked horses towards the cliff.

The water was up to the horses' necks now, lapping against the running board, the wagon starting to drift, tilting. Erhi was already leaping across, scrambling up the cliff.

Finally, the soldier realised how absolutely fucked he was. Finally noticed the rising water.

He was even younger than Hogelun thought. Younger than the Princess. She'd always believed – they all did – that hardened soldiers, not conscripts, protected wagon trains. And yet here was one next to her, terrified out of his mind, attacking her with fruit and fists.

He didn't deserve this. No one forced into the army did.

She'd get him up onto the cliff, it wouldn't take much, she could probably pick him up, throw him at—

And just like that, the soldier made the worst decision possible.

He pushed Hogelun away, and leaped – *off the wrong side of the wagon.*

Maybe he thought she was trying to smash them against the cliff. Maybe he wasn't thinking at all. Hogelun made an attempt to grab him, her fingers closing on air. Then he was gone, pulled under the rushing torrent. She got a split-second look at a hand flailing above the water, and then: nothing.

Hogelun had never shied away from killing on a raid – not if someone stood in her way with something sharp, wanting to stick her with it. That big bastard with the shiny sabre from before? No problem. The archers she'd swept off the side? If she hadn't, they would have done her like Sarnai.

But this . . .

All he'd done was throw some fruit at her.

He was terrified out of his mind, had no idea what to do, and he didn't deserve to die. As much as she told herself that she'd been trying to save him – and that she couldn't have done anything to stop him leaping the wrong way off the wagon – Hogelun didn't quite believe it. At that moment, the guilt was as sharp as any arrowhead.

"*Fuck.*" She turned and flung herself at the cliff, grabbing at it with her fingertips, the same way she'd grabbed hold of the wagon.

Only this wasn't a hard surface. It was slippery, crumbly, and the second she grabbed hold, it dissolved under her grasp.

A hand flashed out of the storm. Erhi, wrapping fingers around Hogelun's wrist. The archer leaned back, teeth bared as she pulled her lover up onto the cliff. Rain-slick fingers slipping, heels digging deep into the mud.

Inch by inch, she hauled Hogelun over the top. The two of them sprawled on the edge of the flood plain, panting, shuddering. Behind them, the wagon overturned, toppled by the flood; a distant, extended crunch, mixed with the horrible sound of the horses going under. Hogelun hated that, hated that she didn't have time to cut them free.

Erhi got up on all fours. Rolled back onto her knees, fingers flying. *Where's the Chief?*

Hogelun looked around, sure she was going to spot Chimeg walking up out of the sheeting rain. But there was nothing.

She and Erhi were alone.

"Chimeg!" She scanned the hills, the water, shielding her eyes against the rain. "*Chief!* Where are you?"

Thirty-One

Sayana

S ayana was really starting to loathe the fucking *araatan*.
It had been three days since it gave her that scrap of food.
And it had no problem eating the antelope they brought it —
which Sayana could understand, because who wouldn't want
three humans waiting on you day and night while you curled
up next to your favourite stalagmite?

But whenever they brought it that food, it wouldn't let them
get closer than about ten feet. Every time they did, that rumbling growl started deep in its throat, getting louder and louder
the nearer they got. They weren't making progress any more;
instead, they were going backwards.

At least its wound hadn't caught the rot; the puffy flesh had
calmed down, less raw and inflamed.

Chimeg and the others would be back any day now. Sayana
knew how that conversation was going to go: *Yeah, Chief, it's
working out perfectly. It shared its food a few days ago, and it's
actually letting us stand a whole ten feet away. Sometimes. Pretty
sure we'll be riding it any day now.*

At least she didn't have to worry about Tuya training the

animal to do her bidding. Right now, it didn't look like it could be trained to do *anyone's* bidding.

For what must have been the thousandth time, she started her approach. Making sure it knew she was coming, moving very slowly, stopping for long periods, letting it get comfortable. Her hands and forearms were slick with blood from the hunks of antelope meat she regularly tossed the beast; she'd long since got used to the smell, to her skin being constantly sticky.

What she couldn't get used to was the endless ache between her shoulder blades, the twinges from her thighs and calves. Turned out, forcing yourself to move slowly and deliberately for days at a time really, *really* fucking hurt.

Sayana stopped, fifteen feet away. Waited, ticking off the seconds in her head.

"Watch its shoulders," Tuya called from the ledge. She was exhausted, with dark circles under her eyes. "If you see them go tense, back off."

"Yeah, you told me last time," Sayana muttered, a little too loudly.

"Move like a dancer — it's all in the torso. Strong and firm. Give the beast an anchor."

Sayana expected her patience with Tuya to run out long ago. The woman was relentless, making her approach the lizard again and again, barely allowing her time to eat and sleep.

Weavers knew, she was no expert on keeping prisoners, but she was pretty sure that a fundamental part of it was that your captive shouldn't be allowed to work you like a pack horse.

Sayana would give her this, though: she worked just as hard. Which made sense — after all, it was her life on the line — but it was more than that.

Tuya was still angry, still resentful, still occasionally a sarcastic bitch ... but there was something else too. A kind of fascination, like a child with a shiny new toy. She couldn't keep her eyes off the *araatan*, and when Sayana finally insisted on taking a break, she often jumped in herself, approaching and backing off, trying to get the beast used to having a human in close proximity.

Didn't matter that she couldn't do any better than Sayana: she came away from her attempts with her cheeks flushed, eyes wide, exhilarated.

Occasionally, she left the cave, always under Khun's careful eye, to bathe in the pool or to feed Ayanga, who swooped down to see if his mistress was still alive. But before long, she was right back inside.

Three more steps. As always, the growl began rumbling through the cave, the lizard's body vibrating with it.

"Steady," Tuya said.

Sayana braced herself for the growl to rise in pitch, like it always did. But when she took the next step, the growl stayed the same. Was it her imagination, or did the *araatan* look just a little more relaxed?

Hardly daring to breathe, she took another step. Then another. Closer and closer. Khun whispered something inaudible from up on the rock ledge.

Sayana's world shrunk down to the few steps separating her from the *araatan*. It blinked as it stared at her, long and slow. Six feet. Five.

Was she supposed to do what Tuya did, when the *araatan* attacked them in the pool below the falls? Put a hand on its snout? Would it accept that? Or would it just take her arm off before she could pull away?

Four feet.

Slowly, despite every part of her body wanting to get as far away as possible, Sayana stretched out a hand.

The *araatan*'s growl got louder, all at once. Its lip couldn't curl, but it bared its teeth anyway. Sayana took the hint, slowly retreating. Heart hammering in her throat.

She kept facing the *araatan* until she was fifteen feet away, as if the beast was a Khan and this was a throne room. When she finally turned, her legs nearly betrayed her, her knees turning to jelly as she walked back towards Tuya and Khun.

Tuya slid down the slope before Sayana even got there, and she was vibrating. Actually vibrating. "What did you do different?" she said, before Sayana could so much as open her mouth. "Was it your hands? You had them by your waist . . . no, hang on, I did that too, and it didn't like me, maybe you . . . did you look at it a certain way? Eye contact?"

"I . . ."

Tuya put a hand on Sayana's shoulder, fingers trembling with excitement. "That was the closest we've got yet. Other than when it came through the waterfall, and I had to . . . but I couldn't see why it let you get close this time, it doesn't make sense, it . . . " The eagle hunter's words failed her then. "Fucking amazing," she said finally, a glowing smile on her face.

Sayana was beaming too. And before she could stop herself, she put her hand on top of Tuya's.

There was a moment, a heartbeat, when Tuya let her. Where they were skin on skin. It had happened so suddenly that neither pulled away. Tuya was still smiling, but there was a curious look in her eyes . . .

Sayana didn't get a chance to find out what the look meant. Because right then, her legs almost gave way. "I . . . I think I need to sit down."

"What? Oh. Yes. Right, of course."

Tuya helped her up the slope. Sayana's head felt far too light, like it was about to float away. Khun came up behind her, squatted down, wordlessly passed her a wild pear, one only slightly shrivelled. Sayana smiled her thanks, took a shaky bite as Tuya lowered herself to the edge. The ghost of the hunter's touch still lingered on Sayana's bare shoulder.

The *araatan* was pacing back and forth, as if inspecting its territory. Whenever it did this, Sayana expected it to leave the cave – it always looked restless, like it wanted out. But after a few moments, it settled down, rolling onto its uninjured side.

"You know, I had this instructor," Tuya said. "In the mountains, when I was learning to fly Ayanga. Mean old bastard named Temujin who actually lost his arm to an *araatan*. The thing took it off at the elbow, and for years, he was the one we all listened to.

"He was the only one who'd actually got close to one, and survived. He told us they were predators. Eat, sleep, breed, repeat." She nodded at the *araatan*. "If he knew what that thing could do, he'd shit himself."

"How do you mean?" Sayana asked, around a mouthful of pear.

"It doesn't just run on instinct. It . . . " Tuya struggled for the words, clicking her fingers. "It perceives the world. It understands how things are connected."

"Isn't that all animals though?"

"Some, sure. Ayanga can . . . look, I'm not explaining this right, what I mean is, the *araatan* is much smarter than I ever thought it would be. It's got base responses, like attacking when it's surprised, but . . . I genuinely think it recognises us now. After only a few days! Do you understand how unusual that is? For a big predator?"

"So we'll be able to ride them? Eventually?"

And just like that, the shutter on Tuya's face came down. As if Sayana had reminded her that she was still a prisoner. That failure might get her killed.

Sayana wanted to apologise, but what would that even mean? Tuya *was* their prisoner, and Sayana had to stay focused. If she couldn't ride the *araatan*, use it in battle, there was no point to any of this.

"We'll keep trying," Tuya said, in a flat voice. "See how far we get."

Silence fell on the cave. Awkward, uncomfortable. Khun, unsurprisingly, didn't notice. She tossed Tuya a fruit of her own, then started fiddling with the strap on her leather pouch.

"Hey." Tuya pointed at the pouch. "What's in there, anyway?"

Sayana swallowed a mouthful of the pear. "Don't bother. We've asked her a thousand times and she's never—"

She stopped talking.

Stared, open-mouthed, as Khun casually reached into the pouch and pulled out the contents.

At first, she thought it was a ball of fabric, little scraps and threads. But it was moss: the kind that grew on rocks near water, thick and luxurious. That looked damp but was actually dry to the touch. The ball was the size of two fists, held close together.

Tuya tilted her head. "I don't understand?"

There was a gentle smile on Khun's face as she peeled part of the moss away.

Nestled inside was a tiny plant. Shorter than Sayana's little finger. A thin, bright green shoot with two narrow leaves, sprouting on either side of a fragile white bud.

Sayana had to work hard to get her jaw moving. "Are you serious?"

Tuya gave her a funny look. "What's the problem?"

"Khun, every time we ask you what's in that pouch, every single time, you ignore us or laugh at us or say you'll . . . you'll make us eat our own livers or something. *Two years*, Khun. Two years we've been asking, all of us. And now she comes along—" jerking a thumb at Tuya "—this person you barely know, she asks once and you just show her?"

Khunbish shrugged. "I find her interesting."

"Are you serious?"

"I had an arranged marriage," Khun told Tuya, as if Sayana hadn't said a word. "I didn't want it, even thought about running away a few times, like Hogelun did, but my parents insisted. And I got lucky – he was a good man. Kind, hard-working. He treated me well, with honour and respect. I fell in love with him."

Khun could be lucid, sometimes, but Sayana didn't think she'd ever heard the woman speak like this. She watched as Khun gently stroked the moss, smiling, holding the little plant close to her chest.

"We had a son." Still in that casual tone of voice. "A wonderful little boy. I never thought I would be a mother, but . . . he was my everything. Nothing else mattered. My little Timur."

She lifted her eyes to Tuya. "Like you, I was a hunter. Altan, my husband, he tended matters at home – even he admitted I was more skilled with a bow than he was. I brought home antelope, gazelle, the odd wild horse. One day, when Timur was no more than three, I came back from a hunt, with the carcass of a wild boar on my horse, and Altan and Timur were gone. A snake had come into the *ger*, a fat old pit viper, and bitten them both."

Sayana sat, transfixed. Even the *araatan* seemed to be listening.

"It was my fault," Khun went on. "We had enough food for

ourselves. I was greedy that day, and restless, and Timur had been loud. I wanted to be on my own. If I had been in the *ger* when the viper attacked . . . "

She let out a shaky breath. The only sign of emotion she'd shown so far. "I killed the viper, of course. Buried my husband. My son. And then, I tried to join them. I could not face life without them in it."

"Oh, Khun," Sayana murmured.

"But my knife wouldn't pierce my flesh, no matter how hard I tried. Our *ger* was by a lake, and I walked into it, but my legs wouldn't take me past the shallows. I knew I could starve myself or stop drinking, but I thought I might just linger in agony.

"And that is when Father Sky spoke to me, through the body of the boar, resting on the back of my horse. Its mouth moving as the rest of it lay still."

It was a few moments before she continued. "He said he would not permit me to die, and join my family. Not until I atoned for what I'd done. Not until I made something as pure and perfect as my son had been."

She gently touched one of the leaves of her plant. "This is a Dawn Whisper. It takes nearly twenty years to bloom, and it only flowers for an instant before the petals fall. They need constant care, just the right conditions, precise amounts of water."

Sayana thought back to their raid on Karkorum, when they'd taken Tuya. That soldier . . . he'd got a hold on Khun's pouch. She'd torn him to pieces.

"I have nurtured it for eighteen years." Khun carefully, lovingly, placed the moss cap back over the plant. "After it blooms, after I witness a perfect, pure flower, then Father Sky will finally permit me to join my husband and my son."

Eighteen years.

What did losing your family like that do to your mind?

But Sayana knew the answer to that. She lived with it. She was looking right at it.

Khun tucked the moss ball back in her pouch, favoured them with a bright smile. "Of course, it's a gift as much as a curse. Until the flower blooms, I am protected. Nothing can harm me: no blade, no arrow, no lightning or wind or angry beastie. Father Sky will not let me take the easy way out." She poked Tuya in the ribs. "You could try and stab me right now, take my knife and plunge it into my chest, and it would bounce right off."

Which didn't make any sense. At all. Sayana had *seen* Khun with nicks and scratches – they all got them from time to time. You couldn't avoid them if you lived in the Tapestry. But when she hunted for a specific memory, a single instant where Khun was badly hurt, she couldn't think of any. No broken bones, no gashes. Not so much as a cold.

Khun stood, stretching, her back creaking and clicking. "I think I may go outside for a while. There are some stars I'd like to talk to."

Moments later, she was gone.

Tuya hugged herself. "Is that all true?"

"I don't know." Sayana still couldn't process the fact that she'd seen inside the pouch. "Sometimes with Khun, it's hard to say."

Neither of them spoke for a long time.

"Why do you do this?" Tuya asked, eventually.

"Do what?"

"Be a raider. Live out here." She gestured to the rest of the cave, to the Tapestry beyond. "If you were at court in Karkorum then you had everything you could ever need. All the riches in the world. You gave all that up, to . . . what? Hide in a cave? Scratch out a living, taking what isn't yours? Killing people for their bones? What are you doing? Did they exile you for something? Did you—"

"I didn't get exiled."

Sayana's voice wouldn't cooperate. She wanted it to come out strong, powerful – it was her choice to leave, no one else's. But in the hollow cave, her words sounded very small.

"Then *why*? You can't tell me being out here is better than—"

"You've been there." Sayana couldn't help a note of venom creeping into her words. "You tell me."

"You chose a life where you ... where you kill people. You ride around, you steal, you kill anyone who stands in your way."

"But that's the point." Suddenly, it seemed very important that Tuya understood this. "Chimeg has ... well, not a code, more like a rule. You don't kill anyone who leaves you alone. If you go on a raid, and somebody runs, you let them go. But if they try and stop you, then—"

"You kill them." Tuya's expression had turned sour. "And you take their bones."

For a few seconds, neither of them spoke. The only sound was the *araatan*, shuffling against its stalagmite.

"You never feel guilty?" Tuya asked. "About the ones you—"

"Like I said. They have *every* chance to get out of our way. And for what we have, what we've built for ourselves, that's the price we pay."

When Chimeg said it, it sounded powerful. It sounded *right*. When Sayana said it though ... and when she said it to Tuya ...

She wanted to tell the hunter about the boy she'd saved, back when she'd first ridden the *araatan*. The words wouldn't come.

"But you don't pay that price," Tuya said. "Everyone else does. All so you can live easy out here, without having to do any actual work."

"Let me ask you something." Sayana twisted, facing Tuya. More angry than she'd realised, because what the fuck did this woman know about her life? She spread her hands. "Why aren't *you* a raider?"

Tuya's face scrunched up. "What are you talking about? Why would I be a—"

"Fine, maybe not a raider, but why are you in Karkorum at all? You're an eagle hunter. You spent all that time training in the mountains, bonding with that bird of yours, and then you leave it all behind and go back? You can't tell me you're happy living in that place."

Sayana pointed to the *araatan*. "When you're training that thing, when you're working with it, you look like . . ." She faltered. The way Tuya looked when she was working, the way she glowed, as if a spark had ignited inside her, shining out into the world.

"Like what?" Tuya asked.

The words wouldn't come. No matter how much Sayana tried to bend them into shape, push and prod them into something that would actually make any sense, they refused to budge. It felt small, silly – something Sayana had imagined.

And if she talked about it . . .

It would mean the feeling she got when Tuya smiled was real. That the little backflips Sayana's stomach did meant something.

She was a raider. Her entire life was about taking what she wanted, without having to ask for it. Not ever. And yet, with this . . .

There were some things you could never take. Things that had to be freely given.

And she would never get that from Tuya, not ever.

The eagle hunter chewed the inside of her cheek. "You

want to know why I stay in Karkorum?" she said. "Remember Odval?"

"I . . . who?"

"Odval." The name spat like something she wanted to stick to a wall. "She was in my bed when you took me."

Sayana had barely thought about that woman since they left the city. Hearing her name now – a reminder that someone had been in Tuya's bed – was a nasty little needle in her side.

She never thought that Tuya being with someone else would hurt. Guess she was wrong.

"Look," she said, resigned. "I promise, you'll be back with your lover before you know it."

"She's not my *lover*, you complete and utter fucking child. I was getting her out."

"What are you talking about?"

Tuya tilted her head back, letting out a slow hiss of air. "The Khan is forcing people to come in from the Tapestry. Live in that *place*. The things that happen in there, especially to the weak ones . . . You couldn't even imagine."

Sayana was still stinging from Tuya calling her a child, but she didn't get a chance to respond.

"So if you want to escape," the hunter went on, "if you want safe passage without the army coming after you, there are ways to get it done. Places you can go, where they won't think to look." Her eyes flashed. "I got people out. People like Odval. One of the soldiers wanted her for his own, and so she came to me. I gave her my bed that night so she could get some rest in a safe place, and in the morning, I was going to get her passage."

"I didn't know."

"No shit. Not that it matters, because Odval's probably in the palace dungeon now. That's where they put anyone who tries to run."

"But ..." *But what?* There was no but. Maybe if they'd taken Tuya a night earlier, or later, it wouldn't have mattered, except they didn't, and now this Odval person was in the Khan's hands.

Sayana got a flicker of her face in her mind. Lined, wide-eyed, framed by wispy grey hair. Terrified.

Tuya's telling the truth.

"You want to know why I stay in Karkorum?" Tuya said, in a dull monotone. "Why I obey my sister and the Khan? *That's* why. So I can be there for people when they have nobody else. I wasn't the only one, but I was damn good at it."

For the first time, Sayana got a sense of what Tuya gave up. She could have escaped the city herself, any time she wanted — if anyone was capable of evading the army in the Tapestry, it was her.

Tuya, when she was around the *araatan* — around all animals, actually, even their horses — was a completely different person. Bright, burning fire. She gave that up willingly, staying in a city she hated, pretending to obey. Risking it all for people she didn't know. Risking imprisonment, torture. Death.

They aren't your problem. The little voice in Sayana's head was defiant. *You don't know them. You don't owe them a damn thing. The only people who matter are the Rakada. Chimeg, Erhi, Hogs, Khun. Nobody else.*

But oh, see, that was the problem. Because she'd been right in the middle of court. She'd had access to so many more people than Tuya, so much more information. If she'd walked her path, stayed, helped people escape ...

But she didn't. *All so you can live easy out here, without having to do any actual work.*

Sayana could say she'd picked this life, and that she wasn't going to waste time feeling guilty over her choices. But that was the thing about guilt. It hung around, whether you wanted it to or not.

The silence came back. Heavy, uncomfortable. Eventually, Tuya slid down the slope, dusting herself off at the bottom. "Come on." She sounded weary, fed up. "Work to do."

Thirty-Two

Yesuntei

"Tell me," Yesuntei said.

The wagon pilot – a small, middle-aged man with a razor-sharp beard – took a long sip of *airag*, cup held in both hands. Yesuntei's stomach gave a hollow wrench, and she had to force herself not to wince.

Jochi's *ger* was sparsely furnished, with nothing but a few blankets and a chest of his belongings. Even the stools had to be fetched from elsewhere. From the side of the *ger*, Jochi himself watched, arms folded, face hidden in shadow.

"A storm hit us," the pilot said. "Up where the mountain streams make the Western Mogoi. We did our best to avoid it but it was far too late, so I chose to ride straight through." His eyes flicked between Jochi and Yesuntei, as if they were about to accuse him of lying to them. "There was no other choice."

He told them about the three raiders who came out of the storm, howling, clad in bone. When he was finished, Yesuntei made him tell it again, from the start. Despite her growling gut, she couldn't stop a small smile sneaking onto her face. *Got you.*

The Namag had given them nothing – nothing but soaked

boots and tired horses. No one was there, let alone a group of raiders. They'd headed north again, tracking the line of the Ulaan River. They'd met plenty of soldiers, more than a few nomads making their way in from the Tapestry, but no one had seen any raiders in weeks.

Yesuntei had been doing her best to ignore Jochi's pointed looks, his thinly veiled suggestions that perhaps it was time to head back to Karkorum.

And then today, this pilot arrived, steering a single, battered wagon. The last survivor of a train.

"Why did you ride onto the flood plain?" Jochi asked, after the third retelling.

"I ..." The pilot looked between Jochi and Yesuntei. "*Bahadur*, the horses, they panicked, and I couldn't—"

Yesuntei held up a hand. In the scheme of things, she couldn't give the tiniest shit about flood plains. "Have the quartermaster give you fresh horses, and a hot meal. Then ride for Karkorum. Tell no one you saw us."

He practically tripped over himself as he backed out of the tent, nodding and bowing.

"Do you believe him?" Jochi rumbled.

"He has no reason to lie." Yesuntei stood, brushing herself off.

"You are too trusting. Perhaps he made a mistake, steered them through the flood plain when the Mogoi burst its banks, and lost the wagons. Made up this story to save his skin."

"Why not run, then? Why risk bringing the wagon back to Karkorum at all?"

That, more than anything else, is why Yesuntei thought the pilot was telling the truth. Some people, you tortured for information. Others, you just asked. And if you showed loyalty to the Khan, that counted for a lot with her. "Besides, what about the bone armour? Why would he lie about that?"

"To make us believe his tale."

She finally gave in and drove a fist into her side, grimacing. "He couldn't have known we were hunting the Rakada. If he's lying, then don't you think it's strange that *that* is the clan he chooses for his story?" She chewed her lower lip. "I need a map."

Jochi glowered, but did as she asked. He dragged the chest to the centre of the *ger*, so it was in the light coming from the flap. Unrolled his map with far more ceremony than Yesuntei would deem strictly necessary. Then again, it *was* a beautiful map: paper, not cloth, with the Khan's seal at the top, the landscape laid out in thick black ink.

Jochi tapped the spot at the source of the Western Mogoi, where innumerable streams carried snowmelt out of the mountains to form the river. "I grew up near here. The flood plain is widest at . . . yes, this point." He glanced at her. "If the pilot really was speaking the truth . . . "

"Then that's where they'd be," she murmured.

Only . . .

She kept running over the pilot's tale. How the Rakada came out of the storm, a wave of blades and rattling bones.

She leaned over the map, arms akimbo. "How big did you say this raider clan was?"

"Not large. Fewer than ten, that much is true, maybe even smaller."

"The pilot told us that there were three of them. He specifically mentioned that: three raiders, riding out of the storm."

"Like demons from the nine hells, he said." Jochi snorted. "Pathetic."

"But why so few?" Her stomach pain was fading into the background now, her heart starting to beat a little faster. "If you're going to attack a wagon train, you'd need your full force."

"Maybe there's only three of them left."

But Yesuntei was barely listening. "And why attack a wagon train in the first place? Why go to all that trouble, put yourself in the middle of a storm . . . "

"They have your sister," Jochi pointed out. "They must have left someone to guard her, no?"

The mention of Tuya was like a thin needle through Yesuntei's heart. She straightened up. "They didn't leave a ransom demand. They're not trying to bargain with us. Ever since we left Karkorum, they've been invisible – and now all of a sudden, they're attacking wagon trains? With reduced numbers?"

"Say what you mean."

Did she voice this idea? If she was wrong, if she made a mistake . . .

But Yesuntei hadn't got to where she was by mistrusting her instincts. "They must know we're looking for them. I believe the pilot told us the truth. And I think he was *meant to*." She pointed back at the map, at the Western Mogoi. "They *want* us searching that area. They didn't care about raiding the train – they just wanted to get our attention. They wanted us to know they were there."

From outside, there was the distant sound of an argument. Two raised voices, something about rations. There had been more and more of those arguments lately; Yesuntei had so far left it to Jochi to discipline his men, but perhaps it was time she intervened . . .

"Thin." Jochi lifted his chin. "And in any case, it doesn't help us. All we know now is where they *won't* be."

As much as she hated to admit it, it was a good point. Yesuntei considered the map. Studied the north-east, the area above and below the river, finger tracing west to the Seven Thousand

Lakes — more like thirty, but still easy for a group of raiders to get lost in. If they were even there at all, and not somewhere else entirely.

She kept turning the attack over and over in her mind. It was planned, and carefully; this wasn't something the Bone Raiders did on the spur of the moment. And if Tuya wasn't with them, then they must have made camp somewhere, at least temporarily . . .

Or Tuya's already dead.

No. Absolutely not. She'd believe that the moment she saw her sister's body, and not a second sooner.

She scanned the area between the Namag and the Mogoi. Looking for something, anything that might help her. Could they have been heading north, to the mountains? Trying to cross into Dalai?

The Eastern and Western Mogoi Rivers snaked like the serpent they were named for; the two of them eventually joined to the north of where the 8th were camped, forming the titanic Ulaan, which ran all the way down to Karkorum.

The raiders wouldn't separate their forces for long — not for a band that small. Which meant that the site of their attack would be no more than two- or three-days' ride from their camp, at the most. Close enough for comfort; far enough that if Yesuntei and Jochi *had* taken their bait, they wouldn't stumble across them by accident. They'd be riding up and down the foothills of the Baina Mountains, fording countless streams, spending all their time at the Mogoi's source and wasting long days hunting for their quarry.

Yesuntei had ridden the Western Mogoi before, could see it in her mind. Its waterfalls, its switchbacks. The clutches of birch trees, the caves, the abundant game. Less abundant now that the damn *araatan* had been spotted in the grasslands, but still.

Jochi was right. It *was* thin. It was also the best chance they had.

She rested a finger on the river's sinuous curves. "We track along here, heading north from the source of the Ulaan River. We check every cave, every forest, talk to everyone we see. We'll find them."

Yesuntei had known Jochi for a long time, and even before she was done talking, she could tell he wasn't going to agree.

"How much time are we going to spend doing this?" he asked.

"As long as it takes." Yesuntei had to stop herself snarling the words.

She regretted it immediately. Jochi had her, and he knew it.

The old soldier adjusted his armour. The harsh light from the doorway painted one side of his face, leaving the other in darkness. "The Khan's orders were to search for your sister. But he will not wait for ever – he will expect a report, a full accounting. It has already been too long. He will grant us more manpower, let us fan out across the grass."

Yesuntei could see how that would go. Because it put Jochi in the clear – he'd received his Khan's orders, followed them to the letter, had returned to ask for more soldiers. *What do you mean the Khan never issued these orders? They have his seal – see here. Yesuntei herself delivered them . . .*

Returning to Karkorum wasn't an option. She was *not* going back. Not without some fucking heads. Return with Tuya and the raiders, and all would be forgiven, swept away in a rush of glory. Return without them, and everything she'd built would crumble.

No, that was wrong. It wasn't about *everything she'd built*; it was about everything she was *going* to build. Karkorum, Hanggai, her purpose . . . taken away. Placed in the care of lesser men and women.

And Tuya would be gone for ever.

"Three days." She hated that she had to bargain, but if it got her sister back, it would be worth it. "Three days on the Mogoi. You give me the 8th for three more days, and I'll give you your raiders."

And as she said the words, an idea took root in her head. Slowly spreading through her mind.

An idea she didn't dare tell Jochi about.

He pondered her request for a full minute. Standing like a golem, staring down at her.

"Very well," he rumbled.

At the door of the tent, he paused. "Mark this: there will be no extension. If we have nothing in three days, we return to Karkorum. No debate, no argument."

"Of course."

Said without hesitation. Willing, compliant.

He'd believe her, because that's who he was. Someone without imagination, without vision. Someone who could only understand what was in front of him.

As Jochi began barking orders to his troops, Yesuntei ran a hand along the edge of the map, eyes boring a hole in the Western Mogoi.

Closer and closer . . .

Thirty-Three

Sayana

For Sayana, washing her braid was usually a nice moment of peace. Gently unwinding it, running river water through the locks, letting it dry in the sun. Her own little ritual.

Today, though? Today, *nice* didn't come into it. It was either she wash her braid, or she was going to stab someone important. Probably Tuya.

They were fast approaching Chimeg's deadline, they hadn't actually succeeded in even touching the *araatan* yet, and Sayana had had enough. She'd waited until the beast had fallen asleep, and taken herself outside for a little *me time*.

It was early afternoon, the air crisp and fresh as a newly made *deel*. Sharp blue sky. The water, of course, was frigid enough to make Sayana suppress a small shriek when she waded into the shallows. Her boots were off, and she'd stripped to the waist.

Carefully, she undid her braid, removing the ribbons. She sucked in a short breath, then crouched down in the water. This time, she wasn't able to suppress the sound she made, and it wasn't small, either.

She leaned back, fully submerging her hair, letting it spread out. Working quickly, she scrubbed the dirt from her body – as much as she liked her ritual, she preferred not to wade into a freezing pool more than once – then popped upright with a gasp.

She squeezed as much water out of her hair as she could. Ran a comb through it to get out the knots. The comb was tarnished silver, another object stolen from the palace. She did try to carve one out of bone once, as a little project. But after she broke her third scapula in a row, she'd decided that the Bone Raider life didn't extend to hair care.

Tuya sat off to one side, leaning against a rock. She'd been tending to Ayanga; the eagle was back in the air, turning in long, slow circles.

The hunter glanced at Sayana, then looked away. Sayana caught herself wanting to hold Tuya's gaze, which was a more uncomfortable feeling than the freezing water. Behind them, Khun walked in rapid circles, muttering to herself.

Sayana closed her eyes as she stroked water out of her hair with her fingers. *This is what you wanted. The* araatan *was your idea. So was Tuya. All of it.*

So, as much as the process was driving her insane, she wasn't going to quit. For one thing, she wasn't giving Chimeg the satisfaction. Absolutely the fuck not.

Footsteps through the trees behind her, followed a moment later by a delighted shout from Khun. When Sayana looked round, Erhi and Hogelun were bringing their horses to a halt. They were exhausted, grim, faces streaked with dirt. They both wore their bones – like they'd completely forgotten they still had them on. Dust was caked on Hogelun's shoulder skull.

Sayana hadn't realised how badly she needed a distraction until then. She flung her wet hair over her shoulder and waded out of the shallows even as an uncomfortable thought tugged at her. Where was Chimeg? Why wasn't she . . .

But even as the thought occurred, the Chief rode out through the trees.

She looked worse for wear than Hogs and Erhi, her right arm wrapped up in a makeshift sling. Erhi had to help her down off her horse, and she moved gingerly, like she'd busted her ankle too.

Which didn't stop Khun leaping at her, wrapping her arms around Chimeg and almost knocking her over. Showering her with kisses, which is something she had never done before, and would probably never do again. "I was so worried," she said, after planting a particularly wet smooch on Chimeg's forehead.

"Khun," the Chief grunted. "Arm."

"What? Oh! Yes." Khun disengaged and gently stroked the busted limb like a treasured pet.

Hogelun squatted down, head hanging. It gave Sayana a good look at her club, slung across her back, at the dried blood on the head. Khun stalked up to Hogs, jabbed a finger at her face. "You should have kept your Chief safe. What's wrong with you?"

"Nice to see you too," Hogelun muttered. She gave Sayana a vague wave, then accepted a water skin from Erhi, drinking deep.

Sayana barely noticed the wave. Because for a second there, right before Chimeg walked out of the trees, she'd caught herself hoping . . .

Hoping the Chief hadn't made it.

She actually took a step back when it hit her. The thought was like something under an old rock, pale and shiny, skittering away.

She cleared her throat. "Hope someone paid for that," she told Chimeg, gesturing at the broken arm.

"Whole lot of someones," Chimeg muttered. The very faintest flicker of a smile, which was both amazing to see, and which made Sayana feel even more like a worm.

"Nearly lost her in the flood," Hogs said.

"I'm sorry – *flood?*"

Chimeg waved this away. "Tell me you've made progress."

Sayana had to phrase this carefully, because Chimeg's progress and her progress might be very different things. "We're closer than ever. You should see it, Chief, it actually recognises us, it knows—"

But nobody was listening to her any more. They were all staring over her shoulder. Hogelun had gone the colour of old milk.

The *araatan* was pushing its way through the waterfall, clambering down the rocks. Water cascading off its flanks. The way it moved reminded Sayana of the Chief: careful, hesitant on its injured leg. Even so, it still astounded her how something so big could navigate such uneven ground.

In seconds, it was by the edge of the pool, head tilting from side to side, looking around. Hogelun took a quick step backwards, reaching for her club . . .

"Don't move," Sayana hissed at her. "It doesn't like sudden movements."

Tuya's words coming out of her mouth startled her. But she was already watching its body language, the set of its shoulders, the way it was moving its head. Tuya herself had popped into existence next to her, and Sayana could tell she was watching too. Watching as the beast took a drink, gulping up silty water.

Everything she and Tuya had worked for hung by a thread. If one of the other Rakada did a single thing the beast didn't like, even something small . . .

As it finished its drink, purple tongue flicking, the horses bolted. Sayana's own was tied to a tree further into the beech grove, and it was pulling at its tether, tossing its mane.

The *araatan* twitched, tasting the air, turning its head at the retreating horses. Sayana and Tuya had fed it today, but if it was still hungry, they might find themselves minus a few horses that they *really* couldn't afford to lose. And that was the best-case scenario.

Instead, the *araatan* turned in the direction of the raiders. Claws squashing into the muddy edge of the pool. Behind Sayana, there was the very slow, very soft sound of Chimeg drawing her spear.

"Chief, stop." The whisper came out of the corner of her mouth.

"Princess, if we don't—"

"Just *wait*."

And – oh, Weavers, it was going right for Hogs. The lizard fixed her with a beady stare, quickened its pace.

Sayana couldn't speak. Could barely move her eyes. Forget her throat: her heart had climbed all the way up into her head, shaking her skull with booming thuds.

The *araatan* utterly ignored her and Tuya. Didn't even look at them. Just lumbered past, making a beeline for the one Rakada who was most terrified of it.

As slowly as Sayana could, she turned to watch. Desperate to salvage this, without having a clue how to do it. *Please, Hogs. Please don't do anything stupid.*

But as the *araatan* closed the gap, got within two feet, Hogs . . .

Relaxed.

No – that wasn't the word for it. What she did took effort, real effort. Sayana could actually see it. Hogelun slowed her breathing right down, forcing it deep. She lowered her shoulders, holding the tension at bay. Mouth very slightly open, not look-ing away from the *araatan*. Hand off her club now, arms cocked out to the sides.

Sayana could swear that right then, the waterfall itself stopped. The flow of the river hanging, suspended.

The *araatan* was so close now that Hogs wouldn't even have to reach out to touch it. A single forearm movement would get the job done. And as its hot breath twitched her *deel*, it lowered its head and nudged her with its nose. Pushing it into her ribs.

Not trying to knock her over, either; it was a gentle motion, like a horse wanting to know if you had a snack for it.

Sayana wasn't jealous. She was too amazed to be jealous. It was as if . . . as if the *araatan* knew Hogs was scared of it, some-how, and it wanted to reassure her. Sayana had no idea how that was even *possible*.

Seconds ticked by. Hours, maybe, Sayana didn't know. Time was suddenly all over the place.

The lizard gave a satisfied snort, then abruptly turned away. Marched past the rest of them, climbed back up the rocks and into the waterfall. Vanishing, like none of it had ever happened.

At some point, Ayanga had landed on the other side of the falls; the bird watched the beast with a beady eye as it passed, then took off again, swooping down the river.

"I'm going to sit down for a minute," Hogs said faintly.

She didn't get to. Erhi wrapped her arms around her, the archer shaking so hard the arrows rattled in her quiver. Eyes squeezed shut.

Khun cackled. "Beastie found a new friend," she told Hogelun, who still looked like she just took a trip to the afterlife and came back to tell the tale.

"What the fuck just happened?" Chimeg muttered.

Tuya and Sayana looked at each other. Sayana opened her

mouth to speak, closed it again. She did this twice before she decided that, actually, she didn't have the first clue what she was going to say.

Erhi spun the unprotesting Hogelun around, held her at arm's length. Tears were streaming down her face. Sayana blinked – had she ever seen Erhi cry? Over anything?

The archer's hands flashed so fast that it was all Sayana could do to keep up. *Are you hurt? Did it do anything to you?*

"I'm fine," Hogs said, still sounding as if she just took a fist to the forehead.

Sayana finally figured out what to say. "So, Chief—" Her voice came out as a cracked, squeaky mess, tongue flopping around like a landed fish. She tried again. "So, Chief, what do you think? How's that for progress?"

Chimeg didn't appear to hear her. She was staring up at the waterfall, a puzzled frown on her face. Like the water had just turned a strange colour.

"Chief?"

"I don't know," Chimeg said, not looking away from the falls.

Sayana pointed a shaking finger at Hogelun. "It almost *ate us* a week ago. Now it's Hogs' new best friend."

Hogelun made a weak little wheezing sound.

Tuya picked up the slack. "It's letting us approach it now. We've got it used to our presence."

And *still* Chimeg didn't move. Just kept staring up at the falls.

Exasperated, Sayana threw her arms out. Which wasn't smart, because she nearly knocked Tuya over. "Sorry, shit – sorry. But Chimeg, come on, you asked for us to show you it could work, how is that not—"

"I don't *know*, Sayana." The Chief finally looked her way. "I am three days out from a hellish raid, I broke my arm, twisted up my ankle, and I've had maybe three hours' sleep. An *araatan* just casually snuggled our cook, then fucked off like it was nothing. Can I please just . . . just have something to eat and get my feet under me? Before we talk about what happens next?"

She didn't wait for an answer. Just marched past, cradling her smashed arm, then dropped to her knees by the pool and scooped cold water onto her face with her good hand.

Sayana was starting to process what had just happened, and it was getting more amazing by the second. She couldn't stop a smile cracking her face. "That was brilliant, Hogs."

Khun dug a closed fist into Hogelun's shoulder. "And you used to be so scared of the beasties. Even the small ones made you squeal like a mouse in a tiger's mouth."

"It . . ." Hogelun disengaged from Erhi, shrugged helplessly. "It didn't . . . I mean, the big one, it doesn't *move* like the little ones do. It doesn't go side to side. And up close, when I got a look at its eyes, I . . ."

She laughed then: a tiny little hiccup. "It's like it *knew* that I was scared of it. Like it understood. I don't really know how to describe it."

"You're doing a pretty good job, actually," Sayana murmured.

Hogs' face split in a delighted, relieved grin, as if she really did need to be reassured. "Where do they come from?" she whispered, looking up at the falls again. "The *araatan*?"

"Depends on who you ask," Tuya said. "Father Sky made them, or Mother Earth. They came from Dalai, or Ngu, or they were here with the First Riders. Someone once told me they're part of the mountains, rocks brought to life. There's so much we don't know about them." She clicked her tongue at that one. "I even heard a story that they used to have wings."

Hogelun's eyes went wide. "You're telling me . . . you're saying they *flew*?"

"I'm telling you no such thing. It's just a theory. An old man I knew, when I was a child, he said they soared like eagles. And that they were bigger – a *lot* bigger. Big enough to block out the Father's eyes."

Sayana actually looked up at the sky. Like a giant, flying, fire-breathing lizard really was about to swoop down and torch them all. It was hard to imagine the *araatan* soaring through the air; hard to imagine living in the Tapestry at all, when one of them could take you at any second.

Maybe that was why no one really knew anything about the First Riders in the Tapestry. They'd all taken one look at the sky, went "Nope", dug a big hole, climbed in, and never emerged.

"I'm going to check on it," Tuya muttered. She headed back to the falls, hopping up the rocks. It had become almost automatic for her – same for Sayana. They knew exactly how to get up there now. They could do it in the dark. Khun followed, skipping merrily after her.

Erhi's tears had stopped, but her eyes were narrow, furious slits. *I don't want you anywhere near it*, she told Hogs. *You stay out of that cave, understand?*

Before Hogs could even get a word in, Erhi turned to Sayana. *You don't let her in. It's you, and Tuya, and that's it.*

"Um . . ." Sayana cocked her head. "Not sure that's my call to make?"

She couldn't remember ever seeing Erhi like this. The woman was usually calm, collected – even when she was angry, like she was when they'd come back with Tuya, it was an icy anger. This was anything but. Chimeg watched from the edge of the pool, studying the archer.

"I wasn't planning on it," Hogelun told Erhi, a little hotly. "I just . . . That wasn't how I expected that to go, is all." She jerked her thumb at Sayana, with a sly grin. "Maybe the Princess has a point about all this, yeah? About riding the things?"

I said no. The way Erhi snapped her fingers and thumb together for the last word, like she was trying to snatch something out of the air, was the same as one of them shouting. Abruptly, she stalked away, heading for the horses. As she did, she cast a dirty look at the Chief – like this was all Chimeg's fault.

Erhi had always been protective of Hogelun. But Sayana had never known her to give orders like that.

"What's got into her?" she muttered.

Hogelun shook her head. Shoulders slumped, her excitement gone. When she spoke, her voice sounded empty and deflated, like a discarded *airag* skin. "I don't know."

Thirty-Four

Yesuntei

Found you.

Yesuntei lay prone at the top of the waterfall, studying the Bone Raiders.

Three of them stood in a tight group near the trees — they were having an argument of some sort. One of them, an archer with a quiver on her back, was using sign, hands moving in quick, angry jerks. A fourth, wounded, with one arm in a sling, squatted near the edge of the pool. All but one of them wore bones.

There was no sign of Tuya.

For a heartbeat, Yesuntei wondered if she got this wrong — if she'd read too much into the finger bone she'd found, if Tuya had been taken by another group entirely. But it didn't matter. Tuya or no Tuya, these raiders had signed their death warrants long ago.

She took a few more moments to study the pool, the surrounding forest. There was a horse tied up, at the edge of the trees, which made sense — if there was a cave behind the waterfall, it would have been difficult to access on horseback. She took it all in, deconstructing it, finding places where they could launch an attack. But the angle was all wrong: they needed to be at ground level, with a full view of the river and the falls.

She squirmed backwards, making sure she was out of sight, then got to one knee. Behind her, fourteen soldiers waited, looking at her expectantly. They were on foot, their own horses a short distance away.

Fourteen. All she could peel off from the 8th.

She hadn't been prepared to stake everything on the raiders hiding along the Mogoi. Even if they were, three days simply wasn't enough time. Jochi was never going to bend, and it was pointless to try, so she'd taken another approach.

While they'd searched, riding hard across the grass, she went recruiting.

She noted the soldiers who seemed unhappy, marked the ones loyal to Hanggai — not just their commander. A quiet word here, a whisper there, a plea, an offer. Glory. Victory. A grateful Khan. Riches. Rewards. Whatever it took.

When Jochi had finally given the order to return to Karkorum, Yesuntei and her new recruits were ready. They'd taken up the rear of the column, then, at her signal, had peeled off.

Fourteen soldiers were nothing like the hundred-strong 8th, but it would be more than enough. When they returned with Tuya, with prisoners, Jochi would have no choice but to fall in line. The orders? No one would question them, and the Khan wouldn't care, not in the face of such a dramatic victory. Hells, Yesuntei would let Jochi claim credit, if he wanted. She would have Tuya back, could return to Karkorum victorious.

But it had to work. It had to. If her gambit failed, everything Yesuntei knew would lie in ruins.

The soldiers were the same rank — the few others who held command in the 8th were all loyal to Jochi, and Yesuntei didn't go near them. But every group of soldiers had its leaders, rank or no rank, and the one the others listened to here was named Chuluun.

He had a narrow, ratty face, with a wispy moustache and soft lips, and didn't look like he could fight his way out of a sack. But Yesuntei had seen him work, when they fought the Thunderhead, and she pitied whichever Bone Raider took him on.

"We need to get to the forest," she said. "See what we're dealing with."

Chuluun scoffed. "Why bother? We could take them from above." He waved a dirty hand at the others – every man in the 8th had a bow, and knew how to use it. "Wipe them out in one go."

Yesuntei resisted the urge to roll her eyes. Jochi would never have suggested something so foolish. But she didn't have Jochi, just Chuluun, so she had to work with what she had.

"Waterfalls have caves," she told him. "And there might be more under the trees. Last thing we need is to give away our position."

"Who cares? More of us than them."

"And if you're wrong?"

Chuluun suppressed a smirk, looked sideways at one of the soldiers, a friend of his who everyone just called Sticks. A hulking monster of a man with perhaps a third of a working brain. The kind of person Yesuntei would *never* have recruited for the 8th when she was in charge.

"Doesn't matter how many there are," Chuluun said. He thumped his chest, and the others echoed it.

"And if they barricade themselves behind the falls?" said Yesuntei. "If there *is* a cave? We'd have a siege on our hands."

"We've trained for sieges. Maybe that happened after you

left." He waved at the land beyond the falls. "We'd have food and water, as much as we needed. These raiders would starve. Even if they slaughtered their horses, we'd smoke them out."

Sticks chuckled, like he was looking forward to seeing that.

"What if there's another exit?" Yesuntei did a little waving of her own, taking in the surrounding hills. "One that comes out somewhere we don't know about?"

That shut Chuluun up. Yesuntei kept going: "Not to mention the fact that they have a hostage. Or have you forgotten why we're out here?"

She looked at them, one after another, making them meet her eyes. The ache in Yesuntei's gut had gone beyond the familiar gnawing sensation into an actual *burn*, like her stomach acid had found an exit, chewing through her. "I will *not* put my sister in danger. Not for anything. Am I understood?"

Every approach carried risk. She had to remember that. No situation, in the history of military campaigns, came without the possibility of defeat.

She might lose Tuya today. It was a truth that hurt even worse than the feeling in her gut.

There had to be ways they could lower the risk, though. She pictured the area: the trees, the falls, the pool, the horses . . .

An ember of a plan began to glow in her mind.

"We watch," she told them. "We observe. We confirm their numbers, and where my sister is."

Chuluun was about to protest, again, so she plunged on. "And then we kill them. Every last one of them."

Thirty-Five

Hogelun

You never sat next to a fire while you were on watch. That was a good way to get an arrow in the face.

Not only would you be a well-lit target, but you'd inevitably find yourself staring into the flames, hypnotised. Which meant if, by some miracle, whoever was sneaking up on you couldn't shoot for shit, your eyes wouldn't be accustomed to the dark. Your first indication that something was wrong would be the dagger sticking out of your chest.

Of course, on nights like tonight, with a bright moon shining down out of a cloudless sky, it made zero difference whether you had a fire or not. Hogelun could see everything in crisp, sharp detail, even pick out the rippling surface of the pool.

But could she have a fire, to keep off the autumn chill? The fuck she could. Chimeg wouldn't listen, even after Hogelun protested that when the moon was out, she may as well have been dancing around naked waving multiple torches.

She huddled deeper in her blanket, yanking it up to her chin – something else the Chief wasn't a fan of, saying it delayed action if they got attacked. Well, the Chief was curled up in the *ger* off to Hogelun's left, nice and cosy, and if Hogelun wanted a little extra warmth during a boring watch she would damn well take it, thank you very much.

Besides. An *araatan* touched her today, and she hadn't shit herself. She deserved a little treat.

She shivered, a breeze tracking across her shorn head. Good thing the *araatan* wasn't nocturnal – amazingly, it actually slept during darkness. Last thing she needed even on a moonlit night was a giant lizard stalking around. Then again, it was cold out here, and lizards couldn't heat themselves, could they? You saw them basking in the sun all the time, they . . .

Hogelun frowned. One of the things she was pretty sure the lizard *hadn't* done, in the nine days since they'd found it, was bask in the sun. Which was weird as shit, when you thought about it, because that's what lizards *did*. Then again, the bastard could breathe fire (another shiver, this one nothing to do with the wind) so it probably didn't have an issue staying warm.

Come to think of it, an *araatan* sitting next to her right now would actually be pretty helpful. Like the world's biggest guard dog. Not only could it probably sense anybody who wanted to put an arrow in your face, it could make you a nice fire, too, and you could just tell your Chief it did it all on its own.

Hogelun studied the stars splashed across the sky. Trying to imagine telling her past self that not only would she not *mind* the thought of a lizard hanging out next to her, but that she'd actually welcome it.

A shadow moved towards her, coming from the direction of the *ger*. Hogelun stiffened – but it was just Erhi, wrapped in a blanket of her own. She sat down next to Hogelun on the rock.

Erhi was a heavy sleeper. Waking her up for her watch always took an age. She didn't love hanging out in the dark – understandable, for someone who needed light to communicate, and who had to keep a metal pot with her to wake the others if necessary. Hogelun vaguely recalled a suggestion from Chimeg at one point that Erhi be spared watch duty, and the gigantic row that ensued. One of the few times they'd fought . . .

Well. Until the last few days, anyway.

Erhi and the Chief had been fighting a *lot*.

Tonight, of course, it was light enough for Erhi to read sign. Not that Hogelun felt like talking. She kept her hands still. Erhi had frozen her out again, after that thing with the *araatan*. Made herself scarce. Which had stung, and there were a few moments when Hogelun felt the familiar, hot flash of guilt – the same guilt she'd felt after she, Sayana and Khun had come back from Karkorum.

Familiar. That was the thing she was struggling to wrap her head around. How long had those guilty feelings been there? They weren't new – now that she thought about it, they'd come many times before, whenever Erhi had shown even a flicker of disapproval.

She'd explained them away, told herself not to be so sensitive, had gotten used to just . . . doing it. Telling herself that it was easy, that she just had to be better, that she wouldn't make the same mistake next time.

But over the past few days, those guilty feelings had been replaced with irritation. As if the part of her that processed them had begun to smoulder and crackle, finally burning out.

Because truly, what had she done? Did Erhi *want* her to lose her cool, when an *araatan* got close? And then all that dog shit about *You will not go into the cave under any circumstances* . . . what was that? Really?

Erhi could be loving, and Erhi could be kind. And sometimes – more and more lately, if Hogelun was being honest – she could be a giant dick.

They sat together. Neither of them moving. Buried in their blankets.

Eventually, it got a bit much. Hogelun was about to ask if Erhi wanted anything, but the archer's hands moved first. *Fox.*

Hogelun raised an eyebrow. *Sorry?*

You asked if I'd rather be a fox or a tiger, Erhi signed. *People hunt tigers. Other animals try to fight them, take their territory. But a fox can just slip through the grass, and no one pays attention to them. Tigers need big kills, but if I'm a fox, I can eat just about anything. Everything's easier.* She wrinkled her nose. *And you were right. Foxes do have more fun.*

Hogelun didn't quite know what to say to that. Or what this even was. She didn't reply, just shrugged, gazing out across the pool. The moon painted a white, gently rippling streak on the water.

A moment later, Erhi touched Hogelun's elbow, then rubbed a closed fist on her heart. Slow circles, round and round. *Sorry.*

Hogelun huffed a tired laugh, took Erhi's free hand in hers. Squeezed once, then gave it back.

So, she signed. *You going to tell me what the problem is? Because I'm not saying sorry for Karkorum, I did that already.*

She expected Erhi to dance around it. Try to reassure her, maybe even get annoyed. Instead, Erhi's signs were quick and clear. *I'm scared.*

You are?

I don't want to lose you.

The words were so startling that Hogelun actually began to make the sign for Erhi to repeat them. She stopped herself half-way through, blinking in astonishment.

Lose her? Erhi was worried about losing *her*? How could she possibly have made Erhi feel this way? What had she done?

I'm not going anywhere, I promise! Hogelun's hands moved

automatically, urgently. *And I go on raids all the time. We
all do.*

Erhi's smile this time was warm and wide. *Never been worried
about that. But raiding is different.*

Hogelun wondered if she was dreaming this entire conversation. None of it made any sense. *Say what you mean.*

*Ever since the araatan stopped us raiding that village, I feel like
you've been taking too many risks. Like you're not yourself. You –
no, please, let me just finish – I know you're the same person, of
course you are, but it's just made me think about what I would
have if I didn't have you and . . .*

Her hands faltered. Tears on her cheek glimmered in the
moonlight. *So, yes: I'm scared.* Erhi wiped the teardrops away,
jabbed a finger at the cave behind them. *I don't like any of this.
This isn't who we are.*

Usually, this was the part where Hogelun would pull Erhi
into her arms, hold her close, desperate to make it all right.
She almost did it, too. Those parts of her were well travelled:
deeply rutted roads that she'd been back and forth on many
times.

But tonight, she took a different path – amazed even as she
was doing it, not fully understanding the signs she made even
as she was making them.

You need to trust me, she said.

Erhi blinked.

*I'm not smart like the Chief is, and I don't have Sayana's
courage, but I'm not going to die. You're never getting rid of me.
We'll be a hundred years old and I'll still be following you around,
annoying the shit out of you.*

She stared deep into Erhi's eyes. *But if you don't believe that,
if you think I can't take care of myself, then we'll never make it.*

Erhi digested this. Her nod was slow. Thoughtful.

I trust you, she signed, after a long moment. *I'll be better. I swear.*

You won't give me shit when I—

No. I'll listen. I won't just talk over you.

And you'll stop being a dick all the—

Erhi smacked her on the arm. *Don't push it.*

The stillness this time was far more comfortable.

You hear about Khun? Hogelun asked. Sayana had told her about what was in the woman's pouch – a story Hogelun still wasn't sure she believed.

The Dawn Whisper? Erhi let out a long breath. *You think the story's true?*

With Khun? Who knows. But Sayana and Tuya swear blind that Khun really did show them, so . . .

Bound to happen sooner or later. Things change.

Might have to get used to that, Hogelun signed.

Which is when the horses went nuts.

Erupted in a burst of panicked shrieks, over from the trees.

Hogelun was on her feet in under a second, Erhi too – the archer might not be able to hear the horses, but she didn't need to.

Horses hardly ever made noise, and they only shrieked if they were in extreme pain.

Despite the moonlight, their mounts were nothing but dark shapes in the birch grove. Chimeg joined Hogelun and Erhi as they sprinted towards it, her spear in her good hand, arm still slung tight to her chest. Khun too, a blur of pumping arms and flashing knives, doing a little shrieking of her own. Hogelun didn't have the faintest idea how she got there so fast; she and Sayana slept in the cave, taking turns to keep an eye on Tuya.

Yesuntei found us.

But how? Had she seen through their wagon train attack? Tracked them all the way here?

In the trees: horses up on their hind legs; men with spears and swords, slashing at them. Hogelun's eyes went wide; if they'd hurt Hoof Monster, if they'd so much as scratched him . . .

As they reached the grove, two horses bolted – one of them was Hoof Monster, and Hogelun couldn't tell if he was hurt or not. Windwalker was still tied to a tree, completely losing her shit, mouth open, froth on her lips, blood streaming down her flanks. Midnight, Khun's pony, was spinning in furious circles.

Hogelun hefted her club, hunted for someone to smash.

Only: there was nobody. The forest was empty.

In the instant before the trap was sprung, Hogelun realised just how badly the Rakada had fucked this up.

She didn't get a chance to react. Suddenly, there were soldiers. Everywhere, on all sides, all of them with drawn bows, far too close to miss, yelling at them to surrender.

Shit.

Thirty-Six

Yesuntei

Yesuntei would never admit it, but she got the idea from Chuluun. It was his comment about slaughtering horses for food in a siege.

She and her men had spent hours observing the camp. She'd finally, finally seen Tuya, under close guard, led out of the cave to bathe and eat. It had taken everything Yesuntei had not to leap from her hiding place, behind the rocks where the pool became river again. She'd desperately wanted to tear the Rakada apart, right then and there.

Somehow, she'd stilled herself. Tuya wasn't hurt, that much was clear, and there did appear to be a cave behind the falls. As Yesuntei suspected, that was where they were keeping her.

The Rakada were few, far fewer than she'd expected, but she wouldn't let herself underestimate them. And it wasn't just a numbers game: if they attacked directly, out in the open, they risked the Rakada retreating to the cave. They risked a siege.

A surprise attack was the next best answer. But it wouldn't be enough on its own. Not when the enemy knew the terrain, not when you had to wait for them to gather. And in any case, some of them might just withdraw to the cave anyway, abandoning the others to save their own skins. That was the thing about raiders: ultimately, they were all out for themselves.

But if you could draw the bulk of them away . . .

Even then, the solution wasn't perfect: there was no way they'd leave Tuya unguarded. One way or another, there would be someone in that cave when Yesuntei and her men went inside. But if it was only one, two at the most, that changed the odds. They might even be persuaded to surrender.

Yesuntei didn't want the horses killed. She wanted as much noise as possible. She and her men had scouted the birch grove, positioned themselves perfectly. They gave the Rakada a straight, open path to the horses, and then slipped in behind them. For all the stories about these particular raiders, they had no discipline. They all rushed in, ready to fight, not thinking for a moment that it was a trap.

As her soldiers took aim, as Chuluun bellowed at the raiders to surrender, Yesuntei allowed herself a very small smile. They were confused, panicked, spinning – trying to find a gap in the lines. There wasn't one. Everywhere they looked, there was the point of an arrow.

Yesuntei hadn't lied to Chuluun – every one of these raiders was going to die – but for now, she would prefer to take them alive. If they failed to pull Tuya out of the cave, if the raiders barricaded themselves inside, these four might provide useful information.

And if an enemy had one of your own as a hostage, it was always a good idea to have several of theirs.

Of course, there was every chance the raiders would simply attack anyway. Charge headlong into a storm of arrows, get cut down before Yesuntei could talk to them. And there was a moment, as the four of them bunched together, where she thought that might happen.

She was prepared for it, of course. Taking them as hostages would be useful, but not essential. If they died now, so be it.

None of them moved. But they didn't drop their weapons either.

Between her men shouting, and the panicked horses, the noise was abominable. Yesuntei winced, then knelt and struck a flint. Her torch – one of only two she had left, since she peeled off these soldiers from the 8th – sprang to life.

In the flickering light, she finally got a good look at the Bone Raiders.

The big one was there, with her shorn head and enormous club. The archer, naturally, and the little one with the knives, the oldest. That strange leather pouch on her chest, which she clearly didn't remove, even when sleeping. And the Chief of course, with her mane of black hair.

The only one not present was the younger raider, the tall girl with the two sabres. Unless there were others Yesuntei hadn't seen, that meant she alone was guarding Tuya. She wouldn't present any problems.

Yesuntei paused on the raider Chief. There was something familiar about her face, as if they'd crossed paths before . . .

She shook it off. It didn't matter. They'd all look the same when they were up to their necks in dirt.

With a raised hand, she signalled to her men to stop shouting. Stepped forward with her torch, absorbing the murderous looks from the four raiders. They were back to back in the middle of the trees, weapons ready. The archer lifted her bow, tracking Yesuntei, but her Chief gestured at her to wait.

"It's over," Yesuntei told them. "Drop your weapons."

Thirty-Seven

Sayana

Here's something about prisoners nobody ever told you. Unless you had a convenient jail, somebody had to watch them at all times. And that somebody had to keep watching them, even when their buddies all ran off to deal with some very scary noises outside.

Didn't matter that Tuya was probably past the point of running off; Sayana wasn't going to take that chance.

So now she was the only one guarding Tuya, and the *araatan* – who was curled up behind the stalagmite at the back of the cave, deep in the shadows, and hadn't moved a single inch. Khun had left them there, saying she would bring them back an eyeball as a trophy.

Sayana was on the ledge, watching the cave entrance, hands slick with sweat. Fumbling for her sabres. Only . . . what the fuck did she do with them? Did she grab Tuya? Put a blade to her throat? And then what? Did they just stay there? Until either one of the Rakada or whoever was attacking came inside?

How to make things more awkward between her and Tuya:

put a knife to her neck and then just stand around waiting for someone to notice.

How did she and the Rakada not talk about this? How did no one say, *Hey, Sayana, you might want to figure out what happens if sister dearest does ride up.*

But even as the thought popped into her head, she cursed herself. Because that was on her. This whole plan was her idea, and expecting someone else to answer that for her was pathetic.

Which, of course, didn't help her now.

Sayana's gaze slid over to Tuya. The hunter was up on one knee, looking between Sayana and the entrance. If she was going to attempt an escape, now was the time. She could rush Sayana, knock her off the ledge, yell for help.

And if she did . . .

Sayana didn't want to hurt her. She wouldn't. But . . .

But she might not have a choice.

They locked eyes. Sayana would have dearly loved it if hers weren't wide with panic, but that wasn't happening.

"Listen to me." Tuya slowly got to her feet. "Throw down your weapons."

"I . . . what?"

"If you surrender, right now, I'll tell them you helped me. It might make things easier for you."

There was no joy in her words. No satisfaction. She said them like there was nothing else to say, like she had no choice at all.

Sayana kept sneaking glances at the cave entrance, watching the flickering shadows in the torchlight. "You don't even know it's your sister."

The corner of Tuya's mouth quirked upwards. "I recognise the style." She took a step towards Sayana. "You could go back to the palace. I don't know who your family is, but they could—"

"Fuck you. Stay there." Sayana slid down the slope and onto the cave floor, keeping Tuya in her peripheral vision. She didn't think the hunter was going to attack her, but she couldn't rule anything out.

What would have been amazing – really, truly amazing – was if the *araatan* could shake itself awake, and come and help her out. All that food and water they'd hauled in here for it, you'd think it owed them one. But no. When Sayana glanced over her shoulder, she could barely see the beast at the back of the cave. It was just an inert, useless shadow.

She shouted at the beast. "Hey! Lizard. *Araatan.*" Which felt incredibly stupid to yell, but they didn't have a name for it yet. Well, Sayana did, but calling the animal *arsehole* all the time just felt lazy. "Need a hand here."

It was awake. She had been around it long enough to know the difference. But it didn't come out from its spot at the back of the cave – as if it wanted to weigh its options, or simply couldn't be bothered.

Movement in the passage. Two shadows, coming right at them.

For a second, Sayana was dead certain one of them was Hogelun – it was big enough. Whatever was outside, the others had dealt with it, and now they could all have some *airag* to celebrate and laugh about how freaked out they were.

It wasn't Hogelun. It wasn't even the Rakada.

The shadows stepped into the light. Two soldiers – one of them absolutely gigantic, even bigger than Hogs was. Dirt-stained *deels*, gold helmets, with a leaf pattern in a dull green. Both of them armed with huge bows, both pointing right at Sayana.

Oh, fuck.

She lifted her sabres, slipped into a combat stance. Which

wasn't going to help, not even a little, but she didn't know what else to do.

When they saw Tuya, still up on the ledge, unrestrained, they actually stopped. Well, the shorter one did, anyway. The bigger one didn't appear to register how strange it was — that the supposed prisoner was standing free, staring down at them. He just kept coming.

"Sticks, hold," the other one snapped. The big guy — Sticks, Sayana guessed — finally came to a stop. Ten feet away. Sayana didn't think they had spotted the *araatan*, deep in the shadows.

And the time for you to wake up and come to the party would be right . . . about . . . now.

Nothing.

"It's over, girl," the big soldier told Sayana. "Yield. My lady Yesuntei might show you mercy." From the look on his face, Sayana would have had better luck trying to grow wings and fly.

"Suck my ox," she said.

Which . . . didn't make any sense at all. She didn't even know where it came from. But every single part of her was fizzing with energy, and apparently she had no control over her insults any more.

"You want her?" She jerked her chin at Tuya, still stationary on the rocks above. "Come and get—"

The smaller soldier loosed his arrow.

It was like someone punched Sayana in the shoulder. It was such a visceral sensation that there was a confused moment where she thought that was what actually happened — that he'd somehow crossed the space between them, and whacked her. The force of the hit made her stumble backwards, ripping a gasp from her lips.

Tuya yelled something incoherent. Then Sayana's fingers

found the arrowhead, sticking out of the back of her bicep, and that's when the pain rolled over her.

She didn't know why the soldier hadn't hit centre mass. Maybe he was a bad shot, or maybe he wanted to leave her alive for this Yesuntei bitch. It didn't matter. It was all she could do to stay on her feet, the room spinning, trying to wrap her mind around the sheer *wrongness* of this thing lodged in her shoulder.

The *araatan* wasn't going to help. The *araatan* had decided not to get involved, to let this just happen. Sayana didn't know why. For a creature that reacted badly to unpredictable movements, it spent a huge amount of time being an unpredictable bitch itself.

She couldn't lift her arm on the shot side (*the arrow side*, she thought, helplessly). Blood poured down her bicep, soaking her *deel*. She was still holding her sabre, but only just. When she put the other one between her and the two soldiers, the one who shot her smiled indulgently.

There was no possible way the other Rakada had fallen to these fucks. Imagining it felt too big, too crazy. When Sayana tried, her mind recoiled, refused to consider it.

They were going to take her. Take Tuya. And there wasn't a single thing she could do about it. The hunter would never finish training the *araatan*, never step foot outside the city again. She would be back performing for the Khan, wasting her life doing tricks with jackals and eagles, never getting to . . .

Sayana's eyes went wide.

Because that wasn't what was going to happen at all.

Odval – the woman in Tuya's bed, when they'd taken her. If she was a prisoner, they would have tortured her, which meant they knew what Tuya did.

They knew she smuggled people out. That she was working against the Khan.

Which meant when they returned her to Karkorum . . .

The sheer weight of it nearly knocked Sayana to her knees, pushing past the pain, blotting everything out. Because it would be her fault. A direct consequence of what she did.

Tuya's smile. Her fingers brushing Sayana's. The way her eyes shone in the torchlight . . .

Sayana would have gone to the ends of the world to keep what the Rakada had. To keep riding the Tapestry. But if she somehow survived this, and Tuya ended up a prisoner, torn apart in the dungeons . . .

The sister wouldn't allow it. Yesuntei would save her. But that was just scrambling, desperate scrambling. Would Yesuntei overrule the Khan? Could she go against him on this?

There was too much to explain to Tuya. Maybe she'd realised the same thing, maybe not, but it didn't matter. Sayana couldn't save herself, but she could save the hunter.

She lifted her head towards Tuya, which felt like it took a thousand years. "Run."

Tuya gaped at her. "I—"

"*Run!*"

As the word left her mouth, the big soldier loosed an arrow of his own.

Sayana caught it out of the corner of her eye, twisted away on instinct. She must have done it right at the very last instant because she could swear that the arrow parted the skin on her cheek. It was aimed right at her head and was big enough to split her skull in two.

It didn't. It zipped past her, into the darkness at the back of the cave. The sound it made when it landed wasn't the metallic plink of an arrowhead bouncing off rock. It was a muffled thud, as if the arrow—

A gut-shaking, titanic roar rolled through the cave.

Sayana's twist had put her on the ground. In the perfect position to look up at the big soldier. He was staring in confusion at the rear of the cave, clearly wondering why the fuck the shadows had suddenly made such a horrifying noise.

He glanced down at Sayana. Puzzlement in his eyes. As if expecting her to fill him in.

She bared her teeth in a pained, desperate smile. "You might want to duck."

She didn't bother to see if he listened. Just flattened herself against the rock floor, and a second later, the space above her filled with flame.

Thirty-Eight

Hogelun

The hatchet-faced bitch in charge, the one who just *had* to be Yesuntei, barked her command again. "Drop your weapons. Now."

Hogelun, who didn't appreciate being given orders by anyone not named Chimeg, gripped her club even tighter.

Not that it stopped the blood pounding in her ears. She searched for a gap, a place that might provide cover from the archers. The horses were still going nuts and there were arrows everywhere and if they didn't do something in the next few seconds, they were going to die.

On her right, Chimeg shifted. Just a little. Hogelun was desperate to tell her not to give in, to *fight back*.

And in that moment, she understood. Understood the crushing weight on Chimeg's shoulders — every day, every moment, having to make decisions that might get someone hurt, or killed. The burden she had to carry, to guarantee her people, her raiders, a life worth living. The thought was so clear, so startlingly complete, that Hogelun's mouth actually fell open.

Yesuntei lifted her hand. "Last chance."

She was less than three paces away. Hogelun could have crossed that space in an instant, knocked the woman's head off her shoulders . . .

But the arrows were faster.

A sound reached them over the hiss of the falls. A rolling, echoing roar.

Hogelun blinked. She was so focused on the situation they were in that for a few seconds, she genuinely had no idea what might have made the sound.

Then she remembered, and an evil smile slid onto her face.

Oh yeah. We have one of those. Didn't we mention it?

The arrows trembled in the torchlight, the archers looking around, sending worried glances at Yesuntei. The woman herself was staring in the direction of the falls with narrowed eyes. There was another sound now, a series of heavy, crunching thuds, and it might have been Hogelun's imagination, but was there a flicker of light out there too? As if the waterfall was being lit from within.

No point worrying about the Princess, or Tuya. They were in the cave, and Hogelun was out here, and she wasn't going to waste this chance. Should she wait for Chimeg? Wait for her Chief to attack first?

The old Hogelun might have.

The new Hogelun — the one that cosied up to giant lizards and didn't let her lover give her any shit — hefted her club, took two giant steps forward, and swung it at Yesuntei with the force of a boulder crashing down a mountainside.

Yesuntei saw her coming, dodged away, and the head of the club turned the birch tree next to her into splinters. As another roar filled the world, one much closer this time, the grove erupted.

Yesuntei's archers started firing. But their targets were

already moving, dancing across the forest floor, burying spear and knife into soft flesh. Erhi fired arrows of her own, Chimeg spun and jabbed, Khun moved between the soldiers in a blur of flashing metal.

Yesuntei rose up in front of Hogelun like an apparition, chips of wood in her hair and a snarl on her face. Hogelun swung again, but she went too far, left herself exposed. Yesuntei's sabre swing nearly cleaved her in two, scoring a hot line down her side and ripping a pained grunt out of her. She stutter-stepped backwards, blocking the woman's follow-up strike with the haft of her club.

Chimeg impaled a soldier through the throat, and as she turned and shouted an unheard order at the Rakada, the *araatan* finally made its appearance.

Hogelun didn't have the first clue how it knew where to find them. Maybe it just headed for wherever the most people were. But she had never, in her entire life, been so glad to see a lizard.

As the *araatan* crashed into the trees, as the soldiers panicked, Hogelun let out a triumphant howl.

Which turned out to be a huge mistake, because it made the lizard swing its enormous head and charge right at her. She had a confused half-second to think: *We're on the same side, idiot!*

Erhi yanked her backwards, right before the lizard's jaws snapped shut in the space she'd occupied. One of the soldiers, perhaps one slightly dimmer than the rest, tried to stab it in the mouth right when it happened to swing its head low. As his screams filled the grove, Chimeg yelled in Hogelun's ear. "Don't think it cares who it eats right now!"

"What do we d—"

"Get the horses!"

Hogelun's eyes went wide. Hoof Monster and Sayana's still-unnamed mount were gone, but Windwalker was secured to a tree. Midnight wasn't, but he'd apparently decided that what he really wanted to do was stand around, quietly shitting himself.

If the *araatan* decided to go for either of them, then not only would the Rakada lose two mounts, but the soldiers might get a chance to regroup.

Khun was bleeding in multiple places, gashes in her temple, her arms and wrists. But she moved like she hadn't noticed, zipping over to Windwalker and cutting her tether in a single swipe. The horse wasted no time in making a swift exit, and when Khun gave Midnight a whack on the backside, her pony moved as well.

Soldiers circled the *araatan*, sabres out, hunting for an opening. Arrows peppered its scales, porcupining it. Hogelun would give them this: they had spine.

They were also easily distracted, and she emphasised this fact by swinging her club and knocking one poor bastard all the way into the next life.

The *araatan* shook itself like a dog, then lashed out with a clawed foot and kicked a soldier into the air. It somehow snatched him as he flew sideways, and crunched down with a sound like a foot going through a rotten log.

An arrow whipped past Hogelun's head; it was a damn miracle none of the Rakada were hit. Even before she could process the thought, Chimeg and Erhi were pulling her away, forcing her back in the direction of the waterfall. The *araatan* let out a belch of fire, setting the splintered trees alight. Khun streaked past, soaked in even more blood than before, waving something that might have been an ear.

"Get to the cave," Chimeg snapped.

"Uh, Chief?" Hogelun said. "Do we *want* to be in its hidey-hole when it comes back?"

"Better than hanging around out here, don't you think?"

There was a big part of Hogelun that didn't want to leave. Not when there were heads to be cracked. But then she took another look at the forest, currently being torn to pieces by the *araatan*, heard the screams from the soldiers, and decided that in this case, the Chief was probably right.

As they climbed the rocks, she glanced back over her shoulder. There was a figure by the pool, down on one knee, face hidden in shadow. At first, Hogelun thought it was a soldier, but then the figure shifted slightly. The moonlight played across its features.

Yesuntei, face caked with blood, stared directly at her through eyes narrowed to slits. Hogelun grinned back, then flicked her the biggest, most exaggerated Cut she'd ever made. It was so satisfying it sent a shiver down her spine.

Then the Rakada were behind the waterfall, into the cave, the roar from the *araatan* faded into the night behind them.

Thirty-Nine

Sayana

You know what helped when you had to have an arrow removed from your bicep?

Booze. Lots and lots of booze.

Which was a good thing, because suddenly, there was more *airag* than Sayana had seen in her entire life. It just kept coming. Like Hogelun or Khun had a secret stash somewhere, and decided that it was finally time to break it out.

And this wasn't like most *airag*, weak as piss; this was autumn *airag*, when the mare's milk was almost but not quite actual poison.

They were all on the ledge in the cave. Erhi numbed Sayana's shoulder with one of her mixtures, snapped the arrow and pulled it out, staunching the spatter of blood with a wad of fabric. After that, Hogelun more or less held her mouth open and poured *airag* into it.

Sayana coughed and spluttered, the blazing fire filling her stomach. Hogelun was upside down, spattered with blood, eyes dancing. "Princess," she slurred. "That was *wild*."

Tuya sat against the wall, looking exhausted. When her eyes

found Sayana's, they widened. She made as if to get up, make her way over . . . then stopped. Settled for giving Sayana a firm nod instead.

Sayana tried to return it, which made her shoulder squeal with pain.

Erhi was still kneeling over her. *You were lucky,* she signed. *It was clean. The muscle is damaged, but it will recover.*

"Wha—" Weavers, Sayana's mouth felt like the *araatan* had taken a shit in it.

The *araatan.*

Sayana sat up, far too quickly — Erhi tried to stop her, but didn't get there in time and the pain nearly blew her head off.

As she scanned the floor of the cave, Erhi shrugged. *Behind the stalagmite. Came in a while ago, looked at us for a while, then went to sleep.* She sat back on her haunches. *It was hurt again. We'll have to treat it but . . . well, its leg has healed, that's for sure.*

When Hogelun got into the *airag,* her pupils went all wobbly and unfocused. Right then, they were literally two different sizes. She reached out to grip Sayana's shoulder — her bad one — then jumped when Erhi swatted her away. "Sorry, sorry."

"You . . . OK?" Sayana asked.

"Better than OK." Her entire face looked like it was lit from within. "They're gone Princess. All of them, the soldiers and Yeshu . . . Yestan . . . " She waved at Tuya. "Her sister. We fucked 'em up."

"Technically, Sayana's pet did the fucking." It was Chimeg, walking up behind Hogelun. Her hair, unusually, was tied up in a thick ponytail. It made her look younger.

There was someone missing. "Khun," Sayana said, sitting up again, a little more carefully this time. "Tell me she isn't . . . "

Chimeg huffed a laugh. "Someone has to be on watch. Just because we won doesn't mean they won't be back."

Erhi looked grim. *You know she's had more than Hogs?*

"Don't think it makes a difference, to be honest," the Chief said. "I still wouldn't want to fight her."

Hogelun burped, then followed it up with a delirious, rumbling belly laugh.

What happened next was the loose, jittery kind of celebration where they all knew they were lucky to still be breathing. The throb from Sayana's arm was awful, but it was drowned under a torrent of alcohol and laughter. She got to hear the whole thing — the horses, the soldiers, how the *araatan* set the night on fire.

It was one of those stories where everyone tried to talk at once, where the details changed a little every time, getting bigger and wilder. After a while, Hogelun was swearing blind that Sayana had commanded the *araatan* to attack, that she had personally told it to eat Yesuntei's face.

The only one who didn't participate was Tuya. She drank with them, sipping *airag* from an old ceramic cup someone gave her, sitting against the cave wall. She smiled at the stories, even laughed once or twice. But every time Sayana looked at her, she was staring off into the distance.

Sayana was talking as loudly as everyone else, mostly because it helped her ignore the pain from her shoulder, but every time she looked at Tuya, a part of her heart went still. Quiet.

When Yesuntei's soldiers came into the cave, when Sayana told her to run, she genuinely thought Tuya was in danger. But honestly? She had no idea if that was true. It was just an urgent, blaring instinct: a thought too big and terrifying to ignore.

And it was time to stop fucking about with this. She wanted Tuya. She couldn't have her, couldn't even begin to fathom how that would work, but it didn't matter. You couldn't help what you felt, and she was sick of pretending.

Which still left a major question unanswered. If Tuya had

gone with the soldiers, if she had escaped . . . she might have had some explaining to do, once she got back to Karkorum, but she would have found a way. And she *could* have escaped. Sayana couldn't have stopped her.

So why was she still here?

Sayana didn't dare hope that Tuya had the same thoughts as she did. The same feelings. She was drunk, but she wasn't stupid.

Tuya's gaze gave away nothing. And every time Sayana had a chance to ask her, every time the others were going at it and she and Tuya were off to one side, she . . .

Hesitated.

As if, by asking her, she would break something very fragile.

As if Tuya would make her move, right then and there, and leave for ever.

Eventually, Khun came in from her watch. She scrambled up onto the ledge – for some reason, one of her blades was jammed between her teeth. "I see everything," she said, around the knife. "I have the holy, eternal sight of Father Sky. Every leaf, every insect, every drop of water in the Tapestry—"

"I take it Father Sky's eternal sight didn't show you any more soldiers?" Chimeg lay on her side, propped up on one elbow.

Khun ripped the knife from her mouth, waggled it at the Chief. "Not a hair nor hide. They ran like the cowards they are." She swivelled her head, her gaze landing on the *airag* skin in Erhi's hand. She snatched it up, squirted the contents into her mouth.

I was drinking that, Erhi signed.

Khun let go of the skin, gripping the spout in her teeth and leaving her hands free to sign. *And I have heard the desperate whispers of your liver, asking for relief. Truly, I am your saviour!*

Chimeg got to her feet. "My shift," she said. Nobody was

listening: Erhi and Khun were signing at each other, so rapidly Sayana couldn't follow, while Hogelun had one of Khun's knives and was squinting at it like it might reveal hidden truths.

Maybe the *airag* had finally got Sayana to the right place, or maybe the pain in her shoulder had faded enough, because she finally scooched over to Tuya. "Hey," she said. "Can we—"

"Princess," Chimeg said. "Walk with me."

Sayana wavered, but then Tuya touched the elbow on her good arm. "Go," she murmured. "We'll talk later."

It was still a few hours before dawn, and the moon had slipped behind clouds. Chimeg sat on the rocks next to the waterfall, spear across her thighs. Midnight and Windwalker were tied up nearby, but there was no sign of Hoof Monster – and of course, Sayana's own mount was nowhere to be seen. Both remaining horses looked skittish, uncomfortable.

Parts of the forest were still on fire, along with the surrounding hillside, but it didn't look like the blaze was spreading.

It took Sayana a good minute to clamber down across the rocks. Chimeg watched, an amused smile playing on her lips. "Set your feet," she said. The waterfall was quieter than Sayana had thought it would be, and it was easier to hear the Chief's voice. "Makes all the difference."

"Guess you'd know, wouldn't you." Sayana waved briefly at Chimeg's own wounded arm, still in its sling. She collapsed next to the Chief, breathing hard, her shoulder singing.

Chimeg gazed out across the pond, tapping the haft of her spear absently.

The silence went on for just a little too long. The *airag* had made Sayana's mouth taste funny, metallic and sour, and she was suddenly thirstier than ever. "Chief? What did you need?"

"Tell me true," Chimeg said, turning iron-hard eyes on Sayana. Sober eyes – as long as Sayana had known her, Chimeg had never had a drop of booze. "Will we be able to ride that *araatan*? Get it to do what we want?"

"Well, not in the next two days," Sayana said, with a laugh that she barely felt at all. There was a sick sensation in the pit of her stomach – surely Chimeg wasn't going to challenge her on this now, not after what just happened?

"Forget the deadline. Just give me a straight answer. With everything you've seen, do you think we'll be able to use it – them – as mounts?"

Maybe it was her torn mess of a shoulder. Maybe she was drunk out of her mind, and didn't have time for this shit. Whatever the reason, the words that came out of Sayana's mouth were clear and cold. "I don't know what else you want me to do here, Chief."

Chimeg opened her mouth to cut in, but Sayana got there first. "How do you think tonight goes, if Tuya and I hadn't spent the past eight days in that cave? What do you think happens?"

"The soldier shot it," Chimeg said. "It was just defending its—"

"No. *No.* I was in front of the lizard, between it and the man who shot the arrow. It could have scooped me up – I was already down and bleeding. But it didn't. It went right for the soldiers, tore them to pieces, and then kept going."

Sayana pointed at the blazing birch trees. "And somehow, it took out everybody but the Rakada. That wasn't chance. That wasn't an accident. That was fucking hard work."

"You didn't command it. It acted on its own."

"So what?" Sayana's palms weren't just sweaty – they were hot, her fingers tingling with heat. "You're missing the point. Find me another person in the Tapestry – no, Chief, I'm serious, find me *one person* who could get within three feet of those things, other than us. It put its head against Hogelun yesterday, right on her body – did you think that happens without Tuya? Without me? I don't know where we go from here, but we can't squander this. We have to use it."

Because then Tuya could stay. Because then she wouldn't leave.

Weariness washed over Sayana. She did her best to stifle a yawn, and failed spectacularly.

"Maybe you're right," Chimeg murmured.

"Of course I'm right," Sayana replied, sullen. Too exhausted to even celebrate.

The Chief nodded to the waterfall. "Head on back. We'll talk more in the morning."

Sayana didn't need to be told twice. She was very much done with her Chief tonight, and getting back up these rocks in the dark, with one arm, while drunk out of her mind on autumn *airag*, was going to be interesting.

She'd just got her foot on the first boulder when Chimeg said, "I thought it was going to be simple."

There was something in her voice Sayana hadn't heard before. A hesitancy. It made her think of someone stepping across a frozen lake, carefully, carefully, listening hard for the creak of ice breaking. The moon was just peeking out behind the clouds, casting the Chief in a pale, ethereal light.

When Sayana looked over her shoulder, Chimeg was staring out across the pond again. "You were the final piece, you know," she murmured. "A scout. A young fighter I could train up. Oh, I thought I had raiding all figured out." She smiled to herself. "Stay small, don't raid unless you have to, scare the shit out of people when you do."

Her eyes were shining when she turned, although Sayana couldn't tell if it was the moon's reflection, or tears. "You didn't know what it was like before. Erhi and I, after we left Karkorum, we must have fallen in with two or three raider clans, and . . . well, you've seen how they are." She gritted her teeth. "I saw other Chiefs make every bad decision, every communication fuck-up, every mistake. All of it. I swore I'd do things differently. And then tonight, I go and run my own clan into an ambush that I should have known was there."

Sayana was still busy trying to wrap her head around where Chimeg was going with this, but that last part broke through. "Chief, you couldn't have known there'd be—"

It was as if the older woman didn't hear her. "I put the horses out of sight in the trees. And even before that, I had us raid a wagon train in the middle of a storm. I held a knife to one of my own—" Her voice caught.

Sayana was too stunned to reply. She'd never seen Chimeg like this. Not once, in all the time she'd known her.

The moment passed, and the hard look reappeared in the Chief's eyes. "Lot of bad decisions. Lot of mistakes, ones I never would have made before."

"Woah, Chief." Sayana squatted down on the rock – something she was amazed she could do without falling over. "It's . . . it's OK. We're all fine." She pointed at her injured shoulder. "I'll even let you teach me to fight with one sabre, like you always said I should."

That made Chimeg smile, just a little.

"And that lizard? It's only the beginning. All we're doing is adding to the formula: stay small, raid as little as possible, ride giant fuck-off mountain monsters when we do."

"Oh yes." The smile grew a little wider. "We'll have to, if we're going to stay out here. You were right about that, at least. But sometimes I wonder if I . . . If it should have been me who . . . " She trailed off.

"Chief?" It came out a lot smaller than Sayana intended, almost a whisper, buried by the sound of the falls.

"Relax, Sayana." The Chief reached across, patted her knee. "I'm still your Chief, for now. I just need to figure this out."

"Sure," Sayana said, not convinced at all.

Chimeg reseated her spear across her thighs. "Go on back. I think there might have been a drop or two of *airag* left." She winked at Sayana. "Be a shame to let it just sit there."

Forty

Yesuntei

As the very first flickers of dawn lit the eastern horizon, Yesuntei approached the pool.

She moved gingerly, on a swollen ankle. *Deel* and leathers soaked with blood from half a dozen cuts. One sleeve of the *deel* was burned away, blistered pink flesh beneath. It was a damn miracle that was the worst she suffered.

The Rakada's Chief hadn't moved for hours, still as the stones around her, but Yesuntei knew better than to assume the woman had drifted off. All the same, she was amazed at how close she got: right to the bottom of the rock fall before the raider noticed she was there.

In an instant, that gigantic spear was pointed right at her, the raider on her feet, face hidden in shadow, body poised to attack. Balanced perfectly on the rocks.

Yesuntei lifted her hands, wincing as her burned arm complained. "Peace, Chimeg. I'm alone."

It would hardly have mattered if she wasn't. Of the fourteen soldiers she'd peeled away from the 8th, she had three left. Three. And one of those might not last the night.

She forced a smile. "Making my sister train an *araatan* for you. That was clever. I admit, I didn't even know it was possible."

Chimeg tilted her head, just for an instant, then attacked. Springing across the rocks, spear point flashing.

Yesuntei quickly stepped backwards. Tensed her stomach, without meaning to, as if it would somehow stop the blow. "Wait. Chimeg, wait, I just want to talk."

The woman stopped. Spear trembling, less than a foot from Yesuntei's chest. "You know my name."

A flash of anger shot through Yesuntei: she could reach out, grab the weapon, get inside the woman's reach . . .

And then you'd get taken apart.

"Not just your name." It was hard to keep her voice even, but she had to. It was the only way this worked. "I know who you are."

"Then you know what happens to your bones after I'm done with you."

"I know you're from Karkorum. I know you once served the Khan, like I do. You were a soldier."

"Good for you." Chimeg huffed a breath out of her nostrils, like an animal about to charge.

"I know what you did."

That, finally, gave the Rakada pause.

"When I saw you, in the forest." Yesuntei pointed at the smouldering ruins of the trees. "I thought I recognised you. It took me a while, but then I remembered."

In her chest, her heart was starting to slow, just a little. She flicked a glance at the waterfall. "Do they know? About you and the archer?"

Chimeg said nothing.

Slowly, Yesuntei lowered her hands. "What did you tell them,

I wonder? About who you were before?" She shook her head: slowly, left, right, back to centre. "What would they say, do you think, if they knew about that night? I admit, I can't remember what sparked it — was it an argument? Over a game of *shagai*, perhaps?"

"Stop." Chimeg's voice was barely there.

"Maybe if you hadn't been drunk, you and the archer both, you wouldn't have got the wrong house, and things would have turned out differently. What you did to that man . . . and in front of his family . . ."

A cold wind played with her hair. "Quite the scandal. I was still with my unit then, and we all heard about it. You were supposed to go on trial but . . . " She held up a closed fist, popped it open. "Gone. Nobody knew how you two escaped."

All at once, the spear tip was at her throat. Chimeg's control was pinpoint, the tip of the giant weapon just grazing Yesuntei's jugular.

"Doesn't matter," the Chief hissed. "They won't believe a word that comes out of your mouth."

"Of course they won't. I'm not an idiot, and that's not why I'm here anyway. I have a proposal for you."

The spear tip didn't move from her throat. But it didn't go any deeper, either.

"You can return," Yesuntei said quietly. "You get your old rank back — you and your archer friend. You must know my position in the palace now, so you know I can make it happen." She actually leaned into the spear tip, just a little. Eyes locked with the raider. "Give me my sister back. Leave your clan behind. Pick up where you left off. Reclaim your life."

Long seconds ticked by.

"You'd kill me as soon as I turned her over," the Rakada said, lips barely moving at all.

Yesuntei had to stop herself from laughing. She thought this was going to be harder. "And waste a fine soldier? Who knows this land like she knows her own reflection? Why in the name of the Weavers would I do that?"

She had to admit: she was impressed with these raiders. Even if the *araatan* hadn't come charging out of that cave, she had an idea that they wouldn't have surrendered.

"There is so much work to do," she told Chimeg. "Dalai in the north, looking to expand their borders. Ngu, where there are already rumours of another rebellion. And pale men, from beyond the desert – who's to say their rulers aren't ambitious?" She clenched a fist, lifted it to her chest. "You could do so much good with the Khan's seal on your helmet. With an army at your back."

Slowly, she lifted her hand higher. Gently touched the spear tip. If she was wrong, then this was the moment where Chimeg would ram it through her throat.

But the Chief of the Rakada let her push the blade down. Yesuntei took a casual step backwards. "You need to ask yourself if these raiders of yours are worth it. If having that . . . that beast is going to be enough to save you, in the end."

"Didn't save your men," Chimeg muttered.

"A small force, against a single *araatan* – one that hardly seemed in control. That's a very long road to travel. What I'm offering is a way to reclaim your honour. No questions asked, all forgiven. Your life back, just as it was."

If nothing else, she had planted the seed in the Chief's mind. She would let it sit, grow, let doubt and worry nurture it.

Of course, she had her own doubts – insidious ones, which wouldn't stay buried no matter how deep she pushed them. Because if the Chief *did* turn her down, then she would need to return to the 8th. To Karkorum.

You've done all you can.

Without another word, Yesuntei walked away from Chimeg, into the darkness. Surprised to find that her stomach hardly ached at all.

Forty-One

Sayana

When Sayana woke up, it felt like the *araatan* had taken a dump inside her mouth. Then decided to chew on her skull for a bit. As for her shoulder . . .

Actually, she didn't want to think about her shoulder.

After ten thousand years, she sat up, squinting, rolling her jaw. Which hurt too, and how was that fair?

The cave needed torchlight, even during daytime – assuming it actually was daytime. Khun and Hogelun were awake, bringing in an antelope carcass to feed the *araatan* – which was in its usual spot, looking as satisfied as a giant lizard could be.

Erhi was nowhere to be seen. Chimeg hovered in the cave entrance, watching Khun and Hogs struggle. Arms folded, face shrouded in shadow. She was unhappy about something – spend enough time with someone, and you learn to read them even if you can't see their expression – but right then, Sayana didn't have it in her to ask.

A few feet away, crouched over a small fire: Tuya.

She must have caught Sayana out of the corner of her eye.

When she turned her head, it was with that same look from the night before. Curious, hooded.

Sayana gave her a little wave. It just happened, and it felt ridiculous even as she was doing it. But right then, a thousand questions were buzzing around in her head, and she didn't know which one to ask first.

She was never going to get a better chance than this. She stood up, unsteady, putting a hand on the cave wall for balance — her good hand, because she still couldn't lift her injured arm. Below, on the cave floor, Khun barked at Hogelun to turn the carcass just so; Hogelun, looking wretched, let out a gigantic yawn.

Sayana squatted next to Tuya. The hunter had a pot going over the flames: millet broth, the smell earthy and warm. Before Sayana could say anything, Tuya dipped a cup into the pot and handed it to her.

Sayana took a sip, which got her voice working. Sort of. "Thanks," she croaked.

"Don't thank me." Tuya yawned too, shielding it with the back of her hand. "Your archer made it. Just tending the fire for her."

She wouldn't meet Sayana's eyes.

"You're still here." Sayana didn't even realise she was going to say it until it popped out.

"Where else would I be?" Tuya jabbed at the embers with a stick, knees together. "I try to sneak away, whoever's on watch would put an arrow in my back."

Which was certainly true now . . . but wasn't true last night.

Tuya could have escaped at any point. Run off while the *araatan* had everyone preoccupied. Weavers, Sayana *told* her to run. She didn't have to go with those soldiers — she could have escaped into the Tapestry herself.

Sayana took another sip, putting in a real effort to actually get these chaotic thoughts in order.

"OK." She set the cup down, half finished. "That wasn't a good enough answer."

"What do you mean?" Jabbing at the fire like it insulted her.

"You told us your sister was coming for you. And when she did, when she nearly took most of us out, you . . . what, just froze?"

"I didn't freeze."

"You didn't run, either. To her, or anywhere else."

It was a long moment before Tuya answered. Below them, Hogelun sat down with a thump. Even Khun looked exhausted, bent over, hands on her knees. The *araatan* was already chewing on the carcass.

"I wanted to see how far we could take the beast." Tuya still wouldn't meet Sayana's eyes. "The last few days, we had . . . I never thought we'd get this far. I wanted to—"

"Dog shit."

"Excuse me?"

"You could have taken everything you'd learned in this cave, gone and found another lizard. Started again, without actually being forced to. You can't tell me you *prefer* it here, with us watching you."

"It's not just as simple as finding another," Tuya muttered.

"Then—"

"What do you want me to say?" Tuya's voice echoed off the walls. Hogelun, collapsed on the floor of the cave, gave the two of them a strange look. Khun was sitting down too now, more subdued than she usually was. "Seriously, Sayana. Tell me what you want."

Sayana took a deep breath. "I—"

And stopped.

What she wanted, what she truly wanted Tuya to say was: she'd stayed for Sayana.

That she felt the same way.

That the moments between them, the tiny little jolts . . . that Tuya saw them too.

But the words wouldn't come. Sayana had no idea what to say.

Tuya drained her broth, wiped her mouth. "Well?"

"Never mind." Sayana got unsteadily to her feet, done with that conversation, done with everything. She was going back to bed. She was wounded, after all, so it wasn't like she would be expected to do much that day.

Her first two steps were fine. But the third one . . .

It was like it happened in slow motion. Like her foot was suddenly moving through oil. She blinked, not sure what was happening.

She was listing to one side. She had to lean on the wall for balance. *Must be in worse shape than I thought . . .*

She yawned then, big and hard. Weavers, she could sleep for an age. Which was a problem, because she wasn't going to make it back to her nest of blankets. The next step she took was more of a drunken shuffle, like the *airag* was still coursing through her veins.

What . . .

She turned her head. It took a whole year to do it. Tuya was slumped by the fire, chin on her chest. Her cup rolled free of her loose fingers, found the edge of the slope, dropped away.

"Tuya," Sayana said. The word came out soupy. Hogelun and Khun were lying flat too; Khun tried to push herself up, couldn't make it, collapsed onto her back. Sayana couldn't see Chimeg anywhere.

The *araatan*. It was swaying. Eyes unfocused. As Sayana

watched, leaning against the cave wall, it collapsed, rolled onto its side.

Panic roared up inside Sayana, but it had nowhere to go. Somehow, she was still awake, even if the others weren't. She stumbled towards the slope, not sure what she was planning on doing but unable to stop herself. What happened was she went right over the edge, landing hard, right on her wounded shoulder.

Pain obliterated everything. The world went grey and red, flecks of light danced like dust in water.

When she came back, Chimeg was standing over her. Spear in hand.

She was beyond movement then; her arms and legs had turned to stone. Horrible, horrible thoughts slid into her head. If their Chief was still standing, and her Rakada weren't, what . . .

"S-Sayana . . . " Chimeg's lips barely moved. She tilted sideways, caught herself, then went to one knee. Breathing hard, like she couldn't get enough air into her lungs.

What the fuck is happening?

Chimeg made one last effort to get on her feet. Even used her spear for balance. But it was no good, and a few moments later, she was on her side. Clawing uselessly at the dirt floor.

There was something in the broth. And in the *araatan's* meal. It was Yesuntei – she'd got one of her people in, dosed their supplies.

Footsteps reached Sayana. Multiple boots, scuffing against the dirt. "Look at that," said a male voice. "Should have done that in the first place."

"Quiet, Chuluun."

All Sayana could see were her black boots, but it was Yesuntei. Some people just sounded evil. "Bring my sister."

She had to do something. And she had to do it now. Right fucking now.

Somehow, she managed to push herself up on her elbow. She was drooling, her mouth flopping open, slick spit running down her chin. The soldiers were there, and Yesuntei. She was doing something with her hands, moving them like . . .

Erhi. Watching Yesuntei sign at her, eyes narrowed. Awake and standing.

There was no possible way Sayana was seeing this. She was hallucinating. Erhi wouldn't do this, not ever . . .

Erhi noticed her then, and both she and Yesuntei looked her way. The glint of triumph in Yesuntei's eyes was straight out of a nightmare.

Erhi paused for a moment, then stepped closer, until she was a few feet away from Chimeg and Sayana. She rubbed a closed fist over her heart.

Sorry.

Forty-Two

Yesuntei

There were many things Yesuntei needed to pay attention to, in that particular moment. It would have been so, so easy for the Rakada to spring a trap. Erhi could have set the whole thing up, conspired with the other raiders. They might have just been acting, ready to spring to their feet and cut Yesuntei down.

But as she spotted her sister, slumped on her side on a small ledge of rock above the floor of the cave, all of it went away.

Yesuntei's ankle had got worse: an agonising lump of swollen flesh. The burns on her arm were going to hurt for weeks. It didn't matter. Before she could stop herself, she was running, scrambling up the slope and skidding to her knees next to Tuya.

Her sister wasn't injured, she knew that, but reality had ceased to matter at that moment. If they'd hurt her . . . if they had drawn a single drop of blood . . .

But she was fine. Her skin and hair were filthy, but there wasn't a scratch on her.

Yesuntei realised she was crying. Shaking with silent sobs. The last thirteen days had built and built, the panic and the dread and the rage swelling inside her, and now it all came out. She lifted her sister up, held her close.

"What . . . ?" Tuya's voice was barely there. "What . . . happened?"

"Shhh." Yesuntei stroked her hair, couldn't stop herself from doing one last check of Tuya's face, making sure she was unhurt. "You're safe. I'm here. You're safe."

In that moment, everything else went away: the Khan, Hanggai, the army, her position at court, the 8th. Fuck every single part of it. None of it mattered.

Because if you couldn't protect your family, what was the point? You could build the greatest nation in the world, the most powerful empire since the First Riders, but it meant nothing if you let your family down.

Tuya had saved her, once. Fought for her to have a place of her own. Got her into the army, gave her discipline. Purpose. And when Tuya was taken? Ripped from her home in the middle of the night? Yesuntei had stepped up, with everything against her. The Khan's advisors wanted her to fail, Jochi and the 8th had turned their backs on her, and just when victory was within her grasp, a fucking *araatan* tore it all to pieces.

But she'd persisted.

"Yesuntei." Chuluun had long since stopped calling her *bahadur*. "What do we do with them?"

That snapped her out of it. Her sister wasn't truly safe, not until she was back in Karkorum.

Gently, she lowered Tuya to the rock. "Sleep," she murmured in her sister's ear. "We're almost home."

She dropped back down the slope, her gaze hardening as she took in the unconscious Rakada. One of them – the raider with a ridiculous braid – was still awake. Glaring at her.

The *araatan* let out a long, groaning sigh. For a few seconds, everyone froze, eyes fixed on the slumbering shape. Yesuntei's fingers wrapped around the hilt of her sabre . . .

But it didn't move. It was as unconscious as its masters.

The original plan had been to simply kill the raiders. Cut their throats while they slept – well, with the exception of the big one, the archer wanted her as part of the deal. Erhi had argued for the Chief too – protested, even – but Yesuntei had turned her down. One or two raiders was fine, something she could explain away, but more than that and there would be awkward questions.

For a time, she thought it might have been a dealbreaker. That the archer was going to reject her offer. But after surprisingly little argument, Erhi had relented; Yesuntei had the distinct feeling she didn't much care for Chimeg any more.

She looked over her shoulder, studying Erhi, wondering if all this was even worth it. Why shouldn't she just put a blade through the archer's throat? Her lover too? After all, they were as responsible as the others . . .

As soon as she had the thought, another idea came to her. There was a much better use for these women. One that would cement her position at court for ever.

"Get my sister," she told Chuluun. "Get her out of here. And we're bringing the raiders, too."

"All of them?"

"Yes. All. Get moving."

Forty-Three

Sayana

S ayana did everything she could to form words. To ask Erhi *why*. It had to be a mistake, it had to be.

But her voice was mush, her limbs floppy and useless.

I'm so sorry, Princess, Erhi signed. *I'm just trying to keep us safe.*

It was that sleeping medicine – the one they'd used on the *araatan*, so they could treat its wounds. She'd put it in the broth, the antelope carcass.

The soldier Yesuntei called Chuluun came into view again, Tuya slung over his shoulder. Sayana didn't have the energy to turn her head, and despite praying as hard as she could, Father Sky did not reach down to blast the shitty little rat-faced fuck from existence.

Yesuntei crouched next to Chimeg. Stroked the hair from her face, almost tenderly. She spoke so quietly that Sayana could barely hear her. "You thought you were the only one?"

She stood. "Bind them," she told her men. "We'll take them to the God's Heel. Rejoin the 8th."

Erhi looked sick. Good. Sayana hoped she felt sick for the

rest of her life. She didn't know what Yesuntei had offered the archer, but somehow, she didn't think it would be enough to get the taste out of her mouth.

It went beyond betraying the Rakada. She'd betrayed Hogelun. The love of her life. Sayana's *friend*.

Her anger right then was so huge that it felt like it could block out the suns.

One of the soldiers grunted as he flipped Chimeg onto her belly, pulled her arms behind her back. As he did so, the *araatan* made a sound. A choked little moan.

All activity in the cave stopped. Froze solid. The moan came again, louder this time. Sayana couldn't turn her head to look — her neck just wouldn't do what she told it to.

"Why isn't it asleep?" said the soldier kneeling next to Chimeg. "You said it would be dosed."

"It was." There was a very satisfying note of panic to Yesuntei's voice.

Sayana had got to know their beast pretty well over the past few days. It had never made this sound before: that horrible, weak, choking moan. She didn't need to see it to know that it was in bad shape. But . . .

But the moans were getting louder. And they were changing, too: growing deeper, huskier.

Erhi, just in view, was frantically signing. *I gave it the right dose. It's probably just taking a little time to work through the . . .*

The next few seconds were very hard to understand.

Sabres ripping from their sheaths. The sound of clawed feet crunching on rock and dirt.

Shouts.

Roars.

The *araatan* moved past Sayana, right above her head.

A huge, scaled mass, twisting and bellowing. The furious, blinding satisfaction she'd felt as the beast came alive vanished in a wave of terror, because it was going to crush her. It was panicked, confused, and at any moment, one of those giant claws was going to punch through her ribcage.

All the antelope she'd brought it, and the stupid thing wouldn't even notice when it stepped on her.

Sayana didn't know where she found the strength to do what she did next. She flailed her good arm. Threw it up and outwards. Closed her fingers on the top edge of one of the *araatan's* scales, on its back left leg, right above one of the claws.

Held on.

She was pulled across the cave floor, her body dragging. She didn't have the first clue how she was going to survive this, but it was the only thing she could think to do. She closed her eyes and channelled every single bit of energy she possessed into her fingertips. Into not letting go, no matter what.

The pain as she slammed off the rock floor again and again was indescribable. It was through her whole body now, her muscles screaming as the surface scraped skin from her shoulders and arms.

Just hold on.

Thunder.

Water. Everywhere. Cold and sharp. Rushing over her.

Blinding sunlight.

Then water again. Deep. All around her, choking, pulling her under the surface.

Just hold on.

But she couldn't. She couldn't breathe, couldn't think, couldn't move. In the distance, the *araatan* roared.

Hold on.

Sayana was dragged through the water. Her head popped out, just for an instant, but before she could take so much as a single breath, she was under again.

Hold—

Forty-Four

Hogelun

Hogelun had always liked the legend of the God's Heel. The story was, when Father Sky and Mother Earth first wove the Tapestry, Father Sky got drunk one night, lost his footing, and stepped on their creation.

She rather liked the idea of one of the all-powerful gods getting completely shit-faced.

The Heel was a giant depression in a vast, flat plain of swaying grass, a day's ride north of Karkorum. It was a full mile across, with a surprisingly steep drop off from the rim. The Rakada had passed it plenty of times, riding back and forth across the Tapestry.

Of course, Hogelun would have preferred that it wasn't filled with soldiers.

The Heel was a giant camp, with big, drab-coloured *gers*, cookfires everywhere, the earth beneath the soldiers' boots a muddy, churned-up mess. And there were dozens of warriors, a hundred of them – while she was no expert on these things, they looked like hard bastards. Like her club would bounce right off them.

Erhi would fit right in.

The thought was like fingertips brushing a burn that hadn't healed yet. Hogelun squeezed her eyes shut, trying to concentrate on something that might actually help. She couldn't confront Erhi if her hands were still tied and there was a boot on her back, after all.

She, Chimeg, and Khun lay on their stomachs in the dirt, near the bottom of the depression. The poison Erhi had given them had made the past two days' ride a groggy, hazy mess.

A pair of boots strode into view. Hogelun had become quite familiar with them. She'd seen them from ground level a lot over the past two days, and once, they'd even kicked her in the stomach. She'd have loved to say it was a weak kick, but she'd give Yesuntei this: the bitch was strong. Hogelun's abs still hurt.

Hogelun lifted her chin off the dirt to take in the woman herself. Yesuntei barely glanced down at her captives. She wore no *deel*, just a leather tunic, and her left arm and shoulder were a mess of scratches. Dried blood crusted on her skin.

The scratches were from the eagle. At least, Hogelun thought so; she couldn't tell if that had actually happened, or if she'd dreamed it. Tuya's eagle, swooping down out of the sky, talons flashing. Yesuntei getting her arm up, just in time.

Was the damn bird even still alive? Hogelun didn't have the faintest idea.

Yesuntei marched over to a giant of a man, as big as Hogelun herself, who looked like he wanted to tear her in half. Which would have been very helpful, and would have saved Hogelun the trouble. Instead, the two of them engaged in a low, hissed conversation, with lots of pointing at the Rakada.

Off to one side, a soldier supported Tuya. The eagle hunter looked like she didn't know where she was, like she could barely remember to put one foot in front of the other. The soldier led her away, towards one of the *gers*. Yesuntei watched her go: a deep, satisfied smile spreading across her face.

"Hogs." It was Chimeg, lying a few feet away. "Still with us?" Hogelun grunted, decided that wasn't enough and made herself speak. "So far."

Khun spoke, out of sight on Hogelun's left – she, at least, sounded moderately awake. "If you don't take your foot from my back, I will gnaw it off at the ankle."

Her words turned into a choked gasp as whoever had the foot on her back kicked her. Hard.

The Princess. Was she here too? No – she was gone, Hogelun remembered that. Yesuntei and her three friends had talked about whether they should go after her. Probably at the bottom of the river, one of the soldiers had said.

Hogelun had a sudden, desperate urge to talk to Erhi. She wasn't even angry any more; she just wanted to understand, wanted to ask *why*. But no matter how hard she looked, she couldn't see the archer.

Why weren't they dead? Yesuntei had her sister back – why was she even keeping the Rakada alive?

Before she could think about it, Hogelun lurched upwards, getting a foot under her and bucking off the soldier with his boot on her back.

She howled like she was on a raid as she plunged towards Yesuntei: stumbling, awkward, hands still bound, but who gave a shit? She was still going to tear the woman's head off. She would do it with her teeth if she had to.

Yesuntei watched her come. Her expression didn't change, not even when the other soldiers brought Hogelun down. Three of them pinned her to the dirt, forcing her mouth into the mud, muffling her curses.

Somehow, she managed to buck them off a second time. That got her an iron fist to the jaw, and the world went away for a while.

As stars flickered in her vision, she was pulled up to her knees. An arm wrapped around her throat, squeezing, forcing her to take panicky sips of air.

Yesuntei turned back to the soldiers' commander – the big man she was talking to when they arrived. "Still fighting. You have to admire that, at least."

"You disobeyed a direct order." The man had a voice like rocks tumbling down a mountainside. "Stole my men."

"And yet, here we are. My sister safe, her captors in chains." A disdainful look at Chimeg, then back to the soldier. "I'll overlook the fact that you abandoned the mission."

Before he could answer, she raised her voice, addressing the others. There was a note of smug satisfaction there that made Hogelun want to wrap her fingers around the woman's neck and squeeze and squeeze until they met in the middle. "You *all* abandoned the mission. But the 8th can still return to Karkorum victorious – or is there anyone here who'd rather not?"

No one answered her. Some of the soldiers glanced towards their commander, but nobody moved.

"Thought so." Yesuntei turned back to the big soldier. "Here's what we're going to—"

And suddenly, Erhi was there.

Hogelun didn't recognise her, at first. Her silk *deel* was gone, replaced by a grey one, worn over hardened leather armour. She wore a helmet – something Hogelun had never seen her do, not once.

So much for not being angry. The rage came on like a thunderclap, obliterating every trace of exhaustion. But she was hurt, couldn't move, could barely breathe.

You swore to me, Erhi told Yesuntei. *You swore you'd let her live.*

"And I will," Yesuntei said, signing back as she spoke.

Let her go.

"Not yet. Not until this is over."

Until what's over? What are you trying to—

Hogelun didn't catch the rest. She was back by the waterfall, sitting on the rocks under the full moon, hearing herself tell Erhi: *If you think I can't take care of myself, then we'll never make it.*

And Erhi's response: *I trust you. I'll be better. I swear.*

But she hadn't.

Right then, it was impossible for Hogelun not to run through every moment of her relationship with Erhi. Every conversation, every sparring session, every joke, every criticism. All of it.

Because there was no way, at all, ever, that the person she loved would do this. Not to her. Not to Chimeg, and Khun, and Sayana.

Only . . .

She thought of all the times Erhi spoke for her. It had been much worse since the *araatan* came into their lives, but even before, Erhi often overrode her. Told her what was best. And Hogelun had agreed, because . . . because Erhi was wise, and cunning, and beautiful. A fox. Because the guilt of disappointing Erhi was worse than anything else.

But was all that even true? Was it really the reason Hogelun had let it happen? Or had Erhi just been able to control her, safe in the knowledge that Hogelun was too scared of losing her to do anything about it?

What did Yesuntei promise Erhi? What could possibly have made this worth it? And why just her? Why not Chimeg as well? The Chief wouldn't have gone for it, not ever, but surely Erhi wouldn't have done this without . . .

With her hands bound, Hogelun couldn't sign. She spoke anyway, and despite trying to keep her voice even, it still broke. "Why? Erhi, *why*?"

Erhi stared at her, miserable.

Chimeg's voice was winter wind. "She'll fuck you over," she said, speaking slowly and clearly so Erhi could read her lips. "She's not going to give you your post back. You're not walking away from what we did."

What we did? Hogelun twisted to look at Chimeg, even as the arm around her throat held her back. What did that mean?

"I will visit you in your dreams," Khun said to the archer. The words were a sweet whisper, as if Khun was making a promise to a child. "I will tear your mind to pieces. You will see my knife in every blade of grass, my teeth in every pool and river. I will——"

One of the soldiers punched her in the face. Khun twisted away, letting the fist glance off her cheekbone — then twisted back, whip-quick, and buried her teeth in the back of his hand. Held on as he shrieked, cackled when he finally tore his hand away, blood spattering the dirt, coating her lips.

The cackle dissolved into grunts as the rest of the soldiers closed in, burying Khun under a barrage of fists and feet.

And somehow, Khun still managed to speak. "You can't kill me. Father Sky won't allow me to——"

"Someone shut her up." For the first time, Yesuntei sounded weary. Then she said: "What's that? On her chest? That's not armour."

"It's nothing," said the soldier with his arm around Hogelun's throat.

"I told you to search her, Chuluun."

It took Hogelun a second to understand what they were talking about. It only clicked when Khun wailed — furious, desperate, anguished. There was the sound of metal on leather, and one of the men holding Khun down passed the pouch to Yesuntei.

Hogelun had never seen inside the pouch herself, but Sayana had told her what was in there. Not that it made one bit of fucking difference; Yesuntei holding Khun's pouch in her hands was wrong, deeply wrong. Like the entire universe had shifted, become just a little darker, more twisted.

Erhi's eyes met hers, and Hogelun silently pleaded with her. Whatever Erhi had done, surely she wouldn't permit this?

"Khun," she said, through numb lips. "It's OK."

Khun didn't hear her. She was shrieking now, like a wounded animal.

Erhi stepped forward, signing, fingers trembling: *It's nothing important, just let her be.*

Yesuntei barely looked at her, just pulled open the pouch. "Weavers' Breath, someone shut her up," she snapped.

"It's just some plant," said Chuluun, the one with his arm around Hogelun's neck. "Had a look while she was asleep. Didn't even think it was worth taking."

As Hogelun watched, Yesuntei plucked out what looked like a ball of moss, peeled the layers back to reveal a tiny stalk, an even smaller leaf, a bright flash against the brown and grey of the camp.

Hogelun's eyes went wide. The Princess had been telling the truth.

"Yesuntei," Chimeg said, words turned to mush. "You don't need to do this. It's nothing. Just a . . . a good luck charm. That's all."

They had Khun squashed into the dirt now, her face turned sideways. Hogelun had never seen her look like she did then: mad with rage and terror, eyes rolling in their sockets.

"Stop!" It was Tuya. Stumbling across the dirt towards them, moving in big, ungainly strides. Barely upright.

"Get my sister to the healers," Yesuntei said, still studying the little plant. "She isn't herself."

"Leave her alone!" Tuya shouted. That drew an irritated look from Yesuntei, but only for a moment. She waved a hand at her sister, and more soldiers stepped in, pulling her away.

"Please," Khun whispered, and the desperation in her voice, the despair, turned Hogelun's heart to ash. "Please don't."

Yesuntei glanced at her, then back down at the little plant. She rolled her eyes, and without another word, she dropped it to the ground. Crushed it under her heel, not even looking at it.

Khun wailed, collapsing in on herself, somehow forcing her chin to her chest even as she was held down in the dirt. Her whole body shook. She was saying the word "no", over and over again, the words coming out in a desolate whimper.

Tuya roared in anger. Hogelun made Erhi meet her eyes, forced her to do it. This time, she said nothing. She didn't have to.

"Put them somewhere safe," Yesuntei said, turning away without a backward glance. "And see to my sister."

Forty-Five

Sayana

S ayana finally sat down.

She didn't really have a choice. She could tell her body to keep putting one foot in front of the other for a while, even a long while, but at some point it just went, *No, actually, go fuck yourself. We're stopping now.*

There was a rock to sit on, at least. A flat little boulder in the grass. She thumped onto it, head hanging, doing her best not to rub at her torn, useless shoulder. At least Erhi had put that anti-rot shit on it before . . . before . . .

No. She wasn't going to think about Erhi. If she did, she'd just start hitting the rock with her bare fists. Then she'd have torn and useless fingers to go with her shoulder, and be no closer to mounting Erhi's head on a sharpened wooden stake.

Without the movement of her feet to keep her mind off things, the thousand aches and pangs of hunger came rushing back. All at once, coursing through her body.

She didn't have the first clue how she'd survived getting

dragged out of that cave. She'd woken up on the riverbank, coughing, choking. It hurt to move, hurt to breathe, and for a long time she didn't actually know where she was.

The *araatan* was gone.

She'd lost her boot again, because of course she fucking had. Ripped away by the current. At this point, Sayana was starting to take it personally.

She followed the river back to the falls, walking lopsided in her one remaining boot. She didn't have the faintest idea what she was going to do when she got there, but she didn't have a choice. Yesuntei wasn't there any more, of course. Same for the Rakada, all their supplies, and their remaining horses. Nothing but an empty cave and cold cookfire ash.

Sayana vaguely wondered why Yesuntei hadn't come after her. Maybe the bitch thought she was dead.

Or that I wasn't worth the time.

Sayana had wondered – hoped, actually – that the *araatan* might go back to the cave. Only: it wasn't there, and in the hours she'd waited, sitting on a rock staring at nothing, it didn't come back.

When Erhi poisoned it, tried to put it to sleep, she'd . . . got it wrong. Didn't give it enough. And it didn't attack, it just escaped. Like it knew the cave was no longer safe, and that it wouldn't be able to fight.

Not that it mattered. It hadn't come back, and the Rakada were gone, and everything Sayana had worked for was dust.

So she started walking. She didn't know what else to do. Heading south-west, in the direction of the God's Heel – that's where Yesuntei had said they were going, hadn't she?

Along with her boot, the river had taken one of her sabres. Torn it from its sheath.

She didn't know how long she'd been walking for – a

night and a day, at the very least, but who knew, really? Her back screamed at her, her bare left foot a blaze of aching flesh.

She'd found a couple of muskmelons early on. Some pools of water that hadn't looked too stagnant. There had been rain at some point, and she remembered tilting her open mouth up to the sky, but she didn't know when that had been.

Just get to the God's Heel.

And do . . . what, exactly?

Yeah. She was still figuring that one out.

It was midday, the sky overcast, hiding the suns. A chill wind toyed with the grass, covering the rolling hills to the south. There was a deer on one of them: one with huge antlers, studying Sayana. If she had a bow . . .

But she didn't. She had nothing. The clothes on her back and a single sabre and one damn boot.

She closed her eyes, tried to remind herself that this wasn't the first time she'd been out in the Tapestry alone. When she'd left Karkorum, days had gone by without seeing another person. This was like that. She just had to keep going, find the Rakada, make this right.

Except: those few days after she had left Karkorum, when she had been trying to find a group that would have her, had been among the lowest of her life. Because what she hadn't realised was that being alone – truly alone – had made room for all the thoughts in her head to start crowding in.

While she'd been in the palace, she could pretend they hadn't mattered. Forced them to shut up by imagining the things she was going to do when she got out. It had been easy, because she'd been surrounded by people who had made her want to do nothing more than escape. They were right there, a tempting bone to gnaw on. Now . . .

Sayana started walking again. The stag watched her go, utterly unconcerned.

The hills gave way to a flat plain, stretching to the western horizon, riddled with tall, jagged rocks. The grass was thicker here, resisting as she pushed through it. The muskmelons hadn't done much; she was already hungry again. She surprised a little sable, perched on the other side of a rock, made a half-hearted grab for it before it vanished. Not that she'd have been able to do anything if she'd caught it: she didn't have her flint, nothing to start a fire.

The flint made her think of the cave. The other Rakada. Erhi. And the burning rage at what she had done gave way to a desperate need. A need to be back with Chimeg, with Hogs and Khun. Because without them . . .

No. That was crazy. She'd been in the Tapestry for years now, and she could figure this out.

She was muttering to herself. Meaningless nonsense, half-finished sentences. The plain stretched before her, the huge, grey sky watching over it.

What if she never found the Rakada? What if she was too late? Unless she could find a horse – and there was nothing, not a single animal on this entire plain except that fucking sable – it would be *days* before she got to the Heel.

Thoughts crowded her, far too many of them.

What if no one else would have her? The other raider clans . . . when the Black Hands stopped by the waterfall, their leader said they were all heading for the desert. Sayana's imagination took this, ran with it, spiralling away before she could stop it.

With no raider clans, she would be on her own out here. Where would she go? Even if she found someone to be with, how long would it be before the army forced whatever group she chose to move back to Karkorum?

She didn't know when she started crying. Didn't know how long the tears had been there. She was walking so hard now that her strides left deep prints in the earth, as if she could stamp out the thoughts. Boot print, heel print, boot print, heel print. But the thoughts just kept coming, and they brought a healthy dose of shame with them. Shame that this was what it had come to. That this was all she was.

Tuya's voice, mocking her: *If you were at court in Karkorum, then you had everything you could ever need. All the riches in the world. You gave all that up, to ... what? Hide in a cave? Scratch out a living, taking what isn't yours? Killing people for their bones? What are you doing?*

There was a wagon. Tracking across the plain ahead of her, north to south.

Before Sayana could stop herself, she was running. Sprinting. This wasn't a raid, not with her and her one little sabre. She didn't have anything to trade for food, but that was fine, she would figure it out. If she could stop the wagon, talk to whoever was there, force these fucking thoughts out of her head ... even for a little bit ...

It was a small wagon, two-wheeled, with a colourful fabric roof stitched in bright oranges and reds. Pulled by two horses that looked like they'd been foals around the time of the First Riders. Other than the pilot, there was no one else on the wagon that Sayana could see; the rest of them walked behind it, either on foot or on horseback. A mix of young and old, men and women, children and babies. There were about twenty of them, dusty *deels* telling the story of a long journey.

Sayana didn't want to startle them, so she called from a way off. The pilot spotted her first, pulled the reins as he brought the horses to a stop. A few of the men drew rust-bitten sabres, but didn't look like they were about to use them.

By the time she reached them, Sayana was breathing hard. It took her a second to catch her breath, hands on her knees. "Where are you headed?"

The pilot – an older man with a nasty-looking set of pimples and a sour twist to his mouth – peered down at her. "Same place you should, unless you want the Khan's people after you."

Another recipient of that blue banner. Of course.

"Oh, I am," Sayana said quickly. "I was with my ... my people, but there was a storm and I got separated ..."

It would have been a great idea to get her story planned out *before* she tried this, but she wasn't in the right headspace. Even the idea of *being* in the right headspace was laughable at this point.

"Anyway – listen," she said. "Can I ride with you? Or walk, I don't need a horse or anything."

She would love a horse. Her screaming, complaining, bootless foot would love a horse. But at this point, she'd settle for not being alone – at least until she could figure out what in the nine hells she was going to do next.

She pulled her sabre partway out of its sheath, which made one of the men nearby step in closer, scowling. "I can fight," she said quickly. "I'm good with a blade. If you run into any trouble on the way, I can help."

The man who'd stepped closer glanced down at her bare foot, saying nothing.

It felt wrong to have her other hand empty, to not have a second sabre there. She pushed past it, tried on a smile. "All I ask for is some food and water. It's ... been quite a while since I ate."

Her smile wasn't returned.

Come on. She just needed to ride with these people for a bit, just so she could get her head straight, get some proper food in her, come up with a plan ...

"A storm you say?" Pimples stroked his wisp of a beard.

Sayana's heart gave a little leap, although she was careful not to show it. "A bad one. A few days back. My horse got spooked, bucked me off."

After a long moment, he nodded. "Very well. You can—"

"I know you."

It came from the man who'd scowled at her when she'd shown her sabre. He had moved a little closer, staring at Sayana through narrowed eyes. He cocked his head to the person next to him: a broad-shouldered woman who also happened to have her weapon out. "Gerel, am I going mad? Is she—"

The woman's eyes widened, and then blazing fury twisted across her face. "It's a raider," she snapped. "Raiders!"

"Woah, hey." Sayana held out her hands – well, hand, her right arm still wouldn't lift without blazing pain. "Not true. Not a raider. I'm not raiding you!"

Saying that felt wrong – like she was betraying Chimeg and the others, like she was disowning them. Her words were lost as the group erupted, as multiple sabres were drawn, as the pilot fumbled with a bow that had to be bigger than he was.

The oddest thought: if she was with the Rakada, and they were raiding these people, it would be over in seconds.

How the fuck did they recognise her? How did they know who she was?

The scowling man came, swinging his sabre back, getting ready to skewer her through the chest. Sayana didn't bother drawing her own blade; she stepped to one side, swept her leg into his, knocked him to the ground. Self-defence – they would see that, surely? She wasn't a raider, not right then, and she didn't care where they knew her from, she could convince them . . .

An instant later, she was on her back in the dirt. Arms pinned, and a bunch of extremely angry people towering over her. Her shoulder wound howling as a knee pressed on it through the bandage. Half of them were watching the horizon, as if they were expecting the Rakada to come riding through at any moment.

They must have raided these people before. Whatever settlement or village they had been in, wherever it was on the Tapestry, they'd hit it. It was the only explanation. Sayana didn't have the faintest idea how that arsehole recognised her, how he even remembered her face without its paint. She certainly didn't know who he was.

Didn't matter. She *had* to make them believe he was wrong.

She put that smile back on her face. Something that was hard to do, when she was on her back with twitching blades inches from her face and a knee driving into her very clearly wounded shoulder. Did they not see that? Did they miss the bandage? Or did they just not give a shit?

"I swear on the Father and the Mother," she spat, "I'm not a raider."

Blasphemy, but it wasn't like either of the Weavers had been looking out for her lately.

"Lies," the scowling man said. He had a smile of his own now too, and it wasn't a pleasant one. "Last time I saw her, she had bones on her *deel*, face all red-painted." He waved his hand in front of his own face, up down, teeth flashing behind his fingers. "Scouting, were you?"

"We've nothing left to give," the woman – Gerel – said, rapping a fist on the base of the wagon. "You took it all."

"Raider scum."

"Where are the rest of them? Why's she alone?"

"Who gives a shit? Gut her. Leave her for the jackals."

Sayana did her best to shout above the din. "I wasn't trying to raid you. I was just looking for some food!"

The scowling man – the grinning man, now – had a blade.

He spun it, trying to do it in one smooth movement, but he fucked it up, and the sabre thudded into the dirt. Sayana kicked at it, desperate now, and got nowhere. In moments, he had it back, angled right down towards her throat. One of his friends pulled her own sabre away, made it vanish.

This couldn't be how it ended. She wouldn't let it. But there were too many people holding her down, and no matter how hard she fought, she got nowhere.

"Hold."

The speaker was an older man, so stooped and shrunken that his *deel* billowed around him. But he had eyes of flint, and a voice that age hadn't touched. "Leave her be."

There was an upswell of angry noise from the others, but the man silenced them, snapping up a raised hand.

"Listen." Sayana jerked her chin at the old man, which was about the only movement she could make. "I'll go, OK? You'll never see me again——"

"Quiet." The man with the blade curled his lip at the new arrival, put the point to Sayana's throat.

"Who are you to take a life when you do not need to?" the old man asked him. He spoke softly now, so softly that Sayana had to strain to hear him. The skin on the back of her neck prickled, and it had nothing to do with the cold metal under her chin. "Who are you to unpick the Tapestry?"

"She's a raider," someone spat. "She's the one who takes lives. She doesn't deserve to——"

"She will face her judgement, when the time is right."

The old man's eyes found Sayana's, and her lungs just . . . stopped working. Her breath hung frozen.

His irises were a deep orange, flecked with yellow, like the last clouds at dawn before the suns burned them away. But it was his pupils that almost stopped the heart in Sayana's chest. They were black, black, black. Deeper and darker than midnight.

Right then, she wanted to be small. She wanted to curl up and shrink until she was nothing, until she could hide behind a single blade of grass. It was such a powerful urge that she actually pulled her knees up – or tried to, because her legs were still pinned in place. Her ears were ringing, blocking out everything else.

She had a strong sense that the others, the men and women around the wagon, weren't seeing what she was. That they had no idea what was behind the man's eyes.

Deep in her mind, she heard Khun's voice. Telling the story of how Father Sky had spoken to her, through the body of a dead boar.

The man – if that's what he was – lifted his chin very slightly. Smiled. The tiniest little quirk of the lips.

"I think this one still has many miles to walk."

And just like that, he dismissed her. Turned away, shuffling back to his horse.

Sayana's captors held her a moment longer; then, with a final few muttered curses, they let her go. She barely heard the insults they threw her way as the wagon got moving again. Barely managed to even lift her head from the dirt, until the sound of their horses had faded, until there was nothing left but the wind.

She sat up, which was when the shakes started. She felt as if something enormous, something the size of the whole world, had held her very lightly in its fingers for a brief moment . . . then let her go. As if she was a moth, captured and examined, wings fluttering helplessly.

She had no idea why she'd been released. She didn't know why she was even alive. It was too big for her to take in, too much to process. Not that it mattered.

She was alone.

Forty-Six

Yesuntei

If you wanted to get clean in a military camp, you splashed yourself with cold water. Nobody wasted firewood to give someone a good, hot soak.

If you were lucky, and you had people working under you who didn't completely hate your guts, you might persuade some of them to fill a tub, which at least meant you could do your whole body at once.

When she was still a soldier, Yesuntei used to get washing over with as quickly as possible. A few quick splashes from a basin in the morning, and that was it. But after six days out on the grass, after everything that had happened, she luxuriated in it. Whole head in the basin, holding her breath, relishing the delightful shock of the cold water. For a moment, she even forgot about her ankle, her cuts and burns.

She surfaced with a gasp, rivulets cascading over her face. As she wrung out her hair, head tilted, Tuya slipped through the open flap of the *ger*.

Yesuntei's heart leaped – she suspected that would be happening for quite some time, whenever Tuya walked into the room. But she controlled herself, flashing her sister a smile as she squeezed the last of the water from her dark hair. "Did you eat? Get something to drink?"

"You have to let them go."

Yesuntei didn't answer immediately. The *ger* was Jochi's, sparsely furnished as always. The only light came in from the flap: a single beam of hard, bright daylight which somehow didn't quite penetrate the interior.

"You know," Yesuntei said, slipping her *deel* back on, wincing as the sleeve caught on her burned arm. "I've seen this before. During the Ngu Rebellion, when we rescued some of our people, they acted as if their captors were their friends."

"You're not listening. They don't deserve—"

She stopped when Yesuntei limped over and wrapped her in an embrace. Even then, even when Tuya was standing right there, in the middle of a camp with a hundred soldiers around her, Yesuntei still had to remind herself that her sister was safe.

"I can't even imagine what you went through," she said. "With that thing, that animal. But it's all right." She pulled away, beaming. "We're going back to Karkorum, and I promise, no one will ever touch you ag—"

"None of this happened like you think it did."

Yesuntei raised an eyebrow, amused – although she couldn't help but feel a tiny twinge of annoyance. "You ... weren't kidnapped?"

"Well ... yes, look, of course I was, but ... "

"And we shouldn't have come after you? What would you have had us do instead? Shrug our shoulders and hope you enjoyed your new life as a slave?" Yesuntei laughed, reaching for a water skin on Jochi's chest.

"I wasn't a slave."

"Listen, when we get back to the city ... actually, before we leave, there should be time, I want a full debrief. I want to know everything that happened, everything you saw." She held out the skin, but Tuya didn't take it. "If this particular bunch of raiders got it in their head that these *araatan* could fight for them, then others might come after you. We need to plan for that."

Tuya lifted clenched fists to her chest, and for a bizarre moment, Yesuntei wondered if she was about to throw a punch. Then her sister bowed her head, lowering her hands to her sides. "You got me back. That's what this was all about, wasn't it? You don't have to keep the raiders — just let them go, they aren't worth it."

That little twinge of annoyance had stuck, like a barb in Yesuntei's flesh. Tuya hadn't thanked her for the rescue, not once. Sure, she had been under stress, probably still feeling the effects of that sleeping potion, but she was lucid enough now.

"I'm asking you," Tuya said quietly. "As your sister. As a favour to me: please just let them leave."

"A little difficult." There was something in this *ger* that stank — rotten meat, a scrap that had fallen into the chest, maybe. It had been at the edge of Yesuntei's mind, but all at once it was overpowering, and it made her stomach lurch. "One of them, the archer, has decided to be a soldier again. I'm pretty sure the other raider, the big one — her lover? Yes? — won't want to leave without her."

"But—"

"*Tuya*. I'm not going to talk about this. You're going to rest up, you're going to do what Jochi and the others tell you, and then we're going back to Karkorum."

She found her sash, tied it around her waist. "You'll return to the palace, at the pleasure of the Khan. You'll continue to advise me on wildlife matters. And you can continue sneaking people out of the city."

Yesuntei wasn't looking at her sister then – the sash knot was giving her trouble, her burned arm making her fingers tremble – but she could picture the look on her face.

"You thought I didn't know?" she said quietly, pulling the knot tight. "I've known for a long time."

Tuya made a very good attempt to meet her sister's eyes, but didn't hold them for more than a moment. "What are you talking about?"

"Your little side activity. By all means, keep at it."

Tuya's mask slipped. She gaped, hands hanging limp by her sides.

"Why?" she said, after a good five seconds.

Yesuntei smiled tolerantly. "You think I'm an idiot? You think people *want* to leave the Tapestry? Live in Karkorum?"

"I—"

"We can dangle the glory of the Khan in front of them – and for some, it actually works. But when you force people to live somewhere at the point of a blade, they'll resent you. And that resentment can be very, very dangerous."

She stepped to the edge of the light from the *ger* flap. "We bribe, we threaten, we blackmail, whatever we need to do. But we learned early on that it wasn't enough. It would never be enough, and it meant we'd be fighting a battle on a thousand different fronts, every day, until the end of time.

"When I found out about your . . . work, the Khan wanted you brought in. I advised caution. Because in what you were doing, I saw an opportunity.

"People can endure anything, as long as there's a scrap of hope. Even if they themselves will never leave, they can daydream about how they would do it. They know that there's a way, that the court's eagle hunter can help them, and so they convince themselves to hang on until the time is right. Just a little longer."

She shrugged. "It's a small part of building the city, but a vital one. So yes: not only will I permit you to continue sneaking people out, I want you to keep doing it. I *welcome* it. No one will interfere, because for every person you help escape, a hundred more decide to stick it out. Hoping that it might be their turn next."

Yesuntei found her sabre. She needed to get it sharpened, which fortunately wasn't a problem – military camps were terrible for personal hygiene, but if you needed a weapon looked after, you couldn't be in a better place.

From the door, Tuya said, "You're a monster."

"Don't be so naive," Yesuntei snapped. The ingratitude burned at her, a startling feeling. "None of this is about me. It's *never* been about me. I'm helping to build something – something that is going to last long after my death, enjoyed by people who won't even know my name."

"The Tapestry won't—"

"*Fuck the Tapestry.*" Yesuntei didn't enjoy cursing, but sometimes, it felt so good. "The Tapestry is nothing. It does nothing, contributes nothing, it can't defend itself. If Dalai – hells, even if *Ngu* decided to take it for their own, who would stand in their way? You?

"But if we unite – as Hanggai – then nothing can stop us. Our children can grow up with purpose. Not just for their family, or their village, but for a nation. And if a few raiders have to die to make that happen, then so be it."

"But it isn't just a few raiders, is it?" Tuya was angrier than Yesuntei had ever seen her. "It's the people in the dungeons. It's everyone who disobeys the Khan's Will. It's wild animals who wander into the city, who don't know any better . . . "

"Worthy sacrifices," Yesuntei said, through gritted teeth.

Tuya goggled at her sister, her mouth moving silently, as

if going through a dozen arguments without being able to choose one.

"You're fucking evil," she said eventually. "You're an evil, heartless cunt."

"That's eno—"

"You're poison." Tuya spat on the ground, eyes flashing. "When I fought for you to join the army, I thought . . . I thought I was doing the right thing. I thought it would *fix you*. Turns out, there's no helping someone like you."

She spread her arms in a challenge. "When you kill the Rakada, you'd better have saved a hole for me. Because I'm not going back to Karkorum. Not ev—"

Before she could finish, Yesuntei was on her.

She grabbed one of Tuya's arms, twisting it up behind her back. Ignoring her sister's howl of pain, forcing her to her knees. Tuya fought, of course she did, but froze when Yesuntei gave her wrist another quick jerk.

"Don't," she said. "Or you can forget about holding your eagle, ever again. On either arm." She raised her voice. "Someone get in here."

As footsteps approached, she bent down and murmured in her sister's ear, "Yes, you're coming back to Karkorum. And yes, you will obey. Because understand this: *I* allow you to exist as you do. *I* am the one who gives you what you have. You will accept my protection and my grace, and you will be thankful for it."

Another tweak of the wrist, on the border of snapping the bone, bringing a horrified grunt of pain to Tuya's lips. "And if you aren't, if I sense anything from you but abject gratitude and immediate, unquestioning obedience, you will lose everything. *Everything.* And you'll get to find out what happens in those rooms under the palace. In the dark."

Yesuntei didn't know the names of the soldiers who entered the *ger*. Not that it mattered: they obeyed without question. They had *all* obeyed without question, ever since she had returned. Chuluun had become something of a hero within the 8th, and Jochi . . . well, Jochi was still in command, in theory. When she got back to Karkorum, Yesuntei might have to look into that.

The soldiers took Tuya, hustling her out of the flap. "Secure her," Yesuntei shouted.

"Yes, *bahadur.*"

She stood until they led the silent, simmering Tuya out of sight. Stood rigid, framed in the doorway, hands clasped behind her back.

Yesuntei took a deep, shaky breath. Headed over to the basin, began washing her hands, slowly and carefully.

Before she knew what she was doing, she'd launched the basin across the *ger*. A fan of water sprayed the fabric, the basin bouncing into the darkness. Yesuntei put her hands over her eyes, trembling silently.

She stood there for a few moments. When she straightened up, all trace of emotion on her face was gone. She was as blank and hard as stone. She had to be.

She always had to be.

As she retrieved the basin, she wondered about the raiders. The plan was to bring them back to Karkorum in chains, and the 8th had orders to leave for the city tomorrow, but . . .

Yesuntei's eyes narrowed. She thought of the tiger in the granary. Thought of how it had died.

There might be a better way.

She found Jochi at the training circle — or what passed for a training circle on the Heel's uneven ground, anyway. He sat on a rock, bare-chested, hand propped on the hilt of his huge sabre, which was point-down in the dirt. His other arm rested on his knee. He was watching two soldiers duel, calling out corrections.

Judging by the sweat on his back, he had been training too. It was a pity he was no longer capable of leading the 8th: he was a good example to his troops.

When he saw Yesuntei coming, he grunted. "Care to tell me why our rescued hostage is now a prisoner?"

"Give me two of your fastest riders. I need a message sent to the palace."

He squinted up at her. Defiance in his gaze . . . but resignation, too. Not to mention a dull, leaden hate.

She'd beaten him. He had no choice but to go along with her forged orders, and then right at the point when he *could* have challenged them, she'd made it impossible for him to do so. She'd given him victory, and for him to deny it would be unthinkable. All the same, he would never trust her again. Not with anything.

Which hardly mattered. Not any more. With the glory of Hanggai assured, who cared about this small-minded man?

"We're heading to the city ourselves tomorrow," he said. "Why would—"

"No. We're staying right here." She rolled her shoulders, massaged her side, trying to force her burning stomach to be calm. "Karkorum is coming to us."

Forty-Seven

Hogelun

Hogelun had always suspected that it might be tricky to sleep with her arms tied above her head.

Turned out she was wrong. It wasn't tricky; it was impossible.

She, Khun, and Chimeg sat against the walls of their cage, hands bound to the bars. The pricks who had put them in there completely ignored Chimeg's wounded arm, wrenching it above her head. The Chief's skin was a sheen of sweat, and in the flickering light from the camp's torches, she looked horrifically pale.

Hogelun's own arms ached. For the thousandth time, she tried to sleep, letting her head rest on her bicep. No good. Her hands were numb, two big lumps of meat at the end of her screaming arms.

The three of them hadn't said much since they'd been shoved inside. They'd had no food, although someone had come to squirt a few drops of water into their mouths. Mostly, outside of a few muttered insults, the soldiers had left them alone. There wasn't even anyone guarding them; as if the cage and their bonds were enough.

They hadn't seen Yesuntei. They hadn't seen Tuya. Erhi

certainly hadn't made an appearance. Hogelun couldn't decide if she was angry about that, or relieved.

Mostly, she just felt sick. Every time she pictured Erhi's face, her gut gave a nasty little twist.

They weren't dead yet. That meant Yesuntei was keeping them for something, and Hogelun doubted it would be a good meal and a solemn apology.

"You all right, Chief?" Hogelun said through cracked lips, after deciding that sleep wasn't happening.

Chimeg's voice was as tight as a drawn bow. "Please stop asking me that."

"You got any give? In your hands?"

"Don't know." Hissed through gritted teeth.

"Khun? How about you?"

Khun said nothing.

She hadn't spoken for hours, hadn't said a single word since that evil hell-bitch crushed her plant. She had folded into herself, and even in the semi-darkness of the cage, she looked a thousand years old. Head bowed, knees drawn up, tilted to one side. As if she didn't even have the energy to keep them upright.

Hogelun was worried about the Chief, but when she looked at Khun, it went beyond worry into a kind of desperation. The idea of Khun not being . . . well, not being *Khun* was impossible to take.

A snatch of conversation from outside the cage reached them. Two soldiers, talking under their breath, muttering something about messengers. Hogelun didn't bother wondering what that might mean; she just gave her ropes the biggest wrench yet, hoping that maybe, just maybe, this time . . .

Aaaaaand nothing.

After a few more seconds of effort, the muscles in her neck were standing out like cords, and Hogelun collapsed. Panting.

She kicked at the ground, mostly because if she didn't, she was just going to start swearing.

"Enough, Hogs." Chimeg's words were barely audible. "Just leave it."

Hogelun steeled herself, digging deep, trying to find enough energy to work the ropes again. In the light of the torches, something on the ground caught her eye. Something she'd unearthed when she had kicked at the dirt.

A stone. About the size of her closed fist. And for some reason, seeing it made her think of the Princess. Now why would . . .

Hogelun's eyes went wide.

Sayana had told them how she'd escaped, after they encountered the *araatan* for the first time. Hogelun had thought it was the most ridiculous thing she had ever heard, had half believed the Princess had been making it up. But what if she hadn't been?

Hogelun checked to make sure there really were no guards, twisting her head, ignoring the crick in her neck. When she was satisfied, she pulled the big stone a little closer with her foot.

Her heart sunk. It had had an edge, but only just, less than half an inch, and dull as their chances. The rest was smooth.

Still, she tried, kicking her boot off and working with her bare toes. Not like she had a fabulous range of options to choose from.

Turned out, she should have given Sayana a little more credit. Getting the stone turned the right way up, when all she had to work with was her feet, was bloody hard in itself. Hogelun dropped it four or five times before she got the damn thing held right.

OK. Great. Now all she had to do was get it to her hands.

But when she tried, she couldn't do it. She strained and strained and strained, but her hips and back wouldn't let her.

She simply did not move in the same way as the tall, lanky Sayana.

Hogelun dropped the stone – the cramps jabbing up and down her thighs gave her no choice. She hadn't thought she could feel worse than she did before. Turned out, she wasn't even close. Fuck the Princess, and fuck her fantastically flexible hips.

Chimeg licked her cracked lips. "Let me try."

Hogelun kicked the stone over, watched as the Chief went through the same process. But Chimeg couldn't do it either, couldn't even get the stone held between her toes. She was shuddering with pain, no control at all.

"Khun?" Hogelun said. "How about it?"

If anybody had the flexibility to get the damn stone where it needed to be, it was Khunbish. Old she might have been, but her body had always moved like she was a sprig of twenty. As if the ravages of age took one look at her and went *absolutely the fuck not.*

Khun didn't answer. Didn't even look like she'd heard.

"Khun, we need you right now," Hogelun said. Try as she might, she couldn't stop fear from slipping into her words, like a knife between ribs.

Khun murmured something, head hanging.

"Khun, please—"

"I couldn't do it." Khun's voice was barely there. Her eyes – big, watery – found Hogelun's. "I failed."

"No, you didn't. No, you . . . Khun, look at me. Look at me. You didn't fail anyone."

"I can't feel him." Khun blinked – a movement that seemed to take far longer than it should have. "I can't feel Father Sky."

Hogelun had no idea what to say.

And why would she? What could she, Hogelun, possibly

tell Khun that would matter? She didn't know anything about having a child, a family, and certainly not what it was like to lose them.

She stared at Chimeg, willing her Chief to do something. Anything. Chimeg just shook her head, mouth slightly open. Which made no sense, none at all, because it was the *Chief*.

Back at the village, before the *araatan* showed itself, Chimeg had stood firm in the face of a thousand flying arrows, aimed her spear carefully, taken out the soldiers' leader. No fear, no indecision: just clear, cold action. An approach that had built the Rakada into the scariest motherfuckers in the Tapestry.

All gone. Drained out of her. As if all of it, every action she'd taken as Chief, every moment, had all led her here. As if she'd lost control, and didn't know how to get it back.

Which left Hogelun herself.

She shouldn't have been the one doing this. Chimeg was right there, and she, Hogelun, was just a cook. A cook, and a fighter. She didn't inspire people. She didn't give orders, she followed them, and that's how it should have been because she wasn't smart enough to know what to do when . . .

At that moment, a very small voice whispered in the back of her mind: *Who's saying that? You? Or Erhi?*

Hogelun's eyes went wide.

Erhi had never used those exact words. She had never told Hogelun she wasn't smart enough, or that she should stick to cooking, or that she should be a good girl and follow orders. She never had to. She had communicated those things through a look or a shrug or a stare, all the time. Through comments that sounded sweet but which held pure poison.

And Hogelun had *liked it*. That was the crazy thing. She *liked* someone telling her what to do, especially if that someone was Erhi.

In that moment, the disgust was overpowering. How could she have put up with that? How could she have let it continue for months and years? Especially when it had led her here. To this cage, facing Weavers knew what, betrayed by the one person she thought she could trust.

And bubbling up from under the disgust: anger.

Rolling, roaring anger.

Chimeg had always expected them to respect the Weavers. She didn't ask them to believe, but she did ask them to be mindful. None of them had ever had a problem with it; you found that attitude across the entire Tapestry, from the smallest group of nomads to the palace itself. It was no hardship.

Hogelun thought for a brief second, and decided that under the present circumstances, she couldn't give the tiniest shit.

"Fuck Father Sky," she told Khun. "Fuck him. You ever stop and think why he let that snake into your house in the first place? Him and Mother Earth?"

Her voice had gone very hard. "None of us saw Erhi coming. She sold us all out. But if you want to blame someone, blame me. *I* should have seen it. *I* should have done something. But I'm not going to let you quit. Not like this. You think your son would want you to just . . . just give up? If he were here?"

"Do not," Khun snarled.

Hogelun didn't even pause. "What about your husband? What would he say? You think he'd be proud?"

"Hogs," Chimeg said quietly. "That's enough. Let her be."

"Nope." Hogelun wrenched at her ropes, yet again, because she didn't know what else to do. "Khun, your son isn't here. Your husband neither. I don't see Father Sky anywhere, and that bitch Mother Earth can *kiss my arse*." She lifted her backside off the ground, thumped it down for emphasis. "But you know who is here, Khun? Me. Me, and the Chief, and you."

Her voice softened. "I love you, Khun. And you, Chief. I even love the Princess – although I'm still not sure I love that lizard of hers."

Chimeg smirked at that. Even Khun smiled, just a little.

Hogelun kept going: "I love the Rakada. I love what we have. And I'm not ready to let it go."

She made Khun meet her eyes. "Remember what you told me? Back before we ran off to Karkorum? You said I didn't choose to be a raider. That I just let it happen." Her words had become a snarl: a deep, animal sound that came right from her chest. "Well, I fucking choose. I choose raiding. I choose not to die in this cage. Now are you going to help me? Or am I going to have to somehow gnaw through these ropes with my teeth?"

Khun held her gaze for the longest time. Opened her mouth to speak, more than once. Hogelun stayed silent, because she didn't know what else to say.

But then, after a whole minute, Khun slowly nodded. "There was a flame," she murmured. "A light in the deep places." She reached out a foot for the stone, pulled it effortlessly towards her. "I saw to the end of time, and it turned me to ash."

Hogelun and Chimeg exchanged a glance. "Don't look at me," Chimeg said, as Khun winkled her boot off and positioned the stone between her toes. "I never know what the fuck she's talking about."

Like the other two, Khun's hands were tied to the bars above her head. The older raider scooched her arse forward, then bent her back in a frankly ridiculous curve to lift her feet to her bound hands. She didn't look the least bit uncomfortable, which was fine, because Hogelun felt that discomfort for her. She felt like she'd run a thousand miles.

But for the first time in days, her head was clear. Like a boot turned upside down so you could knock the dirt out.

It took Khun no more than a few seconds to get the stone to her fingers, but it took an age to saw through the ropes. The Princess must have been bloody lucky with her stone, found one with a very sharp edge.

Eventually, with much grunting, Khun's ropes popped loose. Hogelun had to suppress the urge to squeal. Khun slowly got to her feet; she still looked old, still didn't look like the raider she used to be . . . but there was a glint in her eye that wasn't there before. "I feel like eating some tendon," she muttered, as she worked on Hogelun's bonds. "Let's go get some."

"Khun," Hogelun said, as her aching wrists came loose. "We get out of this, I'll cook you as much tendon as you want."

"With onions?"

"All the onions. I'll make you a whole *mountain* of fried onions."

They freed the Chief, helped her lower her arm down. Hogelun quickly used the scraps of rope for a makeshift sling, which would have to do for now. As she worked, Khun attacked the rope tying the cage door shut.

And all the while, the three of them listened hard to the camp around them. All they needed right then was a soldier coming on or off watch, strolling past the cage, glancing casually inside . . .

After Hogelun had tied the last part of the sling, Chimeg crouched down. "OK," she said, flashing Hogelun a grateful smile. "Here's what we're going to do. We need to get some distance between these fuckers and us, which means horses." She pointed between two nearby tents. "I think they're keeping them that way. Edge of the camp. We'll need to be careful — they'll definitely have some bodies there."

"We could find some weapons." Hogelun's fingers flexed — the numbness was giving way to horrific pins and needles.

"No. The quicker we're out of here, the better. If we take someone down and don't raise the alarm then by all means, but I don't want us wasting time hunting for blades."

Moving as quietly as they could, the three Rakada pushed their way out of the cage. There were no stars or moon, and the shadows between the *gers* were black as the nine hells.

At a glance from Chimeg, Khun took the lead, padding across the muddy earth, skipping nimbly around a deep puddle that would have splashed if she'd stepped in it. She looked naked without the pouch on her chest, but she moved with purpose.

There was an open area past the tents – no horses, not yet, just a wide avenue through the camp, dimly lit by flickering torches. Nothing and nobody there – just an abandoned cook-fire, embers still glowing. A gnawed bone discarded on the ground nearby.

And out of sight, beyond the next clutch of *gers*: the gentle whuff of a horse.

Khun took a single step out into the avenue – and then ducked back into the shadows so quickly that she nearly knocked Hogelun over.

A second later, Hogelun heard them. Two voices, approaching from their left. She, Khun, and Chimeg shrunk back into the shadows, hardly daring to breathe.

"Two whole battalions, apparently," one of them was saying. His footsteps were uneven, like he was limping. "And I heard the Khan himself, too."

"Nah." The other voice was croaky, words blurred and messy, like its owner had spent the night drinking *airag*. "He'll never leave that palace of his. He'll send one of his people."

"I still don't understand what she's thinking. All this for a few raiders. What's the point?"

Hogelun raised a questioning eyebrow at Chimeg. The Chief shrugged, but she looked grim.

The other soldier gave off a drunken chuckle. "Careful. People hear you questioning her, you might end up like them."

They walked past, two dark shapes in *deels* bulked out with thick leather underneath. The first speaker said something inaudible, and the second scoffed. "Even he's doing what she says these days. It's going to be an interesting ride back, you catch my meaning."

The Rakada waited until their voices had faded. Then, with one last peek past the tents, Khun stepped out, gesturing them to follow. Another horse noise came from beyond the next line of tents: the sound of one of them stamping at the earth.

Before long, the animals were in view. There was no enclosure, no fence: just big poles, jammed deep into the ground and used to secure the horses. Hogelun picked out at least two guards, standing perhaps twenty feet away, bored faces just visible in the torchlight.

She peered into the darkness, but couldn't see any others. If there were any, they were on the far side of the horses – it was just two men in this area.

Her heart started to beat just a little faster. If they could do this quietly, they could be mounted and on the run before—

Behind them, in the distance, there was an angry shout. Multiple angry shouts. Which meant someone had finally decided to check on the cage. The two sentries stiffened, glancing at each other.

"Hogs, go left," Chimeg murmured, cradling her broken arm. "Khun, take the right."

Weavers, what Hogelun would have given to have her club right then. Still, she was quite capable of using her hands when she had to. She tensed, ready to spring.

At that moment, one of the sentries jerked his chin at the other. The second man nodded, started jogging. Heading right for where the Rakada crouched, directly between the *gers*.

"Khun," said Chimeg. "Take him."

Khun paused, just for an instant, waiting until the soldier slipped into the tent's shadow. Then she exploded, leaping out of the darkness. The man had just enough time to take a quick, startled breath, and then Khun had a hand over his mouth and an arm around his throat and was squeezing hard.

Unfortunately, the soldier managed to let out just the tiniest little yelp.

"Tabudai?" said his friend.

Fuck. Hogelun didn't wait for her Chief's command. She thundered towards the soldier, banking on her size to scare the living shit out of him, knock him on his arse before he could even think to yell.

But even as she reached for him, she could tell she wasn't going to get there quickly enough.

A split second before she cut off his voice with a titanic punch, he yelled for help. His head snapped sideways, blood and teeth flying, unconscious before he hit the ground.

Hogelun stood over him, trying to look everywhere at once. Someone was hammering an alarm, iron on iron, and the camp behind them was going nuts.

"Quick." Chimeg materialised on Hogelun's left. "Before they—"

And just like that, soldiers poured out of the darkness.

Hogelun spun, fists up, ready to knock back any idiot who even thought of coming within range. But everywhere she looked, she saw arrows. Pointed right at her, at Chimeg and Khun. Every direction. Khun let out a deranged shriek, baring her teeth at the soldiers.

There was a moment where Hogelun thought Erhi was among them. Where she was absolutely certain she could see the woman's tight bun, her angular face. But it wasn't her: just a female soldier, yelling at her to surrender.

Fine. She would take them all on, tear their fucking heads off. But before she could move, Chimeg put a hand on her chest.

"I'm sorry, Hogs," she muttered. "It's over."

Forty-Eight

Sayana

How many people had Sayana killed?

Simple question, really. One that had an answer. A number.

She liked to think she'd never killed anybody she didn't have to. That was the whole point of being a Rakada, wasn't it? When you were the scariest raiders in the grass, nobody fought back. And if they did, they couldn't say they weren't warned.

All of which meant she should have known the answer. It wasn't thousands of murders here: it probably wasn't even fifteen people. The soldier who happened to be in the wrong place when they raided those wagons along the Ulaan River; the woman who came at her from a *ger* as she rode past, swinging a sabre so rusted it was a wonder the metal didn't disintegrate.

But there were more. And as she walked, as she kept trudging through the grass – not even sure what direction she was heading in any more – she couldn't stop thinking about them.

At first, she told herself it was just so she didn't have to focus on the hunger. The exhaustion. But it was like she had no choice: she had to at least get to a number, a single figure.

The harder she tried, the more desperate and frantic she got. Starting from the beginning a dozen times, telling herself to go slowly, to remember. But did she kill that young archer, over by the Seven Thousand Lakes, or did Erhi get there first? There was a man with a huge crop of angry pimples, she remembered him – Chimeg had got him in the gut, and Sayana just finished the job. He was dead anyway, so did she add him to her tally? *Stop.*

She had never regretted becoming a raider. They had existed long before she came along, and when she died, they would continue to ride the Tapestry. No matter how tight the Khan squeezed, there would always be those who slipped through his fingers. Being a raider brought her Chimeg. Hogelun, and Khun. It brought her a life she wouldn't trade for anything.

They'd all talked about what would happen when they died. It had come up on long rides, or around the fire. When they raided to survive, there was definitely a chance that Father Sky and Mother Earth would send them to one of the nine hells when they died.

Chimeg had agreed with Sayana. Said that what they had was worth killing for. When the alternative was arranged marriages, fealty, obligation, conscription, a thousand different humiliations in the service of others, then they would pay the price.

When Sayana faced the gods, after some lucky motherfucker had put an arrow in her throat, she would stare them dead in the eyes and thank them for their Tapestry. She would tell them she had ridden it as it was meant to be ridden. And before they sent her to the nine hells, she would flick them the Cut and tell them that if they hadn't meant for her to become a raider, they shouldn't have created people like the Khan.

Which sounded great around a campfire, with skins of *airag* and the taste of meat in her mouth. But now, stumbling through the grass, with no horse or sabre or even a destination, it shrank away to nothing. She couldn't remember how many people she had killed, and she didn't realise there were tears streaming down her face until her skin was soaked with them.

Thoughts whispered, yelled, clamoured, demanded attention, and she couldn't shut them out. Her shoulder throbbed, each rolling wave of pain reaching to the back of her skull. Her bare foot was agony.

This was crazy. She didn't know where she was – she didn't have the first clue where the Heel was, or what she was going to do if she ever got there. She lowered herself to her knees, then onto all fours, telling herself to take deep, long breaths and completely failing to listen.

At the very least, she should turn south. She was pretty sure the Heel was in that direction, and if she kept going, maybe she'd spot some landmarks. Something she could use.

At some point – she thought it was late in the day, but she wasn't sure – she reached the crest of a particularly tall hill, and got a view over two glimmering lakes. She was almost certain she'd never seen them before. The water reflected the low clouds, slate grey and still. In the north, the hazy mountains loomed.

A sound reached her. High-pitched, whistling chirps, carried by the wind. Just an eagle, riding the thermals far above, probably scanning the grass for some . . .

An eagle.

She had to look at the bright grey sky through eyes narrowed to slits, fighting the glare. But the shape was unmistakeable. The bird was maybe a hundred feet up. Tilting its wings on the breeze.

No way it was Ayanga. If he'd be anywhere, he'd be with Tuya, at the Heel.

But as the bird swooped off towards the lakes, Sayana's legs moved on their own. They got her up off her knees, and got her walking.

Halfway down the hill, the bird plunged, landing in a wild flap of wings on a rock. It studied the grass for a moment, then cocked its head at her.

She didn't know for sure that it was Tuya's bird. She hadn't spent nearly enough time with it, not enough to get familiar with its markings. But there was something in the way it was looking at her, the way it cocked its head, as if it was saying: *You coming?*

The voice of the old man, stopping the people at that wagon from cutting her in two. The one with the black eyes, old as time.

Sayana still couldn't think of him without wanting to flinch, but his words were seared into her mind: *I think this one still has many miles to walk.*

She watched, open-mouthed, as Ayanga – and it was him, Sayana was sure of it – took flight again. Soaring with effortless grace towards the water. For the first time in days, the thoughts in her head were quiet.

The lakes were much bigger than they looked from the hill. The nearest was a vast expanse of water with a muddy, uneven shoreline. She couldn't even see the far shore. The water was so grey it was almost black.

Everywhere, fish were jumping. Ayanga took one as she watched, ripping it out of the air, rolling in place and climbing into the sky with his prize. In the distance, off to her left, a herd of wild horses grazed the water's edge. And to her right . . .

She knew what she was going to find there before she saw it.

The *araatan* was next to a messy tumble of boulders on the shoreline. Even with its back to Sayana, even before she caught

sight of the wounds on its side, she could tell it was their beast.
She had spent far too much time in its company, and she knew
what every inch of it looked like. It was gnawing on a kill,
head bent.

It didn't like being surprised. She knew that too.

When her mouth opened, when she heard herself speak, it
was like her mind was floating three feet above her head. "Hey."

It stiffened, but didn't turn around right away. Sayana waited
until it did, hands loose at her sides.

How did it get here? How did *she* get here? Was she following
it the whole time, without knowing?

This one still has many miles to walk.

As it turned to look in Sayana's direction, it felt like they
were the only two living things in the entire world. Two
heartbeats, under a vast, grey sky, caught in the bowl of the
earth.

The *araatan* studied her, shifting its massive body until it
faced her head on. Snout and teeth covered in the blood of its
kill. That low growl, familiar, rolled through her stomach.

Sayana took a step toward it . . .

Other sounds reached her. Other growls. But these weren't
the low, rumbling growls she was used to. They were scratchy,
uneven. And there were a lot of them.

What . . .

And that's when she saw the other lizards.

Much smaller than their own *araatan*. The biggest was only
just larger than an ox. They crawled out over the boulders,
tongues flicking, snarling and growling, claws clicking on the
hard surfaces. Five – no, six of the things.

Sayana took a step back. Then another. And fully planned to
keep stepping back until the *araatan* and its many, many friends
were out of view.

Her eyes went wide.

Not friends.

Young.

Weavers' Breath – their *araatan* wasn't an *it*. It was a *she*. A mother.

She couldn't know this for sure, but it was like when she saw Ayanga – she could feel it in her gut. Their *araatan* had a brood, and she had finally found them.

Sayana didn't know how the lizard had got back to this place. She didn't know why she'd waited, why she'd left her children to fend for themselves for so long. She couldn't even begin to fathom how the lizard had crossed the distance between the pool, and these lakes – how she moved so fast across the Tapestry. But judging from the blood on their snouts, they had been eating some of her kill too.

If Tuya could see this . . . if she could be here, with me . . .

But she wasn't.

And there was only one way Sayana was going to get her back. Get *all* of them back.

She made the big *araatan* look at her. Lifted her hands, set her body just like Tuya taught her. There was a good chance that the little ones would tear her to pieces anyway, the second she got close, but . . .

Hogelun, laughing, a hunk of meat in her hands and juice running down her chin.

Khun, catching up to Sayana as she rode to Karkorum, cackling with joy, whipping her mount into a frenzy.

Chimeg. Sitting on a rock outside the falls, talking about how she'd made mistakes.

And Tuya.

Her touch. Her eyes.

Her smile.

Yes: there was a good chance this would go horribly, disastrously wrong. But Sayana had to try.

The growls from the younger lizards rose in pitch as she stepped closer, boots squelching in the mud. She couldn't listen to them. She had to listen to *her*. The big one. And right then, that growl was holding steady.

She kept walking. One step at a time. Aware of every single muscle in her shoulders and arms and face. Listening harder than she had in her entire life. She felt like she should be breathing hard, but her breaths had slowed. No more than one or two a minute.

When she was inside ten feet, the closest spawn – the biggest, with a mottled gold streak down its side – opened its mouth and snarled at her. A dot of fire glowed in its throat.

No—

Mama barked at it – it really was like a dog's bark, a high, jagged snarl – and the smaller one backed off. Just a little.

Closer and closer. The world shrank down to Sayana, and the *araatan*, and nothing else. Even her children faded away, blurred shapes at the edge of Sayana's vision.

Her good arm stretched out. Fingers inches away. The *araatan* stared at her. Unblinking. Head lowered. She opened her mouth a little wider – and Sayana gave out a snarl of her own. Tuya, speaking through her.

The snout was just within her reach. Her fingertips brushed it . . .

Slowly, ever so slowly, she rested a palm on the beast's scales. Held it there for a moment. The lizard's enormous purple tongue flicked out, gently touched her forearm.

The world stood still.

Sayana was barely aware of moving, but then she was sliding alongside the lizard's head, staring into her eye as she crossed to her neck and shoulders, stepping over her left foot, gently nudging past one of her children. She wasn't scared any more. She knew what she had to do next . . .

Even if she didn't have the first clue how to do it.

Or how she was going to do it with only one good arm.

When you mounted a horse without a saddle, you used the mane and the base of the neck as a fulcrum to lever yourself up – and even then, some of the time, you ended up flat on your back. The *araatan* was . . . a *lot* taller than a horse.

For all the ground she and Tuya had covered, they'd never actually got to how you mounted the thing. Sayana didn't think it would take kindly to having her clamber onto its snout. The tail? Maybe, but a single flick and she'd be in the lake. Undignified at best, lethal at worst. The rocks around them were too sheer to climb, and it wasn't as if one of the younger lizards would let her climb on their back . . .

And all at once, she understood.

The *araatan's* scales weren't smooth and uniform. They were rough, hard edged, flaring slightly from its body. Just enough for her to get a hand into the gap.

She put one foot up. If the *araatan* decided she had had enough, that she didn't in fact want to be ridden, then that moment was when she would attack.

The beast didn't move. Sayana took in one last breath, and began to climb.

It took an age. Her injured arm made it almost impossible. But slowly, carefully, she clambered up the beast's leg, onto the hump of its shoulder, scale by scale, and then . . .

Then she was on the *araatan's* back. Legs thrust out on either side, feeling like her heart was about to punch through her ribcage. Lungs searing, muscles on fire.

The sun didn't break through the clouds. Father Sky and

Mother Earth didn't appear to applaud her bravery. The wild horses on the far side of the lake didn't even look up.

But it didn't matter. Sometimes, when the world changed for ever, you were the only one who knew about it.

Sayana leaned forward, wrapped her hands around the two little grey horns at the base of the *araatan's* skull. Truthfully? She had no idea how to actually control it, beyond simple steering. She and Tuya never got to that part either. But she had a feeling she would figure it out. She couldn't even begin to describe how, but she could tell her mount was relaxed. Ready.

Like she had been waiting for Sayana all along.

Ayanga swooped down, gliding over the water on her right. Beady eye fixed on her. She squeezed the lizard's flanks with her calves. It snorted, flicked its tongue, and started to move. Big, rolling strides.

For a few seconds, it was all Sayana could do to actually stay on top. It was different to horseback riding; she couldn't rely on her legs to keep her up there. Her core kicked in almost immediately, her abs and lower back contracting. Her shoulder, agonising a minute before, was strangely muted.

She had forgotten about the *araatan's* young. But as she looked to her left, her eyes went wide. They were coming too. Running with their mother, as if this was the most natural thing in the world. All of them pounding across the muddy shore.

It was as if . . . as if they did what she did. Went where she went. They might have been waiting here, by the lake, for weeks – waiting for her to come back. Now that she was here, they were never leaving her side again.

Tuya's voice, in Sayana's head: *There's so much we don't know about them.*

She could figure out all that later. She was already thinking ahead, visualising the God's Heel. If Yesuntei and her soldiers were still there, then she would need to plan this carefully. Even with the smaller lizards, none of this guaranteed her a victory.

And that assumed the lizards didn't have to stop to rest. That they didn't have to hunt. If Sayana was going to take on the Khan's army, she would need to . . .

The idea, when it came, was so ridiculous that her mouth actually fell open.

It was risky: it would add days to her journey, might give Yesuntei the chance to retreat to the city.

But the more she thought about it, the more she liked it. So instead of turning the *araatan* south, she kept it pointed west. Leaning forward, gripping the horns a little harder.

"Let's go girl," she murmured. "Time to do something stupid."

Forty-Nine

Sayana

Khunbish had once told Sayana a story about the Broken Valley.

It was gorgeous. Lush and fragrant, bursting with trees and flowers, the kind of place you would expect to be a haven for animals. But there was this ravine, splitting it down the middle: a jagged rip, like Mother Earth had tried to tear the place in two.

The ravine was deep enough that you couldn't see to the bottom. Khunbish swore blind that a demon lived in there. "If you're not a bird or a tiny, tiny fly," she had hissed in Sayana's ear, "you stay well away. It likes to eat. It likes to *feast.*"

Sayana had no idea if that was true. She *did* know that whenever they passed by, a handful of times since she had been in the Rakada, they hadn't lingered. There was something about a stunning valley without even a single antelope in it that made the skin between your shoulders try to crawl up your neck.

Some places just said, *You're not welcome.*

Sayana stopped at the bottom of the hill leading down into the valley. Two hundred yards away, there were a whole whack of raiders. Sayana squinted, shielding her eyes against the sunslight. There must have been five or six separate raider clans. All of them, presumably, planning to join forces and forge a new life in the Great Desert. A fine plan, except for the fact that right then, they were in the middle of a civil war.

Sayana, her *araatan*, and the *araatan*'s children moved down the valley towards the fighting. As they got closer, Sayana spotted signs that things had been going well – a smouldering cookfire, some *gers* – but at some point, the clans had clearly all decided that what they really wanted to do was beat the living shit out of each other. If there was in fact a demon in that ravine, it was going to have plenty of bodies to snack on.

Now she could see clan markings. She spotted the Black Hands. The Jackalborn, with their rust-red *deels*. Two or three other groups she didn't know. Arkan's Eagles – just the Eagles now, apparently, because there was old Arkan, lying face up, with a spear through him.

Sayana squeezed her eyes shut, hoping that when she opened them, this would all be a horrible dream. Turned out, that wasn't a great idea, because she immediately started to drift off to sleep.

It had been two days since the lake. She now knew how the *araatan* had managed to get so deep into the Tapestry after she left the mountains: the lizards had stamina like you couldn't believe. Stamina to let her keep going after Sayana rode her off a cliff, and stamina to run fifty miles in one go if they had to. Even the young had barely flagged.

Sayana couldn't say the same for herself. She was doing her best to ignore the arrow wound, the aches in her arms and neck, the burns.

They had been fortunate with game; the *araatan* had more or less been able to hunt on the move, and Sayana had the good sense not to get in the way when she spotted her quarry. The few minutes when she and her children had stopped to eat were when she had got off to stretch her legs, forage for food of her own, for water.

They'd only stopped once to sleep, the *araatan* curling up with the young ones in a way that would have been adorable if one of them hadn't snarled at Sayana when she came too close. She got the message, snatched a little sleep of her own. When she woke up, the mother *araatan* was staring at her, silent, those yellow eyes never blinking.

Sayana stared back. Then she made her way over, sat down next to the lizard, and put a hand on her leg. The beast's only reaction was a resigned sigh, but ... she allowed it.

Sayana jerked upright, and refocused on the raider civil war.

They looked to be about a hundred, engaged in a tight, rolling battle with each other, a short distance from the ravine. She couldn't pick out sides, and they were so intent on fighting each other that not a single one of them had noticed the six *araatan* standing fewer than fifty yards away. Did they really believe they were all just going to band together like best friends, then roll out across the desert?

One of the *gers* was on fire. Someone came stumbling out, wreathed in flames, waving wildly and banging off a nearby horse, which panicked and bolted right off the edge of the ravine. Nobody took any notice of that either. Sayana spotted Oktai, the idiot who led the Black Hands, going up single-handedly against one of the biggest raiders she had ever seen – bigger than Hogelun even – wielding a sabre as long as her leg. He slammed it into the earth, sending up a huge burst of dirt as he nearly cut Oktai in two.

One of the *araatan*'s kids looked up at her – she still wasn't able to tell them apart, and she hadn't the faintest idea how the mother controlled them – or if it was control at all. But whichever one this was, it was giving her a look that said: *Get on with it.*

Sayana found her voice. "Um. Hey. *Hey!*"

Not a single one of them looked her way. She put her fingers in her mouth, sent out a piercing whistle. Might as well have been a whisper. She waved her arms frantically as Oktai rolled away, as another raider from a clan she didn't know got an arrow in the throat.

Right then, the *araatan* let out one of the loudest roars she had ever made.

It was so loud that it knocked every thought out of Sayana's head. The roar rolled across the Broken Valley, and it stopped the battle in its tracks.

Every raider — every single one — just froze. Half of them with weapons raised, quivering in the air, staring in total confusion.

Staring at an *araatan*, with a person on its back.

The roar faded away. After the din of the battle, the Valley was eerily silent. Oktai was still on the ground, gazing up at Sayana with a look that she would describe as deeply befuddled.

The *araatan* grunted loudly, as if it was glad it had their attention, then started to close the distance. A few of the raiders stepped back, looked frantically around for help, but most of them just stayed put.

Sayana had no idea how the *araatan* knew she needed their attention. It was like it knew what she was thinking. Like it wanted to help.

She towered over the gathered raiders. The ravine sat in the background, dark and silent. For a moment, Sayana pictured the demon inside it springing loose, coming at her and her ride. Now *that* would have been a battle; she could just picture Khun's face when she heard about it, when she told her that . . .

Sayana gritted her teeth, pushing the thought away. Because if she didn't figure this out, she would never get to tell Khun anything again.

In her head, she saw herself giving the other raiders a rousing speech. Getting them to mount up as one and follow her, her own army, an honour guard that would help her save her friends. She would inspire them, appealing to their love of the Tapestry, their hatred of the Khan. She would make them believe that if they united, if they helped each other, then everything would be fine.

But she'd given a lot of speeches lately, and she was sick of the sound of her own voice. So instead, she said: "What in the name of the Weavers are you fuckwits doing?"

Because, to her surprise, she was angry. Not just angry: furious. Her friends, her people, were in danger. Their entire way of life was in danger. And these idiots couldn't even manage to run away properly. They couldn't even be in the same space for a few days without trying to kill each other.

The smaller *araatan* had fanned out from the big one, and they seemed to be having fun snapping at the heels of the raiders. "I don't even know why the Khan bothers sending the army after us," Sayana said. "What's the point? Sooner or later, we'll just kill ourselves."

She hunted for Oktai, and it took a few moments to find him. He still hadn't moved from his back, still hadn't wiped that stupid expression off his face.

"I'm going to make this very simple," she said. "You can keep beating the shit out of each other, or you can find a horse and come with me."

"Where?" someone said.

Sayana squinted. "Sorry?"

The speaker was a woman – one of the Jackalborn, Sayana

thought – with a long face and a red *deel* spattered with mud. "You didn't actually tell us where you were going."

"Yeah," said another raider – the one who had tried to tear Oktai in two. "Also, who are you?"

Another piped up. "She used to be in the Thunderheads, I think."

"Thunderhead."

"Huh?"

"It's Thunderhead, singular. One of them."

"What, there was only one raider in the clan? Don't be dumb."

"That's not what I meant at all. And who are you calling dumb?"

And just like that, up came the weapons again. It was like they had completely forgotten that she was sitting there on a fucking *araatan*.

Well, most of them. One of the raiders had circled round behind her. A very large circle, keeping well out of the eyeline of the *araatan* and her young. The bony knob at the end of the big one's tail rested in the dirt, and he was currently occupied in clambering onto it. Presumably because he wanted to come up behind Sayana, stab her, kick her lifeless body off the side and claim the lizard for himself.

Sayana never got a chance to ask him why he thought this would actually work. The first she knew he was even there was when the *araatan* flicked him up with a single jerk of its tail, then twisted round and snatched him out of the air. Sayana barely managed to hold on as the lizard crunched down.

The remaining raiders shouted, and the *araatan*'s offspring began to move, spreading out, little bursts of flame shooting from open jaws. Sayana's own jaw fell open too, because of all the things that could go wrong, having her potential army get burned and/or eaten in front of her was right up there.

She let out a short bark, just like the ones she'd heard Tuya make. Pulled hard on the two horns, leaned forward until her torso was almost flat on the *araatan*'s back. Willing her to listen. Willing her to give back control.

There were a few seconds where she thought it wasn't going to be enough. Where violence simmered in the air like heat off desert sand. Then, slowly, the big *araatan* subsided. She growled at her children and, one by one, they stopped moving. Sullen, hungry-looking . . . but still.

Tuya's voice, in Sayana's mind: *It doesn't just run on instinct. It perceives the world. It understands how things are connected.*

She'd shown the other raiders she had control. Now she had to make them believe.

"You have two choices. Well, fine, three. You—" She took a deep breath. "You can run to the desert. Try to make a life there. You can kill each other next to this ravine. Or you can decide to fight the people who are chasing us out of the Tapestry. You can come with me, and my *araatan*, and these six little fuckers running around, and we can show them all."

She rapped her hands on the tough scales between the horns. "They took my clan – the Rakada by the way, the Bone Raiders, I'm sure you've heard of us. They've got them at the God's Heel. A whole bunch of the bastards. I'm going to beat the shit out of them, and it would be *amazing* if I didn't have to do it by myself."

Sayana lifted a closed fist. "It's our Tapestry. Nobody kicks us out."

Look at that. She'd ended up making an inspiring speech after all.

Even then, they hesitated. Exchanged nervous glances. Two

of them, who Sayana swore she'd seen trying to smash each other's heads in minutes ago, leaned close for a whispered conversation.

"God's Heel is two days' ride," Oktai said. He was still on his back in the dirt. "How do we know your friend won't eat us? Or our horses?"

The other raiders murmured in agreement.

"You let me worry about her," Sayana told them. "And the little ones. We have this all figured out."

They did not. Not even close. She couldn't even believe they had got this far. But she could worry about that later.

Slowly, Oktai got to his feet. Dusted himself off, peered at the *araatan*.

"Can you teach us how to do that?" he said, jerking his chin at the lizard. "Ride them things?"

Sayana almost laughed. The idea of her teaching anyone to ride an *araatan* when she had only done it herself two days ago was ridiculous. But there was no way she was backing down at this point.

She didn't know if the Rakada were still alive. She didn't even know for sure if they were still at the Heel. But she did know that she wasn't getting this done without a lot of backup. And since the good citizens of the Tapestry weren't exactly inclined to help out a bunch of raiders . . .

She looked down at Oktai, and unleashed the nastiest smile she could dredge up.

"Come with me," she told him. "And let's find out."

Fifty

Yesuntei

Yesuntei insisted on digging one of the graves herself.

She picked her moment, waiting until the battalions arrived from Karkorum. Until they poured into the God's Heel, joining the 8th. Then she'd found a shovel, stripped down to bare leather, and started to dig.

Underneath the layer of churned mud, the ground was hard, resistant to her efforts. Before long, she was soaked in sweat, the midday suns baking her arms and shoulders. But she could feel the eyes of the soldiers on her, and that was the main thing.

The Heel now held three hundred troops; the camp was a rolling, noisy mess, cheek by jowl. It had taken them three days to get there, and until the first riders crested the lip of the Heel, Yesuntei didn't know if her messages had been heeded. She kept expecting her messengers to arrive instead, telling her that the Khan commanded she and the 8th return to Karkorum.

Moving multiple battalions simply to witness the death of three raiders was overkill. One didn't, after all, hold a parade when a few rats were stamped beneath a boot heel. It would have been more logical to bring the raiders back to the city in chains, or simply execute them, and move on.

But sometimes, the logical answer wasn't the right one. Not if you wanted to tell a story.

And oh, the opportunity for a story here was irresistible. A tale that would stretch beyond the palace and into the city itself: how Yesuntei, right hand of the Khan, had publicly executed the most fearsome raiders in Hanggai in front of three hundred assembled troops. How she took revenge on those who had wronged her, who had wronged the Khan. How she dug their graves herself.

Even so, she didn't know if she could pull this kind of troop movement off. But her assistant had come through for her; Timur had got her request to the Khan, and as she suspected, he had been curious. Hadn't come himself of course – he had sent that oily shit Baagvai – but it didn't matter.

She smiled as she wiped sweat out of her eyes, quietly amazed at how much she had missed her assistant. And when she was back, Tuya could . . .

Her smile vanished. She started digging again, driving the blade harder into the earth.

A shadow fell over her. Baagvai's orange silk *deel* was smeared with dirt, hanging limp and sweat-stained. His face had actually gone red. Yesuntei couldn't see his ankles, which were hidden beneath ornate and entirely useless boots, but she could bet they were more swollen than ever. "The Khan sends his finest wishes," he muttered.

Yesuntei took her sweet time planting the shovel in the dirt, clambering out of the deep hole. She sat on the edge, not deigning to stand, taking a long swig from a water skin. "I am grateful for his attention, *bahadur*," she said. "Please convey my thanks."

Baagvai glowered at her. "We were of course delighted that

you had found your sister. And captured those responsible." He frowned at the graves. "Although I do wonder what our Khan would say when I tell him of your . . . methods."

Yesuntei shrugged. Now that she had stopped, her muscles were stiffening up – a surprisingly pleasurable sensation.

"And only three raiders." Baagvai clasped his hands at his waist. "One wonders why they are worth so much trouble."

"Perhaps you're right. Perhaps you will convey that to the Khan. I'm sure he would be interested in your theory about why we should make *less* effort to punish those who steal citizens from his city."

Baagvai was clearly trying to glower even harder, and wasn't doing a very good job. "Just get on with it," he snapped.

"As you command, *bahadur.*"

It wouldn't take her long. The soldiers digging the other two graves looked like they were nearly finished too.

She spotted Jochi, loitering near one of the *gers*. She wouldn't have thought him capable of loitering, but it turned out a lot could change in a few days.

She called him over. "Assemble the companies."

Three hundred troops wasn't a huge number, compared to the rest of the army. But it was still a sight to see them in formation under the blazing midday sky. As Yesuntei inspected them, standing before the graves with her chin raised, Baagvai's words lingered. Perhaps she should have found a way to lure a few more raiders here; let them look upon the might of the Khan's force, let them witness.

Baagvai himself stood off to one side, apart from the troops, looking hot and miserable as soldiers hauled the prisoners before the graves, hands bound, forced to their knees. They looked like they didn't know where they were, blinking in the hot sunlight.

The soldiers stared at them, impassive. Yesuntei got the tiniest little jolt of annoyance. They should have been proud. They should have been delighted. This was the power of Karkorum, of Hanggai, of their Khan.

Yesuntei's gaze lingered on Chimeg. The Chief of the Rakada, who had thrown a promising military career away for . . . what was it again? A drunken murder? It didn't matter. She deserved this. Yesuntei had given her a chance at redemption, and Chimeg had turned her down flat.

There was a commotion on her left. One of the soldiers had broken ranks – it was the archer, the former Rakada. She was now in uniform, with a regulation sabre on her sash. She sprinted towards Yesuntei, her arms moving frantically as she signed. The movements were so jerky that Yesuntei only caught a few words: *stop* and *please* and *we agreed*.

It was Jochi who got in her way. He threw out a huge arm, swinging it like a club, knocking her to the ground. She scrambled up almost immediately, her hands still moving as she signed something at one of the Rakada. The big one – her lover? Yes, that was it.

"Get her out of here," Yesuntei snapped.

Jochi paused, but only for a moment. Then he obeyed, hauling the archer up. She tried to fight, getting her sabre halfway out of its sheath, only for Jochi to take it away. It was as easy as taking a toy from a baby.

The big woman, on her knees, stared after the archer. She worked her jaw for a moment, then spat what little moisture she had onto the hot dirt. In a strange way, Yesuntei actually respected her for that.

"Indecorous," Baagvai muttered, as if Yesuntei herself had orchestrated all of this.

She ignored him. "Soldiers of Hanggai. *Hear me.*"

There was the slightest shift in the assembled troops, the

soft hissing of fabric on leather as three hundred looked her way. Chuluun, of course, was in the front row of the 8th's line, standing like a proud parent. She would have to remember his contribution, once they got back to Karkorum.

"One of your own was taken. A citizen. Stolen from the shadow of the palace. Stolen by these three raiders." She swept her hand at the prisoners, her lip curling in contempt.

It was a shame Tuya couldn't witness this. She was still under guard, of course, and would be for some time. No matter. She would come round.

Yesuntei lifted her chin even higher, started walking towards the prisoners. "But the brave soldiers of the 8th Legion answered the call. *They* marched out into the grass. *They* scoured the land. *They* would not rest until our fellow citizen was returned to us."

They looked like they'd rather be anywhere else. That little jolt of annoyance came again, sharper this time.

"This is their triumph," Yesuntei marched behind the three Rakada. "Let this stand as a testament to their honour."

From between swollen lips, Chimeg said, "Fuck me, you talk a lot."

Yesuntei planted a foot on her back and kicked her into the open grave.

With her hands bound, Chimeg couldn't break her fall. She landed on her injured arm, and her scream was delightful.

"Chimeg!" The big Rakada tried to get to her feet. Yesuntei shoved her over, and she wriggled in the dust like a worm.

"You took my son from me," said the last Rakada, the older one.

Yesuntei cocked her head. "What?"

"Killing me won't save you." The raider bared teeth crusted with blood. "I will haunt you from the deepest reaches of the nine hells."

Yesuntei's stomach twinged. Weavers, she was going to be happy to have these bloody Rakada out of her life.

She snagged the shovel, moved over to the dirt next to the grave. Without ceremony, she started filling it. Chimeg had somehow managed to get up on one knee, but even if she got to her feet, she wasn't getting out of that grave. Yesuntei would bury her with her own hands, witnessed by all.

"Chimeg! We're here!" They had to restrain the big raider, two soldiers pinning her to the dirt. "Just . . . just listen to my voice."

"It's all right, Hogs." A maddening smile on the Chief's face, even as Yesuntei shovelled dirt on her head.

"No! No, Chim—"

"I love you both. Remember that." The smile became a vicious grin as Chimeg stared up at Yesuntei. "Thanks for trusting me, all these years."

The big one's shouts dissolved into meaningless nonsense. The other one, the one who said she'd haunt Yesuntei, was chanting now, in a language Yesuntei didn't know.

She kept going, ignoring the ache in her arms and back. The dirt rose to Chimeg's knees, her waist, her chest. She made no attempt to fight it. Just stood in the hole, smiling gently. Like she had chosen to be there.

The earth rose to her waist. Her chest. Her shoulders. It ran down her face and smeared her neck and cheeks and caked in her hair. Still, she kept smiling.

There was a rock in Yesuntei's latest scoop of earth, a big one. She was going to take pleasure in throwing it at this infernal woman's head.

She was so focused on her task that she almost missed the shift. The change in the soldiers, the low murmur that rolled through them.

Irritated, she glanced up, shovel poised. They weren't even looking at her. All of this trouble, this effort, and they couldn't even pay attention.

Without meaning to, she followed their gaze. All the way up to the rim of the Heel.

Riders. Silhouetted against the blazing blue sky. Ten, then twenty, then forty. Not an army, Yesuntei could tell that immediately, just from the way they assembled. Ill disciplined, swerving every which way. Raiders.

So. Perhaps they *did* hear what was happening today. They organised themselves, got together to save the Rakada. How sweet.

Yesuntei wiped sweat off her forehead. This was *perfect*. No group of raiders, no matter how large, could stand up to three legions. They would wipe them out at a single stroke – and what better way to add to the story? Everyone there would return to the city a hero, and *she* as the one who made it happen.

"Soldiers of Hanggai," she called. "Prepare for . . . "

The words didn't make it out of her mouth. Another shape had appeared on the rim.

A shape *much* bigger than the surrounding horses.

A panicked murmur rolled through the soldiers, and Yesuntei didn't have to catch it to know what it was. What they were whispering.

Araatan.

She squinted, trying to understand what she was seeing. There was someone on the *araatan*'s back. A slim shape against the blue.

"Fuck yes, Princess," the big Rakada growled.

"Weavers protect us." Baagvai's voice was little more than a breath.

As Yesuntei stared, raider arrows arched into the sky. Arrows trailing coloured powder, bursts of red and yellow and green. A few moments later, a sound rolled out across the Heel.

A roar.

Big.

Angry.

Hungry.

Fifty-One

Sayana

A few things that happened on the two-day ride to the God's Heel:

One of the Jackalborn got it in his head to try and mount a baby *araatan*, while everyone was asleep. So the *araatan* ate him.

A member of the Black Hands, the woman with the big scar on her face, thought it might be fun to bait a second lizard as a silly game. She was now missing two fingers.

The Eagles, formerly Arkan's Eagles, decided that they actually didn't want any part of this, and left.

They were replaced by another group of raiders Sayana didn't know, but the newcomers decided to raid the raiders. There was a lot of confusion and shouting and some poor bastard got an arrow in the knee, but in the end, they joined up too.

Then again, a whole bunch of things could have happened that Sayana simply didn't remember. Since they'd left the Broken Valley, she'd had perhaps three hours of sleep. Between keeping the peace, keeping the *araatan* and her children fed, and trying to keep everyone focused, sleep sort of became a thing she once did but then grew out of.

She couldn't remember what she actually ate last. Or when that was. Her *deel* was a torn mess, she was pretty sure her shoulder wound had a little rot, and she still couldn't lift her arm enough to swing a sabre.

Her braid ... well, it was still attached to her, but that was all she was willing to say.

It didn't matter. They were here.

They'd made it.

"Right," Oktai called up. "So. That's *way* more soldiers than you said there'd be."

Above him, on the back of the *araatan*, Sayana shrugged. In the sky, Ayanga rode thermals, like he hadn't noticed any of this. He had been with them the whole time, watching over them.

Oktai chewed his lip, shrugged. "You think your friends are down there?"

Sayana shielded her eyes, hunting for the other Rakada. But they were just far enough away that she couldn't tell who was who. "No idea. Don't care. Didn't ride all this way just to turn around and leave."

He grinned at that. Took a slug from a skin, then leaned back in his saddle and hurled it up to her. It was a miracle she caught it at all.

"This might help clarify things," he told her.

It was the strongest *airag* she'd had. Strong enough to make her eyes fly open, to tear a cough from her throat.

The *araatan* grumbled underneath her, and one of the kids let out a high-pitched yelp. Sayana was still amazed at how much distance they could cover, although she supposed that getting to chow down on that idiot from the Jackalborn helped.

"You like it?" Oktai winked. "Solmon adds a secret ingredient. Fermented muskmelon." He frowned. "Or maybe it's wolfclaw root. I forget."

Sayana tossed the *airag* back to him, turned to stare down at the massed soldiers.

"Hey." Oktai made her look at him. "You gonna be all right? When we get down there?"

She gave him a weary smile. "Helps if I'm a bit drunk."

He laughed at that. It was actually kind of amazing: he was one of the few people who *hadn't* been a problem over the past few days. Sayana still thought he was an arsehole, but he was smarter than she had given him credit for.

"I never asked," Oktai said. "Your pet. She got a name?"

Sayana blinked, pulled out of her thoughts. "What?"

"Your lizard. What's she called?"

"She isn't called anything. She's an *araatan*."

"Not having that." He looked imperious, pouting magnificently. "A mount needs a name. That's the Raider Code."

"No such thing as a Raider Code."

He looked over his shoulder, studying the others. "Not yet."

Which was . . . a little too much to deal with right then.

"Anyway," he said. "Doesn't matter. Bad luck to ride into battle on a nameless mount."

Sayana's mouth opened and closed for a minute before she decided, actually, she didn't have time to debate this. Besides, there was an answer to his question.

"Princess," she told him. "Her name is Princess."

He chewed on that for a moment. "Not bad. Got a decent ring to it." He hawked a gob of spit into the dirt. "Archers are ready," he told her. "You want to . . . ?"

"Nah." She jerked her chin. "Go ahead."

Oktai raised a hand, and there was the twang of bows loosing. Arrows arced into the sky, their lightweight cloth bags trailing clouds of bright powder. Was Sayana annoyed to find out that the Rakada weren't the only raiders to do that, before a raid? Of course she was. Turns out Erhi had stolen the idea.

Erhi. She was down there. Even if . . .

Even if the others were dead, she wouldn't be.

As the arrows reached their apex, their powder trails faded away, the contents spent. Oktai waited a beat, then looked over at Sayana. "So, are we doing this, or . . ."

"Oh. Shit. Right. Yes. Sorry." She leaned forward to grab the *araatan*'s horns. Princess's horns. The soldiers below them were moving all right, mounting up, horses running back and forth.

"Hold on." Oktai sounded offended. "You need to let us know to attack."

"I *am* letting you know. I'm about to start moving, aren't I?"

"No, I mean like, you need to lift your sabre or give a speech or something."

Sayana stared at him like he'd lost his mind. "Since when did you ever need an invitation to—"

Right then, Princess let out the biggest roar Sayana had ever heard her make. So loud that she was half convinced the mountains on the horizon shook, just a little.

As the sound faded away, she caught Oktai's eye.

"There's your damn speech."

Then she gave Princess the heels.

And as they tilted downhill, as the *araatan*'s claws kicked up huge clods of dirt, as every raider she could find came rolling behind her, Sayana tilted her head back . . .

And *howled*.

Fifty-Two

Sayana

Scholars in the Tapestry had long been divided over the question of Father Sky.

Specifically, they had spent centuries arguing about whether he was a being who actually lived in the sky, or whether he *was* the sky.

A fringe group had once argued that he in fact dwelt *beyond* the sky itself, peeking in from time to time to see how things were going, But they'd murdered each other in a horrible disagreement over primary sources, and nobody had raised that point of view since.

(Sayana, of course, could have told them something about a man with black eyes, one who made you feel as small as a speck of dust. Nobody had asked her yet, and if they ever did, she still wasn't sure she'd be able to talk about it at all.)

Whatever Father Sky was or wherever he chose to make his home, there was no question that he had the best view in all of creation.

And if, on this particular day, he had glanced down in the direction of the God's Heel — which he had supposedly created with a stumble on a drunken night – he would have seen something that had never occurred in the Tapestry before.

Men and monsters, marching as one.

Well, marching might be a bit of a stretch. You couldn't even really call it an advance.

In Sayana's mind, she'd seen the Raiders riding behind her in a tight V, with her and Princess at the tip of the attack. A spear with which she would pierce the Khan's army.

That didn't happen. For one thing, the horses were a lot faster than the *araatan*. For another, the slope was a lot steeper than she'd expected. For a third: there were six baby lizards, who everyone was trying to stay out of the way of. Which meant that their advance to battle came in the form of a giant, chaotic, rolling hellstorm, thundering down the hill towards a rapidly panicking army.

Still, this wasn't an army of conscripts, most of whom would have broken the second the *araatan* appeared above them. They were hardened soldiers, all of them, and despite their panic, they fought back.

The first arrows appeared when the raiders were halfway down the slope. Sayana had absolutely no defence, no shield to lift, and she was riding the biggest target around. If even one arrow made it through . . .

They thudded into the dirt around her, other raiders falling. Every muscle in her body tensed, her shoulder twinging as it remembered what an arrowhead felt like. But the impact didn't come.

There were two figures, kneeling in the dirt ahead of her, off to her left. She couldn't see their expressions, couldn't tell who they were, but she didn't have to: they weren't dressed like soldiers. It was the Rakada. There should have been three figures, not two, and a hundred awful possibilities filled Sayana's mind.

It didn't matter. Nothing mattered except what she was doing, right then. Sayana howled again, as the first mounted troops launched themselves towards her.

She had absolutely no idea how to make Princess breathe fire. It turned out, she didn't have to. The lizard tilted her head up, and with a sound like a thousand metal bars being quenched in a thousand pails of water, she shot a stream of flame.

The soldiers tried to scatter, but they were simply too close together. The inferno engulfed six of them, turning both riders and mounts into screaming balls of fire. Some of their brethren stared in shock, but there were just as many recovering, spreading themselves, shouting panicked commands.

One of the soldiers, cannier and faster than the others, was on Sayana's flank. He kept an eye on the *araatan*'s head, clearly expecting another jet of fire. Bow out, arrow tracking her.

She twisted the *araatan*; Princess turned her thundering run into a skid, simply sweeping both horse and man aside.

The claws raked along the side of the horse, ripping open the rider's leg, sending both of them crashing to the ground in a detonation of blood and dirt. The *araatan* closed her jaws over horse and rider, tearing, swallowing.

Raiders and baby *araatan* surged around them. The smaller lizards made Sayana think of excited puppies; they thundered back and forth, breathing fire at anything that moved, attacking whatever was in front of them, raider and soldier alike, snapping and biting.

Oktai, howling, already bloodied from a gash on his temple, reared his mount up and knocked a soldier from his own horse. Sayana got a glimpse of another raider — a Jackalborn, she thought — down on one knee, no horse in sight, firing arrows faster than anyone she'd ever seen. Two of the smaller lizards were snapping at a big charger, the man on top panicking. Tents burned.

She couldn't see the Rakada, and she certainly didn't have a clue where Yesuntei was. She didn't get a chance to look, either. Two riders came at her, big soldiers in black *deels*, bows raised to plant an arrow in her chest.

Princess let out another belch of fire, but it wasn't as strong as before — she must need time to recharge between bursts, something which Sayana really wished she had thought about before then. The two riders steered their horses around the flame, but Sayana leaned too, yanking on Princess's horns, digging in her heels.

The *araatan's* tail, with that huge knob of bone at the end, came whipping round. It hit one of the horses with a thud Sayana felt in her teeth.

Princess lunged forward, snatched the second rider off his mount. Sayana got a brief look at his arms, thrown up in the air, like he was asking the Weavers for help. Then he was gone.

She didn't know if the soldiers had overwhelmed the raiders, or if it was the other way around. Everywhere she looked was chaos — burning tents, burning horses, arrows flying everywhere.

And in that instant, she spotted Hogelun and Khun. A hundred yards away, off to her left.

Their hands were tied, but that clearly hadn't stopped them. They were both on their feet, Hogelun kicking out at two soldiers, keeping them away, Khun's face twisted in fury.

Sayana howled again, turning Princess and crashing across the battlefield towards them. An arrow thudded into the *araatan's* flank, somehow got caught between the scales. The lizard barely noticed.

The soldiers didn't look around until Sayana was right on top of them. And when they did, when they glanced over their shoulders and found the space behind and above them filled with scales and teeth, they didn't even have time to scream.

The *araatan* came out of the smoke and skidded to a halt in front of the Rakada. Hogs and Khun looked exhausted, and at some point in the past few days, someone had beaten the shit out of them, but . . .

But they were alive.

Hogelun's grin was enormous. "Just for the record, you had better have the best explanation of all time."

"The prophecy has been fulfilled!" Khun yelled, dancing on the spot. "The age of men has come to an end. *Now is the age of the lizard!*"

The lizard in question lunged for her. She darted backwards, nearly toppled over, Princess's jaws snapping closed above her head. The *araatan* only stopped when Sayana yanked back on the horns, when she yelled at her to quit it.

They hadn't got around to training her how to distinguish friend from foe, and having her eat the people Sayana had come to save would have been . . . less than ideal.

Her eyes went wide. "Chimeg? Tell me she's not—"

"Down here!"

Their Chief was buried in a hole, practically up to her neck. She shook her head in wonder as she gazed up at Sayana. "Took your bloody time."

Sayana made a sound that, in a different world, might have been a laugh, and wheeled Princess around. "Hogs, find something to fight with, then you and Khun—"

Hogelun lifted her bound hands. "Little help?"

"Um . . . Right." Sayana pulled out her sabre – not like it was much use to her where she sat – and tossed it down. It clattered to the dirt close to Hogelun's feet.

Hogs stared at it, then looked back up at Sayana. "Fuck am I supposed to do with that?"

"Cut the ropes, what do you think?"

"Cut the ... our hands are tied, you idiot. Climb down and help!"

"Do you have *any idea* how long it takes me to get on and off this thing?"

Technically, it wasn't that long – she'd had plenty of practice over the past couple of days. But if she dismounted now, she wasn't sure she'd have the energy to clamber back on.

"Just ... just lie on your back," she called down. "It's not hard!"

"How would you know? Get off and help!"

"What's happening up there?" Chimeg shouted. "I can't see a damn thing."

Khun came out of nowhere. Hands untied. She scooped up the sabre, and darted behind a startled Hogelun. "Used the beastie's claw!" she shouted up, as she sawed at the ropes.

"Of course you did," Sayana muttered.

In seconds, Hogs was free. Both she and Khun looked murderous; tired, beat-up, hungry, and *more* than ready for payback.

Chimeg was still buried, locked in place by the dirt. Hogs took a step towards her, and nearly got stabbed in the face.

The soldier came out of the smoke, a blur of black and flashing steel. He was so quick that Hogelun tripped over her feet, fell backwards on her arse. Before he could skewer her, Khun was on him. She all but cut him in two with Sayana's sabre.

"Thanks," Hogelun huffed. Glared at the lizard, as if to say, *Appreciate the help.*

Something pulled Sayana's attention. It was Khunbish – and it took her a second to realise why. "Khun. Your pouch. Your ... the little plant. Was it here? What did they—"

The most awful sadness crossed Khun's face then. Like a cloud in front of the sun.

"Yesuntei," Hogelun spat. Which told Sayana all she needed to know.

Hogs and Khun dropped to their knees next to Chimeg, scooping like crazy, trying to dig her out.

"Leave it!" Chimeg shouted. "Just go."

Sayana thought she'd heard wrong. Hogs paused, mid-scoop: "Chief?"

Chimeg bared her teeth in what might have been a grin. "Don't worry about me. Just get some weapons and get in there."

"What are you talking about?" Sayana shouted down. The idea of leaving Chimeg . . . it didn't make sense. However much she and the Chief had clashed over the past few days, she couldn't even imagine doing this without her.

"Stop." Chimeg turned to Khun, snarling the words. "Khunbish, *stop*. It'll take too long to dig me out, and I can't fight with this arm."

Khun stared back at her, chewing her lip. It was Hogelun who spoke then. "Chief, if someone comes—"

"*Just fucking go.*"

Sayana couldn't help but picture the last few days. How the Chief wouldn't listen when she heard the plan to tame the *araatan*. How she put a knife to Sayana's throat, after she and Tuya first made contact. Her scorn, her disbelief that this could ever work.

And that moment following Yesuntei's attack, staring out at the moonlit pool, when she told Sayana how many mistakes she'd made.

Chimeg had ruled the Rakada with an iron grip for years. Taken everything onto her shoulders. Always at the front of every raid, always taking the hardest tasks. Building the greatest clan in the Tapestry.

And now here she was, saying, *This isn't my fight. Don't worry about me.*

From her prison, the Chief locked eyes with each of them in turn. Craned her neck so her gaze could bore into Sayana.

"Do *not* fuck this up," she spat. "You don't need me for this one." A wry smile snuck onto her face. "You're the Rakada. Act like it."

Hogelun took a breath, as if to protest . . . then nodded.

"Oi!"

Oktai, still on his horse, came thundering out of the smoke — then had to rear up when Princess, startled, nearly took a bite out of him. Sayana pulled the lizard back, hissing at her to relax.

Oktai's face and *deel* were soaked in blood, gritty with soot. "I was hoping I'd run into you," he said, wheeling his horse.

"Are we winning?" Hogelun made it sound like this was just a little game of *shagai*.

"No idea." Oktai's sabre was chipped, looking like it was about three hits away from shattering completely. He jerked his chin at Sayana. "Thought you should know. There's some woman in a cage back there, keeps shouting your name."

Tuya.

Sayana had no idea why she would be in a cage, but she couldn't leave Hogs and Khun. Not right after she'd just found them. The idea stuck in her throat, sour and sharp.

But Hogelun just grinned. Gave her sabre an experimental twirl, then pointed deeper into the camp. "We'll be fine. Go get her."

Fifty-Three

Sayana

The only thing Sayana could hear was her own breath. To her, the entire battle had gone silent.

As she and Princess stomped through the camp, the world around them was a complete and total shitshow, and it happened without a single sound. Nothing but her breathing, hard and heavy in her head.

A raider stumbled across the path in front of them. Burning, clothes on fire, mouth open in an ugly, silent shriek.

One of the baby lizards, jaws locked around a horse, the larger animal wide-eyed with terror, frothy blood at its mouth.

A soldier, still wearing one of those ridiculous conical helmets, impaling another raider on a spear. He heard Sayana coming, whirled in place, yanked the spear free – and then he was gone. Vanished under Princess's thundering bulk.

Arrows were everywhere. Everywhere. Filling the sky.

Oktai said he didn't know if they were winning or not. But as Sayana spotted yet another raider, face down in the dirt, an arrow sticking out of their back, she knew for sure.

They didn't have enough. They couldn't take on these many soldiers, not even with the *araatan*, not even with her young.

She had no idea where she was in the camp. It was a gigantic mess of tents. She would never find Tuya — or worse, she would crash into her cage before she knew it was there, trample her.

"Tuya!" Her voice was muffled, barely audible to her. How could she hear Tuya calling her name if she couldn't even hear herself?

With real effort, Sayana focused, getting at least some of her hearing back. The din was wild, a mess of screams and impacts, the air stinking of smoke.

As Princess's swinging tail flattened another *ger*, Sayana kept shouting her name. Where was that fucking eagle when you needed him? It had no problem showing her the way to the *araatan*, out by the lakes; why was it being shy *now*?

If the araatan had wings, like Tuya said they used to, this would have all been so much easier.

Princess was flagging — she was breathing hard, her movements sluggish. After days of riding hard, and then down into this fight, she had finally had enough. "Come on, girl," Sayana muttered. "Just a little longer."

At that instant, she heard Tuya. It was so buried in noise that she almost missed it. She pulled back on the horns, Princess fighting her. Hardly daring to breathe.

Tuya's voice reached her again. "—ana! O—here!"

It was coming from behind. Sayana turned Princess around — she actually fought, like she didn't want to go. Blood hammered in Sayana's ears, eyes huge, finding Tuya's voice, losing it again . . .

Turned out, she had actually shot right past her. Her cage sat next to one of the *gers* Sayana's mount had destroyed. Ayanga was perched on top, preening, looking like he didn't have a care in the world. Like he was just waiting for them to show up.

The bird was very, very lucky Sayana didn't have a bow right then.

"You did it." Tuya pressed herself against the wooden bars of the cage. Despite the entire world exploding around them, a smile played on her lips. It shot a delightful little jolt through Sayana. "It trusts you."

"She." Sayana still couldn't quite believe Tuya was in front of her. "And she's a mother."

"What?"

"Doesn't matter."

This time, she did dismount. The cage door was held shut with thick, oily rope. Tuya wasn't bound, but it would have taken her for ever to pick it loose.

Sayana cast around, but of course, there wasn't a single blade anywhere. No sabre, no knife. And she wasn't exactly sure how to ask Princess to bite through the rope . . .

Arrows. A bunch of them, scattered on the ground, next to a discarded bow. No sign of whoever had been using it. Ignoring her desire to pop an arrow into that damn bird, Sayana went to work. This was going to take ages; the rope was a huge, knotted mass, the thick strands parting at the rate of about one every millennium.

"How did you know I was even here?" Sayana said.

"It – sorry, *she* – she roared." Tuya looked dazed. "Got pretty used to how she sounds. But where did you even—"

"Long, long story," Sayana pointed at Ayanga. "He helped."

The arrowhead jumped, burying itself in her thumb. She yelped, pulled back, kicked the cage in frustration as she jammed the wound into her mouth. Princess was turning in a slow circle, sniffing the air, as if hunting for her next target. If she ran now, Sayana didn't know how she'd catch her.

Her gaze landed on that bony lump at the end of her tail.

"Get back," she told Tuya. "Other side of the cage."

She didn't second-guess herself, clambering back onto Princess. Groaning as she got her feet over, a weary, bone-deep sound. Her shoulder was raw *pain*.

Tuya realised what Sayana was about to do, and her eyes went wide. "Wait. Hold on, let's just keep going with the arrow, maybe—"

"Nope. Sorry."

Sayana backed off, giving Princess a little more room to work, then turned her so she faced the cage. The oddest thought, then: without the last few days spent riding her, she wouldn't have been able to do this. But she'd learned how to control her, learned how the lizard responded to commands.

"Back up!" she yelled at Tuya. And then, in one big movement, she spun her mount. The tail dragged in the dirt, and there was a moment when Sayana was convinced it wasn't going to pick up enough speed. But at the last instant, Princess lifted it, pulling it free of the mud. The cage bars splintered as the knob of bone crashed into them, breaking them apart.

Tuya, fortunately, had the presence of mind to duck. And now that the way was clear, she didn't waste time giving Sayana shit. She clambered free, squirming out through the narrow gap, then started scooping up the arrows littered across the ground. The one Sayana was using on the rope was still embedded there, sticking sideways out of it.

"Why were you in a cage anyway?" Sayana shouted down.

Tuya just jabbed a thumb over her shoulder at Princess, snatching up the bow as she did so. "Reckon she'll be OK with two of us?"

"No idea. Look, you need to get out of here, find somewhere safe to—"

"Fuck that." And before Sayana could blink, Tuya clambered onto Princess's back, doing it the same way she did.

It was really quite unfair how effortless she made it look.

The lizard grunted, taking the weight . . . but didn't buck her off. It was startling to suddenly have Tuya this close, this *there*. Sayana half expected her to fade away, like she was hallucinating this whole thing. Like she was drowning in that river, and all of this was her imagination: the last flickers of her mind before it winked out for good.

Tuya nocked an arrow. "You ride," she snarled. "I'll shoot."

Sayana picked a direction, the place where the fighting seemed loudest, and urged Princess forward.

She had been so focused on training the *araatan*, so intent on actually getting it to do what they wanted, that she hadn't given much thought to how she'd actually use her in battle. She had no control over how the beast attacked.

Spinning her to use her tail as a weapon was one thing, but biting? Using those giant claws? That was all her. All Sayana could do was point her in the right direction, move her where she wanted to go. She didn't think it was possible to feel both absurdly powerful and utterly helpless at the same time, but it was.

They thundered through the camp, sweeping *gers* aside, until they reached the outskirts. It was a brawl: a gigantic mass of sabres and spears, panicked horses, fire and smoke. There was no point trying to get Princess to avoid the raiders and take out only the uniformed soldiers; Sayana would just have to hope the Black Hands and the Jackalborn and whoever else was still there had the good sense to get out of the way.

Turned out, when you plunged an *araatan* onto a raging battlefield, most people didn't actually notice. There was just too much going on.

Two mounted soldiers spotted them, brought their horses

around, coming up on their flanks. Tuya twisted, nocked and fired. The first arrow hit its mark, right in the throat, toppling the rider from his horse. The second went wide. Before Tuya could fire again, Princess roared, letting out a burst of flame that immolated the second soldier – it wasn't as powerful as her first, but you try telling that to the blazing heap of human collapsing to the ground.

Sayana had no idea if this was going to help them turn the tide, but *Weavers* it felt good.

She thought she spotted Hogelun, a dark blur in the melee. Before she could get a fix on her, she was gone. Oktai roared past, shouted something at her, didn't bother to stop. It felt like every single *ger* was burning now, like the whole Heel was filling with smoke.

"Two!" Tuya yelled.

"Two what?"

"Arrows. I've got two left."

"Well, that's not g—"

All at once, they weren't the only ones on the back of the *araatan*.

The soldier sprawled across Princess's back, just above her tail. He must have found something to climb, tracked their path, jumped at just the right time. Either that, or grabbed hold as the lizard thundered past, and hung on.

Tuya kicked out at him. He batted her away, snarling, getting to one knee and drawing his sabre.

He wasn't looking up. Which meant he was completely unprepared when Ayanga dived out of the sky and buried two sets of talons in his face.

The eagle clung on even as the man shrieked, toppling off the back of the *araatan*, vanishing out of sight. The bird shot skywards, talons dripping red.

Tuya suddenly stood – literally stood, like you would in stirrups, balancing on the *araatan*'s scales – and fired. "One left." She held on tight as Princess suddenly leaned left, opened wide, and snatched a soldier off his feet in the instant before he split a Jackalborn's skull. "You got a sabre for me?"

"No! I don't have a fucking sabre for you! *I* don't even have one!"

"You came to a fight without a blade? What's wrong with you?"

"Do you not remember me smashing your cage open? Did you think I—"

Princess went insane.

She roared, high and terrified. When she tilted her head back, there was—

There was something sticking out of it. No: worse than that. It was an arrow, and it was in her right eye.

Sayana's mount was making the most horrible noise now, a panicked moaning. Before she could do anything, before she could reach over and pull it out, the *araatan* twisted sideways so violently that Sayana and Tuya tumbled off her back.

If it had been a straight fall, both of them would be done. Broken ankles at best, broken backs at worst. But Tuya reacted quickly, grabbing hold of a scale, snatching at Sayana's *deel*. Gripping a handful of fabric, slowing them just enough to arrest their fall. A second later, the *araatan* twisted again, roaring in agony, and Tuya's grip faltered. She and Sayana crashed to the ground, limbs tangled.

Mercifully, Sayana hadn't landed on her injured shoulder. She scrambled to her feet, ears ringing, just in time to see Princess stumbling off. Still making that awful sound. Half of Sayana wanted to give chase; the other half wanted to find whoever fired the arrow and peel their skin off.

They were on the edge of the fighting, near a stack of water barrels that were still miraculously intact. Sayana couldn't see anybody with a bow, no one who could have fired that shot. "Come on," she told Tuya. "We need to—"

The next arrow passed so close to her chest that it brushed her *deel*. She spun, trying to find the archer – right as Yesuntei nocked and fired again.

She'd appeared in front of the water barrels, out of thin air. Black *deel* torn, one arm soaked in blood. The second arrow nearly took Sayana's head off.

She reached for a third, but the quiver on her back was empty. Possibly because she was the one who'd fired at Princess; Sayana didn't know. With a sneer, Yesuntei threw the bow aside, drew her sabre. Automatically, Sayana put her right hand to her sash – which not only hurt like a bastard but reminded her that she didn't actually have a weapon.

"Yesuntei – stop. Just stop." It was Tuya, hands out.

Yesuntei didn't speak for a moment. Didn't move. Just held her sabre at her side. Sayana kept expecting the battle to reach them, for the tide of soldiers and raiders to come their way, for one of the *araatan's* young to intervene.

Run, she thought. But her feet wouldn't listen. She couldn't see Princess anywhere. Couldn't spot her in the mess of smoke.

Yesuntei's mouth worked for a good few seconds before she actually spoke. When she did, it was through gritted teeth, the words slow, crunchy.

"I want to," she told Tuya. Her eyes were wet. "I wanted to help you." She glanced at Sayana, and the sneer came back. "But you chose your side."

She attacked. Standing still one moment, a blur of movement the next.

Her sabre flashed as she swung it at Sayana's face. She only just managed to dodge, had to do it again as Yesuntei brought the swing back the other way. Tuya made an attempt to grab her, but Yesuntei didn't even pause. With her free arm, she drove an elbow hard into her sister's throat.

Tuya went down, gagging, her face twisted. Yesuntei didn't even look her way. This time, her attack was a thrust, trying to punch through Sayana's stomach. She twisted to the side, the blade scoring a hot line down her midsection, and kicked out. Her boot caught Yesuntei on the thigh, knocking her off balance.

Sayana needed to find a weapon. Anything. She needed to—

Yesuntei recovered appallingly fast. She swept her leg around and knocked Sayana's out from underneath her. She stumbled, didn't quite go down, catching herself with one hand. Her fingers landed in something sticky and wet, but there was no time to look. She rolled, rolled, and then Yesuntei kicked her in the ribs.

The impact knocked her soul from her body. That really was what it felt like: like she was now floating ten feet away.

She curled into herself as Yesuntei flipped the blade, getting ready to stick her.

In the instant before she did, Tuya socked her sister in the jaw. Yesuntei's head snapped around, spit and blood flying. Tuya's face was grey, but she kept going, throwing wild punches.

The problem was, she was no soldier. Give her an animal, and she'd work miracles, but she couldn't handle a trained fighter like Yesuntei. The woman ducked under a swing, hitting Tuya in the throat again.

This time, Tuya didn't get up.

The anger that ripped through Sayana right then was titanic. She surged upright, fingers hooked into claws. Weapon or not, she was going to scratch this bitch's eyes out.

Yesuntei was bent over, her back to Sayana. If she could get an arm around the woman's throat—

Without looking, the woman half turned, lashed out with her boot, and got Sayana square in the crotch.

There was a blinding flash of pain – and an instant later, a horrible, sick, rolling ache. Sayana crashed to the ground, unable to even scream, curled into a ball.

In all the fights she'd been in, no one had ever done that. It was quite remarkable, when you thought about it. Or it would have been, if Sayana had actually been in a position to have any thoughts at all.

Yesuntei blocked out the sky above her. She kicked Sayana onto her back, put a knee on her chest—

And brought her blade down.

At the last instant, Sayana grabbed at her hands, pushing them back. It didn't stop the blade tip from pushing into her leather armour. Yesuntei adjusted, finding a seam, drilling through it. A moment later, metal touched Sayana's chest. Bit.

This time, screaming wasn't a problem.

And Yesuntei was strong. Much stronger than Sayana thought she was. She couldn't move her hands, couldn't put on enough pressure. The woman leaned harder, driving the tip further in, a bloody smile splitting her face.

There was another sound, too. One that took Sayana a second to understand. A high-pitched wail. Getting louder and louder by the second. *"Eeeeeeeeeeeeeehhh—"*

Yesuntei twisted the blade. Just a little. But even that movement was enough to make Sayana nearly black out. This was worse than the arrow, worse than anything she had ever felt.

But through the pain, through eyes blurred with tears, she could still hear that wail. Closer now. *"EeeeeeEEEEEEEEEEEEEHHHHH—"*

And all at once, she understood.

She gave Yesuntei a smile of her own. Hissed words through bloody, gritted teeth.

"You are . . . so . . . fucked."

And then, mustering every bit of energy she still had, she got a knee between them, and shoved the bitch backwards.

As Yesuntei got her balance, as she moved to finish the job, she finally became aware of that wail.

"*EEEEEEEEAAAAAAAHHHHHHHHHH—*"

Sayana didn't know how Khunbish got airborne. She didn't know what the raider jumped off. But Khun was suddenly above Yesuntei, a demon screaming down from the sky, a black shape with a face buried in it, a face covered with gleaming red blood and twisted in absolute, pure *rage*.

Yesuntei had just enough time to get an arm up, and then Khun was on her. A whirling, wailing tornado of blades and teeth. She didn't so much collide with Yesuntei as meld with her, latching onto her upper body, legs wrapping around her torso, momentum sending both of them crashing through the water barrels.

Somehow, Sayana managed to sit up. Blood pouring down her chest, the space between her legs a raging hellfire. Khun was still wailing, plunging her knives into Yesuntei's chest in a blur of steel.

A black-clad arm came up, as if trying to grab something just out of reach . . . then fell.

It didn't rise again.

Tuya, her hand on Sayana's thigh. Crawling, struggling to breathe, but . . .

Alive.

Sayana managed to get herself up – or at least, get herself up to a sitting position. Tried to speak, and got absolutely nowhere.

She didn't bother asking if Tuya was OK. Neither of them were OK. For a long moment, they just stayed there. Tuya kneeling next to Sayana, hand on her shoulder.

Until finally, finally, Sayana wrapped her arms around the hunter, and held her.

Fifty-Four

Hogelun

It was the baby *araatan* who won it for them.

Hogelun would have loved to say it was the raider clans working together, but honestly, she wasn't even sure how Sayana had got them pointed in the same direction. They were outnumbered, undisciplined, and for most of the fight, Hogelun was convinced that every single one of them was going to die. Her included.

But those little fire-breathing lizards turned out to be a gigantic problem for the Khan's army.

The lizards attacked anyone. Friend or foe. More than once, Hogelun saw some poor raider clutching a stump where his leg used to be. But as it turned out, the raiders' lack of discipline was what saved them.

When a lizard thundered into a pitched battle between them and the soldiers, the raiders didn't try to take it on. They got the fuck out. The soldiers, on the other hand, obeyed their honour and duty and whatever other ideals they happened to have, and attempted to destroy these four-legged enemies of the Khan. Which didn't go very well for them. The little bastards might not have been the size of big Mama, but they still had teeth and claws and fire breath and scales that made blades just bounce right off.

Hogelun couldn't pinpoint the moment when the victory happened. She got lost in the fight, and even though she had nothing but a sabre to work with, it was enough. And at some point, standing in the middle of a field of black-clad bodies — more than a few of them on fire — she realised it was over.

The camp was a giant blaze itself now, smoke blotting out the sky. The only living soldier she could see was busy trying to kill one of the baby *araatan*, because some motherfuckers never learned.

She lifted her sabre, let out a trembling howl. No one answered, although one of the other raiders, a woman with wild grey hair, somehow still mounted, weakly raised her own weapon in return.

Hogelun's shoulders slumped, the exhaustion washing over her. Weavers, she missed her club. Gone, now — but then again, maybe it was still there, in that cave. Maybe once they were back together, Sayana and Khun and the Chief, they could . . .

The Chief. Hogelun turned her head around so fast that she actually pulled something in her neck. She started lurching in the direction of where Chimeg's hole was — or where she thought the hole was, anyway.

As she made her way along the line of tents, stepping and occasionally tripping over the odd body, movement drew her eye. A figure, ambling towards her out of the smoke. For a second, she wondered what in the fuck she was looking at, then realised it was Khunbish.

The older raider was covered head-to-toe in blood. Every part of her, from the tips of her hair to her boots, was crusted red and brown. But she was still walking, and as far as Hogelun could tell, she wasn't injured.

"Chimeg lives," Khun said, raising her voice.

Hogelun sagged with relief. "You pulled her out of the hole?"

"She is one with the earth now. The gods have planted her like a stout tree."

"You didn't dig her out, did you?"

"A magnificent testament to the power of the Rakada! The ancient voices will sing of her triumph in the dark and deep places."

"Right." Hogelun tucked her sabre in her sash. "I'll just go . . . handle that, then."

As she passed Khun, the older Rakada laid a hand on her shoulder. "Father Sky will not allow me to die."

Hogelun's heart sank, but she managed to plaster a smile on her face. "I know. That's . . . that's good, Khun."

"But he said nothing of how he wanted me to *live*." Those long, bony fingers tightened their grip. "The world he made for me is treacherous. Things I see, I cannot trust. Voices that whisper deep. But if . . . if he wishes me to walk the Tapestry until I have paid my debt, then I am bound by its laws. There are things here that *are* real. That I *can* trust. You showed me that, Hogelun. You did."

Despite the blood, the wrinkles around her eyes were still visible. A hundred lines, a thousand.

"I will place myself at your back," she told Hogelun. "Always and for ever. You may be surrounded by enemies, attacked by all the demons in the nine hells, and you need not even whisper my name, because I will already be there."

A tiny, flickering smile appeared on her face, just for an instant. "You have my blades, my friend, until every light in every world goes out."

She extended a hand. In a daze, Hogelun gripped her forearm, and Khun squeezed back.

There was so much that Hogelun wanted to say. But she seemed to have misplaced her voice.

Khun let go, raised her face to the blazing suns. The Large Eye, and the Small. Then, as if the conversation never happened, she resumed her jaunty little dance across the battlefield.

"Oh!" she yelled over her shoulder. "I saw Erhi, earlier."

And just like that, Hogelun's exhaustion was gone. As if it was never there. She wrapped her fingers around her sabre hilt, found her voice at last. "Where?"

"At a distance, in the camp," Khun pointed into the mess of blazing *gers*. "Preparing a horse, it looked like. I could not chase her; I was trying to convince one of the little *araatan* to join forces with me, instead of trying to eat me."

Hogelun wavered for a moment, thinking of Chimeg. They needed to get the Chief out, get that arm looked at.

And still, she found herself walking in the direction of the camp, further down the slope towards the bottom of the Heel. Erhi would almost certainly be long gone, but . . .

But she had to know.

It was surprisingly easy to pick her way through the wreckage. Plenty of *gers* were still burning, but others were just ash now, and there were wide avenues to walk down.

All the same, it took less than ten minutes for Hogelun's hopes to die. She could walk this camp for hours and not find Erhi. Reluctantly, she turned to go – only to find one of the baby *araatan* blocking her path. Its tongue flicked, tilting its head as it studied her. The scales around its mouth were covered in dried blood.

Even a few weeks ago, a lizard this size would have reduced

Hogelun to a squirming mess; now, she just sighed. "Are we really going to do this? Now?"

The *araatan* made one of those little growly-yelp noises.

"Your mother likes me, you know. We're friends."

The stand-off went on for a few more seconds, and then the *araatan* vanished behind one of the burning tents, its tail snaking in the sooty mud. Hogelun didn't know if it had eaten its fill or just couldn't be bothered. Not that it mattered. She . . .

Hogelun cocked her head. Someone was shouting, the voice drifting on the breeze.

It took her a few minutes to find the source, near the other side of the camp. At the end of a wide path between the tents, running east to west, the rim of the Heel visible in the distance. It was that idiot with the fancy robe, the one who had stood around while Yesuntei was trying to bury them.

He was hanging off the side of a saddle, begging the horse's rider to allow him to climb on. The horse looked put out, annoyed at this weight hanging off it, and Hogelun knew who the rider was going to be before she looked.

Sometimes, the universe just wanted you to know.

"I am the representative of the Khan!" The man's voice was a frantic wheeze. "You are commanded!"

Erhi glowered at him. Her eyes were narrowed, in the familiar way they did when she was trying to lip-read. In that moment, it was as if there was a hook in Hogelun's heart, tugging gently on it.

Erhi gave up. She planted a foot on Baagvai's shoulder, and shoved him back. He toppled into the mud with a peeved "Oh!" Erhi's horse — not Windwalker, of course, just a brown-and-white mare — was loaded up with saddlebags. As if Erhi had a long ride ahead of her.

In the instant before she gave the mare heels, she spotted Hogelun.

They were perhaps fifty yards apart. Too far, if Hogelun gave chase; Erhi would be gone before she was halfway there. The air between them was silent; the only sounds were Baagvai's pathetic snivels and the soft rumble of burning *gers*.

That hook again. The little tug.

Forgive her.

It was a soft thought. Seductive. But even as it was forming, Hogelun understood: she couldn't forgive Erhi. She would never be able to. She would never be able to think of this woman and let her betrayal go. It already tainted every memory she had of the two of them, and that was going to be with her for ever.

Erhi did not deserve forgiveness. Erhi deserved to face Khun. And Chimeg. And Sayana. Erhi deserved to face her. Deserved to answer for making her feel small, for keeping her guilty, keeping her scared.

And then she deserved to feel the crushing weight when the Rakada turned their backs on her.

What do I deserve?

Hogelun blinked, because the answer was right there. Fresh and clean as dew on the grass, as the suns crested the horizon.

She deserved her own thoughts. Her own life. She deserved not to have to think of Erhi, ever again.

She wouldn't get that – not really. Erhi would always, always be there. But in a way, it didn't matter, because it was what Hogelun chose.

All of this was her choice.

Hogelun raised her sabre to the sky, then tilted her head back, and for the second time that day, let out a howl. This one dwarfed the first. It shook Hogelun's stomach, rattled her skull. The wind picked up then, amplifying the sound, rolling it through the camp.

Erhi couldn't hear it of course, but she would understand.

Without a single backwards glance, Hogelun turned, and walked away.

Fifty-Five

Sayana

P rincess was under an overhang at the edge of the Heel, pushed back against the dirt wall. She was alive, her chest rising and falling, with two of her young curled up next to her. Yesuntei's arrow was still lodged in her eye socket, which was a raw, red mess of tissue. The shaft had snapped off, leaving only a stub of wood. Looking at it made Sayana want to go back and find Yesuntei's corpse, work out how to resurrect her, and kill her again.

Tuya was ahead of her on the slope, and came to a wobbly halt, her hand out for Sayana to do the same. "Easy now," she said, gesturing to the big lizard. Her voice was still shredded. "Not sure it . . . *she's* in the best mood."

"Is she going to be OK?"

Tuya puffed out her cheeks. "Well, you healed her once, no reason you can't do it again." She winced. "You'll need some more of that sleep gunk your archer friend used on us, and some treatment for rot. You'll probably have to get her used to your presence again, not to mention her little ones, but . . . well, lizards depend more on smell than sight anyway. It's worth a shot. Depending on what you want to do next."

They looked at each other, and all at once, it was awkward. Sayana didn't think she had the faintest idea what she wanted to do next.

And she didn't think Tuya did, either.

They sat down on the slope, watching the chaos at the base of the Heel. Sayana thought they had won. Or at least, there were more raiders than soldiers, and the camp was finished.

Sayana cleared her throat, touched the cut on her chest. She was quite proud of the fact that she didn't scream. "About your sister . . . I'm so—"

"Don't." Tuya's voice was quiet, brittle.

Sayana had just enough good sense left to listen.

They sat there for a few minutes in silence. Tuya's face was blank, but the sadness in her eyes . . .

It made Sayana want to hold her. To grab hold and squeeze tight and never, ever let go.

"Yesuntei went down the wrong path," Tuya murmured, after another minute. She took a shaky breath. "There was no other way. I know that."

She wiped her face, even though her eyes were dry. "When she was a child, she used to hide in my bed, when she got scared of . . . ' Tuya trailed off.

Sayana had an idea that she never would find out why little Yesuntei used to hide.

"Anyway." Tuya gave a thick sniff. "Anti-rot stuff. For your *araatan*. You'll need that."

"Guess we'd need to find some rot treatment for us, anyway." Sayana forced a laugh. "The Rakada, I mean. We're all pretty banged up."

"Sayana . . . "

"You're probably fine, I don't see any blood or anything, but you should get checked out anyway, your neck—"

"Sayana, it's time to let me go."

Turned out, Sayana was lying about not knowing what to do next. She knew exactly what she wanted to do. She knew exactly who she wanted to be, and who she wanted to be with. Except . . .

Tuya wasn't their prisoner any more. She had done everything she said she would, everything they wanted her to. Sayana couldn't ask any more of her.

The slope beneath Sayana suddenly felt too loose. Like the earth was starting to slide, pebbles and tiny clumps of soil carrying her down to the bottom. All she could see was the stunned delight on Tuya's face when she'd touched the *araatan* for the first time, the excitement when Sayana got close, later on in the cave. If Sayana let her go . . .

She would never see that smile again.

She would never see *Tuya* again.

"I . . . I was hoping . . . "

Tuya looked at her expectantly.

"Do you . . . do you think you could hang around a little longer? Just . . . just until we fix Princess – that's her name, by the way, I named her, I—"

"Is that all you want?" Tuya whispered.

And *still* Sayana couldn't find the words. Tuya was right there, and she was stumbling. Throwing up a thousand ways to say it, rejecting them all, a hot flush creeping up her neck and onto her cheeks.

Which was when fifteen-year-old Sayana piped up. The same part of her that insisted she ride to Karkorum in the first place, that refused to accept what Chimeg and the others were telling her. *For someone who hates being alone*, she said, *you're making this very difficult.*

"You know," Sayana said, "I never answered your question."

"What question?"

The words came in a rush. Because if she didn't do it, right that instant, they would stay locked behind her teeth for ever. "When we were back at the falls, while we were training Princess. You asked why I left Karkorum. Why I left it all behind to be a raider. I never answered you. I left because I was alone."

Sayana closed her eyes. "It was the worst kind of alone. Where you're surrounded by hundreds of people, and you can't talk to a single one — not in any way that mattered. So I left. I got a new life, as a raider, because I thought it was the only choice.

"If I had to take what wasn't mine, if I had to kill, to never be alone again? To live out here, in the Tapestry, with the life I'd always wanted?" Sayana gripped her knees hard, knuckles turning white. "Then I'd do it. That was the price, and I paid it. It's why I took you. Because I thought there was no other way to keep what I had."

There was a strange lightness in her chest, a trembling in her shoulders — like she'd been carrying a heavy weight, and had finally set it down.

"But it isn't true. It *can't* be true. Because there's nothing that I do as a raider, absolutely nothing, that makes me feel the way you do. When I watch you with the *araatan*, with Ayanga, with *any* animal, it makes me feel like . . . like I have all the choices in the world. Like there are *thousands* of paths for me to take. That's what you do for me. You open up the whole Tapestry. The whole world."

Sayana laced her fingers in Tuya's. It was all coming out, all of it.

"I don't know if you feel the same way," she said. "If you hate me, for what I did to you, I . . . I guess I understand. But you can't tell me you aren't meant to be out here. You can't tell me that isn't what you were meant to do. Please stay. I don't even care if we're together or not, I just . . . "

She did. She cared very much. She wanted it more than she had wanted anything.

But she couldn't make Tuya do this. This was something she couldn't take.

There was no raid in the world that could bring her what she wanted.

"Please stay," she said again. "Stay with me."

Tuya said nothing. Just studied Sayana. Her face was a perfect, total blank.

After a long ten seconds, she took her hands back. Leaned over, her fingers brushing Sayana's skin, planting a kiss on her cheek.

And she whispered: "No."

It took Sayana a moment to understand. "But . . . "

"I'm sorry."

Tears pricked the corner of Sayana's eyes. The weight was back, resting on her shoulders, crushing her.

Tuya looked regretful then. Like she had made a choice of her own, and she still didn't know if it was the right one. The tiniest hope flared inside Sayana – and it died when Tuya said her next words.

"I can't forgive you for what you've done," she said gently. "Not just to me, or Odval, or all the people I could have helped if I was still in the city. You're a raider. I wasn't just helping people escape the Khan – I was getting them away from people like you. Maybe one day, I'll be able to see past it, but—"

"I'm not lying." The tears were flowing now, hot on Sayana's face. "I mean it, I mean every word."

"And I'll never forget it. But tell me this: are you ready to give up being a raider?"

She nodded to the three figures, making their way up the slope towards them. Hogelun. Chimeg. Khunbish. "Are you ready to leave them?"

"I . . ."

Tuya smiled. A smile filled with sadness.

"You need to think about what you want, Sayana. I'll never force you to leave the Rakada – I've watched you too, and I've seen how happy this clan makes you. But I couldn't be with someone like that. And I have so much more work to do."

She gave Sayana's hand one last squeeze. Let go, stood, massaging her throat.

"Where will you go?" Sayana whispered. She couldn't bear the thought of her going back to Karkorum. To a place where she wouldn't smile.

"I think I'll go to the mountains," Tuya said. "Find some of the people I've helped. Check in on them."

She leaned down, gave Sayana one last kiss on the cheek, fingers just tilting her chin up.

It was one of the worst things Sayana had ever felt.

"I will remember you," Tuya said.

And then she was gone.

Walking back down the slope. Right past Chimeg and the others, giving the Chief a guarded nod. Chimeg paused for a moment, as if wondering what the right thing to do in this situation was, then shrugged and returned it. The Rakada and the Eagle Hunter passed each other, and they let each other go.

A few moments later, Hogelun thumped down next to Sayana on the slope with a weary huff. Khun followed, then Chimeg, still cradling her injured arm.

They stared out at the burning camp. Or the rest of them did, anyway. Sayana was watching a lone figure mounting a horse, slowly making her way around the edge of the *gers*. She watched Tuya until she crested the lip of the Heel, and vanished.

Above them, the Large Eye and Small Eye stared down out of a gorgeous blue sky, like it was just another day in the Tapestry.

Hogelun rubbed the top of her shorn head with a closed fist. "So. You and Tuya."

"Me and Tuya," Sayana muttered.

"Anything you want to talk about?" Chimeg asked.

"Not right now."

Hogelun gripped Sayana's knee briefly, then let go.

Khun — still covered in Yesuntei's blood, along with who knows how many others — gave a firm nod. She lifted a hand to her chest, where her pouch used to be. Her fingers wavered, fell to her lap. "One cannot tame the heart," she said. "One might as well try to swallow the suns."

A beat. Then Hogelun said, "Careful, Khun. You almost made sense there for a minute."

Behind them, the *araatan* groaned in pain. Hogelun looked over, winced when she caught sight of the arrow. "Fuck. Is it gonna be OK?"

"She, not it," Sayana told her. "And she'll be fine, if we can find a healer."

Nobody said anything then. All of them thinking of Erhi.

"Suppose we'd better," said Chimeg. "Things are going to change, now there's an *araatan* on our side. What do you say, Sayana? Are you up for it?"

"Princess," Sayana said.

Chimeg lifted an eyebrow. "Don't tell me you actually prefer that nickname now."

"Not me." She jerked her thumb at the lizard. "Her."

"What do you mean, her?" Hogelun asked.

"Her name is Princess."

Hogelun's face scrunched up. "But . . . but *you're* the Princess."

"Not any more," Khun said happily, as if this wasn't news to her either. Chimeg made a *hmph* sound, but there was a smile playing on her lips.

After that, they just sat. Each of them lost in their own private world. Sayana scanned the horizon for a figure on a horse, riding further and further away, but didn't see one.

Eventually, Hogelun said, "What the fuck do we do now?"

The words came out before Sayana even knew she was about to say them. "I have a couple of ideas."

Chimeg snorted. "Why am I not surprised?"

Fifty-Six

A Few Months Later

T he best thing about being the Khan was the pears.
Etugen pondered the one in his fingers, marvelling at
it. It was perfect. Dusky skin, firm flesh under his fingertips.
Everyone else could eat pears that were woody and fibrous,
or mushy and overripe. But he was the Khan, and he had an
entire kingdom dedicated to getting him pears at precisely the
moment – the very instant – when they were at the perfect
ripeness.

His chambers, just off the throne room, were magnificent.
Oiled wood and brass, fine incense burning. A single table and
a carved bench, the wood glowing from the sunslight, which
flowed in from the room's tall window.

The window looked south to where the Ulaan and Khar
Rivers met, below the city. Etugen could smell the spray. He
much preferred this view to the one from the northern side of
the palace, down to the tent city.

Perhaps one day, when the walls were built and the tents
were buildings, it would be a view worth lingering over. Still,
one had to make many sacrifices while building a nation.

The Khan was a stout man, with broad shoulders and a wide chest, neatly trimmed beard dyed black to hide the grey. He had been a soldier, once, and while his body had begun to run to fat — something his advisors assured him happened to all men of fifty years — he tried to stay in shape. Weekly sparring sessions, the odd run around the palace grounds, as much as he could squeeze in. Lamentably little, these days.

This pear was something he had been looking forward to all morning. It had been difficult: news of more attacks, more raiders. Absurd stories of men riding *araatan*, the enormous beasts from the mountain.

He had grown weary of trying to separate fact from fiction; it would have been easier if that woman were still around, the one who used to lead his Guard. She always had a handle on what was happening.

The Khan curled his lip. He couldn't remember her name just then, but she had lost her life in some quest or another — something about a missing sister? And had taken three hundred good men with her.

He lifted the pear to his mouth, careful to lean forward — it wouldn't do to stain his silk *deel* with juices.

Before he could take a bite, there was the sound of soft footsteps. It was one of his advisors — Baagvai, yes, that was his name. The Khan didn't much care for him, but the man's wide eyes and trembling lip held his attention now.

Sighing, he put the pear down. "What is it?" he said, failing to keep the irritation from his voice.

"Great Khan . . . there's . . . "

"Spit it out."

Baagvai told him.

The plain beyond the city was more mud than grass now. The intake of citizens coming in from the grasslands had slowed to a trickle, and that day, there were none. Etugen rode at the head of his Guard: thirteen hardened warriors, bristling with steel. He himself was in full armour, conical golden helmet lined with gold leaves. A bow on his back, in keeping with tradition, although he could barely remember the last time it had been fired in anger.

Behind the guard: every soldier in the city, and in the surrounding barracks. The hooves of a thousand horses hammered the ground. Overkill, one would think, for the single figure waiting at the base of a small hill, a little over half a mile from the city. But after the stories coming in from the grasslands, Etugen wasn't taking any chances.

Winter was almost here, and the grass was patchy with snow. The sky was a bright, frigid blue, the air crisp and clean. The *araatan* squatted at the hill's base. Tall as two men, with a thick, muscular body, lined with scales the colour of summer grass. Feet the size of a soldier's shield, with splayed, hooked claws.

At first, Etugen thought some of its scales were white, or crusted with snow. But they weren't scales.

They were bones.

Big femurs and tibias, human and animal, strapped across its shoulders and snout.

A fearful murmur spread through the guard behind him, the soldiers beyond. The beast caught his eye, bared hideous teeth, a low growl rolling across the grass.

But the *araatan* wasn't what drew Etugen's eye. It was the woman standing next to it. She too wore bones, woven into the shoulders and front of her grey *deel*. Her braid too: little white knots.

He studied her for a moment, wondering if this was some dream. Then he turned to his guard. "Leave us."

"But *bahadur*—"

"Leave us."

When he and the woman were alone, he turned his horse sideways to her, eyes narrowed. His voice, when he spoke, was low and controlled.

"Daughter," he said.

Sayana smiled. "Father."

It had been years since he had seen her. She wasn't his only child, far from it, but she was easily his greatest disappointment. Even if she had somehow managed to tame this beast, had it standing silently as they talked, like an obedient dog.

The chill breeze played with her hair, blew away the puff of white vapour when she breathed. Etugen eyed the lizard, wondering how it could withstand the cold. Then again, it lived in the mountains . . .

Not any more.

He shook off the thought, irritated. "You would stand against me?"

"Well." Sayana shivered, hugged herself against the cold. "You are kind of an arsehole."

It took all the self-control he had not to nock an arrow right then. Only the presence of the *araatan* stopped him. "You ungrateful pup. I gave you everything. I gave you a life that most in Hanggai could only dream of, and this is how you repay me—"

"Oh please. You didn't even tell people I was your daughter – hushed that up nicely, didn't you? How many brothers and sisters do I have anyway? No, you know what, don't answer, pretty sure you've lost count."

He actually laughed. The temerity of her. "You act like I cast you out. You were raised by my loyal servants, given a place at court, everything you could possibly want."

She kissed her teeth, leaned against the *araatan*. It didn't seem to mind.

"Want to know the weird thing?" she said, absently scratching its snout. "I'm not actually angry about that. If you can't keep your dick in your pants, I would much rather someone else raise your kids." Her voice turned hard. "But that wasn't enough. You didn't just want us gone: you wanted us *controlled*. Quiet little birds at your court, never speaking, never getting in the way. Good little obedient servants."

"So all this to get my attention?"

"*Get your attention?*" As if the words were rotten in her mouth. "This had nothing to do with you. I hadn't thought about you in years – well, fine, maybe a bit here and there, but I genuinely didn't give a shit. You'd never have heard from me, after I got out – probably would have been better for you, you know? No need to control one of your daughters at court if she just vanished over the horizon, never to be seen again. Not like you made an effort to hunt me down, did you?"

With a grunt, she mounted the *araatan*. Quickly clambered up one leg, hand over hand, fingers gripping the scales. Moving with natural, practised grace.

There was a saddle, of sorts – a thin leather pad, strapped to its back. His daughter straddled it, glared down at him. "But *then* you started fucking with my world. Fucking with the Tapestry. Fucking with people's lives, telling them where they could live, what they could do, making them join your army."

"I'm trying to secure the future of Hanggai. I'm trying to build—"

"I don't give a shit what you're trying to build. It ends now. No more conscription, no more stupid blue banners, no more ordering people to leave their homes." She jerked her chin at the city. "And you don't get to keep people here any more. That's done."

He actually laughed at that. Glanced back at the massed ranks of his Guard, his army. "And who would stop me? You?

I'm impressed with your new mount, daughter, but if you think you'll be able to beat my entire army on your own—"

"*On my own?*" she said. Eyes wide and innocent. "Whoever said that I was on my own?"

She put her fingers to her lips, and sent a piercing whistle out into the crisp air.

It faded away. For a long moment, nothing happened. Etugen scoffed, but as he was about to ask what on earth she was doing, the other *araatan* came over the crest of the hill.

They were markedly different from the one his daughter rode. As were their riders. The one in the centre was ridden by a giant of a woman, twin skulls on her shoulders and sharp ribs jutting out from her chest. Her animal was enormous, with a snout that must have been a yard long, jagged teeth sticking out every which way.

On the woman's right was an *araatan* that looked almost bird-like. Thinner legs than its brethren, eyes narrowed to slits. The rider was tall, a spear jutting up from her back. Lanky black hair framed a face painted blood red.

The leftmost rider was absolutely covered in bones, every inch of her *deel* and hair. She grinned at Etugen, then cackled, tongue flashing. Her *araatan* was smaller than the rest, with yellow scales. The scales were smeared with dirt, as if the *araatan* had been rolling around in the mud.

Etugen stared.

"You thought we'd stop at one?" Sayana pursed her lips. "Sorry, Dad. You really should get out more. It took us a few months to train them up, but it's easy when you know how."

More raiders joined the three lizards at the top of the hill. Dozens of them, on horseback. Etugen couldn't help noting how some of them looked at the *araatan*, at the flashes of jealousy he saw on their faces.

"So like I said." Sayana clicked her tongue, and her mount began to turn. "Stay out of the Tapestry. It's ours now. Ours, and whoever lives in it. They're under our protection."

Etugen found his voice. "And what will you do, I wonder? When Dalai crosses the border, in the north? When the pale men cross the Great Desert to take our lands? When Ngu revolts again?" He lifted a clenched fist – he was angry, angrier than he had been in years. The realisation was startling. "Will you—"

The *araatan* lunged. A quick, sinuous movement, twisting, mouth opening wide. Etugen squawked and tumbled off his horse, which took off running.

As he lay in the dirt, blinking, his ears ringing, the great Khan was aware that not one of his Guard – not a single one of his soldiers – had come to his aid.

A shadow fell over him, and Sayana smiled.

"Take a wild guess."

She squeezed the side of her mount, began to march back up the hill. She conversed briefly with the raiders at the top, the three riding the other *araatan*.

Etugen rose up on his elbows. Whatever Sayana was saying, it made the others laugh. There was a moment where he couldn't look away, where all he could see was the four raiders, laughing together, as if they didn't have a care in the world. An eagle soared through the skies above them, a dark blur against the searing blue.

Without another glance in his direction, the Khan's daughter turned her mount, and her raiders followed. A moment later, they were gone.

The story continues in…

Book Two of the Rakada

The Bone Raiders

Writer: Jackson Ford
Early readers: Nicole Simpson, George Kelly, Werner Schutz,
Dane Taylor
Sensitivity Reader: Tuga Namgur
Historical consults: Jack Weatherford, Enerelt Enkhbold
Agent: Ed Wilson
Editors: Anna Jackson, Bradley Englert
Publisher: Anna Jackson
Managing Editor: Joanna Kramer
Editorial assistant: Serena Savini
Copy-editor: Sandra Ferguson
Cover artist: Thea Dumitriu
Map artist: Rebecka Champion
Design: Duncan Spilling, Jo Taylor
Production: Tom Webster, Narges Nojoumi
Audio: Jessica Callaghan, Louise Harvey, Sarah Shrubb
Marketing: Madeleine Hall, Aimee Kitson
Publicity: Nazia Khatun, Ellen Wright

Sales: Drew Hunt, Caitriona Row, Hannah Methuen, Ginny Mašinović, Jess Dryburgh, Daja Din, Andrew Hally, Dominic Smith, Frances Doyle
Ops/stock: Kellie Barnfield, Millie Gibson, Sanjeev Braich

Thanks to our families and friends.
Special thanks to booksellers and reviewers worldwide.
Extra special thanks to you.

Jackson Ford would like to thank The HU, Nine Treasures, Big Gee, Hanggai, Tengger Cavalry, Refused, The Unseen, Passcode, Zeal & Ardor, Unleash The Archers, Awich, Alien Weaponry, Arion, Lindsey Stirling, A$AP Rocky, and Amaranthe.

Sign up for "Sh*t Just Got Interesting" — Jackson Ford's weekly newsletter — at jacksonfordauthor.com/newsletter, or scan the following code with your phone:

meet the author

Brooke McAllister

Jackson Ford splits his time between London, Vancouver and Johannesburg. He is the author of the bestselling Frost Files series, beginning with *The Girl Who Could Move Sh*t with Her Mind*. He was a journalist for over a decade, writing for the *Guardian*, *Wired*, the BBC and others. This is his first fantasy novel. He wishes someone had told him how hard it is.

Find out more about Jackson Ford and other Orbit authors by registering for the free monthly newsletter at orbitbooks.net.

Follow us:

f **/orbitbooksUS**

𝕏 /orbitbooks

▶ /orbitbooks

Join our mailing list
to receive alerts on our
latest releases and deals.

orbitbooks.net

Enter our monthly
giveaway for the chance
to win some epic prizes.

orbitloot.com